# FIGHTING FOR

# FOREVER

**Also by JB Salsbury**

Fighting for Flight
Fighting to Forgive
Fighting to Forget
Fighting the Fall
A Father's Fight

# FIGHTING FOR
# FOREVER

JB SALSBURY

Fighting for Forever

JB Salsbury



Edited by Theresa Wegand

Cover by Amanda Simpson of Pixel Mischief Design

To every girl whose been judged unfairly. No one can truly understand your struggle until they walk a day in your shoes.

"For I know the plans I have for you," declares the **Lord**, "plans to prosper you and not to harm you, plans to give you hope and a future."

--The Holy Bible, Jeremiah 29:11

# PROLOGUE

## Four years ago . . .

It's cold. Way colder than I thought it'd be. Even as my bare legs quake and I shove my hands into the pockets of my shorts, I'm shocked at how it's possible to be so cold and yet sweat simultaneously.

Lana would hate this. She despises the cold.

Reality washes over me in a sickening wave, intensified by the stagnant smell of death mixed with the pungent stench of formaldehyde. Lana can't feel the cold. Not anymore.

"Miss Langley." The chill of the coroner's voice is absent of emotion. Sterile, just like the room. "Are you sure you don't want to wait for your parents."

"No. They . . . they aren't coming." Her body has already been identified through dental records. There's really no reason for me to even be here, other than the fact that I just *have* to see my sister to believe she's truly gone.

"The remains are"—he fumbles with a set of keys in his coat pocket—"disturbing. I just want to make sure you're fully aware of what you're about to witness."

*The* remains?

"Her, not *the*. My sister is a her." A twinge of anger boils behind my chest as I glare at the middle-aged man. His hair is short with only a few hints of silver that give away his age. His slim stature and thick glasses combined with the formal way he speaks would classify him as a nerd. A dead-body-studying nerd. "I'm aware."

He nods. "Very well, follow me." He directs me down a short corridor to a private room that is intended for family viewings. Motioning to the door, he studies me when I don't move through it. "I'm happy to stay, or I can leave you if you'd like."

I nod, staring blankly at the wood panel that separates me from Lana. Not Lana, but her corpse.

He clears his throat. "Miss Langley—"

"I'm good," I whisper. "I'd like to be with her alone."

He stalls for a few seconds before walking away, the only sound the squeaking of his shoes against the linoleum, which plays second to the pulse in my ears.

I lift my hand to the door and watch in eerie slow motion, as if my arm isn't an extension of my body. Deliberately, inch by inch, I push into the room. A stark white sheet draped over a table reveals the telltale lumps of her body. First her feet then the dip of her legs, belly, chest, and finally the contours of her face all shrouded in white.

I'm stuck. My hand braces the door open, but I'm unable to move. Images of the last time I saw her flicker through my mind. She was headed back to campus after having dinner at the house. It was chaos as dinners usually are, and she was smiling. It was rare, but she was smiling. Dad walked her to her car and prayed for her safety as he always did.

He prayed for her safety.

I pinch closed my eyes and shake off the fury that wants so badly to be released to the surface. That was the last anyone ever saw of her.

She never made it back to the dorms. Her roommate assumed she'd stayed at home for the weekend. We'd assumed she was too busy studying to call. It wasn't until almost forty-eight hours later that we got the phone call.

Her car had been found.

Abandoned.

Along with her body.

Her body, so warm and full of life when she left, now lies still in a cold room, alone.

I force my feet to move and they carry me in. I fight the urge to squint against the bright light that bounces off the bleached surroundings. My legs lock up just before my belly hits the table.

"Svetlana?" My voice shakes; nerves and emotion have me rattled. "It's me." My eyes tear up, and my heart lodges in my throat when she doesn't reply.

Even though I know she's gone, I'm so desperate to hear her voice just one more time that I close my eyes and try to conjure it from memory. Yet nothing comes.

I blink open my eyes and scrutinize her form. I step closer. Her face. Even under the sheet, something's different. Off somehow. My hand hovers just above her chest, and I flex my fingers, taking in the lack of warmth. She's really gone.

Why? A single tear escapes my eye, followed quickly by another. Why would a God so full of love and grace take the only real blood connection I have?

Other than the three years between us, we were almost identical: same eyes, hair, similar features. We'd always said we were meant to be twins.

I can't even glance in the mirror without seeing her, and now I'll never see her again. This will be the last time before her body is committed to the ground and . . . A sob rips from my throat.

"We've been inseparable. How will I live without you now?" Slowly, I lower my hand to her chest as tears stream down my cheeks to drip off my jaw. "*Moya sestra. Moye serdtse.*"

Hovering, I move my hand up to the sheet at the end of the table. My fingers shake as I grip the hem. Pulling it back, my knuckles brush against something soft, and I register immediately it's her silken hair. The dark blond locks she always wore long used to play gracefully against her light skin.

Suddenly desperate to see it, itching to touch it again and be reminded of how it felt against my cheek when we'd hug, I yank down the sheet.

The visual hits me in the chest. I stumble back, fall to my bottom, and scramble away, kicking with my feet. My heart races as my mind tries to process.

That's not Lana. It can't be her.

My breath saws in—out—in—out. Pulse pounding, I peer up at her, but dart my eyes away.

Oh God, no . . . please . . . what did they do to her?

Slowly, I crawl onto my knees and push to standing on wobbly legs. Unable to take more than a few seconds at a time, I allow my gaze to fall on the gory resemblance of my sister.

What used to be thick and beautifully arched eyebrows are replaced with deep gashes that've been stitched together. Her once high cheekbones are gaunt and sliced through on both sides, as if there was an attempt to remove her lower jaw completely. Peeling the sheet off her body, I see more of the same. She's sliced up everywhere. Her chest, arms, belly, leg . . . There isn't a single space that hasn't been marked.

Monster. Whoever did this is evil.

What did they put her through? How many of these cuts were made before she passed out from the sheer agony of it? Did she scream for help that never came and wondered why, calling out to God for rescue?

My tears dry. Sadness is replaced by a rage I've never felt before—a crazed desire to return this kind of pain, to act out the vile and torturous treatment on the one responsible for inflicting this on her.

A war wages within my soul, the struggle between what is right, what is holy and honorable, and what is wrong but brings relief.

Revenge.

Vindication.

Whoever did this to her needs to pay a penalty that the law can't deliver. He deserves to take every slice just as she did. I will ensure that happens.

For Lana, I will become the monster. Even if it costs me my very soul.

# ONE

## Present day . . .

### MASON

It's like being in the damn Twilight Zone.

The dance floor is crowded with fighters, who are big enough on their own, and watching them all crammed on the dance floor twirling their women around is a sight I wouldn't believe if I weren't sitting here watching it. They spin their girls under their arms, wear big goofy grins, and dip them like they're Fred-freakin'-Astaire and Ginger Rogers.

I'm almost embarrassed for them, but there's something about the expressions they've been wearing all night that assures me I'm missing something. I mean here I am at the singles' tables, throwing back bourbon while they dance to Celine Dion or some shit as if they're the only couples in existence.

Weddings are lame. Blake and Layla's was better than most, only because they both insisted on a live band, and that band being Ataxia, the music fucking rocked. But the party's winding down and a DJ took over. Judging by the mushy stares the guys are giving their girls, I'm guessing it won't be long before they all disappear behind their individual closed doors.

I groan and throw back the last of my drink as the party song to kill all wedding receptions blares through the speakers. I swear on my grandfather's grave, if my boys start dancing to "YMCA," I'm out of here.

Wade drops down into an empty seat next to mine, pulling his giggling date to his lap. "Mase, man . . . you've been warming that chair all night."

I don't look at him, but I see him follow my gaze out of the corner of my eye.

Shit. I've been caught staring. *Again.*

I drop my chin and force my eyes to the bride and groom, who are locked in a slow dance even while the Village People croon their noxious song.

Wade drops a quick kiss on his date's shoulder. "Babe, why don't you grab your coat?" He gives her a shove off his lap before leaning into my line of sight. "Baywatch, you need to let her go. She's happy with Cam, and I know you want her to be happy . . . right?" He lifts an eyebrow, daring me to contradict him.

Do I want Eve to be happy? Of course. Would I rather she be happy with me? Fuck yeah.

I shrug, and feeling suddenly suffocated, I pull at the neck of my dress shirt and tie only to realize they're hanging open and loose. My throat is dry, and I force myself to swallow. "I'm happy for them, really. No hard feelings."

Such a line of bullshit, but it's the one I've been feeding everyone since Eve chose Cameron over me. Every time I think I've moved on, that I'm over it, I end up being forced into the same room with them and realize I'm not.

After Eve took over for Layla while she's on maternity leave, I see her at the Training Center every damn day—her and Cam with their hands all over each other—and the anger of rejection burns like a bitch.

I seek them out accidently, as if the thought of them naturally brought my eyes around, only to find them whispering against each other's lips on the dance floor and looking all the cheesy romantic couple that they are.

When did I become such a cynic? I was the guy who loved love, wanted to share my time with just one girl, unlike every other guy I know. I was looking for *the one*, and I'd thought I found her at fifteen. I was wrong.

What going away to college introduced me to, life as a UFL fighter in Vegas slammed home: Women don't like nice guys. When given a choice, they'll always choose dudes that treat them like shit and give them something to fix.

My stomach plummets as Eve brings her hand up to Cam's jaw and leans forward to brush her lips against his. He grips her ass and pulls her close, and the jealous rage that's always hovering close to the surface flares.

The asshole and the ice queen. They deserve each other, and if I didn't still care so much for Eve, I'd congratulate them on their relationship with a big-ass grin and move the hell on. But I can't control the pull I have toward the woman, can't just turn off my feelings.

*That should be me with her.* My hands on her ass. My tongue in her mouth. My heart in her hands. I growl at my own pussy-ass thoughts.

Fuck 'em. Fuck 'em both.

God, I can't help myself from being such a dick. I suppose I owe Cam and Eve a hearty thank you. They've turned me into an asshole, every girl's wet dream.

"I'm out." I push up from my chair and grab my suit coat, and I'm ready to burn off some of this shit cartwheeling through my head.

Wade studies me in a way that makes my skin crawl. He's well aware that I'm full of shit, and he's calling my bluff. "You takin' off?" He stands and crosses his arms over his chest, his head tilts slightly, and I can't help feeling like he's reading my mind.

"Yeah, my brother's in town with some friends." Why they're in town I have no idea, but something tells me it's not vacation. A sour taste floods my mouth at the thought of facing The Brotherhood; although, avoiding them isn't an option either.

"You're not driving, are you?"

I almost roll my eyes at Wade, who's apparently been nominated to play Baywatch's babysitter tonight, not that I'm surprised. All the guys have been keeping a close eye on me lately, covering for me when I fuck up, making sure I don't end up shit-canned by the UFL or arrested for acting like a jackass.

"Nah, I'll grab a cab." I pull on my jacket, patting all my pockets in a quick check for my phone and wallet. "It's just down the strip."

He opens his mouth to say something but slams it shut just as his date struts up and tucks into his side with her coat and purse. "Don't forget about tomorrow. You're up on rotation. Cameron will have your ass if you don't show."

"What're you? My secretary?" I inwardly groan because I had actually forgotten about tomorrow.

Wade reads me and nods. "You have to be there by nine a.m."

For the past few months, Cameron has been having fighters donate a few hours every Sunday to The Community Youth Center for Sports and Rec. Jonah found fighting through a similar program and claims it saved his life, Cameron thinks it'll do us some good to play Good Samaritan, and after all the mud the UFL has had to scrape off, a little positive publicity doesn't hurt.

"Got it." I fish my phone out from my pocket to quickly set an alarm reminder. Last thing I need is to get into more trouble with our fearless leader. "Tell Blake and Layla good-bye for me, will ya? I don't want to interrupt."

"Sure thing."

Tossing Wade a chin lift, I move through the crowded ballroom with my head down, reading text messages to avoid having to draw out my departure with a ton of good-byes.

I shove out into the large corridor of The Four Seasons and, as the door shuts behind me, take my first full breath. The muffled music and murmured voices fade away as I make haste to the lobby.

I click open a text from Birdman.

**Caesars. Nobu Sake Suite. Don't be a bitch. Come hang with your bros.**

One more came in three hours after the first.

**Drake's asking for you. Hurry up.**

Another came in ten minutes ago, this one from my brother Drake.

**I'm hiiigh as hell. Get your ass over here.**

Shit, that's exactly what I was afraid of.

---

Fifteen minutes later I'm tossing some cash to the cab driver outside Caesars Palace. I move from the taxi and through the glass doors into the casino where I'm hit with the sensory overload that comes along with Vegas casinos: the pinging and trilling music of the slot machines, the occasional cloud of pungent cigarette smoke, and then the subdued high-rollers section, tense with concentration, sanctioned off to the side.

I follow the signs that point me to the Nobu Hotel inside Caesars until I find the check-in and elevators. My damn dress shoes echo against the marble flooring, and I regret not dropping by my pad for a change of clothes before coming. I pull out my phone to text Birdman and ask for a floor and room number.

I notice a sign indicating the restrooms and figure while I'm waiting for the return text I'll take a leak. As I move around the elevator bank, my phone pings in my hand.

**Tenth floor #1098**

Something slams into my shoulder.

"Shit!" My phone skids across the marble floor. "Watch it, asshole!" I bark at the offender who just crashed into me from out of nowhere.

"Oh my God, I'm sorry."

With my glare stuck on my pinwheeling phone, I hear her voice before I see her, and when I see her, it's from behind and only because she's scurrying after the palm-sized wireless device.

Her tiny frame hunches over, arms outstretched to the ground, as she click-clacks in heels that look way too tall for any human being to negotiate on the slick floor. She's dipped in a skin-tight, long-sleeved black dress, which covers every inch of her skin to her ass then cuts off to expose a pair of very bare and toned legs.

The phone stops its slip-n-slide when it hits the wall and she scoops it up. "Aw, crap." She's facing away from me, her head down. "I'm so sorry." Shaking her head, she turns.

I didn't notice from behind, but now I can see her long platinum blond hair has a few bright purple panels that streak through at random. The loose waves that hang over her breasts create purple candy-cane-like swirls through her mane. She closes the space between us and finally looks up at me.

Whoa . . . her eyes, they're blue, but not like any blue I've ever seen. Maybe it's the purple in her hair that's setting them off, but they appear lavender.

"Look. I'm really sorry about your phone. I just stepped out of the ladies' room and crashed right into you." She hands me the device.

The screen is shattered. "Damn."

"Yeah, bummer." She chews her bottom lip.

The sweetness in her voice and sincerity in her expression stoke a fire of irritation I can't name.

"I feel like shit about—"

"You need to watch where you're going." I spit the words like throwing stars and almost grin at the shock that registers on her face. Yeah, I'm a dick. Sue me.

Her eyes narrow. "I said I'm sorry."

"*Sorry* isn't going to fix my phone." I thrust it, cracked screen forward, toward her face, just in case she forgot the shit she caused.

She recoils, her eyes pulling into tight slits. "It was an accident!"

"Accident?" She's right, I wasn't paying attention either, but I'm so sick of women fucking with me. Tired of being a doormat and feeling like a beaten dog. "Typical chick. Movin' through life worrying only about yourself." I step into her space and lean forward, intimidating her with my size, or at least trying to.

She doesn't budge.

"Newsflash, sweetheart . . . it's not *all about you.*"

And then she shocks the shit out of me and smiles. *Smiles!*

Her shoulders relax and she lifts one eyebrow. "Huh . . ." She taps her chin with one white-tipped, manicured finger. "You know what? You're wrong. It *is* all about me." She rips the phone from my hand and flings it back across the floor so it skids and lands just like the first time, but this time with a crack.

My jaw clenches. "What the hell is—?"

"I was sorry the first time; I'm not sorry the second." She flips the long waves of her bi-colored hair and struts away like a black panther on heels.

I watch her go, drawn to the feminine sway of her hips and fixed on the perfect curves of her tight little ass. A tight little ass that deserves a series of firm swats.

"Bitch." The word falls from my lips on a whisper before I move to retrieve my phone that, upon further inspection, is now in three distinct pieces.

Doesn't matter if I'm the nice guy or the asshole; I'm always going to be an easy target for strong-willed women.

Well . . . not anymore.

# TWO

## MASON

"Fuckin' A, Mayhem! You made it!" Charlie wraps two beefy arms around me, pounding me on the back in a bro-hug.

"Charbroil, long time, brother." I hug him back, oddly comforted by the familiarity of being around one of my old friends from back home.

Charlie and I grew up together, along with Birdman, Harrison, and Jayden. Drake and I were only a year apart in school, despite our two-year age difference, so we had all the same friends. When I went off to college on a full-ride wrestling scholarship, Drake stayed behind with these guys on the high-school-dropout plan.

"Get your ass in here, man. Drake's been asking for you since we pulled into town." He closes the double doors to the penthouse suite, and I'm immediately hit with the stench and smoky haze of chronic along with the rhythmic beats of Sublime.

Fuck, some things never change.

As I move through the Asian-inspired space, the cracking of pool balls and murmured curses of male voices get louder. We round the corner, and the room opens up to sky-high ceilings, glass walls, and furniture draped with the bodies of Santa Cruz's most notorious surf gang, The Bone Breaker Brotherhood.

"Mayhem! You motherfucker!" Birdman calls the attention of the room, and I'm surrounded in hugs, back pats, shoulder punches, and fist bumps.

"Long time, brother." Harrison rubs my head, messing up my semi-styled mop that I'd tamed for the wedding. "You clean up nice, little bitch."

I shove him, but laugh. "Yeah, you're looking more and more like your brother." I slap his stomach just as his twin brother Jayden hooks Harrison around the neck. They're identical twins, and although the joke is old and not even funny, it's comforting to fall into our childhood ribbings.

"He wishes he looked like me." Jayden flashes his golden-boy smile that contradicts his edgy look. With a shaved head and tattoos all over his neck, including a small cross on his cheek just below his eye, he carries the hardened look of a criminal.

We continue giving each other shit, and the few guys I'm not familiar with stand off and greet me with chin lifts.

"Well, well, well . . . our UFL all-star has decided to grace us with his presence."

Just the sound of his voice makes my stomach clench with worry, but I shake off my unease and turn toward my little brother.

Drake struts out of a dark bedroom while pulling on a button-up shirt. He's ripped in a way that doesn't look natural, swollen muscles that are definitely bigger than they were the last time I saw him over a year ago. Inked across his chest and up to his shoulders are the scripted words *"Bonded by blood, loyal beyond death."*

Fuckin' A, he's in deeper than I thought.

What started out as a harmless surf gang has escalated to levels I'm afraid to even imagine. He saunters toward me, smiling and holding his arms out.

"Look at you, bro." I give him a back-thumping hug. "All grown up."

He pulls back, and I study the scar that he picked up after a weekend camping with his dad when he was sixteen years old. Our mom was pissed that he didn't get stitches, but Drake seemed more proud than I'd ever seen him. He said he'd gotten into a fight, and he wore that damn slice through his face like a badge of honor. Crazy little shit. His eyelids are heavy, eyes bloodshot, no doubt from whatever it is he was doing in the hotel bedroom.

"Brother"—he takes me in from top to bottom—"you look like a homeless Michael Bublé."

"And you look like Tupac's gay white twin." My teeth grind together in frustration. My little brother is a gold tooth and a shit load of talent away from that being true.

A warm smile breaks through his tough façade, and he moves in, throwing an arm around my shoulder. "It's been too long."

From the looks of it, way too long. "It has."

He guides me to the sliding glass doors that lead to a large patio complete with fire pit. I turn around to see all the other guys have stayed inside as Drake drops down on a long semi-circular couch. He props his feet up on the fire circle, knee cocked, one sole of his high-top blue Chucks on the edge.

"How's the UFL-superstar life treating you?" He pulls a joint out of the breast pocket of his Dickies shirt and pinches it between his lips to light it.

"Good, man. I've got no complaints."

"We caught your last fight on TV," he says between drags. "Made ten grand on that fight."

"You're running numbers now?" How does he get himself into this shit? Honest to God, it's like trouble chases *him* down; he finds it without even looking.

"Dabbling here and there." He offers me the joint, but I just stare at it until he shrugs with a "Suit yourself" and continues to puff on it.

I scan the horizon, the Vegas lights practically blinding even from this height. When I first moved here, I thought they were downright mystical. Now they just hurt my damn eyes.

I swing my gaze back to him. "What brings you to Vegas, D?"

He picks something off the tip of his tongue, tilts his head and studies me. "You know what."

Fuck. I'd hoped it wasn't what I thought. I lean forward, resting my elbows on my knees. "How deep are you in with him?"

A small, but confident grin curves his lips. "I'm his son." He says it like it's the most obvious thing in the world.

"Drake—"

"Save it, Mase, really. I mean"—he holds his arms out and motions around—"look at this, all this. I'm living a life you only see in movies, man."

"Yeah, the ones where your character gets gunned down in the end."

"In a flame of glory."

"Or in the trunk of a car and a shallow grave." I shake my head and feel the beginning of a headache throbbing in my temples. Whatever buzz I was riding when I left Blake's wedding is now non-existent.

"You don't need to worry about me." He stubs out his joint on the edge of the fire pit. "*My* dad didn't float my ass through high school with new cars and shit or pay my way to a Big Ten school like yours did, but I'm doing alright now."

No, his dad didn't do the things for him that mine did for me. I'd always felt like shit having the nicer things and tried to share as much as I could, but the fact of the matter is, my dad was a successful plastic surgeon married to my mom. Until Drake's dad came to town and caught her eye. My dad didn't realize Drake wasn't his until after he was born and it was obvious he looked nothing like him.

A simple DNA test told my dad everything he needed to know. I swear to this day, after my parents got divorced, he set me up financially just to torture my mom. Drake would always be her reminder of what she'd given up for a quick fling with a bad boy.

"You two done making out?" Harrison saunters on to the patio, clearly high or drunk as hell. "We've got plans for the night that start, like, now."

"What happens in Vegas . . ." Drake lifts an eyebrow before standing up to head in.

I do the same and fight the urge to yawn as exhaustion sweeps over me.

Once back inside the suite, I let my gaze slide through the room, taking in all the booze, drugs, and money that are cast around like part of the décor. Confirmation that my little brother has been pulled deeper and deeper into the world his immoral leader had created.

Jayden has his nose practically buried in a mound of white power while Birdman sorts through small square tabs, bagging them in Ziplocs the size of a quarter.

Drake's dad had a horrible reputation in our town. He was accused of everything from robbery to assault with a deadly weapon, but none of it ever seemed to stick. Our mom tried to get Drake's dad to be part of his life, but he wasn't interested until shortly before my brother's seventeenth birthday when his Dad had lured him into his world of corruption and God knows what else.

I school my expression so they can't see the look of disgust, disappointment, and worry that I'm feeling. The sound of a doorbell rings through the room.

Harrison jumps up from the couch. "I think the entertainment just got here." His eyes light and he rushes to the door.

"Looks like Pops hooked us up with this sick-ass suite *and* female companionship for the night." Drake leans in, blowing pot smoke in my face. Another joint? Fuckin' hell. I hold my breath, knowing that if a drug test picks up even a trace of that shit, Cameron will kick my ass, rip up my contract, and sprinkle it over my bloodied body.

He lifts one eyebrow and grins through his higher-than-Sputnik expression. "And you wonder why I'm in this business." With a shrug, he slouches deeper into the couch as if his point has been proven.

"Helllllo, boys . . ." The soft female voice purrs, and when I turn, I'm met with a pair of violet eyes.

No fuckin' way. "We meet again."

Her bright eyes turn feral. "*You.*"

"Looks like I made an impression."

---

## TRIX

That arrogant son of a prick!

After the way he treated me in the lobby, he has the nerve to try to be charming? That slanted smile and glare, a wicked combo of primal masculinity, won't work with me, buster. Nope. He wants to exercise his magnetism; he's barking up the wrong dancer.

All that blond hair, tan skin, and impressive build, he thinks he can push girls around and we're just going to fall to our knees reaching for his zipper. Ha! Not likely. No way. I'm a damn professional; restraining myself against the pull of attraction is my job.

But really, what is he doing here? What are the chances?

Shake it off, Trix. It's all about the job.

It actually hurts. The glare I'm aiming at this damn man is making my head ache and my eye twitch. I'm not at all surprised that he's pinning me with a similar scowl that only manages to piss me off more.

Handsome men think they can win women over on looks alone. All good-looking guys are just that—good to look at.

Then they open their mouths, and I'm reminded that God seemed to give up on making real men about twenty-two years ago. Instead, he's created stuck-up, self-serving, prima donnas who wouldn't know how to take care of a woman if their wieners depended on it.

I pinch closed my eyes, immediately feeling guilty for my blasphemous rant. *Sorry, God. You know I don't mean that.*

I shift my eyes from the icy-blue stare of this Abercrombie-model-looking jerk and settle on Angel. She's already plopped down on the lap of a big guy with a strong roman nose and a goofy smile.

It takes all of five seconds to do a quick assessment of the type of men we're dealing with. They're rough, but not scary. Sure they've got the tattoos, one even has a scar, but everything else about them softens all that. Tan skin seems to make all their eyes appear light, and even the brown eyes look tawny in comparison. Sun-bleached blond and brown hair adds sweetness to their wannabe hard looks.

"We've been hired to keep you guys company tonight," Angel says, addressing the room. "This is Vegas, but that doesn't mean we don't have rules. You boys keep it respectful, and we won't have to get Santos over there to feed you your own blood. Sound good?"

Santos is a huge Mexican-American, who I'm pretty sure spends more time in the gym than anywhere else in the world. He's been a bouncer at Zeus's Playground since before I started working there and thinks of all the girls as his little sisters. I've seen him break fingers, arms, and noses. The dude doesn't mess around.

"You girls got names?" A shorter guy, probably not much older than I am, asks, and I do a double-take. He looks exactly like the guy leaning against the pool table only his light brown hair is longer than the shaved-headed, tattooed version. Twins.

I avoid broken-phone guy's eyes and move to the pool table twin to lean next to him. "I'm Trix. This is Angel."

"You girls gonna stand around and talk all night or get naked?" The second biggest guy in the room looks a lot like the rest save for the scar and the fire of irritation in his eyes. I zero in and size him up.

He's dressed nicer than the others, although not as nice as the guy I ran into downstairs, but the way the room quiets when he talks says a lot.

He must be the head dickhead 'round here.

I move to him slowly, making sure he tracks every roll of my hips, until I'm standing between his feet. "You tell us, big guy. What do you want?"

His expression turns from annoyed to hungry, and his hand darts out to my thigh. "Depends. What're you offering?" He rubs from my knee up under my dress to almost my hip.

This guy has balls. "Dancing." I still his hand before he's able to continue his course that's leading to my bare ass. "That's it."

"Oh, come on." He licks his lower lip, and I have to give him credit. He's handsome in a dangerous kind of way. "For the right price, I bet you'll change your mind."

A low rumble catches my attention, and I turn to find cell-phone guy shooting daggers at the guy's hand as it caresses my leg.

I gasp as the hand clenches my flesh. "What do you say, Trix? You feel like getting fucked—"

"Drake." Cell-phone guy growls in warning, and for a second, I want to tell them both to fuck off, until I see the barely concealed rage in his eyes.

"We're here to party, *Mason.*" Drake says his name, and it drips with contempt and sarcasm as they stare off. "I'll make sure she spreads the love."

Something is off between these two.

“Boys, boys . . . No sex. Just dancing.” I swivel out of Drake’s hold and over to the stereo. “Relax.” I turn up whatever they’re listening to, well aware that men respond better when they’re able to listen to their own tunes, and Angel and I can move to anything.

I take a deep breath and push back the part of me that hates what I do. I tell myself that my body is my superpower. My sexuality works like kryptonite, weakening men and making them pliable. I remind myself why this is necessary, and with every article of clothing I remove, the power surges from within.

For me, nakedness doesn’t equal vulnerability. It’s strength in its purest form, used by women since the beginning of time, and I’d be an idiot not to take advantage of it.

# THREE

## MASON

I hate this. I hate every fucking thing about this, and yet I can't leave.

From the moment I walked into this fancy, freakin' suite, I've been battling two opposites: the pull toward my brother and the anger that pushes me from him. Throw into the mix the violet-eyed panther who's currently shaking her G-string-clad ass in Jayden's face, and I'm damn near homicidal.

But why?

This girl with the fruity cereal name, Trix, and her associate, Angel, aren't here against their will or being taken advantage of. As a matter of fact, they seem to be the only ones in the room, with the exception of their bodyguard, in total control.

After they started dancing and ended up in nothing but small strips of satin between their legs, I sat there as long as I could. Trix kept her distance from me, choosing to focus on everyone else, not that I'm surprised. My guess is I'm not her favorite person after our less-than-pleasant meeting. And for some stupid fucking reason that bothers me.

The uncontrollable urge to touch her becomes too much, and I make my way to the small bar in the corner of the room. My annoyance is curbed by a sense of sympathy for Trix and Angel. It's not healthy for a woman to expose the most private parts of her body to a room full of strangers, letting every man fantasize about a body meant for just one man. Her man, whoever she ends up with.

And yet I'm hard as steel. My conservative opinions apparently have zero effect on my dick's response to Trix. Something about her, maybe it's the yin and yang of our earlier argument to the sultry enticement of her moves, but the stirring in my pants ignores my command to chill the fuck out.

Why I even care about any of this is stupid. This girl hates me. Hell, I hate her. Okay, maybe I don't hate her, but I sure as shit don't like her.

Jayden palms her breast. *Don't fucking touch her.* A low growl rumbles in my chest. I take a step forward to remove his arm from his body, but Trix takes care of it with less bloodshed. Rather than shove him away, she simply grabs his wrist, moves it from her body and shakes her finger in his face while biting her lip. He drops his hand to his lap and grins like a good little puppy.

"What's wrong, Tiger?"

I dip my chin to the pretty dark-haired girl, Angel, as she runs her hand from my forearm to my shoulder.

"Whoa . . ." Her wide dark eyes meet mine. "You're big." She squeezes my bicep a few times. "You must work out."

With a slow grind of her pelvis to my thigh, I grip her wrist. "Don't."

Her eyes widen, and I immediately release my hold. "It's not you. It's just"—my gaze slides to Trix—"strippers don't do anything for me." I'm such a fucking liar.

"Well, thank gawd. I needed a break." She pushes into the spot next to me and smiles. "So, what do you do for a living?"

I have a hard time keeping my eyes from her perky naked breasts and wonder how she can so easily have a conversation while standing here topless. "I'm an athlete. Universal Fighting League."

"Ah, well that makes sense." Her eyes shift around the room. "Are all you guys fighters?"

"No, just me." I shrug and settle back, at ease now that I realize she's more interested in conversation than anything else. "Can I get you a drink?"

"I'd *love* a Diet Coke." She nods toward the mini-fridge. "Think there's any in there?"

My lips curve into a smile, and I reach down to grab a Diet Coke from the fridge. I pop the can open and hand it to her. "Here ya go."

"Thanks." She takes a few greedy gulps and then shifts to lean her back against the counter in a casual way, like we're just two friends in bar. "So, you're the only fighter. These guys your groupies?"

"No, Drake's my little brother." I nod toward him, and I try to avoid staring as Trix moves to straddle his lap. "They're in town, visiting."

"Visiting from where?" She takes another pull off her soda.

"Santa Cruz, California."

She tilts her head up, eyebrows pinched in thought. "Is that north of Los Angeles?"

"Mm-hm." I nod.

She shrugs and takes another pull from her drink. "Anywhere near San Jose?"

"Yeah, but coastal."

"Trix knows—"

"Drake . . .?" We all still, heads swiveling toward the small frame of a woman as she comes into view from a darkened bedroom off to the side of the living space.

My eyes dart to Drake, whose mouth is in Trix's ear while she straddles his lap on the couch, her perfect tits pressed to his chest and her blond-and-purple-streaked hair tossed all around him. The woman steps into the light, and my breath catches in my throat.

Long golden hair parted in the middle cascades over her shoulders to her ribs. She's wearing a tank top and floor-length hippie skirt, which hangs off narrow hips, showing bare feet.

She's aged since I last saw her; time combined with rough living has made its mark on her once youthful face, but it's her.

"Babe, get your ass back to bed." There's no kindness in Drake's command, not even a hint of shame at being caught red-handed with a naked stripper on his lap.

Trix cringes and pushes off Drake, her expression twisting in pure disgust and hatred. "I'm taking a break."

"No, stay right where you are." Drake reaches for her, but Santos moves in, and with one look, he sends Drake's hand back to his lap.

"Drake, what are you doing?" Jess moves farther into the room, her pained expression meant only for him.

"I said go the fuck back to bed!"

I move to him in a few long strides. "Drake!"

He jumps up, whirls toward me, and within seconds we're in each other's faces. Nose to nose, fury charges the air between us, and years of time dissolve as old feuds resurface.

"Mason?" Jessica's voice shakes.

"Back off, Mason, or I swear to God—"

"You'll kick my ass?" I push back my anger, telling myself taking my little brother to the ground in front of her will only make matters worse. I step back and relax my stance. "Love to see you try, *brother*."

I slide my eyes to Jessica and force a smile. Her eyes glaze over and a shaky smile touches her lips.

"Hey, Jess."

She rushes to me and throws her arms around my neck. "Mason, what are you doing here?"

"Jessica, get the fuck over here." Drake holds out his arm for her.

A muffled whimper sounds against my chest, but she ignores his command. "I've missed you."

Drake glares at me from over her shoulder, and the rest of the guys shift uncomfortably around the room.

"Yeah, hey . . . shhh, me too, Jess. Shhh . . . it's okay." I run my hand up and down her back, hoping the touch is soothing enough that she'll drop the death grip from my neck.

"Jess, now." Drake's not giving up, clearly jealous by her clinging to me. Fuck him. She may've chosen him after three years of dating me, but right now, she's choosing me.

I squeeze Jess a little tighter, noticing how different she feels in my arms now compared to when we were in high school. Fragile and frail rather than the muscled track star she was back then. "How are you?"

Took years for me to get over them being together. She was my first everything, my first love. Back then, I thought we'd end up married with two point five kids and a damn retriever. That is until a month before I left for Penn State and I caught her and Drake fucking in his room mere feet from my bedroom door. That was it. She wanted the bad-boy version of me, and she fuckin' got him.

I should feel some kind of vindication over the shitty way he's treating her, but my chest aches at how broken she's become. The lost look in her eyes I feel in my gut.

"I'm okay." She releases me and turns to the strippers, who are now fully clothed and whispering heatedly with their bodyguard. "Why would Drake hire prostitutes when I'm right there in the next room?" A single tear rolls down her cheek.

Can she really be that clueless?

"Oh, them? Yeah, um . . . they're not prostitutes. They're with me." Fuck, I don't know why I said that. I don't want to protect Drake, but the big brother in me can't help it. That and I'd say anything to wipe the look of sheer betrayal from her face.

Her eyebrows pinch together. "With you?"

"Yeah." I hold my arm out to the girls and hope that one of them is smart enough to follow my lead.

Trix click-clacks over and tucks into my side. The second her heated body hits mine I bite back a groan. Damn, she feels good. And smells even better.

"Hi, I'm um . . . I'm really sorry about all this. We actually have a policy that we only entertain couples when both parties agree." Trix tucks a strand of hair behind her ear. "If I'd known you were here and not in favor of our being here, we would've terminated the contract."

I squeeze Trix tighter to my side, proud of her quick thinking and relieved by Jessica's now-relaxed smile.

"See, Jess? It's fine, and really, it's my fault. I had no idea you were here."

Trix looks at her wrist and taps it even though she's not wearing a watch. "Yep, and our time's up, so we'll be leaving."

A few of the guys grumble from behind me, well aware that their time is not up. I shoot them a quick glare to quiet them. They groan, but don't protest further.

"See? We were just leaving." I keep Trix close, safe from the horny group of men who look like they're about to pounce.

"You're leaving too?" Jessica asks and pleads with watery-gray eyes.

"I am, but, um . . . you guys are going to be here for a few days, right? I'll see you again." I run my hand along her upper arm.

"Okay." She hugs me close, and Trix ducks out of my hold to avoid the group hug. Reluctantly, I let her go, but pat Jess and pull away, hoping to grab Trix before she takes off.

There's something I need to say, and I know if she gets away I'll never see her again.

## TRIX

Santos, Angel, and I move from the penthouse and toward the elevators, eager to get hell out of there.

Talk about an uncomfortable situation. That poor woman who walked out of the bedroom looked like she'd been kicked in the gut and spit on when she saw me on her boyfriend's lap.

I'm no stranger to asshole guys. I'm also not naïve to think that every man I dance for is available, but a striptease is all about the unattainable fantasy—something to indulge in before going back to your woman who'll bring the illusion to life. But planting an exotic dancer in your girlfriend's living room to let her watch is a first-class dickhead move.

We step into the elevator. "Easiest gig we've ever worked." Angel presses the button, which lights up to indicate we're headed to the lobby. "Paid for two hours and only had to work for one." She pulls an invisible slot machine handle. "Cha-ching."

"I left them VIP passes to Zeus's so they'll get their money's worth." Santos leans back, his thick hands shoved into the pockets of his jeans. "Quick thinking with the rule about couples."

"Yeah, well, there *should* be a rule about that. I felt so bad for that girl." I pull a rubber band out of my clutch and have Santos hold my purse while I wrap my hair up in a messy bun. I'm off duty for the night, ready to wash my face, throw on some pj's, and pass out. "You remember the last girlfriend who got pissed and filed a complaint saying we were hooking. Never trust a pissed-off girlfriend. Speaking of couples"—I stare at Santos and watch his big cheeks turn pink—"did Diane like her anniversary present?"

The blush on his cheeks intensifies and I grin. After shoving piles of lingerie catalogs in our faces one night, begging for us to let him in on what women think is sexy, we made a ton of recommendations. I guess he took our word for it.

"She did," he says, "but probably not as much as I liked seeing her wear it."

"Ha! I bet." The elevator pings and we walk out and toward the valet through the casino. "You're a good man, Santos."

"Nope, I'm fuckin' lucky is what I am." He snags our tickets and goes to the valet stand to drop them off.

"Whoever those guys are, they must have serious cash. Did you see the shit they had lying around?" Angel pulls off one fake eyelash followed by the other and tucks them in her bag.

"I did." Illegal shit, but yeah, there was a lot of it. All of it reminded me of my time with Hatch. It's been a year since he took off and I've heard not a single word. The night he stopped in Vegas before he went on the run he'd told me he was headed to Mexico. I wonder if he ever made it or if the guys who were after him found him first.

If he's dead, I'll never get him to confess all he knows.

Sadness overwhelms me at the thought of going back to my parents' home empty-handed. All I want to do is bring them the peace of mind they deserve. After all, they've given me everything, despite the shit I continue to put them through. They've given hope to kids who never had any. Made a family where there once was none.

"Trix, babe . . ." Santos dips his forehead toward my car, which the valet pulled up and is hopping out of.

"Right, I'm teaching tomorrow, so I'll see you Monday." I give Angel a hug, and Santos walks me to my car, tipping the valet and standing there until I get in, shut the door, and strap on my seatbelt. I mouth *thank you* and head home.

At a stoplight, I catch a reflection of my eyes and am reminded of the girl from the hotel room. Her eyes were sullen, almost haunted. It was obvious she and that Mason guy are old friends, and if her expression when she saw him was any indication, I'd say they were close at one time.

What surprised me was the sweet way he treated her, completely opposite of how he was with me. I mean, sure, I broke his phone, but even after that, he disregarded me like I was scum. Most likely, he takes some kind of moral offense to being in the presence of a woman like me.

He's the type who needs a woman who sees her body as some kind of prize to be won. The way his hands ran over that girl's arms like they were made of glass . . . He whispered soothingly into her hair, close enough that she could glean comfort from the heat of his breath. Yeah, he's a woman-worshiper.

When he threw his arm over my shoulder and tucked me tightly into his side, I felt a sliver of what he's capable of. Strong, deliberate, and aware, he's probably a gentle lover, firm and deep, but slow and attentive. The kind that lasts all night and late into the day.

He's the kind of man a girl like me doesn't need.

Or maybe the kind I don't deserve.

Not that it matters.

# FOUR

## MASON

"Mister"—Sylvia Thomas, the Community Youth Center Director, studies a slip of paper she has pinned to a clipboard—"Mahoney?" She squints up at me through magnified glasses that make her eyes look bulbous.

"Yeah, call me Mason."

"Mr. Mason . . ." She scribbles what I assume to be my modified name on a sticker nametag and then slaps it to my chest. "Great, follow me, and I'll show you where you'll be working today."

The Community Youth Center doesn't look anything like I thought it would. It's sleek and modern, and judging by the smell of fresh paint and new floors, I'd say it's recently had a major facelift. We move through a series of hallways before we come to a big open gym. As tired as I am from having to drag my ass out of bed this morning, the scent of rubber mats, sweat, and the sounds of human exertion perk me right up.

"How long have you guys been at this location, Mrs. Thomas?" I raise my voice to be heard over the sound of squeaking sneakers and kids' voices.

She smiles back at me, pride shining in her eyes. "We've been here for nearly thirty years; although, you'd never guess it by looking at it. The place was a wreck until Mr. and Mrs. Slade funded the complete remodel."

Ah, Jonah and Raven. That explains it.

The gym is filled with kids of all different ages: some as high as my thigh and others that could stand with me almost eye-to-eye. They're grouped off according to activity. A dozen are playing volleyball, and fewer are on a half basketball court. There's a group running sprints, some doing tumbling on a large mat, and others simply sitting on the bleachers, watching.

"The children are allowed to pick whatever it is they're interested in. Most days they're happy to hop around from class to class, but we do have those who choose not to participate." Her face twists in disappointment. "This is where you'll be."

The large section that's sanctioned off for MMA is top of the line. It's padded for safety, and a small pile of gloves, hit pads, and kickboxing bags is set up in the corner.

She hands me a slip of paper. "Here's the sign-up sheet for today." She waves over a group from the bleachers. A few kids amble over, dragging their feet with cautious expressions. "You guys are in for a treat today. This is Mr. Mason, and he's a professional fighter with the UFL."

I nod to the kids and take in their wide eyes.

"Alright, I'll leave you to it." Mrs. Thomas grins and walks away, but turns back, snapping her fingers. "Oh, I forgot! If you need anything, you can ask Trix."

My expression falls and my jaw goes slack. Did she say Trix? No. I must've imagined . . . I follow her pointing finger to a group of girls who are lined up and seem to be working through some sort of dance routine.

"She's our veteran volunteer. Been here longer than anyone. Any questions you have, she'll have the answer."

And sure enough, the stripper-phone-crusher from last night comes into view. Her tiny white shorts, tan legs, and blousy tank top are conservative compared to what she had on last night. Her long hair is pulled back into a ponytail, and she's grinning big, clapping out a count while encouraging the young girls she's teaching.

"Have fun."

"Great, okay." My eyes are fixed on Trix as my mind tries to make sense of what I'm seeing.

An exotic dancer who volunteers to teach kids?

She must feel my eyes on her because she stops clapping and searches me out. Her body goes rigid when she sees me no more than ten yards away, staring. A tiny grin pulls at her lips, and her eyebrows dip in confusion.

"Mr. Mason, can you teach me how to kick someone's butt?"

I rip my eyes from Trix and focus on the kid, who appears to be around eight years old, staring up at me. His shirt is two sizes too big, and I can see his mismatched socks through the holes in his shoes.

"What's your name, kid?"

He flashes a mouthful of crooked and missing teeth. "Denny."

I cross my arms at my chest. "Alright, Denny, whose butt needs kicking?"

He shifts on his feet and studies the blue mat below them. "My stepdad. He's always tellin' me what to do." He wipes his nose along the length of his little forearm.

My chest tightens, and I squat down to meet Denny's eyes. "Not sure it's a good idea to go after your stepdad, bud, but I'll tell you what." I nod to his feet. "Take your shoes off, and we'll work through some moves so that, if and only if you're in a position to defend yourself or someone you love, you can take down a man five times your size."

His eyes grow even bigger. "Really?"

"Really." I push to standing and ruffle his hair. "All of you take off your shoes and socks and meet me at the kickboxing bags."

—

## TRIX

"And *that* is exactly why I love coming on Sundays." Alize, one of the teenage girls I've been teaching dance to for the last few months, points over her shoulder.

I don't even have to ask who she's talking about. I saw him earlier with Sylvia.

"That's what I'm sayin'. What's up with the man candy? Every Sunday it's a different hottie." Isabella has one hand cocked on her curvy hip, eyes focused on Mason as he works on some punching with a handful of boys.

"I think imma need some fighting lessons, girls. Shiiit."

I muffle a laugh. "Alright, alright, that's enough." I wave for them to come in for a huddle. "Desi, if you use that language around Sylvia, she'll make you run laps."

"Miss Trixy, you know I save my best bombs just for you."

"Oh, I'm sure you do," I say sarcastically.

The kind of kids who show up here at the Community Youth Center are rougher than most. I'm not naïve enough to think that anything I do will change the path of their lives. I just want to give them a safe place to be themselves without judgment. God knows they'll get enough of that outside these walls. I've seen what they're capable of when they're not being forced into a mold, when they're given choices and their individuality is encouraged. It's nothing short of a miracle.

"Let's take a break, and then we'll come back and work through the routine from the start." We all put our hands in the middle of a huddle and yell "break."

They move to the bleachers to grab water, but I head over to Mason. I thought we ended on okay terms last night. It seems ridiculous to be in the same room and not say hello.

"Aww, shit. Miss Trixy's gonna make her move," Desi yells, and the rest of the girls dissolve into giggles.

I laugh and scurry to avoid them so they won't see the pink in my cheeks. My heart pounds a little harder the closer I get, and I convince myself it's the girls watching me rather than Mason who my body is reacting to.

"Good job, Den!" Mason's deep voice carries across the space between us. "Keep your hands up. Jab. Left-left-right. Good!"

I stop at the edge of the mat, not wanting to interrupt. He's on his knees, oval pads strapped to his hands, barefoot. His simple white T-shirt and blue, knee-length exercise shorts add a sexy casualness to his shaggy blond hair. My eyes trace down the rippling muscles of his wide back as it flexes and releases while absorbing Denny's blows.

"Yeah, bud, you got this! In ten years, you'll be takin' my job."

Spurred on by Mason's words, Denny's face tightens in concentration, shiny with sweat, as he grunts through every punch. One and then the other, he fires his tiny fists into the pads until he drops his arms, panting.

"Alright, who's next?" Mason rocks back to the balls of his feet and pushes to standing with a fluidity I've never seen on a man of his size. He turns and his eyes catch mine. They register surprise then cautious curiosity. "Trix."

"Mason, hey." I step onto the blue mats and cross to him. "I noticed you over here and wanted to say hi."

He hands the pads he was holding up for Denny to Leon. "Hey, man, you mind holding these for the next guy?" Leon nods excitedly and slips on the pads. After a quick instruction from Mason, he goes down on his knees to take punches.

Mason turns his attention back to me, his towering frame seeming so much bigger now, maybe because I'm not wearing my heels.

"I'm glad you came over. I have to say"—he casts his gaze around quickly—"I didn't take you for the volunteering type," he whispers.

I shrug. "Eh . . . condition of my parole. It was this or pick up trash on the side of the freeway."

His smile fades. "Parole? Really?"

"No."

He grips his chest and shakes his head, a low chuckle rumbling from his wide chest. "Damn, I was gonna say . . . You're full of surprises."

I survey the gym and shrug. "I like the kids, and you know I like to dance so . . ."

"You're training the next generation of strippers, huh?" He immediately cringes. "Sorry, that was supposed to be a joke."

I wave him off. "Yeah, I got that. Funny." An awkward silence builds between us, and my eyes dart everywhere to avoid getting lost in his square jaw and full lips. "So you're one of the UFL guys. I've seen a few of them come through here. Cool thing you guys are doing."

"Wish I could say I came here by choice, but our boss is a demanding ass and forces us."

His statement stabs me with a sliver of disappointment, but I'm not completely sure why. "Give it a chance. You'll learn to love it."

"I can see that." His face goes serious, and he moves in close. "Listen. I wanted to talk to you about last night, but you took off so fast. About my phone—"

"Oh, yeah"—my cheeks heat—"I feel really bad about that."

"Don't. I shouldn't have blown up at you the way I did. I had just come from . . . You know what? It doesn't matter." He meets my eyes. "It was uncool and I'm sorry."

"No biggie, really." I turn to look over my shoulder at my girls, who are all staring with open mouths. "Listen, do you want to have lunch with us later?"

"Lunch?" He rubs the back of his neck. "I didn't even think to bring anything."

"That's okay. I'll share mine."

He squints one eye. "Really? You'd do that?"

I lean in, and he meets me halfway, the organic scent of his skin, like cedar and honey, swirls and scrambles my senses.

I take in a deep breath and whisper, "I'm an exotic dancer, not a monster."

—

## MASON

I put in my hours and am technically free to leave, but instead, I'm sitting in the grass under a tree with Denny and a couple of the older boys I was working with along with Trix and three teenage girls. A slight breeze takes the edge off the Vegas summer heat, and the ground beneath us is cool enough to make the temperature comfortable.

Trix sits with her back against the tree's trunk, her toned legs stretched out in front of her, as she digs through an insulated lunch box. I'm close to her feet, legs out, palms to the grass behind me.

"Mr. Mason said I could fight for the UFL when I grow up, Miss Trixy." Denny digs into a brown paper bag lunch the Community Youth Center provided.

Grinning, Trix tosses me a silver juice pouch. "I don't doubt that, Den. You're pretty spectacular."

The kid pulls all the food from the bag while the older kids huddle on the opposite side of the tree. "Yeah." He chews on a bite of peanut-butter-and-jelly sandwich. "Mr. Mason said I'm a natural."

Her eyes on the boy, her expression softens before she aims her smile at me. "I saw your moves," she says, but doesn't take her eyes from mine. "I think Mr. Mason's right." She hands me a little bag filled with carrots and rips a sandwich in half. "Here. It's just turkey and mustard. I hope that's okay."

I take her proffered food, feeling like a total dick, but also not wanting to offend her by rejecting it. "Are you sure? I can wait until I leave to eat."

"I always bring extra. The Center gives them lunch, but the older kids need more food than they provide so . . ." She pulls out three more bags of carrots and tosses them to the teenagers, who thank her. She takes a bite of her sandwich and nods. "Go ahead."

I pop the slim yellow straw into the juice pouch and take a sip. I can't explain what it is about these kids. I can tell just by lookin' in their eyes that they've lived more life than those twice their age and most of it probably not good. Working with them for only a few hours has me feeling like absolute dog shit about my earlier attitude. *Our boss is a demanding ass and forces us.* God, Trix must think I'm a shallow idiot.

"Wait!" Denny holds up his hand. "We forgot to pray!"

Trix smiles and puts down her sandwich. "Right, good thinking, Den."

Denny snags my hand and Trix's then waits impatiently, staring between my other hand and hers. "Mr. Mason, we need to make a circle."

Trix and I link hands, and her tiny fingers feel so soft and warm against my palm. I try not to imagine what those hands would feel like against my bare chest or wrapped around my—*no, sick bastard! We're about to pray for shit's sake!*

"Close your eyes and bow your head," Denny commands.

I dip my chin and peek over at Trix, who is doing the same with a huge smile on her face. She pops one eye open and then rolls her lips between her teeth to keep from laughing. I squeeze her hand and fight the urge to follow suit.

"Ahem . . . Dear God, thank you for the sun and for our food. Thank you for bringing us Mr. Mason so he can teach me how to fight. And thank you for Miss Trixy, who teaches us how to pray. Amen." Denny drops our hands and dives back into his lunch in a way that makes me wonder when the last time he ate was.

"That was a kick-butt prayer, Den." Trix throws back a gulp of her water.

She teaches them how to pray. I study the woman at my side and mull over all I know about her.

She strips in a titty bar and doesn't bat an eyelash at illegal drugs. She volunteers with at-risk kids and teaches them to pray.

Something doesn't add up.

# FIVE

## MASON

It's Tuesday morning, and I'm stuck in the conference room with the rest of my camp while Cameron lectures us on shit I'm sure I already know.

After my volunteer day at the Community Youth Center, I couldn't stop thinking about Trix. As incredible as she is dancing near naked, she's just as amazing with her clothes on. Her moves weren't nearly as provocative, but she's clearly a gifted dancer. So why strip? Here in Vegas, a thousand different venues would pay well for a dancer with her skill, and she could keep her damn clothes on.

It doesn't make any sense.

What doesn't make even more sense is why the hell I can't stop trying to figure her out. She's like a Rubik's Cube; the more I twist her around in my head, the less she makes sense.

My phone rattles against the conference table with an incoming text. I reach for it and check to see it's from Drake. Shit.

**Meet me tonight.**

A prickle of unease races up my spine. I haven't heard from my brother since that night at the hotel suite. I'd hoped they'd partied their asses off and gotten back home the next day with nothing more to show for their Vegas experience than a nasty hangover. But, no, he's still here.

Which means he's up to no good.

Although we were raised by our mother, our fathers couldn't have been more different. Mine was attentive, always paid child support, showed up for every wrestling match, and bought me whatever I wanted. Drake was lucky to get a phone call on his birthday, and most years he didn't. Because of that, I'd always look out for him. I'd lie and tell my dad I needed new shoes but buy them for Drake and take him shopping with my allowance. It wasn't much, but it was all I could offer. I know Drake was resentful, and I often wonder if that's why he made a play for Jessica. Yeah, I got the college education, but he got the girl.

"Mason! Pay attention!" Cameron's growl of frustration calls me from my thoughts.

I lift my eyes to his, palm my phone, and sink back into my chair with a three-finger salute. "Aye, aye, *Captain*."

"Baywatch." Jonah leans into my line of sight, breaking my glare-off with Cam. "Quit with that shit."

My shoulders lift a tad and I ignore Jonah. It's not like I enjoy making Cam's job difficult or that I have little respect for him after the way he fucked with Eve. Oh, who am I kidding? That's exactly what it is. "Continue." I nod toward the boss standing at the head of the table.

Hard as I try to stay focused, being in a room with Cameron and Eve isn't my idea of a party. The sooner he stops talking, the sooner I can escape and go exhaust myself in the weight room rather than stare at Eve as she jots down notes while biting her lip in concentration. Fuckin' A.

Cameron leans over the table, bracing his weight with two fists. "Thank you for your *permission* to continue my meeting."

"Stop . . . please." Eve's whisper is low enough for only the few of us sitting up front to hear. Her eyes dart to mine and narrow in irritation.

Lame.

I smile wide and act like I'm listening. My foot taps anxiously; I'm so ready to get the hell out of here. A few fighters ask questions, but I remain zip-lipped. I already know everything I need to know. Cameron wants to set up a card with me vs Tanaphon Li, a Muay Thai badass who has been openly challenging me since my first televised fight with the UFL three months ago.

". . . Caleb's training in Europe for another two weeks, and until Blake is back, I want you with Wade and Rex," Cameron's words penetrate because they carry the tone of finality. "Train hard, boys." He's wrapping this shit up. Perfect.

He grabs a stack of papers and hands them to Eve, who shoves them into a folder. A soft expression on his face makes me want to punch a wall. The fighters trickle out one by one.

Rex grips the back of my neck. "Weight room in thirty."

"Yeah." I answer him, but don't take my eyes off Eve, pinning her in place with my stare.

She must get it because, after the final fighter has left, it's just the two of us. She slaps a folder down and glares at me. "What the fuck is your problem?"

A slow chuckle falls from my lips. "I'm surprised you've noticed I *have* a problem."

"How can you say that? You're one of my best friends." Her eyebrows pinch together, and I'd do anything to erase the hurt I see in her expression.

Like she has the right to be hurt. "Was."

"No, *are*. You *are* one of my best friends."

My stomach churns, acid and guilt mixing in an I'm-an-asshole-induced nausea.

"I miss hanging out with you, Mase."

I groan and drop my chin. Why does hearing her say that shoot straight to my gut? The truth is . . . "I miss that too."

I hear the sound of her chair creaking and then shuffling feet. "Then why do you continue to do this?" She props her ass against the table next to me so that I'm eyeing her gray dress pants. "I'm trying to give Cameron a reason to like you, and you're not helping."

"I . . ." I shake my head. She asks a good question, one I can't even answer. "I don't know." I shrug. "You're happy."

"I am." The happy sigh that falls from her lips makes my fists clench. "I want *you* to be happy too, and if you keep taunting Cam, then things are never going to get better."

She's right. I'm a little bitch.

"Oh, I know! We should catch a movie sometime."

"Are you crazy?" I glare up at her, meeting her wide blue eyes. "Cameron would shit himself if we went out alone."

A soft smile curls her lips. "I didn't mean *alone*. You, me, and Cameron."

I flick a balled-up Post-It note across the table. "Fun."

"Just think about it, okay?" The hurt in her voice sounds of disappointment, which tightens my chest.

I nod and avoid her eyes until she gets the hint and grabs her shit to leave me to my pity. God, I'm pathetic. First Jessica, now Eve. Hell, my own mother cheated on my law-abiding dad with a fucking criminal. Sooner or later I'm going to need to suck it up and get the hell over it.

---

"Keep your head down!" Rex is holding the pads, absorbing every punch I throw, which isn't too hard since I'm exhausted. "Come on, Baywatch! Leave it all on the mats."

I growl and throw a left, a right, a left, then drop my hands. "Done." My breath saws in quick bursts. "I'm . . . beat."

"Alright." He drops the pads. "Good job. I think we can call it a day."

"Thank God." I rip off my gloves and toss them to the side of the cage and grab my water.

"You're with Wade tomorrow for sparring. Take it easy tonight, and try to shake off that shitty attitude."

"No clue what you're talkin' about, man—*ouch!* Fuck!" I rub the back of my head where Rex whacked me. "What was that for?"

He faces off with me, his expression serious. "It's been almost a year."

I turn and scoop up my gloves, prepared to end this convo ASAP. "I don't know what you're getting at, but—*ow!*" I rub the back of my head again. "Stop fucking doing that!"

"You keep lying to me; I'll keep hitting you."

I exhale hard and consider what to say next that'll save my noggin from another open palm slap. "I'm over it. I am."

Rex's hand flies, but this time I duck.

"Fine! Okay, fine. I'm pissed, alright! I don't get it. Cameron fucked her up, and she crawled back to him, begging. Makes no sense. She's smart and beautiful and . . ."

"Do you still want her?"

Yes! Well, not really, I mean . . . do I? I shake my head. "I don't know."

He tilts his head and pulls at his lower lip that is usually hooked with a silver ring. "So it's not losing the girl that's pissing you off; it's coming in second place you can't get over."

No. That doesn't even make any sense. Yet somewhere deep in my gut it makes perfect sense. "That's stupid."

"Is it? You're competitive. You have to be to get where you are today. You lost to the underdog, and that shit's been festering for a year."

I blink and shake my head. Fuck, is that all this is? I'm completely over Jessica. Those feelings from high school fizzled out after I found out she was fucking my brother. And although I'd hoped for more with Eve, I don't want to be with someone who doesn't want me.

Am I a better man than Drake, better than Cameron? Yeah. So all this is my bitch ass throwing a fit because Eve chose a guy who isn't as good for her as I know I would've been?

He puts a hand on my shoulder. "Take my advice, bro. Move on. Suck it up. Cut your losses."

"Yeah . . . maybe you're right."

"If you end up fighting Li, you're going to get international attention in a major way. You'll need to focus, give two hundred percent of yourself if you want a chance at winning. The dude is out of your league."

"Thanks a-fuckin' lot."

He shoves my shoulder. "This isn't a joke, Baywatch. Don't let something like hurt feelings get in the way and fuck up how far you've come."

I glare at him, wondering when the hell he got so damn smart. "What're you? The love doctor?"

"Fuck yeah, I am." He smiles, and I twitch with the urge to throat punch him. "You still on for poker night?"

No. Maybe. "I don't know."

"Alright, well . . . let me know. Lane and Wade are in. If you're not, I'll get Talon."

I nod and shove out of the octagon and to the locker room chanting "I am a whiny ass bitch" over and over because everything Rex just said rang true.

I'm just a sore fucking loser.

Great.

---

## TRIX

It's just past five when I pull into the back lot at Zeus's for my shift. My phone tucked between my ear and shoulder, I grab my purse and push the long wet strands of my hair back off my face.

"Did Isaac make the varsity team?" My weekly call home to my folks happened later than usual because of my little brother's football tryouts.

"We won't know until later in the week, but you should've seen him. He did so well. I don't doubt that he—oh, hold on. What is it, honey?" I hear the muffled sound of my mom pressing the phone to her chest, as she always does when our conversations get interrupted, which is often with five kids in the house.

"Mom, I'll let you go." I push out of my car and hope like hell no one notices I'm late.

"Leah wants to talk to you, is that okay?" My mom is the sweetest woman I've ever known, kind and gentle, gracious and loving, and she has the patience of a saint.

"Sure, but I'm late for work, so it'll have to be quick." I lean back against my car, waiting to talk to Leah before I go inside Zeus's, not wanting to expose my little sister, even in voice only, to the debauchery of a strip club.

"Oh, dear. We'll hurry. Here she is." My mom mumbles what I assume is instructions to my sister.

"Hello?"

I grin at the sound of her tiny voice. "Hey, Leah, I miss you."

"H-hi!" My parents adopted Leah from an orphanage in India where little girls are given up freely by their parents. She came to live with us when she was four and has always had the sweetest stutter. "I m-m-miss you."

"I miss you too. How's school?"

"Good, except for the kids who're mean to A-a-ron." Aaron was adopted from Tanzania and is the same age and grade as Leah, so they've been raised like twins. "They call him n-n-names for being black."

My hand grips my phone so tight my fingers go numb. *Those assholes!* "Aw, well kids make fun of things they don't understand. I'm sorry Leah-bear. Tell Aaron he's perfect and that it doesn't matter what anyone else thinks."

My poor parents. Raising eight kids adopted from all over the world and varied in color and ethnicity, Mom and Dad came up with a lot of creative ways to explain hate.

"Okay, Leah," my mom says in the background. "Your sister has to go now."

"I l-love you! Bye!"

"I'll see you in a couple weeks. Bye, munchkin." My heart cramps that I'm not there—that I'm in Vegas rather than home with my mom shouldering the weight of raising kids from the ages of five to sixteen. Being the oldest now, I should be there to help now that Lana is gone. Pain slices through my gut, reminding me exactly why I'm not home. "Mom?"

"Hi, yeah, sorry to keep you. They're so excited for you to come home. We all are. I'll let you go. Have a good night at work, honey." There's a sadness in her voice, but how could there not be? My parents know what I do for a living, and I'm well aware that it rips away at their hearts.

They don't understand why I strip, why I left home at nineteen to become an adult entertainer. Some days, when weeks and weeks pass and I get no new leads, I don't understand either. I get lost in playing the role and forget the reason why I started in the first place: for Lana, always for Lana. And once I accomplish all I need to do here, I swear I'll move home and take care of the only two people in this world who have ever loved and accepted me for exactly who I am.

"Thanks, Mom. Give Daddy a hug and . . . I love you."

"Love you too. Speak soon."

I shove my phone into my bag and mentally prepare for my night. I try to convince myself that this lifestyle hasn't gotten to me, that it's not eating away at my soul, destined to leave me hallow and empty-handed. I've invested too much, given up too much to stop now.

# SIX

## MASON

"Can I get you boys another round?" A red-headed waitress, who I assume is also a stripper, stands with a tray in one hand and the other hand placed on her cocked, lace-clad hip. She's wearing a tight dress made completely of white lace that showcases a blood-red thong and nothing else.

"No, thanks. I'm—"

"Don't listen to him." Jayden whirls his hand, motioning around the table exaggeratedly with big eyes and an equally big grin. "Another round."

She spins on a spiked heel, and we all watch her ass as she struts away to place our order. The music pounds and the glow from the black lights blurs my vision. Why do they insist on making everything in these places glow? The smell of old booze and perfume is so pungent I can taste it. I blink rapidly and check the time. This is miserable. Sooner I get out of here, the better.

I lean over to my brother, who is sitting closest to me. "Why are we here?" I have to practically yell over the throbbing music and don't find it shocking at all that his eyes stay glued to the brunette who's currently grinding against a pole on stage.

His eyes are wide and rimmed with dark circles. It's not uncommon to pull all-nighters in Vegas, but Drake looks like he hasn't slept in days. "Delivery. Figured we'd come early and enjoy the scenery."

So he's here dealing drugs for his piece-of-shit dad. "Makin' the family proud," I mumble.

He grins, quick and shaky, and his eyes dart around the room. "Here's some tequila." He slides a shot in front of me. "Should help dissolve that stick up your ass."

"I'm in training. Can't stay up getting lit all fuckin' night." Irritation flares as Rex's words from today filter through my mind.

*Give two hundred percent of yourself if you want a chance at winning.*

"UFL turned you into a straight-up pussy, big brother." He leans forward and tucks a twenty-dollar bill in the cleavage of the dancer, letting his fingers linger a little too long against her breasts before leaning back. "You always used to be down for whatever . . ." He grabs the shot, throwing it back and slamming it down hard. "Now you're a big ole nerd." His shoulders bounce as he laughs silently and pulls more money from his pocket.

"It's called having a job, Drake. Some would consider that an accomplishment." He wants to piss me off, get me worked up so he can see a glimmer of the old kid I used to be. The scruffy surf kid who would throw a punch if someone simply looked at my little brother wrong.

"Accomplishment." He says the word like he's testing it in his mouth and doesn't like the taste. "Abandoning The Brotherhood is your biggest accomplishment."

My blood fires and I ball my fists. "You've managed to drag every single one of our friends into whatever the fuck it is you're working with your dad, and you think I'm the bad guy? Look at you? You're fuckin' spun out at twenty-one." *Such a fucking waste of potential.*

The waitress returns with our drinks and just in time. I have to keep my cool. I have to.

"Dude, isn't that the chick from Saturday night?" Harrison scrubs a hand over his head, squinting.

What? My head jerks to a small side stage where Angel is swiveling her hips and dropping articles of clothing piece by piece. I breathe through the throbbing in my chest. There was a tiny part of me that thought he was talking about Trix.

They work together. If Angel's here, I'm assuming Trix should be around here too.

"That bitch owes me a private lap dance after the way she and her little blond friend bolted on Saturday." Drake stands up and waves her over. "We've got a paid hour from Saturday night to make up for, boys."

At seeing Drake, Angel's face registers surprise before she nods in recognition and holds up a finger.

"What about Jess?" Fuck, my shoulders are up to my ears and my muscles so tense they feel like they're going to snap.

"Put her on a plane back to Santa *Snooze* yesterday." He flicks another look around the room. "Vegas ain't her thing."

I don't know whether to feel good or bad that he sent Jess home. There's no way the guy is faithful. At least with her gone, he can't fuck someone else right under her nose. That poor girl had no clue what she was getting herself into with my brother.

He fidgets in his seat before tucking more money into a stripper's G-string.

Birdman leans in, looking not all that different from Drake with bloodshot eyes. "That guy got beef?" He jerks his head toward a table of dudes who all seem to be minding their own business.

Jayden and Harrison puff out their chests, drilling holes into a harmless-looking guy with their glares. "That dude?"

Drake pulls up his tee to reveal a gun shoved in his waistband.

I punch his shoulder, catching him off guard and sending him back in his chair. "What the fuck is wrong with you? You can't bring that shit in here!"

"Dude's got problems, giving us looks like—"

"You can't shoot someone for looking at you, dickhead!" I motion to the table of guys. "You're all fucked up on whatever and seein' shit that ain't there."

"Nah, man . . . dude was staring." Charbroil flexes his fists, looking for a fight.

Harrison moves to stand. I grab his bicep and sit him back down just as he jerks free from my hold. "That's it. Come clean right fuckin' now. What the hell is going on with you guys?"

Paranoid. Sketchy. Clearly not sleeping.

"Nothin', man. Just been partying." Birdman wipes his nose almost as if subconsciously.

"Don't get your panties in a bunch." Drake tilts his head, his eyes flicking over to the men at the table and back to me. "We're dropping off some product and then we'll be out—"

"What's *left* of it." Harrison dissolves into a fit of laughter.

Drake aims a glare at him that shuts him right up.

"Hold on." My blood runs cold and my heart pounds heavy in my chest. "So you're dipping into the product you're here to deliver?"

"Shoulda' kept your mouth shut." Jayden shakes his head at his brother.

I lean into my brother. "Do you have a death wish? You think whoever you're dealing to is going to be okay with you using his shit?"

"Why the hell do you care? It's not like dude's gonna show up with a scale!"

"I care because the last thing I need is to call Mom and tell her your ass got dead over . . . You know what? Forget it. I'm fuckin' outta here." I push to stand, but Drake grips my forearm.

"Run away, college boy." His eyes are glossed over, wired and wide, his mouth curves into an unfriendly smirk. "Jess was right. You're a fucking pussy. No wonder she swallowed my dick instead of yours."

My head gets light. Vision blurs. Rage spikes through my veins at the mention of Jessica combined with the worry I have for my brother. How could he be so stupid? The people his dad runs with are hardened criminals, mafia, gangs, the worst of the worst. The kind of men who make people disappear, or worse, make them unrecognizable.

I push up from my seat and move away with staggered steps, hate and remorse battling away in my chest. My feet carry me through the crowd of bodies. Where? I don't know, just . . . away. I push through people, shoving everyone who blocks my path.

"Watch it, asshole!"

I ignore the voices and search for the bathroom, somewhere to splash cold water on my face and calm my shit down. There's a hallway, dark but lit with neon. Possibly the restrooms or, even better, a back exit I can get the hell out and into some fresh air.

My legs carry me back, but my head is stuck on the dilemma of how in the hell to save my brother from himself. Why can't he—*Omph!*

A tiny body goes flying and lands hard. "Ouch!"

That voice. Anger rockets to the surface. I reach down and grab her by her upper arms, lifting her off the ground harder than I intend, mostly because she weighs next to nothing.

I focus on her big eyes and parted lips. Her hair is pulled tight into a sleek long ponytail, and she tilts her head back to glare up at me.

"What is it with you?" I roar in her face. "Why the fuck can't you keep yourself safe?"

—

**TRIX**

"What? You ran into me, jerk!" I try to shrug out of his hold, but he takes two steps forward until my back presses against the wall.

My ass burns, pain slicing through my left cheek. Why is he looking at me like he wants to kill me . . . or eat me?

Whatever softer side of Mason I saw at the Community Youth Center is a memory. The dickhead is back.

He leans in, his eyes on my lips, his angered breath in bursts against them. Silence builds between us, along with something else. Something alive ripples between his chest and mine. His glare, piercing blue fire, lights beneath a wavy mess of blond hair. I'm sucked in, falling helplessly into the draw of his gaze.

Without warning, he pushes closer and buries his nose into my neck, breathing in deep and running it from my shoulder to my ear. My head tilts, unable to resist the gentle touch: so innocent and yet heavy with promise of something more.

"Mmm, what is it about you?" The rumble of his deep voice races goose bumps down my arms. "You smell like heaven."

No, I don't want this. Not when he's mad. His hands glide down my arms to my hips, and his long powerful fingers clench my flesh. My eyes fall shut on a moan.

I'm like clay, molding to his will, helpless in a way I can't explain, but the power of his body and the sense that he's hanging onto the last string of his control are a heady combination. His lips join in the exploration of my neck, not wet, just soft sweeps against my shoulder.

"Mason . . . wha—what are you doing?" I don't want him to stop, but this isn't right. Just seconds ago he looked like he wanted to rip my head off. Even still, I won't push him away. I'm physically incapable of pushing him away, completely at his mercy.

"What are you doing to me, Trix?" He drops his forehead against my shoulder, and his breathing is heavy enough to match my own. He moves and pushes me back, holding my hips so that my backside presses into the wall.

A hiss shoots from my lips.

"Fuck!" He puts space between us, but remains with a firm hold on me. "Did I hurt you?"

I turn slightly so that the neon pink light shines on my bottom, which is on fire like a brutal case of road rash.

Mason squints. "Is it . . . you're bleeding."

Well crap. I am. I shrug and tap lightly against the broken skin. "I broke your phone; you broke my ass." The stinging pain cools a little of the heat he'd electrified earlier with his touch.

"Damn." He squats for a closer look and sucks air through his teeth. "I'm really sorry."

"Nah, don't worry about it. The owner of this place just added this textured sandpaper floor because the girls kept slipping in their heels back here. I guess they never considered what would happen if one of us got slammed into it by a behemoth when we're wearing nothing but lace cheekies."

His eyes flare and study my panties. "Is that what these are?" His finger motions to my hip.

"Oh, uh, yeah." This man is unnerving. His size, good looks, hot and cold demeanor . . . I'm fumbling over myself. And I never fumble, especially around men. "Should've worn my leather panties. They're skid-proof." *Stop talking, you sound like an idiot.*

He peers up at me. "I can fix this. Do you have a first aid kit?"

"Oh, psht." I wave him off. "No worries, I'll take care of—"

"No." He shakes his head then rubs the back of his neck. "I feel bad. Let me fix it."

"Oh, um . . ." I glimpse around, trying to figure out where we can go and doctor my ass while he talks. Rules are restricted to no guys backstage so that leaves . . . "Here." I open the door to one of the private rooms. "Wait here. I'll be right back."

After a quick trip to my dressing table for a small first aid kit that I've only had to use for foot blisters, I go back to the private room to find Mason standing uncomfortably in the corner rather than sitting on the red velvet couch.

I close the door behind me and hit the "occupied" slider. His eyes widen. "Don't worry, it's just . . . These rooms are reserved for private dances. I get the feeling you wouldn't want anyone walking in here and thinking the worst of you. "

"Right, um . . ." He reaches out and grabs the kit from my hand then looks around. "Is it possible to get more light in here?"

I reach over and click on the overhead fluorescent bulbs that are usually only used at the end of the night for cleaning purposes. We both squint as our eyes adjust to the brightness.

"Better." He pops open the kit and motions to me. "Go ahead and stand there." He points to the armrest at the end of the couch.

I do as he instructs, but shake my head. "You really don't have to do this."

"No? You think you can bandage your own ass?" He chuckles, and the sound rolls through me like warm honey.

"I could have one of the girls help me out." Why does my voice sound so weak?

I hear him move behind me before I feel the heat of his huge body close to my back.

"Really, it's the least I can do." He rips open a package. "Hmm . . . if you could, um . . ." His voice is lower, as if he's crouched to put his eyes at ass level. "Just uh, lean forward and arch your back so I can, um, get underneath."

I tuck a grin into my shoulder at the discomfort I hear in his voice, grateful that I'm finally making him as unsettled as I feel around him. I'm all too comfortable shoving my butt in a man's face, clearly something Mason isn't used to. I brace my weight on the chair, arch my back, and just for fun I walk my feet apart just a few inches.

Making a man squirm is one of my most favorite things to do. And considering how shaken up he made me, this transfer of power is one of the best feelings I've felt in a long time.

"How's this?" I peek at him from over my shoulder, and his eyes are fixed, staring straight ahead and right between my legs.

He makes a sound in the back of his throat, like a moan but with more edge. "Good."

His hot breath feathers against my skin, shooting straight between my legs. No, no, no, no, Trix. Rule number one, do not get turned on. Sure, Mason is big, gorgeous, and smells like sugar and earth mixed, but I'm in control.

"This might sting."

Cold hits my wound and I flinch slightly.

He dabs at my raw ass and fire ignites across my skin. "Who knows what kind of shit is living on the floor out there."

I suck in air through my teeth.

He keeps dabbing, but his touch is lighter. "You okay?"

"Fine." I grit my teeth. A whimper falls from my lips.

"Shh . . . almost done."

"Damn, that hurts." I drop my chin and breathe deep.

"I know. I'm sorry. The only thing this kit has is alcohol." He sounds pissed, but his touch is still gentle. "Hang in there."

"Keep talking. It helps."

He laughs low and sexy. "Okay."

And we're back to sweet. The way he is with me now is such a contrast to his loss of control after our accidental run in. Now, he reminds me of that man who gave Denny confidence he'd never had before, or comforted a very sad woman who burst into tears just from being on the receiving end of that kindness.

"That girl, Jess? Is she an ex or something?"

His hand stills for a few pregnant seconds. "Jessica?" The sting of alcohol is back. "She, um . . . She was a long time ago." He stops and rips open more packages. "She and my brother have been together now for years."

"Your brother? So the guy with the"—I pause, trying to think of a polite way to say—"big ole scar on his face".

"Drake, yeah." His finger swipes across my wound, this time warm and smooth like ointment.

"I didn't think you guys were related. I guess there's a little resemblance." The burning begins to numb.

"He's the darker, stockier, uglier version of me." He sticks what feels like a Band-Aid on my backside. "There ya go. All set."

He pushes up, and I turn to thank him, only to realize that he's still just a few inches away, so close I can smell the whiskey and mint of his breath.

"Look, Trix. I feel like an ass. I've run into you twice, and both times I was a dick."

"No biggie." My eyes are locked on his, and I can't look away. "I figured you weren't yourself."

His eyebrows pinch, but his lips curl. "You figured? You don't even know me."

"I know men." I tilt my head and study him. "You don't have it in you to be a full-time jerk. Part-time? Maybe. You're a good guy at heart."

"That's me." His jaw ticks, and I wonder if dickhead Mason is about to reappear. "Mr. Nice Guy."

I cross my arms under my bustier-clad breasts, settling in for the playful argument I feel coming. "Your bandaging my ass only confirms it."

He squints one eye. "It kinda does, doesn't it?"

Silence builds between us, his blue eyes going from mirthful to something heated. My breath speeds along with my pulse, and his eyes track from my chest to my eyes and down to my lips.

"You're beautiful," he whispers, almost as if he didn't mean to say it out loud.

"Thank you." The urge to touch him is overwhelming. Tentatively, I reach out and fork my fingers into his hair. His lips part as I run my nails softly down his jawline. "You're beautiful too."

What am I doing? This is so far beyond professional flirting. This is . . . What is this? I've been in these rooms with more good-looking men than I can count, but none of them have brought out this urge in me: the desire to touch and to learn and to know someone without an end game, without a dollar amount flitting through my head. No calculations, just pure, raw, animalistic desire.

"Mason?"

"Hmm." He steps closer, just one half step that brings his chest to mine.

Breath catches in my throat at the contact. My tongue moistens my lips while I stare unabashed at his full mouth. "May I kiss you?

His eyes flare, the blue turning into pure liquid fire. "Fuck yeah." He grips my hips and tugs me to him.

I hook my arms around his neck, thankful for my stiletto heels that put me not much shorter than his six-foot-something height. My stomach tumbles, my heart throbbing in my chest as he lowers his mouth to mine.

Softly he brushes his lower lip against my upper as if he's asking permission or waiting for me to beg: a simple act, so tiny and yet so hot. Most men I deal with, even the one's I sleep with, are quick. Very little seduction's involved with a sure thing. But this . . . This is something new, foreign, and unbelievably sexy.

I tilt my head and allow the very tip of my tongue a taste of his lips. We groan simultaneously at the touch, and his fingers dig deep into the flesh of my hips. Finally, after a few more light teases, we open to each other, allowing our tongues to finally meet in a slick friction I feel in my toes.

"Fuck," he whispers against my lips. "I knew you'd taste like this." He dives back into my mouth, this time deeper, sucking at my tongue.

My legs wobble beneath the mind-scrambling power of his kiss, and I fist my hands into his hair to keep upright. Alternating between nips of our teeth, pulls of suction on each other's lips, and hands that grasp one another, I lose myself to his mouth.

"Hey!" There's a pounding at the door. "Everything okay in there?"

I rip my lips from Mason's, breathing heavy. "Yeah, Santos. Be out in a minute."

"Time's up, Trix. You know the rules."

Mason's glaring at the door, and his hands continue to hold me close to him.

"Shoot. I better go. I'm up next, and I need to find something to wear that'll cover my injured booty." Not to mention get my damn head together. I release him and take a step back only to have him follow me with a step forward.

"Up next . . ." The softness of his expression turns hard.

My eyes grow tight. "Yes."

His grip tightens. "Why."

The fire of irritation stirs in my belly at the judgment I hear in his voice.

"Because it's my job."

He laughs, but there's no humor in it. "To get naked for a room full of horny dickheads."

And there it is. Judgment.

"Oh, and you're so much better than I am? You beat the shit out of people for a living."

"I can't even believe you'd compare the two!" He steps close, his fingers digging into my skin. "I'm a mixed martial artist. What you do is visual foreplay. Give men something to jack off to."

My breath catches in my throat at his cruelty. Maybe he's not such a nice guy after all.

His eyes narrow. "Do you get off on it?" He sneers.

"Have you lost your damn mind?" I peel his fingers off my hips and move to the door.

"You do, don't you?"

I shove him in the chest. "You have no idea why I do what I do."

"It's not rocket science, *Trix*." His low and condescending chuckle freezes my blood. "You didn't even fucking *flirt* with me at the club with those kids."

The chill of his voice makes my skin prickle.

"Propping your ass in my face and suckin' on my tongue is all part of the job, huh?" He moves past me, grabbing the door and flinging it open so hard I flinch. "I might be nice, but I'm not stupid."

With long strides, he carries himself down the short hallway and disappears into the crowd, leaving nothing but the sear of his lips and an ache in my chest behind.

—

## MASON

Being stuck in a tiny room with Trix, I found her presence all consuming. The delicate scent of her skin combined with her half-naked body overloaded my senses. Then her smile, that tiny curve of her lips, gave way to an innocence that contradicted her overly sexy appeal.

I felt something. Something beyond a simple stir in my pants. Yeah, I felt that too, but I also felt myself falling. The woman she is beneath the lingerie and makeup, behind her seductive looks and dance moves, she's the one I want. But that's not who she is, at least, not entirely. As much as her reminding me she's a damn stripper was unwelcome, it's exactly what I needed to hear to pull myself away.

The back door isn't far from the room I've just stormed out of. I shove past a bouncer and out into the back lot. The place was packed when I got here, so I settled for a spot around the corner and on the street. The sooner I get free of this place, the sooner I can get my shit together.

My feet pound the pavement, and I flex and release my fists to burn off the urge to punch a fucking wall. The muffled sound of angry male voices calls my attention to an alley not far from where my truck is parked. Looks like someone's having a worse night than I am. A pained whimper echoes off the brick buildings, and I move toward the dark corridor.

Slowly, I peek down the alley only lit by a single streetlight. A group of dudes huddles around something, fists swinging and legs kicking. I have only seconds to act, and I wonder if calling the cops would be the better idea. I'm outnumbered and pretty sure whatever's going on here I want no part of. I reverse back out of the alley, pulling my phone out of my pocket when I hear him.

"Not so tough when your daddy's not around, eh, Drake?"

I spring into action, my legs burning up the distance between them and me. "Hey! Get the fuck off him."

They all whirl on me, and I see Drake curled up on the ground, bloody and not moving. One of the assholes grins seconds before I slam my fist into his jaw. Catching him off guard, he rocks back on his heels, cupping his face. Another advances and takes the brunt of my jab. One more, I swing. He grunts and falls back. Before I'm able to throw another punch, my arms are locked up behind me. I roll into it and toss the guy holding me to his back. I'm grabbed again. My left arm gets loose, and I swing hard at the man advancing. He goes down.

It takes three of the six of them to lock me down. "Leave him alone." I'm breathing heavy and still struggling to get free; my shoulders burn as I try to rip from their hold.

The biggest of the group glares at me and wipes blood from his lip. "This ain't your business, man. You should've walked away." He kicks Drake in the back.

"Don't fucking touch him!" I pull my arm free and lunge, but am quickly re-restrained.

"You know this kid?" His eyes move between my brother and me.

"You touch him again . . . I'll break both your arms." My teeth grind together.

He hauls off and kicks him again. Drake's not making a sound. Is he dead?

"Stop!"

He places the sole of his boot on Drake's head, resting it there like my little brother is a prized kill from a recent hunt. "Stop? This kid ripped me off."

Drake moans, and I notice then that the guy is slowly putting pressure on Drake's head.

"No, please don't." Fuck, he's going to crack his skull!

"Don't what?" He presses harder, making Drake squirm.

"Stop. Whatever he owes, I'll pay it. Just fucking stop. Now!"

The guy lifts his eyebrows but doesn't remove his foot. "You're taking on his debt?"

"Yes." Dammit! I'm so used to saving his ass I didn't even consider what the debt is. Not that it matters. They're going to kill him. "If you'll leave him alone."

He saunters over to me, eyes intent. It's then I notice what he's wearing. Leather vest, jeans, chain hanging from his hip, and big heavy black boots.

"You'll deliver three times our original amount exactly one week from today."

Fuck! If Drake survives this, *I'm* going to kill him.

"Same time, right here." He tilts his head to study me. "If you're late, if the weight is off by even a fraction of an ounce, you and this piece of shit are dead."

I flick a gaze to Drake, who has rolled to his back, his face not showing even a hint of skin as it's covered in blood.

"Fine. One week. Here." I swallow hard and contemplate the predicament Drake's sorry ass just put me in. "You give me your word. I follow through. You leave us alone."

He holds his arms out wide. "On my word, brother."

There's coughed-up laughter by the men holding me back. I wrench free, and they step back to avoid me swinging. I don't, but instead rush to my brother.

His face is swollen, puffy slits that don't show even a hint of his eyes, and his nose and lips are busted. My hands hover over him, unsure where to touch him that won't hurt.

"See you soon, sunshine." The biker asshole chuckles through an overgrown mustache and goatee, and they move toward the mouth of the alley.

"Wait!"

They turn around.

"How much? You said three times the amount. I don't know what it was or how much he owed."

The big guy grins wide. "Ask him. Oh, and try to be smarter than your brother and come unarmed." He holds up Drake's gun, grinning, and then tucks it back into his waistband. "Thanks for the piece." He laughs and disappears around the corner.

"Fuck, Drake!" I pull my shirt off and put it under his head. "What the fuck have you gotten us into now?"

---

It took me an hour to get Drake cleaned up enough to assess the damage those guys did. Figured dragging him through the casino and lobby of Caesars like a slab of raw meat wouldn't be the best idea, so I brought him home to my place.

He's banged up, probably could use a few stitches, and I'm pretty sure he has a broken rib, but he refuses to let me take him to the hospital. A few ace bandages around his torso and butterfly Band-Aids on his eye will have to do.

"He's good. I loaded him up on pain meds, and he's sound asleep on my couch." I watch my brother's chest rise and fall, making sure he's not dead and that I'm not lying to Jayden.

"He didn't even tell us he was going; fucker just disappeared. We should've been there. Had his back. I can't believe this shit!"

"Pack your shit and get some fucking sleep. You guys are gone tomorrow, understand?"

"Mason—"

"Just fucking tell me you understand!"

A few beats of silence are followed by Jayden's long exhale. "Yeah, man. We'll be gone first thing."

"Good. Pick Drake up on your way out of town. I'll text you the address."

I don't wait to hear him confirm and press "end" before setting the alarm on my phone to go off every few hours.

This is going to be a long fuckin' night.

I drop down into an overstuffed club chair and drop my head back, rubbing my forehead.

I knew their coming to town would end up biting me in the ass. I go from volunteer work at the Youth Community Center to drug dealer in less than a couple days.

My head spins, and I try to force myself to think clearly. Between Drake and his dad's connections, they should be able to get what's needed by the time I need to deliver it in a week. After that, I'm cutting ties with all this: my brother, his lifestyle, all of it. I've lived too many years of my life, saving Drake from himself, but now I have way too much to lose, and he's going to have to start making healthier choices.

Or better yet, have his dad bail his ass out of trouble from now on.

After all, he's the one who got him into this bullshit in the first place.

# SEVEN

## MASON

"There's no way Tom Curren is a better surfer than Kelly Slater." Wade tosses his cards into the center of the table. "Fold."

"He is, bro. Google that shit." I scan my fanned-out cards and pull two, flipping them face down and pushing them to Rex. "I'll take two."

After my brother dragged ass back to Santa Cruz with a bruised body and a shattered ego, my life picked up right where it left off, starting with poker night at Rex's. Drake swears his dad will take care of everything from here on out and that I'll have exactly what I need to deliver in less than a week. He better be right, but history proves I shouldn't be too optimistic.

"I wouldn't fuck with Baywatch, man." Rex slides my cards toward him. "He lifeguarded with Hasselhoff; he would know—"

"Real fuckin' funny." I throw a chip at Rex's head, and he dodges it easily.

"I can't find my keys," Gia calls from across the room as she makes her way to us. Her flowing orange hair falls just past her shoulders in loose curls.

Rex's eyes dart from her to his cards. "Must've lost them."

"Right." She moves in behind Rex and runs a hand over his messy hair before bending over to kiss his head. "Hand 'em over."

He feigns innocence and pulls her hand from his shoulder to place a kiss on the underside of her wrist. "No clue what you're talkin' about, babe."

"I'm not taking the bike. I just need my house key." She rolls her eyes and acts as if this isn't the first time her man has put her motorcycle on lockdown.

"Oh, in that case, they're in the freezer." He slaps down two cards and passes them to me with a slanted grin.

"You're annoyingly sweet when you're protective." Gia ruffles his hair again and moves to snag her keys. "So, who's winning?"

Lane, Rex's guitar player, organizes his chips. "Like you have to ask?" He motions to his stacks with a big dramatic sweep of his hand.

Rex grabs Gia as she passes and pulls her down to his lap, his finger moving to play with the single diamond she has hanging from her neck. "Where are you girls going tonight?"

"Dinner, but I probably won't be home until late. We always get to talking and lose track of time."

"You having a girls' night out?" Wade perks up in interest. "Is it with that dirty little blond waitress from The Blackout?"

"Dude, whatever happened to the girl you brought to Blake's wedding? That was, like . . . a week ago." I put my cards face down and take a long pull from my beer.

"She's a sweet girl." He grins.

The doorbell rings and Gia jumps. "Oh, that's her." She scurries off to the front door, and Lane lays down three of a kind.

"Nice, but . . ." I fan my royal flush and lay it down. "Bam!"

Rex and Lane groan, and before I pull all the chips to me, a voice tickles my ear. So familiar, I can almost taste the lips that it came from.

My entire body ignites, blood thunders through my veins, and my skin prickles with anticipation. I haven't been able to stop thinking about her since that kiss . . . fuck, that *kiss*.

"Son of a bitch." I mumble the words, and before I can even turn to look, Gia is at the table.

"Guys, this is my friend Trix."

No shit.

I turn to look up at her and my breath catches. Dammit, she's pretty.

She's in baggy jeans that hang off the flare of her hips, ripped and rolled up to her calves. Her top is fairly conservative, a loose-fitting charcoal gray tank that has the words "Life Starts at Midnight" scrolled across the front. She's wearing her hair more natural, aside from the purple, than I've ever seen it: long and wavy like she's been hanging out at the beach all day. And fuck me: the girl's wearing flip-flops, her toes tipped in pink nail polish.

"These are two of the guys Rex fights with, Wade and Mason." Gia saying my name pulls my attention back to Trix's eyes.

Her expression registers shock for a second before she wipes the look clean. She shifts uncomfortably on her rubber sandals and stares between us. "Nice to meet you."

That damn voice makes my skin hot, and everything below my waist come to life, including my legs' urge to run the hell out of here.

I don't know how to act around this woman. I mean, she's a stripper for shit's sake. She has seduction down to an art and uses it freely as a way to earn a living. That's all this is. My feelings, her face invading my thoughts, it's what she's trained to do, what she gets paid for. And I'm just the shmuck to fall for it.

"And I know you know, Lane," Gia says in a knowing way that makes my fists clench and my gut burn.

Lane grabs Trix's arm and pulls her into his lap. "Mm, baby . . . I've missed you." He buries his face in her neck, and I'm so stuck on the visual I can't move.

Dammit to shit.

Trix's eyes dart to mine a split second before she pushes Lane's head back and moves to try and stand. "Fuck off, Lane."

"Oh, come on, baby . . ." Lane pouts but releases her. "Don't act like you don't miss me."

She straightens her shirt and shakes her head. "You're a dick."

I can't see her face through the thick waves of her hair, so I can't tell if she's okay, and not knowing fills me with unease.

"No, I got a dick." He pushes his chair back, legs open. "It's ready if you're willing, baby."

"*Lane*." The word rumbles through my clenched teeth, and it's taking every ounce of my strength to keep my ass in my seat. "Enough."

The room goes silent except for the sound of Alkaline Trio playing on the stereo. Lane's eyebrows pinch together, in confusion more than aggression, and the air around me is charged with tension.

Rex clears his throat. "Where are you girls off to?"

Gia's wide eyes swing between Lane and me, and then she blinks and focuses on Rex. "Oh, um . . . we're going to check out *I Love Burgers*."

Rex nods toward the door, a silent *maybe you should get the hell out of here* to his girl.

She gets the message and grabs Trix. "Bye, guys."

"Yeah, nice meeting you, Wade," Trix says from behind me.

A surge of jealousy rages inside me. "Yo, Trix." I cock my head to see her, my muscles tense.

The room is still quiet, and all eyes move between the mauve-eyed beauty and me.

"Yeah?"

"How's your ass after our last run in? Better?" I immediately regret being such an ass as muffled laughter sounds throughout the room. Fuck if the high of being a jerk isn't short-lived.

A small grin tilts her lips, and she straightens her shoulders. "Yeah, Mason. Why wouldn't it be?" Her eyes slide slowly down to my crotch and back to my eyes, defiance shining behind them. "I barely felt it."

The room erupts in a series of *awww shits* and *she told yous*, but I ignore them.

I lock eyes with Trix as she stares at me, anticipating something. Our gazes tangle, and I can't help but get lost in the violet depths. Seconds pass before her expression falls. Her eyes dart among the guys, now painfully obvious about avoiding mine. Shit, why am I such a mess around this girl?

"Later." She waves with a flick of her perfect hand and moves through the room to the door, Gia following behind her.

Way to go, genius.

Couldn't have fucked that up any better.

## TRIX

"God, I feel like I might explode." I lean back in my seat, hoping it'll stretch out my belly enough to give the food I just ate somewhere to settle. "That was so good."

Gia makes a pained face. "So damn good."

We moan and groan for a second, and I consider how grateful I am for good friends. If this were a date, I'd have stopped at half a burger and passed on the fries, but with Gia, I can stuff my face until my heart explodes.

"Phew . . ." I take a swig of my beer. "I'm gonna sleep like a baby tonight."

She tilts her head with tiny tilt to her lips. "You sound like an old man."

"Sometimes I feel like an old man." I rub my stomach and fake burp.

We laugh, and when it dies, she leans in with her elbows propped on the table. "How are you doing?" All that bright hair and those lightly freckled cheeks give her an innocent appearance that contradicts a painful past that shines through her thoughtful steel-colored stare.

I swallow and play stupid. "Whoa . . . call the party foul police." I motion to her with my beer bottle hand. "Holy serious face, batman."

She simply lifts one eyebrow.

I roll my eyes. "Gia . . . I already told you—"

"I know what you told me, but I don't believe you."

"Hatch and I hooked up." I shrug and force myself to look casual. "Nothing more."

"I think you miss him."

My thumb rolls back the soggy label from my beer bottle. "I don't." I just need him.

She worries her bottom lip for a second. "You seem, I don't know, different. Preoccupied maybe?"

"No." I shake my head and shrug. After Mason's blow off at Zeus's and then again tonight at Gia's house, I'm starting to think the guy despises me, but I just can't figure out why.

"Crap. If it's not Hatch, then . . . is it Mason?"

My eyes bulge out of my head. "What? Why . . . why would you? No!" I pull my hair back and twist it behind my head, thinking. How do I explain without outing myself? "Yes, I mean . . ." A long exhale falls from my lips, and defeat weighs heavy as I consider how to lie to my friend.

Would it be so terrible to let her in just a little? She could help me find the answers I'm searching for. After all, she lived with Hatch for longer than I've ever spent time with him. Neither she nor Rex talks about it openly, and she's never divulged anything more than the basics of her time there. But maybe if she knew, if she understood the reasons for my searching, she'd offer something helpful.

"Gia?" I keep my gaze down, but feel her staring at me. "Do you know what it's like to need someone you hate?" I peek up at her, and her expression is blank. "You almost have to become someone else to get close, and when you do, you realize you'd do anything, give up anything, just to get closer, even though you can't stand the person?"

She recoils at my words, and I instantly feel like shit. After Gia took off and ended up living with Hatch at the Wild Outlaw MC compound, she was so messed up and dependent on him she could've died.

I depended on Hatch for information. She depended on him for survival.

"Gia, I'm sorry. That didn't come out right. I meant that—"

"No need to apologize." She shakes her head as if she's trying to shake free the memories. "I know exactly what you mean, and of course I have. I know the feeling well." Her fingers toy with the ripped ends of her paper napkin. "Rex, he, uh . . . he doesn't like to talk about it."

"I don't blame him. You should've seen him the night he found out where you were." A shudder runs through my body at the memory.

She nods. "Yeah, I know, but how can we move past it without talking? He never brings it up, refuses to even mention Hatch's name. Even in therapy he shuts down. And the nightmares . . ." A long breath escapes her.

"Give him time. I'm sure he'll come around."

"Anyway what you and Hatch had was not the same as what I had with him."

"It wasn't what it looked like. I just . . . I need to find him and have him be okay." Just, not for the reasons she might think.

She takes a deep breath, and upon exhaling, her shoulders relax. "It's weird. Part of me wants him to be okay, but then there's this other part of me that hopes he's not." She sits back and slumps in her chair. "If Rex ever gets his hands on him . . ."

Only nightmares could do justice to what Rex would do if he were confronted with Hatch again. Rex and Gia are like one soul, bound together for life and beyond. I've never seen anything like it, except for with my parents. Their love transcends all understanding, survives through the most tragic of life's events, even death.

What would it be like to feel that kind of love? I can't even imagine being at a point in my life where I'm free enough to experience it.

"Anyway, I'm sorry I brought it up." She waves me off with a flick of her slender fingers.

I pick at my warming beer bottle. "Can I ask you a question? What was it like living in the MC compound? Did you, I don't know, hear or see anything that freaked you out?"

"I was out of it most of the time. If I wasn't, I'm sure it all would've been pretty freaky." Her eyes go unfocused over my shoulder. "They had prospects that they'd push around: young guys who one day would be serving drinks and taking their shit and then swagger in with their cuts and emblems as full-fledged members. They would talk a lot about rites of passage and being bonded by blood." She tucks her bright orange hair behind her ear. "I didn't really hang out to listen."

"I'm glad you got out of there. That could've ended very differently." A shiver tracks down my spine.

"Because of you, Trix. You saved my life by going to Rex. I'll never be able to repay you for that."

"No need to. That's what friends do."

A wicked grin curls her lips. "Speaking of friends . . . I don't care what you say. I know there's something going on between you and Mason."

My stomach bottoms out at his name. "There's not—"

"Stop denying it!" She slaps her palm on the table and leans in to whisper. "Mason was going to rip Lane's arms off right there in my kitchen."

I groan and drop my head into my hand. "Nothing's going on. I'm just as confused as you, I promise." I push back and down the rest of my beer. "We keep running into each other, and every time we do, I can't tell if he wants to kiss me or kill me."

"In my limited experience, I'd say if he likes you he wants to do both."

Likes me? Mason likes me? Do I like him? A swarm of butterflies takes flight in my belly, answering my internal question.

Oh shit! That's not good. Sure, his hot-cold routine keeps me guessing. He's definitely not hard on the eyes with his casual just-walked-off-a-Quicksilver-photo-shoot look. My body heats at the thought of his strong hands on me, his mouth covering mine, and his breath at my neck.

I slurp down some water, hoping to cool the heat, and search for a quick subject change. "You guys still looking for a house?"

She glares. "Nice try." Her eyes study me so intently that it takes everything in me to not give her what she's asking for and admit I maybe kinda dig Mason. "Fine, I'll leave you alone for now. Just know he's a really good guy, Trix. You could do worse."

"Ha! All I've ever done is worse." Mason's too good for me. Too clean. Unburdened.

We sit and chat for another hour before our butts numb and our jaws are exhausted.

I drop Gia off at home and drive blindly the few blocks to my place. Most of our casual girls' nights out aren't littered with the heavy conversation we had tonight. Next time we'll stick with a more standard less thought-provoking topic.

I pull into the garage, thankful that my roommate's car isn't there. She spends most nights during the week with her boyfriend. Not that I mind. She pays her rent on time, and I get the house to myself.

Grabbing my hobo-chic purse in the dark, I hear the contents ping-ponging down between the seats. "Dammit." I reach over and fish up much as I can, shoving it back into my bag.

I push out of the car and, in one step, almost slam into the towering figure of a man. I gasp and clench my chest. "Holy shit!" My eyes tighten into a glare. "What are you doing here?"

# EIGHT

## MASON

What am I doing here? Excellent question.

I was forced to listen to Lane talk about Trix while playing poker, so caught up in his graphic descriptions of his time with her that I ended up losing all my money along with my patience. He'd called her a "groupie," said she was "fun to play with," and as if that weren't enough to have me wanting to lunge, he'd made reference to the fact that the whole band had had her.

The whole band!

When I turned my glare to Rex, I fantasized about the next time we'd step into the octagon together. I imagined crushing his throat under my forearm until the fucker passed out. He must've felt what was coming because he quickly clarified that he was excluded from that statement. He had never been with her.

Saved from an ass-kicking.

I left, unable to take being in the same room with a man who had been more intimate with Trix than I had. Trix . . . What a stupid fucking name! And if the stories Lane told are true, it would seem the name matches the girl.

She blinks up at me, hand still to her chest as if to calm a racing heart. "You gonna tell me why you're here?" Her eyes narrow. "You followed me."

I nod toward the door that leads into the house. "We need to talk." The words come out on a growl that shocks even me. I have no right to demand answers. All we did was share a meaningless kiss. Even as the words filter through my head, my gut roils at my lie.

"Talk." Her eyes are still narrow, and her lips quirk in a way that makes me want to suck them. "You expect me to just invite you into my home after you followed me home like a damn psychopath?"

I step into her space, her body heat drawing me in. "Are you afraid of me, Trix?"

She pushes back with a step of her own. "I'm not afraid of anyone, but you haven't been overly nice since—"

"Did you hook up with Lane?" The words fly from my lips like arrows and strike.

She recoils slightly. "What?"

"Cut the bullshit. Just tell me the truth."

"Why do you care?" Her question is barely a whisper.

"I have no fucking clue." I rip my hands through my hair. "Answer me."

She swallows hard. "Of course I did."

Ouch. I knew she had, but why does hearing her confirm it piss me off? "Why?"

Her eyebrows pinch in confusion. "Why not, Mason?"

God, hearing my name from her lips, the light ring of her voice, I imagine what it would be like to hear her crying out my name in pleasure. I bite back the urge to take her mouth and press her up against her car. "Because your body . . . you . . ."

"My *body* is a tool, a means to an end." She holds out her arms then drops them hard to her sides. "It's just flesh and bones and nerves. I make money with it, and I have fun with it. And if you're going to stand here and judge me, you can turn your sexy-as-hell ass around and go home."

The air charges between us and I stop breathing. "You think I'm sexy."

"You're an idiot." She moves to push past me.

I grab her elbow and pull her back to face me. "I don't like you."

She juts up her chin. "I don't like you either."

"You fascinate me." I reach out and rake both hands through her hair, pulling it off her shoulders and face to fist it at the back of her head. "And you're so fucking beautiful it hurts."

Her lips part, breath catches. "Mason . . ."

That voice . . . This time it's heavy with something that makes my blood pound in my veins. "You're gonna break me." I tilt my head and crash my lips to hers. She opens to me without hesitation, welcoming the intrusion of my tongue into her hot, slick mouth.

We moan in unison, as if we'd both been holding back and are finally reveling in the release. Her hands grasp at my arms, my biceps, and then pull at my shirt to bring me closer. I suck her bottom lip into my mouth, then the top one, and walk her back until her ass hits her car.

I rip my lips from hers, running them along her jaw to her neck. The light salt from her skin mixes with the rich smell of her hair, and my eyes roll back at the sensory overload. "God, you taste good."

She holds my head to her neck. "Please, don't stop."

I flex my hips, grinding into her body, desperate for the friction on my aching dick. I want to get lost in the feel of her naked body against mine, the warmth of her legs wrapped around me while she whimpers in ecstasy. If I could bathe in her scent, let it wash over me and wear it like skin, I would.

But this is her. What she does and how she gets through life. She's a master of seduction, and holy fuck is she mastering me now.

I slide one hand from her hair and down her body, palming her breast over her shirt. Full and round, it fits perfectly in my hand, and her hardened nipple rakes against my thumb.

"So perfect."

"Yeah, well, they better be." She drops her head back, and I nip and lick at her pulse point. "I paid a fortune for them."

I pull back and meet her heated stare, eyelids dropped low, and lips parted and pink from my kiss. "They're fake?"

She shrugs one shoulder. "Is that a problem for you?"

I bring my other hand down and cup both her breasts, groaning at the feel of their weight in my hands. "No, they're gorgeous." A small grin ticks against my lips. "They feel really good."

She looks down at my hands on her boobs, and I almost laugh at the awkwardness of it all that for some reason doesn't feel that awkward. "I had an excellent plastic surgeon."

"Huh." I squeeze her breasts, and we both burst into laughter. "Sorry." I drop my hands and do a quick readjusting of my shorts to alleviate the discomfort.

"No need to be sorry. I'm not ashamed that I have breast implants."

I shove my hands into my pockets, my palms raging to be pressed back into the softness of her chest. "Occupational necessity I suppose."

She shakes her head and smooths her hair tangled by my hands. "Necessity? No, but you're right, being well-endowed doesn't *hurt* in my business."

I push down the reminder of what she does for a living. Feeling brave, I reach and tuck a swirled purple-platinum lock behind her ear. "I like your hair."

A tiny blush hits her cheeks. "Thanks." She ducks her chin. "I get bored, so I'm always changing it." She runs her teeth along her bottom lip, eyes darting to the door. "Listen, um . . . do you still want to come inside?"

Fuck if this shy side of her isn't getting me hotter.

"I thought you weren't stupid enough to invite in a psychopath." I lift an eyebrow.

"I'll take my chances."

Silence builds between us for a few seconds before she clears her throat and grabs her purse from the ground where she'd dropped it. "Come on. I want to show you something."

—

## TRIX

This is stupid. I shouldn't invite him in. His presence alone takes up all the space in my head and the air in my lungs.

He followed me to ask me about Lane, and when I told him the truth, he was jealous. I've never had a guy get jealous over me before. Even the men I've been intimate with have always understood what I am, what I do. It's a mutual agreement of no attachments. I've never had an opportunity to have a real boyfriend, not that I'd want one. Since the beginning, I've been on a fact-finding mission. Relationships are a distraction I don't need. Not that anyone's offered me a commitment. I get naked for strangers for a living for crying out loud, not exactly the kind of woman a guy wants to settle down with.

I move through the kitchen, flicking on lights, and hear Mason's heavy footfalls behind me. He doesn't say anything, but I catch him checking out the place from the corner of my eye.

My place isn't a dump; it's a nice two-bedroom house in a subdivision where all the houses look the same. My furniture isn't anything to brag about, but it's comfortable and serves its purpose. But something about having him in my home makes me wish I had things he'd be impressed by.

We move through to the living room, and I click on a lamp at the side table. "Make yourself at home. I'll be right back."

He doesn't sit, but meanders to the back sliding glass door and parts the vertical blinds to peek outside.

I head to my bedroom and pull open a drawer at the bottom of my dresser. Tucked in the back, beneath my everyday clothes, is a stack of pictures, and I grab it to sort through them until I find the right one.

A questioning voice in my head asks why I'm exposing this part of my life to a guy I hardly know. I've had plenty of guys in my home and in my bed, and I'd never dream of opening myself up to them like this. But something about Mason feels . . . different.

When I saw him with the kids at the Youth Center, he seemed genuinely invested. Then came the night at the club, our kiss, and his brief rage of jealousy about me having to go back to work. No one has ever expressed that for me before. And as much as it pissed me off, it flattered me. That he would think I'm special enough to keep hidden from the pervings of other men was sweet, even if his actions right after were just as infuriating.

I find the photo I'm searching for, shove the rest back into the drawer, and head out to the living room.

"You live here alone?" He's studying a row of DVDs in my entertainment center.

"No, after Gia left, I found a roommate through a girl I work with." I plop down on the couch, lean on the armrest, and tuck my feet up under me. "She's a nine-to-fiver, has a serious boyfriend. I rarely see her."

He holds up a DVD. "You watch cartoons?"

I squint to read the title. "It's not a cartoon; it's Disney."

"Still a cartoon," he mumbles.

"*Animated movie.*" He wouldn't understand what something like Disney means to a young Russian orphan, how Svetlana and I dreamed of becoming the princesses we'd seen in those movies, swept off our feet and rescued by a handsome prince. What a joke.

He studies the cover with confusion etched on his face and tucks it back into its spot. "Strangest stripper I've ever known."

I hold up a finger. "*Exotic dancer*."

He scrunches up his face adorably. "There a difference?"

"*I* think so, and if I'm the strangest one you've known, can I assume you've known a few?"

"No." He moves toward me and drops down on the couch, not putting too much distance between us but enough that we're not touching. He nods to the photo in my hand. "What's that?"

A sudden unease washes over me. Is this a mistake? Too late now. What am I going to do? Shove the damn thing down my shirt and run away?

I thrust the photo in front of him before I can change my mind. He takes it, tilts it toward the light, and studies it before turning to me. "Are these kids from the Youth Center?"

I lean over, hit for a second by the scent of his cologne and warmth of his leg now against mine. "No, um"—I point to the scrawny girl in the middle, eighteen years old, flat-chested and knobby-kneed with long mousy-blond hair—"that's me."

He jerks his eyes to mine, his crystal-blue gaze roaming my face, and then back to the photo. "Wow."

Heat floods my cheeks. "Funny, right?"

"No, you're cute." He checks me out again and then goes back to the picture. "Mickey Mouse shirt. I see the Disney obsession started young."

"Sad thing is I'm eighteen in that photo."

He chuckles, and the sound soothes my racing heart.

"Was this taken at camp or something?" His fingertip glides along the photo. "Who're all these kids?"

I worry my bottom lip with my teeth. "Oh, um . . . those are my brothers and sisters."

Another jerk and his eyes are huge, framed in dark eyelashes that curl up at the ends, and twinkling with interest. "No kidding. That explains why you're so good with the kids."

"You're not so bad either, ya know."

Is he blushing? "So who's who?"

I lean closer and point out individual faces. "That's Isaac, Leah, Zander, Zoe, Aaron, Josiah . . ." I move through them all until I end on the last. "And um . . . that is, or was, my older sister Lana."

"Was . . ." There's sadness, a longing in his voice as if he feels her loss too just from that one word.

"Yeah, she died shortly after this picture was taken." I study the photo with him, and he tilts it more toward the light.

It was just weeks before her twenty-second birthday. She'd followed in the path my parents laid out for us, drawn to ministry and selflessly serving others. I can't remember a time where she was even in trouble, whether it be school or at home. She was the perfect daughter.

Unlike me.

"I'm sorry to hear that." He clears his throat. "So most of them are adopted." He runs a finger over the faces that represent almost every color, race, and nationality.

"Not most of us, all of us."

He grunts in recognition. "You and your sister look like you could be related."

"We are . . . were, I mean." I lick my lips nervously and clear my throat. "We were both adopted from an orphanage in Rostov-on-Don." He peeks up at me in a funny way that makes me smile. "Russia. My parents adopted all of us from different countries, ya know, before Brad and Angelina made it cool."

He nods and goes back to studying the photo. "What was that like?"

"I don't remember much from living there. I was too young. Lana was seven, and she remembered it being bad."

He hands me back the picture but doesn't meet my eyes. "That had to be hard."

"Not for me. I always had Lana. She protected me from it all, more like a parent to me than a sibling." I run my sweaty palms down my bare legs.

"I know the feeling." His eyebrows drop low as he studies the carpet, and something tells me his thoughts aren't on my sister or me.

"Yeah?" I'm grateful we've managed to skate over the details of her death and focus on him. It's a morbid story that has the capability of ruining even the darkest moment.

"Drake's always been a little shit. I swear the guy would've been arrested a dozen times if it weren't for me." He runs a hand through his hair, the blond waves sliding through his fingers like silk.

I grip his thigh and squeeze, and his eyes dart to where I've made contact as if my hand conducts electricity. "You're a good brother. If he's anything like me, he appreciates it."

"I put my ass on the line for him more times than I can count." Slowly, he moves his focus from my hand, up my arm, his gaze like a caress as it settles on my lips. His earlier, easy expression is now shrouded in worry. "Trix, I—" He blinks and leans away. "Shit, hold on." He pulls his phone from his pocket. I breathe through the heat of the moment as the device vibrates in his hand. Whatever he sees on the caller ID has him hitting a button to silence it and shoving it back in his pocket.

"New phone?"

He turns toward me, his expression still etched with concern, which he quickly wipes clean. "It is." We lock eyes as silent seconds tick between us. "My last one was shattered by a magnificent creature exiting a bathroom."

I fight the urge to grin huge and goofily. "I'm sorry to hear that."

He cups my jaw and drops a slow lingering kiss against my lips. "I'm not." His eyes slam closed, and it isn't until seconds later I register the vibration coming from his pocket. "Shit."

"What is it?"

He pulls away and scrubs a hand through his shaggy blond hair with a groan. "I gotta go."

"Oh, uh . . . okay."

He blows out a long breath, either out of relief or frustration, I can't tell, then tilts his head to peer up at me from beneath this lashes. "Go out with me."

"Right now? But you said—"

"No, let me take you out. A date."

"A date?" My voice is high with excitement. I've never been on a date. "Like a real date?"

A crooked grin tilts his lips. "No, the fake kind."

I rock into his shoulder hoping to hide my blush. "Ha, ha."

"When do you have a night off?"

"After tonight? Not until Tuesday."

"I'll pick you up Tuesday." He grabs my hand and kisses my knuckles. "Seven o'clock."

Warmth bursts in my chest. "Okay."

He leans forward and leaves one last kiss on my lips, no tongue, but deeper than friendly. "See you then." He stands and moves to the front door, turning before he passes through it. "Lock up when I leave."

"Yeah, I will." God, I sound so breathless.

"Later, Trix." He winks and he's gone.

What are we doing? Kissing without sex, sharing about our families, a date?

If I didn't know better, I'd think this was the beginning of a relationship. I nibble a fingernail and feel the pound of my pulse in my neck.

Holy shit! I'm in unknown territory.

—

**MASON**

After waiting to make sure Trix locked the door behind me, I jump into my truck and hit call back on my phone. He answers on the first ring. "Birdman, what's up?"

"Drake took off. Took Jessica with him."

Fuck. "What do you mean *took off*?"

The sound of a long exhale is followed by a short cough. "Went into hiding 'til all this clusterfuck blows over."

"That's probably best. He make sure to get a hold of the shit so I can deliver it?"

And as soon as I do, I'm washing my hands of this, and Drake can face the consequences of his decisions for once in his fucking life.

The heavy press of guilt weighs down on my shoulders when I think of what Trix said earlier: the way she spoke about her sister, the longing and pain that hung on every word. I never want to imagine that kind of hurt. I'll never be able to just sit by and allow my little brother to get taken out if there's something I can do to stop it.

"He did. You'll have what you need."

"After this is over, if you guys have more than shit for brains, you'll all get the fuck out of this before it's too late."

"Mason," he whispers, and I can hear the shuffling through the phone like he's searching for a quiet place to talk. "Things aren't like they used to be, man. Back then it was parties and chicks, fuckin' hanging with our bros and dipping into some minor shit. S'not like that anymore and I'm fuckin' freakin' out over here."

"Why're you guys still involved? You've gotta break ties with—"

"I wish it were that easy, man." I hear his deep inhale and almost have to laugh at the irony of him smoking weed while neck deep in a no-win situation with their drug-dealing hero.

"It is that easy. Get a job, stop going to the parties, and pull yourself out."

Birdman clears his throat. "They don't just let you leave. You have to pay to get out. Blood for blood."

"What the fuck does that mean?"

"Forget it. I gotta go."

"Bird—"

The line goes dead.

Fuck! I grip my phone in my hand tightly then toss it in the passenger seat of my truck to avoid crushing it.

Blood for blood. So they get jumped out? Take an ass-kicking in order to walk away. Seems worth it to me. Taking the beating and walking away with the rest of your life free and clear sounds like a pretty good fucking deal.

# NINE

## TRIX

"As soon as they take a break!" I'm leaning into Angel, yelling to be heard over Ataxia as they dominate the room at The Blackout. "You take the back. I'll hit the front!"

"Yeah, okay!" She nods, and the nod turns into bobs of her head as she sings along to the music.

I put in four hours at the Youth Center this morning. I wasn't surprised that Mason didn't show up. He'd explained that all the fighters rotate shifts, and the guy who showed up was just as good at drawing the attention of my dance girls. I was happy to see the new guy take to Denny, and I wondered if Mason had anything to do with that. I wouldn't be surprised if he had.

After that, I worked my shift at Zeus's, and it was busy as always. On Sundays, it would seem some go to church, as I did every Sunday growing up, and some go to strip clubs. Worshiping the flesh over the spirit, turning Sunday into *Sin*day.

My chest aches as I consider what I do. It never used to ache. Back before Hatch took off and I was closer to my end game, I would've done anything back then. Information is a powerful thing, especially when it brings vindication.

Every day that Hatch is gone, I feel further and further away from finding Lana's killer. I start to forget why I'm here, why I take off my clothes for strangers, slip into backrooms and perform things I'm even ashamed to admit to myself. And the more I forget, the more it aches. Like my soul is pushing me to quit. To move on and start living my life. Not the life of a girl on a mission. Not the life of a girl who has been playing a role for so long she's completely forgotten who she is.

The music rings throughout the room and the crowd cheers. Rex announces that he'll be back, and I push back from the bar with the stack of Zeus's promo cards in hand.

"Let's go." I motion to Angel, who has her stack in hand as well. "I'll meet you in the middle." I move on heeled feet, making sure to take short steps due to my very short and very tight skirt.

I've had a drink, but not enough to be tipsy. Technically, we're on the job, making a commission off every card that comes back to Zeus's. I spot a group of guys up front and approach, smiling big and batting my eyelashes. They each take a card and promise to come in the following night. Score!

Table by table I hit up the crowd, both men and women. When I meet back up with Angel, I have only half the cards I started with, and it looks like she had similar luck.

"You want to stay for the last set?" We drove from work together, and my car is back at Zeus's. As much as I'd like to call it a night, I'm at her mercy.

"Yeah, if that's okay with you."

Ugh. "Sure."

"Let's go backstage and leave some cards." She moves to the side of the stage and I follow. "Hey, Brick." She greets the bouncer that got his nickname from the fact that he looks like a brick with a head. "We've got business backstage."

His eyes move up and down our bodies, and we wait until he's finished visually stripping us. "I bet you do."

"Brick, cut the crap." I don't have the patience for this tonight. Usually I'd flirt, and get off on making the man eat out of my hand, but now I just want to hurry this night along and get home.

What if Mason shows up?

No, I refuse to think about that guy any more than I have, which is a lot. And if I count one very hot and steamy dream, it's a ton. Damn, is it warm in here? I use the cards to fan myself just as Brick crosses his arms over his chest.

"Sure, you girls can go on back, but what're you going to do for me?" His eyebrows jump, and I swear if I didn't think I'd break my hand I'd punch him square in the gut.

"Brick! They're good." Gia comes up beside me and pulls me in for a quick hug, an empty cocktail tray in her hand. She shoves the huge bouncer in the shoulder. "You can let them back. And stop sexually harassing my customers."

I laugh at the expression of the big man as he pouts and steps aside to let us through.

We wave a thank you to Gia and move down the long corridor, the sound of our heels clicking echoes off the black concrete walls. We've been back here so many times we'd be able to find the room in the dark, and have, several times. I pinch closed my eyes at the shame that washes over me an instant before I shove it away, refusing to examine it.

Without knocking, we push open the door and step inside the backstage room. The band is there, surprisingly without a single woman.

"Thank fuck some chicks showed up." Talon groans and points at us with one of his sticks. "I swear your woman is out there chasing off all the groupies." He's looking at Rex.

Rex gives us a quick nod and a lip-ringed smile. "Fine by me."

Lane's face twists in offense. "Real nice, dude. Fuckin' sausage party in this place."

"Aww, poor Lane has to actually work to get laid now," Angel says sarcastically with a pouty lip.

"As long as you're here, baby"—Talon leans back in his seat, a beer bottle hooked by his fingers, legs open, and visually molesting me—"come sit on my lap."

That fucking ache in my chest flares. "As attractive as that offer is, I'll pass." I hold up a short stack of cards. "We just came to drop these off. Hand them out to whoever or don't. No biggie."

Heat hits my back, and two big hands come around my middle. "Come on, Trix." Lane, that asshole. The way he embarrassed me the other day in front of Mason, I could've killed him. "You used to be fun."

"And you used to be charming." I try to pull away, but his grip only gets tighter. "Let me go, Lane."

"Lane." Rex glares at his guitar player. "You heard her, man."

"She likes it." His hand slides up to cup my breast. "She just won't admit it."

Rex stands, and I slam my elbow into Lane's gut.

He releases me to double over, and his arms wrap around his belly. "What . . . the fuck . . .?"

I prop a hand on my cocked hip. "I did like that, Lane. Thank you."

Rex shrugs and sits back down. "Serves you right, asshole."

I lift an eyebrow at Talon, daring him to say something, but he remains silent, his face scrunched up in sympathy pain.

I swipe my hands together. "My work here is done."

Lane stumbles over to the couch and drops down next to Rex, who shoves him so hard he tumbles to the floor. "Touch her again; you deal with me."

Angel giggles and follows me out of the room and back into the bar. I'd don't blame the boys for being confused. Up until now, we've had a take-what-you-want-when-you-want-it kind of relationship. I've used them just as many times as they've used me. Funny thing is now I don't want to. Maybe it's me giving up on my purpose, gearing up to move on with my life, knowing that I'll never get to settle the score. The thought is as depressing as it is terrifying. All I've ever known is revenge. What will I do next?

I'm losing touch with my job, my self-appointed assignment to find Lana's killer and put him through the kind of hell he subjected her to. I can't help but wonder if this sudden ache in my chest is my heart giving up, throwing in the towel and leaving me with nothing to do but live.

We navigate our way through the crowd and to the bar, ordering drinks while we wait for Ataxia to play its second set. After a few sips and a couple dodges of drunken men and their grabby hands, Angel leans in to whisper.

"Seems like there're more people now. Let's circulate, try to hand the rest of these out. That way we can take off as soon as the show ends."

I nod and hold up the few cards I still have. The sooner we can get out of here, the better. My feet ache and long for a soak in a warm bath. "Sounds good."

We patrol the room, avoiding those we've already spoken to and chat with some new faces. A table clears and a couple sits to take their place. Might be tourists, but they do love to hit Vegas strip clubs while in the City of Sin, soaking up the full experience.

I motion for Angel to follow me over, but as I get closer, my footsteps slow then freeze and I'm stuck. My stomach lurches into my throat.

Mason.

He's with a girl. Not just any girl, a really, really pretty girl. They're sitting across from one another but leaning over the small table toward each other. She's talking animatedly about something that he seems to like a lot because he's flashing a smile and laughing harder than I've ever seen him.

I prepare to turn, to run and hide, but Angel doesn't notice my semi-freak out and bellies up to their table. Mason's eyes fix on her, registers who she is, and then he immediately swings his gaze to me.

Fuck!

"Trix, come here." Angel's eyes are as big as bottle bottoms as she implores me to get my shit together and play it cool.

We have rules about crap like this: running into customers outside of the club when they're with their significant other. The rule is we act like they're total strangers.

I take a deep breath, throw on a mask of indifference, and advance toward them. Mason's eyes eat me up from hair to heels until I squeeze in between his date and Angel to ensure there's a buffer between us.

Sell the club and walk away. Simple.

"Hey, guys. Hope we're not *barging* in on you." My scowl is tight and aimed at Mason, whose baby blues are wide. "My name is Trix and this is Angel. We're here passing out VIP cards to our club, Zeus's Playground." I chuck a card at Mason that hits him in the chest and falls to his lap. His date takes Angel's proffered card and studies it. "Have you ever heard of it?" My question is directed to the cheating bastard to my left. He answers my question with a drop of his brows, and his full lips pull into a tight line.

"Oh, yeah!" His date holds up the card. "I've heard a lot about this place. You girls dance there?" God, why does she not only have to be pretty but also nice?

"We do." Angel butts in and pushes out her double-Ds. "You guys should come by sometime; we do private dances for couples all the time."

"Whoa . . . really?" The girl's eyes dance with excitement and dart to Mason.

He stares at his beer, his eyebrows pinched, and his jaw hard. The image of them together, on a small couch in a private room at Zeus's flashes through my head: a dancer straddling their laps, running her body along theirs as they suck on each other's lips.

A low growl gargles in my chest. "What's wrong, big guy? You don't like *strippers*?" The word tastes sour on my tongue.

His glare slides up to mine, and as fierce as it seems, I don't back down from it. "Trix . . ." My name is said on an angry rumble that I feel deep in my belly.

I prop an elbow on the table and lean toward him. "Are we offending you? Breaking up your *date*?"

"Cut it out." His jaw is clenched, teeth bared.

"Cut what out? I'm just here doing my *job*. What exactly are *you* doing?"

The beautiful blonde holds up her hand and looks curiously between us. "Wait, am I missing something?"

I turn my head toward her and the anger dissolves. She's really pretty and clean looking. Not fake in any way. Natural light hair that probably doesn't reek of hair bleach, highlights from the sun rather than streaks of candy-color, little makeup rather than the fake eyelashes and lip-plumping gloss slathered all over my face. She's perfect for him. Better for him than me.

Disappointment crushes my lungs. "No, you're not missing anything." I push back from the table. "Sorry to bother you."

I turn on my heel and head toward the door, needing to get the hell out of there with or without Angel. I hear Mason call my name from behind me, but embarrassment pushes me forward. I'm weaving in and out of clusters of bar patrons until I finally exit into the warm desert air.

"Holy shit!" Angel is right behind me. "What was that?"

"Nothing, it was . . ." God, I'm such an idiot. "I'm done for the night."

She nods, a small smile on her face. "Yeah, I gathered that." Her eyes narrow. "Oh my God . . . you like Mason."

The door swings open so hard it hits the brick wall behind it, and Mason comes barreling out. His eyes hit me, and I curse my damn shoes because if I run in them he'll surely catch up to me.

"Trix . . ." There's softness in his voice, a pleading that reeks of guilt. He eyes Angel. "Hey, could you give us a second?"

Her gaze slides to mine, one eyebrow lifted. "I'll be in the car."

"I'll take her home," Mason says.

"You will not!" I jut out my chin. "Who will you take home first, huh? Me or your date? Oh . . . let me guess. You'll take her home first so you can fuck me after, right?"

His expression darkens. "Stop it."

"'Cause good girls like that don't put out like we do."

"Hey!" Angel stomps a foot. "I don't—"

"Right?" I ignore Angel's offense. "You wine and dine the lady and end it with a good night kiss before you fuck the easy girl to get off!"

His hands shoot out and grip my shoulders, pulling me to his chest so quickly a whoosh of air rushes from my lungs.

I squirm to get out of his hold. "Let me go."

He presses his lips to my neck, his nose just under my ear, breathing me in. "Fuck . . . stop. Why are you doing this?"

"What?" Why? Um, besides walking in on the guy I kissed and let feel me up on a date with another woman? God, I'm such a hypocrite. I have no right to feel as possessive as I do, and yet . . .

"You misunderstood what you saw in there." His big hands slide around my back and down to link just above my ass.

My traitorous body curls deep into his chest. "Mason, you're on a date. The only misunderstanding was me thinking . . . thinking . . ." *That we were more.* How could I be so stupid?

He pulls back, and the anger I saw in his face is replaced with a tenderness that I feel in my chest. "Thinking what?"

I shake my head. "Nothing."

At the sound of a throat clearing, my gaze darts to Angel, her expression soft. "I think you're in good hands." A tiny smile tugs at her lips. "I'm gonna head back inside."

My cheeks heat and I nod. "Okay."

"Thanks, Angel. We'll be there in a sec." She heads back into the club, and Mason forks his fingers into my hair to cup my jaw, locking me in a determined blue stare. "She doesn't need to worry. You'll always be safe with me."

I believe Mason would protect me from harm, but he has no idea how vulnerable he's made my heart. "Am I?" I choke out the words, shocked at how seeing him with another woman has reduced me to this kind of violent jealousy.

His grip is firm, unrelenting. "I care about you, Trix. I care about you enough to want to strangle every man who's had the pleasure of touching you, to follow you home like a damn stalker, to walk away from you when all I want to do is strip you down and bury myself inside you. I care about you enough to ask you out on a *real* date and to chase after you when you run away." He shrugs. "I care about you enough to forgive you for breaking my phone."

My lips twitch, and I hope he sees it as a grin I'm fighting and not the torrential downpour of tears his words have evoked.

His hands cup my face. "Let me explain. Then you can decide if my offense is worth walking away from me for. Deal?"

I nod into his big palms, and my heart flutters as a soft smile tilts his lips. "Deal."

"Okay." He takes my hand. "Come on."

# TEN

## MASON

Holy shit! That was close. For a second there, while she tossed out insults like arrows, I thought I'd lost her. I thought she'd never calm down enough to let me explain.

The crap she says about herself makes me sick to my stomach. That a woman this beautiful could have such little respect for her body is astounding. I take her belittling herself as a personal insult. I almost grin at the challenge she's set before me, to prove to her that she's so much more than the "easy stripper." Her body and the honor of pleasuring it should be a prize to be won, not a tool to be passed around as she claimed the other night. My competitive nature digs in, hell bent on proving her wrong.

I take purposeful steps back to my table, making sure to stay at her side rather than drag her behind me.

As we get closer, she stops. "Oh . . ."

Ta-da! Now she understands.

I encourage her to walk with me with a gentle tug on her arm and tuck her to my side as we step up to the table.

"You're back." Eve's smiling between Trix and me, her hand interweaved with Cameron's.

"We are." I squeeze the tense girl at my side. "I'd like you guys to meet Trix. Trix, this is Cameron Kyle, my boss, and Eve, his girlfriend."

I can almost feel the heat of her blush against my skin as she burrows deeper into me. "Hi, nice to meet you guys."

Cameron's glare moves between us, and his jaw gets soft. "You too."

"Girl, I hate to be annoying, but seriously where did you get those shoes? They're hot!" Eve hops off her stool and studies Trix's shoes. "Cameron, do you see these things?"

Cam grins, and Trix pulls away from me enough so that she can lift her foot up for Eve to study it. They go back and forth, some shit about websites and mall stores that I mostly ignore. When I turn away from the convo, I find my boss staring at me.

"What?"

His shoulders bounce with silent laughter. "Nothing, man."

"Shut up." I fight my own smile, knowing exactly what the guy's thinking.

I've moved on from Eve and am now chest deep into feeling for another woman, who'll probably destroy me.

As I look down at Trix, all decked out and showing off her best assets, my blood roars. Either this girl has worked some kind of voodoo witchery on my ass, or she's the most alluring woman on the face of the planet. On paper, I wouldn't give a woman like Trix a second glance. Even as the thought moves through my thick fucking skull, shame weighs heavy in my gut. She's a stripper, loose with her morals and her body, but that's not who I see when I'm with her. It's the woman inside, beneath the skin-tight clothes, colored hair, and makeup, and damn if even covered in all that she isn't stunning.

"If you guys don't mind, I'm gonna skip out." I give Cam a chin lift and fist bump Eve. "Thanks for the movie." They regard me in a knowing way that makes me want to flip them both off.

The girls say good-bye, and we find Angel to let her know I'm taking Trix home. They share a quick hug before I pull Trix from the room, eager to hear her apology.

—

I'm barely out of The Blackout parking lot when she huffs. I wait knowing that she's most likely working up the strength it takes for a strong woman like Trix to swallow her pride. "Mason . . ."

Here it comes. I pivot and lift one eyebrow.

She turns toward me, angling her sexy little body in that short skirt and off-the-shoulder top. "You're such a dick!"

Laughter bursts from my lips, and if I weren't driving, I'd double over with the force of it. "I'm a dick? What did I do?"

Her sweet lips are pulled wide in a playful grin that reminds me of that picture she showed me of when she was a teenager. "You let me believe you were on a date, for like, minutes." She shakes her head slowly, eyes tight, but still smiling. "If I didn't know better, I'd think you wanted to see me jealous."

Jealous. Is that what she was? I never really thought past the fact that she was just pissed at seeing me with another girl, not because of her feelings for me, but because she felt betrayed in some way.

"Is that . . .?" I clear my throat. "You were jealous?"

I keep my eyes to the road, but catch her expression fall as she turns to face forward. "Well, yeah, I think I was."

My heart slams in my chest, and I grip the steering wheel to keep from pulling her over to straddle my lap.

"That surprises you."

Am I that obvious? "Um, yeah, a little. I didn't realize you'd . . ." Had the same feelings for me as I had for you. How do I say what I want to say without freaking her out?

She doesn't press for more, and dead air thickens between us before she angles toward me again. "Do you always play third wheel on other people's dates? I gotta say it's kinda sad." Her teasing tone, having apparently moved on from the heavier conversation, catches me off guard.

"It's sad that I went to a movie with my boss and his girlfriend and then dropped by The Blackout to catch another friend of mine's band play?" I make a quick turn into a gas station and pull up to the mini-mart.

"Not when you say it like that, it's not," she mumbles and turns to watch out the window. "What are we doing?"

"How do you like your coffee?" I study her stunned expression and smile.

"It's eleven o'clock at night."

I lift my eyebrows, waiting.

"Cream and sugar, please." Her eyebrows pinch together, and she pulls on her lower lip. "Oh, unless they have those flavored creamers, in which case, I'll take a few of those. Vanilla, if they have it."

There she goes being cute.

"Done." I grab the keys and hop from my truck. "Be right back." After the door shuts, I hit lock on the key fob and chuckle when her confused eyes come to mine. "Stay put."

She rolls her eyes, and I turn to head in to the mini-mart, wondering why I feel so drawn to her. The need to protect her is overwhelming. The desire to be close to her is uncontrollable. And the urge to know her, really know her, is irresistible.

—

## TRIX

*Coffee.* What in the hell does he have planned?

I assumed, after my embarrassing display at the club, he was going to drop me at home and try to forget the evening's foot-in-mouth events. At least, that was what I planned to do.

Instead, I'm sitting in his truck, feeling like a high-school girl on a date with the quarterback.

I watch as he moves to the gas station market, long strides from his powerful legs that carry his gorgeously sculpted body through the door. I lose the visual as he gets lost within the market aisles and take the moment to pull down the visor and check my face.

Ugh. Yep, I look like a stripper. I grab a small packet of tissues from my clutch, swipe at my cheeks, and dab my eyes. There's something about being around Mason that makes me want to strip everything away. I want him to see more than the sex and temptation. I want him to see, well, me. Maybe it's because he's so down to earth, so real, that I want to meet him on the same level. A whisper of guilt tightens my chest, but I push it back, telling myself I have nothing to be embarrassed about.

I take my clothes off for a living, and a damn good living at that. I've done what I had to do to get the things I've needed, and there's zero shame in my plight. And yet, when Mason looks at me, he makes me want to be better. He reminds me what it felt like to be unguarded, to live in my skin without playing a role.

"Stupid." Finished removing a good fifty percent of my makeup, I pull my hair over one shoulder and throw it in a quick braid. The car alarm tweets and the door locks flip up. With a final check in the mirror and unable to do a thing about the tight one-shoulder shirt and mini skirt I'm wearing, I flip the mirror closed.

The driver's side door swings open, and Mason folds into the truck with a bag around his arm and two cups of coffee balancing in one hand.

"Here, let me help." I grab both cups and deposit them into the cup holders.

"Thanks." He turns and drops the bag into the backseat, and my eyes go immediately to his stubbled jawline. The dark shadow contrasts with the blond shaggy hair that meets it just in front of his ear. He must feel me staring, because he tenses and turns his liquid blue eyes to mine. His eyebrows pinch as his gaze glides from my hair to my eyes, my lips, and my neck. "Wow!"

"What?" The single word question falls from my lips on an exhale.

His hand reaches for my braid, wrapping it around his fingers and giving it a gentle but firm tug before he cups my jaw. He stares at my lips, and I self-consciously dart out my tongue to moisten them. His eyes flare, and he runs his thumb roughly along my lower lip, sucking his bottom one while watching the path of his finger. "You're so pretty."

I blink to rid the burning in the backs of my eyes. Pretty? Only my parents have ever called me pretty. Sexy, fuckable, a wet dream—those are the things I'm used to hearing. But pretty? My chest warms, and I lean into his hold, lips tingling with the urge to press against his.

He blinks and clears his throat. "We, uh, we better get going." He removes his hand from my cheek and shifts in his seat, a painful expression on his face.

The loss of his warmth and sting of rejection burns in my gut, but the lingering arousal that his simple touch brings doesn't seem to notice.

"So where are you taking me?" I grab my coffee, needing something for my hands to do so they don't reach over and grip at his massive thighs.

"It's a surprise." He peeks over at me with a half-smile. "You don't have a curfew, do you?"

I shake my head and smile into the lid of my coffee. "No."

"Good." He leans forward, his powerful arm pulling the cotton of his blue tee tight around his biceps, and adjusts the stereo. "Do you like Blink 182?"

"Yeah." The scratchy sound comes through the speakers. "Is this *Cheshire Cat*?"

His eyebrows pop in surprise. "It is. I love this album."

"Me too. It reminds me of grade school." Back when things were easy, before life got hard.

"Did you ever see them play live?" He turns onto I-95.

"No, I didn't. You?"

"They came through Santa Cruz and played at—"

"Shut up!" My hand moves on its own and punches him in the shoulder. I resist the urge to shake off the pain from hitting his brick of a bicep. "You're from Santa Cruz?"

He grins, so big and so damn beautiful I feel it flutter in my chest. "Yeah."

"I'm from San Jose." The excitement in my voice rings through the truck cab.

"No kidding? Wow, small world."

"Right? We used to drive out to Cowell Beach every summer growing up."

His eyes dart to mine in surprise. "I learned to surf at Cowell. Did you guys rent a place?"

My cheeks heat, and I'm grateful he can't see it in the dark cab. "No, we didn't really have a lot of money, so we'd just go for the day."

He's completely unaffected by my confession of our being broke, but I suppose that's because he doesn't know all of it. Like the fact that we all didn't even have swim suits and had to share a couple towels between the ten of us. Not that any of it mattered back then.

My fondest childhood memories were from those trips, leaving before the sun came up, piled in our van with a bag full of peanut-butter sandwiches, and leaving after the sun sank into the ocean. Our skin red, hair matted with salt water and sand, exhausted. And Lana.

I clear my throat of the lump the memory brings. "To think we could've been there at the same time."

"Nah, I don't think so." He takes a sip of his coffee then puts it back in the cup holder. "I would've remembered you."

My face feels hot, but this time for a completely different reason. How is it that his compliments turn me into a nervous, blushing mess? "Mason, I was a knock-kneed, mousy kid. I'm sure a guy like you was surrounded by beautiful beach babes. I just . . . blended in with the sand."

"Ha! That's funny." He shakes his head. "That you could *ever* blend in is laughable." He peers over at me for a split second before his eyes go back to the road. "Don't forget I saw a picture of you as a teenager, and trust me . . . I would've noticed you. Noticed and then shown off to get your attention."

My stomach flips over on itself, and I smile out the window into the dark. With the city behind us and the dark mountains ahead, I imagine what it would've been like to know Mason back then. Was he a cocky teenager, a leader-of-the-pack type who was constantly surrounded by cheerleaders? No way would he have paid attention to the shy seventeen-year-old girl with the Disney obsession.

We turn off the freeway onto a road that seems mostly desolate.

"You're not taking me out into the middle of nowhere to have your wicked way with me, are you?" Not that I'd care if he was.

He turns to me and flashes a devastatingly handsome smile that has me catching my breath. "Maybe."

My stomach lurches, and I slug down a few gulps of coffee. If that's his plan, I'm going to need plenty of energy to enjoy it.

# ELEVEN

## MASON

I'm nervous. I don't remember the last time I was really nervous around a girl. I mean, even with Eve, we always had a friendship first that made things so easy when we hung out. That was a big part of what convinced me we were meant to be together. Love should be easy, right?

Trix is different. She constantly has me on edge, walking the fine line of my sanity and hypersensitive to her every move. Although our conversations are light and there's no uncomfortable silence between us, the prospect of being alone with her sends a battalion of butterflies loose in my gut.

I sip on my coffee and let the caffeine charge through my veins, giving me a second wind. Truth is, after the movie tonight, I was ready to go home and crash, but the opportunity to spend time with Trix alone is too good to pass up.

"Hang on." I hit the four-wheel drive and pull off the small road and through the mountains.

Small rocks spit from the tires and knock against the wheel well. She squeals with laughter and holds on to the sissy bar while we blaze a trail over rocks, gravel, and small plants to a clearing up ahead.

I stop and put the truck in park. "We're here."

"That was gnarly!" She's grinning big, childlike excitement in her eyes that makes my chest swell with pride. Her head swivels around, leaning forward to peer out the windshield. "Where are we?"

I jerk my head to my door. "Come on, I'll show you."

"Oh, I don't know." She holds up one long tanned leg, and I resist, just barely, the urge to take in the view she's flashing from between them. "I don't have on my hiking heels."

"Hmm . . . good point." I chew my lip then hold up one finger. "Hold on." I slide from my seat and circle around to the passenger side of the truck.

I open the door to find her staring at me. "What are you doing?" She laughs as I reach over her into the backseat and grab my flannel button up shirt.

"Put this on." When she leans in, I maneuver it around her back and allow myself to get close and drink in her scent as she slips her arms through the arm holes. "Good now . . . " I run both hands from her knee to her calf, groaning at the smooth texture of her skin, and pushing away fantasies of what her legs would feel like wrapped around my hips. Once to her foot, I slide one shoe off, massaging the arch of her delicate foot before moving over to repeat the process on the other. Fuck. I never thought of myself as a foot-fetish guy, but Trix's feet are enough to make me curious.

"Mmm . . . that feels good." The guttural groan of pleasure from her lips makes my dick instantly hard.

"You feel good." Everything about her feels incredible: her voice, her touch, and her lips. Fuck . . . I need to taste her lips. I lean over and hold myself just inches from her, so close I can feel the heat of her body and absorb the vibration of her quickened breath. Her big eyes rimmed in black blink up at me, silently begging. I scoop my hand under her knees, and another behind her back, pulling her from the truck.

Her hands fly to my neck and lock there to steady herself. She doesn't struggle or protest, but willingly gives her weight to me while I move her to the truck bed.

"Hold on, baby." I turn my head and cringe. Shit, the endearment came so easily, and I hope it's not too much to send her running.

She squeezes me tighter, and I release her enough to pop the tailgate and gently place her on it.

"Thank you." She pulls the flannel around her body. Even though it's summer in Vegas and not cold, it tends to run a little cooler in the mountains, and she's wearing next to nothing under my shirt. "It's so dark out here." She looks around. "Are there bears?"

"No." I sit up next to her, close enough that our thighs are touching. "No bears."

She turns her eyes toward me. "So, what is it? Why are we here?" The lust in her voice is so heavy it's all I can do to keep from pushing her back, mounting her, and fucking her senseless.

I lean in and brush my lips along her jaw to her ear. "Lie down."

She trembles and sucks in a lungful of air. "Okay."

Slowly she lowers herself back, and I know by her quick intake of breath she finally sees why we're here.

"Oh my . . ."

I grin into my shoulder and lean back to lie alongside her. "Amazing, right?"

"I've never seen anything like it." The wonder in her voice makes my chest feel light. "Wow, there are so many."

"The lights on The Strip make the stars impossible to see, but up here, we get the unobstructed view."

The dark sky is alight with billions of flickering stars, clusters of some that are lighter and darker, and a smattering of tiny ones that make up the Milky Way. We sit in silence for a few minutes, enjoying the view and the quiet company of each other.

I've been coming up here for a while, and after I found this clearing on a hike, I thought it would be the perfect place to come see the stars. I'd planned on bringing Eve, but after she made it clear she wanted Cameron, I decided she didn't deserve my sharing this with her. But Trix, she makes what is already beautiful absolutely breathtaking.

She lifts her hand and paints the sky with wide brushes of her fingers. "They almost seem so close you could touch them."

"You wanna touch one; just ask."

She giggles as her hand continues to swipe through the sky. "I do, can you get one down for me?"

"Your wish is my command, m'lady." I hold up my hands as if I'm aiming a shotgun, make the "cha-chic" sound of me cocking my rifle. "Look out. It's about to rain stars." I push an impressive explosion sound from my lips.

She laughs and shields her face from the downpour of fake stars. "Oh here, let me get a few for you too." She holds up one delicate hand, three fingers tucked in, pointer out, thumb up. "Pitchu. Pitchu, pitchu, pitchu."

"What the fuck you shooting with? Peas?"

She shows me her gun hand. "Peas! I'll have you know this is a very powerful weapon."

I shake my head, fighting the urge to pull her on top of me and taste her lips. "I don't know. Sounded like a peashooter to me."

"It's not the size of the gun; it's how you use it." She shrugs.

"Is that right?"

"Um . . . no, actually." She grins wide and sexy. "It's more about the size."

We laugh until humor fades into silence as we stare up into the sky.

"So, are you going to make out with me under the stars, or just make me lie here fantasizing about it."

My body springs up, and I rein in my lust enough to slowly lean over and slide my knee between her legs rather than pouncing. "Fantasizing?" I rest my forehead against hers. "Tell me."

Her hands sift into my hair and grip. "Better, how about I show you?"

I tilt my head as she brings it down to hers, and I press into her full soft lips. My teeth rake against her bottom lip, requesting entrance. She grins and opens to me, allowing me to delve into the delicious cavern of her mouth. So slick, warm, and so fucking sweet. She moans and arches her back, pressing her chest into mine, searching for more contact. I slide my hand up under the flannel shirt and splay my hand on her belly.

I hear the sound of her bare feet hitting the tailgate, and then she shifts, pushing herself back further into the truck bed and breaking our kiss. I look to see her breasts are now at my eyes. I trace the line of stomach, moving up and up until my fingertips hit one pebbled nipple and . . . no bra.

"Fuckin' hell." My hips flex on instinct, pressing my hard-on into her leg, searching for the friction that will dull the ache.

Her legs snap together to lock around mine, and she shifts as if she's putting out a flame between her thighs. "You're teasing me." She reaches down and pulls up her tight little shirt to expose one plump breast. "Take it, please."

I drop my mouth to her and suck deep, rolling my tongue in slow torturous laps over the sensitive tip. I feel rather than see her hand move from her belly, lower, and lower until . . . I grasp her wrist just as her fingers dip between her legs. "No. That's mine."

What the fuck? That's *mine*?

I don't know where it came from, and I brace for her to unleash hell on me for claiming her pussy as my own, but she shocks the hell out of me and smiles. I push up and take her mouth in a deep kiss, using my tongue and teeth to pull greedily at her lips. I run my hand along her inner thigh, groaning into her mouth and drinking in her soft sigh when I hit the small piece of satin between her legs.

Her knees fall open, and I run the length of my finger up and down, up and down, over her panties, pressing in deeper with each pass. She rips her mouth from mine, sucking in quick pants of air.

Between her perfect breasts and her full suckable lips, I can't decide which one to hit first. Rather than drown in her taste, I watch her expression as I move her panties aside and dip my fingers into her body.

She cries out, and my jaw locks down, teeth gritting against the urge to pound my fingers between her legs until she screams my name. The visual of her writhing against me, grinding down on my hand and meeting my fingers thrust for thrust becomes too much.

I nip at her bare breast. "Other one."

She complies, popping the other breast free. I take turns lapping at her tits while finger fucking her so hard they jump in my mouth. "Mase . . . don't stop."

*Mase.* My eyes roll back in my head, and I suck her deeper into my throat.

She clenches down around my fingers, her heels to the tailgate, thrusting up hard enough that her ass lifts off the bed while she chases down her release. My mouth waters, wanting to taste her and feel the flow of her orgasm against my tongue, but I can tell I'm too late.

Her tiny body stiffens seconds before she detonates. I push back and watch her back arch, her hips lift into my hand, and her mouth open as a long moan falls from her lips. Her hands fist my shirt as she rides my fingers, milking every last bit of her orgasm.

I rock my hips into her thigh, pretending we've just come together and mimicking the movement of a slow float back to earth. But every rub of my boxers against my dick, every rasp of fabric against the tender flesh, propels me on.

She lies there, my fingers still knuckle deep inside her while I dry fuck her hip. I bend down, suck her tit in my mouth and ride her harder.

"Don't stop." She rolls her hips on my fingers again, ready for more.

I growl, wanting release so badly it hurts, but more than that, wanting to taste her. As I slide my fingers from her body, she shivers.

I move from her breast with a wet pop of suction and kiss down her belly. Straddling her hips, I hook her under the arms and push her up further into the truck bed.

"Mason?"

"Shh . . . gotta taste you." Her skirt is around her waist, and I hook my fingers in her panties to pull them off.

"I . . . I can't." Her hands come to mine in what I assume to be her help. "Stop!"

I tear myself from her body at her command, my heart hammering in my chest. "What?" I blink away the fog of lust and arousal. "Did I hurt you?"

She scoots back, covering her body with the flannel and sitting up. "I'm sorry. I can't let you do that."

If that isn't a cold fucking bucket of ice water to the nuts.

"That's okay." I take in a deep breath of mountain air and try to breathe through the disappointment. "I'm sorry. I'm moving too fast."

She avoids my eyes. "No, it's not that. I mean"—she shrugs—"I know what you're thinking, and you're partially right. I've never been one to say no to a hook up."

Anger flares quick and hot. "No, fuck no. I never thought that about you." Did I? Well, I don't anymore. Unless, is that all this is?

"It's okay if you did." She pulls a rubber band from her hair and shakes out her messy braid. "I'm not going to lie. I like using my body for pleasure, and I'm not above giving it just because I know I can."

I swallow back the sour taste her words evoke.

"But a girl has to draw the line somewhere, right?" An awkward giggle rumbles in her throat.

I sit with one ass cheek to the tailgate and rub the back of my neck, trying to force blood back up and into my brain. "I don't understand."

"I've never had a man, um, go down."

"What?" No fucking way. Curiosity sizzles through my blood. "Never?"

"Nope." She dips her chin and twirls a long strand of her hair. "I know you probably don't believe me, and that's okay, but it's something I've been saving."

"For who?"

She cringes. "You'll think I'm stupid."

I angle more towards her, my fingers itching to comfort and erase her insecurity. "Not at all, but no shit, I'm curious as hell."

"I was raised that a woman should save herself for her husband. Obviously, I messed that up, but I thought if I could save one thing for him, that would be it."

"Huh." I climb up into the truck bed and sit next to her. "So everything else—"

"I've done. Yeah." She picks at a loose thread on the button of the flannel shirt.

"But never—?"

"No. Men only care about getting off, so it's never been a problem before." She shrugs.

"Sounds like you've been with the wrong men." My fists numb and my jaw aches.

She blinks up at me. "Stop staring at me like I've grown a second head."

I move my gaze from her, wondering what the hell I must look like from her perspective and not wanting to make her ashamed or embarrassed.

"What are you thinking?" She whispers and concern etches her question.

"I think"—I meet her stare—"you're pretty spectacular."

With the light from a billion stars, I watch her full lips pull into a grin. "You do?"

"Yeah, Trix, I do." The feel of her name from my lips is off now, like something has changed between us. She's no longer Trix the exotic dancer, but a girl, a woman who is saving a very intimate part of herself for only one man—one very fucking lucky man who will end up being her partner for life, protecting her, shielding her from heartbreak, cherishing her love, and ensuring her happiness.

"Hey, can you tell me what your real name is?" I have to know. With every bit of my soul, I want to know who this woman is outside of the G-strings and stiletto heels.

Her face twists in confusion. "My *real* name?"

"I'm assuming Trix is a made-up name, you know, to create and entice the fantasy."

She bites her lip, thinking. "Hmm. And what would you say is so enticing about the name Trix?"

Seems pretty obvious to me. She can't be clueless about it, but she wants to hear me say it. I'll play. "Trix is a sweet tasting cereal that melts in your mouth. It's like candy, sweet like you."

"Ah, aren't you the charmer." She holds up a finger. "I've also heard Trix implies I 'turn tricks,' like I'm a hooker."

I shrug one shoulder, ashamed to admit it, but . . . "Yeah, that too. Creating the fantasy."

She laughs and drops her chin. "If my dad hears this, he'll wish they'd renamed me," she mumbles.

"So, what's your real name?"

She peeks up at me and smiles. "Beatriks, with a 'k.' It's the Russian form of Beatrice."

"Your *real* name is Trix?"

"Yeah." She laughs, and the sound shoots straight to my groin.

"Wow." I study her: big eyes that, even though it's too dark to see, I know are blue with the slightest hint of lavender, full lips, and under all the blond and purple hair is a natural blond that I bet lightens bright white in the sun. "Beatriks."

"My brothers and sisters call me Bea, like bee-ah."

"Bea." I tuck a few loose strand of her hair behind her ear. "That's cute. I like it."

I like it. I like her, and fuck if all this information about her isn't making me even more curious.

# TWELVE

## TRIX

"Take your pick." Mason holds up a bag. "Peppered"—he holds up another bag—"or teriyaki."

"Hmm . . ." I'm sitting with my back leaning against the pick-up truck cab as I survey my options. "That depends. Are we going to be kissing again?"

He nods repeatedly, even closes his eyes for emphasis. "Oh yeah, there will be a lot of kissing, but"—he tosses me the peppered flavor jerky—"I can tell by the way you're eyeballin' this bag that you like it spicy, and lucky for you, I do to."

I pull out a long piece of smoked, dried meat. "You like spicy? Even secondhand?"

His eyes track to my mouth as I chew. "I'm willing to bet my life that with every taste, taking it from your mouth makes it sweeter."

"I guess we'll find out." I grin and toss the bag back to him, hitting him in the chest.

He rips out a couple pieces and then pushes in next to me. "So, tell me about your sister. Lana, was it?"

I cough on my food and reach for the bottled water that Mason handed me just before he busted out the jerky.

"I'm sorry. Are you okay?" He pats my back a couple times while I slurp down gulps of cool water.

I clear my throat. "Yeah, I'm fine. I wasn't expecting such a serious question."

He turns his gaze upward, his head resting on the back window of the truck. "I'm sorry. I wasn't sure whether or not it was a sensitive issue."

"It's not. I just never talk about her." I set down my water and rip apart tiny shreds of jerky.

"You can trust me."

I nod because, without even understanding why I can trust him, I know with certainty that I do. "Svetlana was, um . . . She was . . ." I hate saying it, hate muttering the words because *brutally murdered* should never accompany my sister even in name alone.

"Murdered."

"Yes, but it was ugly. The papers called it 'sliced,' and that's exactly what she looked like."

"Holy shit, Trix, you saw her?" His hand grips my bare knee, and the firm hold and warmth feel safe, reliable. Protective.

I rip off a small section of jerky and shove it in my mouth. "Mm-hmm."

"God. That must've been terrifying. Walking in on that kind of scene must've been brutal." His grip tightens.

"Oh, I didn't actually walk in." It was cold. The smell of the room was like a mix between disinfectant and death. I'll never forget the scent that death carries. "I identified the body."

"Holy fuck."

"I remember the sheet was shaking. At first, I thought maybe she'd woken up. I know that sounds stupid, but I just couldn't believe she was gone, so . . . I peeled back the fabric, almost expecting her to jump out at me and say 'Surprise, you're such a sucker!' but deep in my heart I knew that wasn't Lana's style."

As kind and generous as she was, she was always serious. My dad said it was her strict Russian blood. I think she was haunted by the past, and whatever happened in that orphanage sucked all the silly right out of her.

"It was my hand holding the sheet that made it shake, and when I pulled it back, what I saw . . ." I pinch my eyes closed to push back the memory. "No one should ever have to see another human being as mangled as she was. I made myself stare at her, wouldn't allow myself to look away because it was her. It was Lana, and . . . God, she was so good. So pure." I blow out a long breath and shake my head. "It should've been me."

"Trix, how can you say that? Tragic things happen all the time, but who's to say one person deserves it more than another? It's random and senseless."

I consider his words: roll them over in my head even as every one of my instincts roars he's wrong.

"What if it wasn't?" I toss the rest of my jerky over the side of the truck bed. "They carved into her body, Mason, when she was still alive." A shiver racks my body, and he throws his arm over me and pulls me close. I curl my arms around my belly, and allow his warmth to envelop me.

"They found her in the mountains, left there like a carcass for the animals to feed on."

"Fuckin' hell," he mumbles.

"Her car was ditched on the side of the road. The cops believe whoever did it had lured her in by faking a flat tire or something. It was so like Lana to pull over and help someone if they needed it."

"Sick sons of bitches."

"After they found her in Redwood—"

"Wait, Redwood . . . the State Park?

"Mm-hm."

"I think . . . I remember this story. She was headed out of town, so no one noticed her missing right away."

I swallow hard and nod. I'm not surprised he'd heard about Lana on the news. The story ripped through all the local towns—a killer on the loose—and scared the shit out of everyone.

"Fucker responsible better be rotting away in prison."

"Hmm." No, he's not. I roll my lips between my teeth to avoid giving too much away. I've already told him too much. "Thank you for listening." I throw my arm over his firm abdomen and hold him to me. "I haven't talked about her in so long. Not even Gia knows." Truth is, by the time we got close enough where I could share it with her, she had enough of her own demons to wrangle.

His body stiffens. He kisses my head, slow firm presses of his lips that send a soothing heat through my torso. As he rests his cheek against my hair, I can feel his clenched jaw tick.

I push up and out of his hold, but he moves his hand back to my thigh, as if he needs to touch me more than I need his comfort. "Enough of the dark stuff, I don't want Lana's story to be what you remember about our date."

"Our date. You say it like there won't be others."

I did? I guess I did. "Will there be?"

"If I have my way?" He grins. "Absolutely."

---

*Find them, Bea. Make them pay . . .*

*Lana?*

*I love you.*

"Trix, we're here." Mason's voice calls me from sleep. "Wake up."

I blink open my eyes and jerk upright. "Shit, shit . . ." I wipe a light sheen of sweat from my forehead. "Sorry."

He chuckles. "For what?"

"Huh?" I blink over at his grinning face as reality seeps to the surface. Just a dream. I peer out the truck window to see we're idling in my driveway. "Whoa . . ." I sit up and stretch my stiff neck. "What time is it?"

"Almost four-thirty." He smiles sheepishly. "Sorry I kept you out so late."

"No, it's fine." I notice the sun hasn't begun to peek up over the mountains, which means I'll still get a decent nap before I have to be at work. A breath crawls up my throat, and I cover my mouth to avoid a full, gaping, ugly, tired yawn. "Man, I crashed on the way home."

"Yeah, you did. Must've been all that jerky."

My cheeks heat, knowing it wasn't all the junk food we ate that made me tired; it was the hot and heavy make-out session and the equivalent of an emotional marathon conversation that followed. Which would also explain the dream.

A tiny tilt of his perfect lips and the memory of him sliding them down my neck send a shiver up my spine. This guy is so sweet and innocent on the outside but sexy in a way that betrays his shining surfer-boy look. And he's a wonderful listener. At times, when I was talking about Lana, I could feel his anger, as if he felt the pain of my words. He's the kind of guy a girl could get used to.

*A* girl. But not *this* girl.

And nothing reminds me of that more than my dream. I'm almost glad I fell asleep on the way home. Lord knows I needed a reminder. I'm living my life for Lana, and until I find her killer, there's no room for anything else.

But God . . . Mason. No, I can't.

"Thanks for tonight." I grab the door handle, and a quick flash of confusion crosses his expression.

"Hold on." He grabs his door handle to get out.

"Mason, you don't have to walk me up." Please, don't come to my door. It'll just make things harder.

As if he didn't hear me, he moves from the truck, rounds the hood, and ends up at my door. Before I can beat him to it, he opens it for me. I snag my clutch, scoop up my shoes, and I slide out.

"What kind of a man doesn't walk a woman to her door?" The insinuation behind his question drops my gaze to the concrete driveway.

Every man I've ever been with.

I tuck my hands under my arms in eighty-five degree weather, feigning cold to avoid him holding one of them. We proceed to the front door in silence, and I busy myself with my keys to keep from looking at him and getting sucked into those gentle blue eyes. "Thanks again. Oh!" I start to shrug off his flannel shirt.

"Don't worry about it." He grabs the lapels and pulls the shirt back up over my shoulders, his thick fists meeting in the middle of my chest. "Hold on to it for me."

"Is this like an earring thing?" I tilt my head, trying to ignore the heat of his knuckles that threatens to rest against my cleavage. Just one deep breath and—no . . . I shake my head.

"An earring thing?" He drops his hands, and I'm immediately grateful as I am equally bereft.

"Nothing. Forget it." I slide the key into the door, hoping to make a quick getaway, because damn if this man isn't magnetic or something.

He chuckles and grips my elbow gently. "Oh, come on. Now I'll be lying in bed all night"—the heat of his chest warms my back, and I fight the urge to moan and sink into his hold—"thinking about you."

Oh no, no, no, no . . . That voice is deep and heavy with something I'm going to refuse to name.

". . . and wondering what an 'earring thing' is."

I turn toward him, my back against the door. Ugh . . . big mistake. He's so close. I attach my gaze to his chin, hoping it's a safe placc to land, or at least safer than his lips or his eyes. Or that hair, all that blond hair. Gah!

"It's what girls do when they want a repeat. They leave something behind, usually of value, so they have a reason to go back." There, I told him. Now if I could just figure out how to unlock my door from behind my back and fall inside the safety of my house.

He crosses his arms at his chest, eyebrows pinched, but grinning. "Go back for what?"

"Usually? Another date, or in some cases, another session of hot sex." My cheeks heat furiously. Fuck!

"Is that what I'm doing?" His hand moves toward my face and I almost flinch. If he touches me, that'll be the end of it. Evading the power of his looks and swagger is one thing, but add on a touch, and I'm screwed. His knuckles glide from my temple to my jaw. "You have no idea what this does to me."

I shake my head, not trusting my voice.

"Making you blush . . . It's almost as satisfying as making you come."

I choke—fucking *choke* on my own saliva—which only manages to make my face hotter.

He drops his hand while I catch my breath and clear my throat, a low rumble of laughter reverberating from his chest.

"I have to admit, making an exotic dancer blush is something to brag about."

I press my palm to my throat and then look up at him, expecting to be met with a playful grin. Oh shit.

His face is etched with irritation, eyes dark and eyebrows low. "Right." He shakes his head, blinking. "I better get going." He hooks me behind the neck and pulls me in for a quick, hard, and chaste kiss to my forehead. "Later."

I stand shocked still for a few beats. "Bye."

Before he's to his truck, I turn and push my way inside, closing and locking the door behind me. My back slams to the door as I try to calm my racing heart.

"What the hell was that?"

The peal of tires sounds on the other side of the door, and I try to assimilate the series of events that led to a pissed-off Mason.

Early into the morning, I still can't figure it out.

Not that it matters. It's better that he not like me.

Better for both of us.

—

## MASON

She's a stripper. How could I forget?

The sweet woman is one of eight adopted kids, loves her parents, and has had to work hard for everything she has. This woman has had to endure the worst kind of pain, witness the gore of the death of a loved one, and talks about it with a fierce protection in her voice that would rival the strongest man. The woman, whose body belongs in a fucking display case as a sample of what perfection and beauty looks like, is a *stripper*.

And not just any stripper, not a part-time, just-to-make-ends-meet kind of stripper, not a working-her-way-through-college stripper, but a bona fide career-as-an-exotic-dancer kind of stripper.

Fuck! And go figure my ass goes and falls for her. Hard.

I slam my palms against the steering wheel, wishing to God things could be different. Can I date a woman who makes money by grinding her panty-clad pussy against the crotches of random men? That shit has to turn her on. I barely touch her between her legs, and she fucking ignites. No way she doesn't get off doing what she does.

The first time we kissed I'd foolishly demanded she tell me why she does it. I wanted so badly to hear that she was as shallow as the stereotype in my head. Rather than answer, she looked at me like I'd asked her to lop off her own arm.

So why? With all the available jobs, why do something as debasing as stripping?

It's because she loves seducing men for money, bringing them to the brink of insanity. It's exactly what she did to me tonight. I suppose I should be patting myself on the back for getting all I got from her tonight for the price of a coffee and some cheap mini-mart snacks.

As soon as the thoughts filter through my head, they sour my stomach with guilt. It's not like she's ever tried to hide who she is and what she does. She's never made any promises, at least, not with words, but fuck if our time together wasn't bringing me the hope of possibility.

What a fucking surprise to find myself here again, longing for a woman who I can't have, or at least have all to myself. Sure, Eve gave me parts of her. By giving me her friendship, she trusted me with the most important parts, but I could never have her the way I wanted: fully and completely, body, heart, mind. And now Trix offers me her body as long as I'm okay sharing her with every man who passes through Zeus's front doors.

I slam my truck into park outside of my modest condo complex. Hitting the alarm, I move through the grassy, well-manicured courtyard and pass by the saltwater pool complete with hot tub and waterfalls that I know are there, all while noticing none of it.

It was stupid to pursue things with Trix. We're supposed to go out on Tuesday, but unless I can convince myself to care for her on a surface-level-only, physical relationship with no attachments, it's probably best if I cancel.

Once to my condo, I push open the door and flick on the lights. It's a clean, modern, bi-level with more space than I need. After signing with the UFL, I moved here with nothing but my clothes, a computer, and my stereo. The organization had the place furnished: overstuffed furniture and sleek tables made of dark wood polished to a shine. It's decorated to catalog perfection and so not my taste it's almost laughable.

I head to the open kitchen for a glass of water before going to bed where I expect to lie there all night, overthinking, while staring at the slow rotation of the bamboo ceiling fan.

A package on my countertop catches my eye. I move toward the foreign mass of brown paper and tape and find a slip of paper sitting next to it. My gaze jerks up to my living room. Someone was here. Are they still?

I move fast, taking two steps at a time up to my loft bedroom, and flick on the lights. No one. Bathroom looks the same as it did when I left this morning. I haul ass down to the guest bedroom, my office, the laundry room . . . all empty.

Dread settles in my gut, a sixth-sense that tells me exactly who was here and what's in the package. I navigate my way back to the package and snag the note.

*It's all here and accounted for.*

"Fuck!" I toss the scrap of paper and grind my teeth at the unsatisfying way it floats to the ground.

Tomorrow night. Zeus's. Dammit to hell.

# THIRTEEN

## TRIX

After getting home at the crack of dawn and catching a few hours of sleep, I woke to my alarm as it pulled me from the most delicious dream: waves, sand, and Mason. I dragged myself to the gym and hit the treadmill hard before coming in for my shift. As much as I enjoyed my time with Mason, things ended strangely.

When he left me at my door, he didn't mention our date we'd set up for tomorrow night. I don't know if we're still on or not, and I can't even call him because I don't know his number. I suppose I could ask Gia, but there's a tiny part of me that's apprehensive. The intensity of what I feel around Mason scares me, and as much as I want him to smother me with it, I'm terrified of being lost to it.

My phone on my dressing table chimes with an incoming text, and my heart leaps. I drop the magazine I'd been mindlessly flipping through and snag the device.

Damn, not Mason.

My brother Isaac.

**I MADE THE TEAM! BooYah!**

I grin at how much my little brother is starting to sound like the teenage boy he is.

**Of course you did! It's your highly-tuned Mother Mary.**

**Hail Mary, Doofus.**

When I spoke to my parents earlier today, they'd mentioned that he was going to find out if he made the football team tonight. I guess they leave for some kind of training camp to get all the players geared up before the beginning of the school year. It's almost midnight, so I assume he's been out celebrating.

My fingers furiously type and I giggle out loud.

**Whatever . . . will I get to see you when I come home or will your big-shot football-playing self be occupied with your admirers?**

I hit "send" and bite my lip to keep from laughing while I wait for his reply.

**Have your people call my people.**

"Let me guess." Angel shuffles over, dressed in nothing but patent leather and metal, having just come from her S&M routine. She drops onto her stool at her dressing table and rips off her spiked collar. "Mason?"

I sit up straighter and curse my eager response.

She dips her chin to motion to my phone. "It's so obvious! You're grinning like a queen at the Pride Parade."

A long sigh falls from my lips, and my shoulders droop in defeat. "Nah"—I hold up my phone and shake it—"it's my little brother. He's just really funny."

"Oh, well"—she continues to unbuckle and remove the painful looking corset until she's bare naked—"never mind. I assumed after all the hot and heavy spit swapping y'all did last night he'd be blowing up your phone today."

I roll my eyes and regret filling Angel in on the details of my time with Mason. The second I got to the club after the way she saw us leave last night, she was begging for the tell-all. I gave her most of it just because it felt so good to share it with someone. Being with a man like Mason isn't something a woman can keep to herself. That goodness doesn't seem real until it's spoken out loud between friends. And even then, it almost seems too good to be true.

"You tease, but it was ah-maze-ing." I check the timer on my mirror and realize I have ten minutes before I'm up. "When was the last time you've been with a man that was content to kiss and feed you jerky?"

I drop my robe and pull on pieces of the costume I laid out earlier.

Angel ties the satin sashes of her black Zeus's robe. "That's easy. Not since high school." Her eyebrows pinch and a slow smile tugs at her lips. "What're you wearing?"

"Huh?" I'm tugging on a pair of board shorts over a bright yellow G-string. "This?" I stand up and loop the yellow triangle bikini top around my neck and tie it at my back. "I'm changing things up."

She stares at me like I slid on a muumuu.

"What?" I hold out my hands and twirl, grabbing at the super long strands of extensions I put into the back of my hair to make it twice as long and board straight. "Don't I look like a little surfer girl?" I pop up on my dressing table, cross my legs, and wiggle my painted toes.

"You're batting your eyelashes." She laughs and shakes her head. "Holy shit, they're gonna love the whole innocent thing you got going on. And barefoot . . . fucking genius."

"Thanks!" I don't tell her where my sexy surf-inspired idea came from.

"Trix, you're on in five!" Santos' call comes thundering through the room.

"On it!" I hop off the table and check my look one more time.

"What're you dancing to, The Beach Boys?"

I turn toward her with what is probably a wicked grin. "'Drunk in Love,' baby." I snap my fingers and move past her. "Beyoncé up in this bi—"

"Trix!"

Angel and I dissolve into a fit of giggles. "Coming, Santos!"

"Kick ass, babe."

And with a smack on the ass from my girl, I'm off to work a crowd.

—

## MASON

As I sit in my truck, not far from the alley that I dragged my brother's broken body from only a week ago, I can't help but wonder how this is going to play out. I don't know why I didn't think of it before, but now, as I stare down the dirty backstreet, a wave of dread comes over me. These guys could easily take my offering—this offending burden wrapped in brown paper and twine—and then leave me with a bullet between my eyes.

I need to stay semi-public to avoid that. Close enough to the back lot of Zeus's that any gunshot would be heard and reported, but far enough away that I won't be seen.

"Pass it on and get the hell out of here." My gaze swings to the red beat-up Honda Civic at the opposite side of the lot and my chest aches.

Trix is here.

I'm tempted to duck inside and watch her dance from a back corner where she won't notice. After the way I stormed off last night, I can't imagine she's interested in seeing me. But as much as my draw to be close to her pulls me in, the reluctance of being witness to her stripping holds me back. The memory of her dancing in that hotel suite is enough to make my blood boil and my fists clench. She seemed to enjoy what she was doing, and I have to wonder how she can possibly draw the line between where her job ends and real physical arousal begins.

The low growl of motorcycle engines pulls me from my thoughts, and I watch as a small fleet of bikers pulls up to the alley. I recognize all four of them from the other night, the bigger one standing out like a bad omen.

Kicking out their stands, they lean the bikes and dismount then linger, lighting cigarettes and settling in.

Fuck. Here we go.

Eager to get this shit over with and go the hell home, I grab the stupid package and shove it under my arm. With long strides, I head toward them and the bikers notice me right away, stilling conversation and all turning to face me.

I don't hesitate in my approach, and the big fucker I dealt with last week steps forward.

"I didn't think you'd pull through." His voice is gravelly and low, jagged in a way that speaks of hard living.

"You didn't give me much of a choice." I hold out the package and he takes it.

He doesn't even glance at it, but passes it back to one of his brothers, keeping his eye on me. "Was kinda looking forward to bloodying that pretty-boy face of yours."

My fingers itch to ball into fists, but leaving this parting peacefully is in the best interest of all involved. "You're a man of your word; you back off me and Drake." It's a statement of fact, a promise that I need to hear him confirm.

The biker grins wide, whiskered lips curling back over the yellowed teeth of a chain smoker. "You tell your boy if he crosses us again he won't live to talk about it."

The guy's eyes dart over my shoulder an instant before I hear the low rumble of male voices behind me. I turn to see a group of guys I instantly recognize just as the roar of motorcycle engines fire to life.

"Mase?" Wade says, his gaze moving between me and the retreating bikers as they mount their bikes to take off down the street.

Dammit, fuck! I dip my chin, hoping to sidestep into the shadows.

He shoves my shoulder. "What the hell are you doing here, man?" There's humor in his voice, but when I turn to face him, his expression grows hard as he takes in the motorcycle taillights. "Those your friends?"

I notice Wade is with a few of the newer fighters, some guys who've just joined our camp and are clearly being given the hot-spots-in-Vegas tour.

"No." The urge to get out of here is so strong my legs cramp with the desire to move. "They were asking for directions."

He nods. "Oh, well then, come with us. I was just taking the boys here to check out all Vegas has to offer." He grabs the back of my neck and motions for me to join him.

"No, thanks." I motion to my truck and act casual. "I was just headed out."

He's back to glaring at me with suspicion. "You were already inside?"

Shit!

"Yeah, but uh—"

"Come on, Baywatch." Pauly, one of the new guys, smacks me on the shoulder. "One drink!"

It's easier to just have a damn drink than to figure out a way out of this that won't get my ass teased for weeks. "Sure. Okay." I shove Pauly—"It's Mason or Mayhem to you, asshole"—and reluctantly follow, thankful that Wade hadn't shown up two minutes earlier and seen me hand off at least ten pounds of drugs. I'll pop in with them and then disappear as soon as I can.

Santos, working security at the back door, recognizes me and holds the door open for us, and we shuffle into a dark hallway. I feel the huge bouncer's eyes on me as I pass, his glare burning into my head. Clearly this guy is protective of Trix. Threat received.

Techno music gets louder as we move down the corridor and get spit out into the main club. It takes a second for my eyes to adjust to the contrast of dark and day-glow as we shuffle through the room to a vacant table in the back. Thankfully, it's busy enough that we've avoided being right up against the main stage. This might keep Trix from seeing me, and I could still get away with slipping out of here unnoticed.

We order drinks from a slutty-looking cheerleader and watch as a few dancers I've never seen before swivel their hips in nothing but a thin string tied between their legs. Judging by their lack of clothing, I'd say we're catching the end of their dance.

"Tomorrow Cam's going to talk to you guys about training partners . . ."

Wade's involved in UFL Training 101, so I tune him out and scan the room, looking for the flash of platinum and purple, and coming up short. That means she's backstage or in a private room. My skin prickles with irritation, and I'm tempted to throw open the doors and bust open skulls.

I shift on my barstool and try to shake off my severe mental discomfort. Fresh off a drug deal, I'm hopped up on adrenaline and *what-the-fuck*. I breathe through a mix of relief and jumpiness. Don't go kicking the ass of someone who doesn't deserve it. After all, this is a legitimate job. Trix's job. It's her fucking *job!* I fist my hair and ready to make my hasty exit when our drinks arrive.

"Here's to a successful fighting year, boys." Wade holds up his beer and clanks bottles with the newbies, but I avoid the cheery "hear, hear" and slug back a good half the bottle.

"Gentleman, have we got a treat for you tonight!" The announcer's voice grates on my nerves, ratcheting my agitation. "You got wood? Because we've got a girl who's ready to grind on that. Put your hands together for the sugary-sweet and sultry—"

Oh, fuck no . . .

"Trix!"

Motherfucker! I slam down my beer bottle as the room goes dark. Rippling blue lights flash on the stage, and the sound of crashing waves trickle from the speakers. The crowd roars and yells at a blank stage. The music builds, waves mixing with some Indian snake charmer music, sexy and seductive. My heart pounds in my chest, and I'm transfixed on what I know is going to be a scene that will destroy me as much as turn me the fuck on.

A soft sultry voice singing about drinking drips through the speakers. Bright lights flash.

And she appears. Bare feet, bikini, and board shorts. No fucking way.

I suck in a quick breath and hold it, spellbound by the way she looks combined with the slow roll of her hips. Hypnotizing. The bass drops, but the tempo stays slow, lazy. Like love-making.

"Holy shit, it's her!" Wade shoves my shoulder, but I'm locked on the beautiful woman on stage, unable to rip my eyes from the vision before me.

Her hands move over her body, sensual swipes of her palms over her belly that move between her legs, reminding me of last night. I shift in my seat, harder than steel, and watch as she dances just for me. All that hair, longer than it was the last time I saw her is draped and thrown around her face, which is fixed in an expression of ecstasy.

She turns, sliding her shorts down with a tug of her thumb, teasing to within an inch of my sanity. My fists clench against my thighs; the urge to rip those tiny scraps of material from her body and sink deep inside her is so strong it's all I can do to remain in my seat.

The shorts drop to her ankles to reveal a bright yellow G-string, and she kicks them into the crowd to get swallowed up by a group of hungry men.

I blink, mesmerized by how she can move her body. Like liquid, she glides. Crawling on all fours, she dips her chin to the floor. Her chest, belly, hips, thighs . . . like a serpent. Fuck, she's outstanding.

My legs push me to standing, and before I realize what I'm doing, they carry me toward the stage.

She pushes up to her knees, legs wide, and her hands glide up over her breasts, squeezing them gently before she moves them to around her neck, and with a flick of her wrist, her top is gone. Adrenaline fires through my veins; lust and the need to pop the eyes from every man in the room battle for dominance.

She drops into a wide split, the globes of her tanned ass in the faces of the entire front row. The song goes on at an erotic pace and sings about swerving on a surfboard. She mimics the motion of sex, her knee cocked as she rolls her hips in waves and grinds down on nothing beneath her.

For a split and selfish second, I imagine this is all for me. I take my head to a place where everything she does is for me and only for me. Where her body and all she has to offer she gives freely to the one man she can trust with it.

Me.

Warmth explodes in my chest.

She inches her gorgeous ass toward the edge of the stage, and hands come at her from every direction. I jerk from my fantasy and blink away the fog of lust as patrons shove as many bills as they can fit into the tiny strings of fabric that cover her most private places.

Rage, hot and welcome, fires beneath my skin. I move, grab the first body that stands between my woman and me, and toss it away. One by one, I pick them off like ants, grabbing the backs of their shirts, flinging them aside to get to her, and making a path that will get my arms around her to protect her from these lecherous animals that can't keep their fucking hands to themselves.

The murmur of chaos explodes around me, but I ignore it. Fists pound at my back and arms, but it's static compared to the drive to get to Trix.

Her head jerks around, eyes wide, mouth agape. "Mason?"

I can hardly hear her over the commotion, but I'm so transfixed on her face I read her lips. In one long stride, I'm on stage. I scoop her into my arms.

"Put me down!" She kicks her legs, but it only makes me squeeze her tighter to me.

"No."

"Mason, please." Her words are rushed and panicked. "I can walk, just . . . trust me. You *need* to put me down."

"No fucking way." I carry her back toward the curtain only to be met by Santos, who's grinning and cracking his knuckles.

He tilts his head. "Hands off her."

"Okay, never mind." Trix's arms tighten around my neck. "Don't put me down. Do *not* put me down."

She's safe backstage and away from prying eyes. "It's okay." I kiss the top of her head.

"No, Mason. Don't." Her hold gets tight, but gravity wins, and her legs drop to the floor. "Oh shit. You shouldn't have done that."

Her mumbled words are the last thing I hear before Santos hauls back and knocks me in the jaw.

Pain splinters through my face, and I brace my weight on my knees. "Motherfuck!"

"Santos! You're such a bully!" Trix drops down to her knees to see my face, concern pinching her pretty forehead. "Oh my God, are you okay?" She grimaces and sucks air through her teeth. "I was trying to warn you."

"Dammit to fuck, that hurt." I rub my jaw and stand up to see a very satisfied Santos.

"Don't look at me." He shrugs. "House rules, man."

Trix pops her hands on her hips, glaring. "Great. And now they're going to ban you!" She throws her arms out to her sides, her breasts bouncing with the force of it, totally unaware that she's practically bare-ass naked. "What were you thinking?"

I run a hand through my hair and breathe through the letdown of adrenaline. God, I stormed up on that stage like a damn Neanderthal. “I don’t . . . I’m sorry.”

She steps in close and peers up at me, her violet eyes searching mine. She’s so tiny now; barefoot, she only comes up to my chest. “You can’t do that. I could lose my job.”

The corner of my mouth lifts as I try to fight off the joy at the prospect of her no longer stripping. I rub the back of my neck and shrug. “Would that be so bad?”

She thwacks me in the stomach. “Stop it!”

“Put a shirt on. And some pants and . . . maybe I’ll think about it.”

Her eyes widen, but a contagious grin curls her lips.

“Come on, man.” Santos throws a big meaty thumb over his shoulder. “I gotta escort you out.”

“Santos, can you give us a second?” Trix turns her pleading eyes toward him, and his expression softens. “Pleeeaaase?” She turns out her lower lip, and the guy is a goner. What guy wouldn’t be?

“Fine. Five minutes, Trix.” He points a finger at me then two fingers at his own eyes. “I’m watching you.”

“Creepy.”

Trix grabs my hand and pulls me deeper backstage into a dark corner. It’s hard to focus on anything other than her perfect naked body.

“Here.” I reach behind me and pull my T-shirt over my head, leaving me in my undershirt. Shaking it out, I put it over her and smile as her glaring face pops through the neck hole.

“Really?” She slides her arms in but shakes her head.

“Yes.” I cross my arms over my chest, locking my hands beneath my biceps. “Unless you want me to throw you up against this wall and do dirty things to that sweet little body, you need to cover up.”

Her breath hitches, and I smile inwardly at how affected she is by the simplest things I say. My fingers itch to run through her hair, to pull her to me and taste those lips that look as if they're dipped in candy. I want to pick her up, have her wrap her legs around my waist and beg me to take her away from all this.

"Mason, tomorrow night I think we need to talk." She turns her head to see Santos standing off to the side, giving us space, but not nearly enough.

Talk. Great, this is where she tells me she'd rather pull out all her own toenails than date a guy like me.

"Trix, hurry it up!"

"Hold on!" she yells at Santos and turns back to me. "Tomorrow at seven, right?"

"Yeah. Tomorrow."

"Okay, here . . ." She grips the hem of my shirt and starts to take it off.

I still her hand, and the heat and softness of her skin make me groan. "No, keep it." I lean in and place a long, lingering kiss on her forehead, staying away from her lips because if I allow myself that I'll never stop there. "Tonight, watching you dance?" I press my forehead to hers. "You took my breath away."

And with that, I move toward the bouncer, grinning like an idiot. Yeah, I might be walking away, leaving her here to get naked for men for the remainder of her shift, but right now she's wearing my shirt, and that screams victory. Even if only a minor one.

# FOURTEEN

## MASON

Not much could make this day any sweeter. After getting home last night and texting Drake that I ran his little-bitch errand, I pushed all thoughts of my brother's problems aside and thought about Trix.

After Santos escorted me out and explained that I'd usually be blackballed from ever returning but that Trix would have his balls if he refused me, I felt like an Olympic champion.

I lay in bed all night, thinking about the talk we're going to have on our date. I'm sure she'll toss out a million reasons why she can't date me, but she's insane if she thinks I'll agree to any of them. There's not an athlete in the world that is as competitive as a fighter, and I'll be dipped in dog shit before I'll give her up.

I'll have to convince her to quit her job, which will be the hardest part. Hopefully, I can convince her I'm worth the risk rather than having to live through the crushing jealousy of her exploiting her body—a body I'm determined to have as mine—for money.

"Come on, Baywatch, you still have to spar." Rex knocks me in the back of the head, and I lie back down on the weight bench, bracing myself to lift the bar. "Fucking, Peter Pan." He's sweating and grinning down at me.

"Since when did I get the stupid fucking nickname award?" I push up the weight and grind through a few reps.

"You earned it," he says as if it's an easy connection to make.

I growl through a few more reps before my chest starts to burn and my arms quake. "Shit." I slam the bar back on the rack. "You trying to kill me?"

"Not with three hundred. Stop being a pussy."

The door to the weight room swings open. "Where's my welcome home party, motherfuckers?"

"Holy shit." I sit up and stare as Blake struts into the room, now with a black band around his ring finger, and an obnoxious grin on his face. "What the hell are you doing here?"

He shrugs then moves in for a fist bump. "Cut the honeymoon short. Jack got sick and Layla lost her shit, thinking he had some island fever or some crap. Came home to find out the kid had a cold. Now he's healthy as a horse."

"That's too bad." I run a towel over my sweaty forehead. "I know how much chicks dig honeymoons."

He flashes a crooked grin. "Every day is a honeymoon in my bed, Baywatch. My woman isn't missin' shit, trust me."

Rex slaps Blake on the back. "You got here just in time for sparring." He jerks his head to me. "Baywatch is all primed for an ass-kicking. Need to knock his little-bitch ass outta the clouds."

"Is that right?" Blake cracks his knuckles and rolls his head on his shoulders. "Fuckin' A, I'm ready."

Great.

---

"Fuck, old man." I dodge Blake's left hook. "Fatherhood made you lazy." He lunges for my legs. I jump back, just out of reach.

"Lazy's still kickin' your ass." He steps in and lands a body shot.

"Baywatch, concentrate!" Rex's command is laced with irritation.

I swing my left and Blake spins away. Shit.

My muscles are loose with fatigue. I move around Blake and focus on his hands, waiting for my opening. Fuck, this guy is a damn machine. Never off his game.

"You looking to fight me or fuck me, Baywatch? Stop flirting and take a shot." His taunts roll off my back as I zone in, ready to put forth all my energy to end this little dance we've been doing.

If he'd just drop his guard . . .

I swing. He ducks and lunges for my legs. I jump back. Not fast enough. His arms lock around my thigh. Shit! I'm airborne. My back hits the mat with a whoosh of air escaping my lungs.

"Fuck!" I pound the mat with my fists.

He shoves my jaw in a mock punch. "Nah . . . but thanks for the offer."

Asshole.

He pushes to stand, and Rex shows up at his side, glaring down at me with his arms crossed over his chest.

"What?" I avoid their eyes, knowing the lecture that's sure to pour from their stupid mouths.

"Where's your head at, Baywatch?" Rex digs the ball of his foot into my ribs. "And I swear to shit if you say it's in the fight I'll sweep your leg Karate-Kid style." He holds out his arms and lifts a knee as if he's Danielson, and Blake chokes on a laugh.

I roll away from them and hop to my feet. "I don't know what you want from me. I'm training my ass off."

Rex's teasing expression sobers. "No . . . you were on fire a few weeks ago. Now you're, I don't know"—he taps his temple with two fingers—"not here."

Blake's squinting at me or, wait . . . just over my shoulder. I turn to see a grinning Layla headed toward us with a little bundle of baby wrapped in a blanket and cradled in her arms.

He grips the chain link. "Mouse, what the hell are you doing here?" A proud smile splits his face as he takes in his woman and their son.

Layla tilts her head and presses a kiss to his lips through the cage. "I wanted to bring Jack by so he could watch Daddy work." She smiles down at her baby, and I don't miss Blake's hands flex on the metal link like he's itching to touch his kid.

"Yeah? Or were you bored and wanted to come shoot the shit with Eve?" He takes two steps back and hops up and over the octagon fence.

She giggles. "That too." Her gaze swings from Blake to Rex and me. "Hey, you guys should meet us out tonight."

"Whoa, what?" Blake plucks Jack from his mother's arms, dwarfing the infant with the size of his arms. "Tonight?"

"Yeah, I was talking to Eve, and we thought it would be fun to go out for happy hour tonight. Ya know, get caught up." She shrugs and waits for Rex and me to answer.

"Oh, um . . . I can't tonight."

Blake glares at me. "Why not?"

"I uh . . ." I shift on my feet and avoid their eyes. "It's, um, I have a date."

"Aha . . . so that's where your head's at." Rex knocks me in the back of the skull.

"Ow! Fucking cut that shit out!" I rub the back of my head.

Rex shakes his head and then answers Layla. "Gia and I will be there. What time?"

Layla grins. "Six o'clock at The Bacon Bar." She swings her gaze to Mason. "Bring her with, Mase, just for one drink."

"Oh, sure. Yeah, okay." I can't think of a single reason to say no other than to tell the truth, which is that I don't want to share Trix with anyone tonight, but I suppose a drink before dinner would be alright.

After all, if she agrees to date me exclusively, she'll have to meet my UFL family. She seemed to get along great with Eve, and she's already tight with Gia. What could possibly go wrong?

# FIFTEEN

## TRIX

I'm sitting at my kitchen table, pounding a furious beat with the heel of my shoe. My calf burns, but nerves insist I continue. I check my phone for the time, wondering what the surprise detour Mason told me about earlier could possibly be.

The text came in shortly after I woke up. I'm assuming he got my number from Gia. I click through and open the message again.

**Surprise detour. Be ready at six. :) Mason**

An explosion of flutters takes flight in my belly. "It's only a date! Teenagers do it for crying out loud." Jeez. I push up to pace the small kitchen, smoothing the front of my white dress.

I searched for my most conservative outfit for my first date, and although this dress hangs loosely off my shoulder and around my body, it's shorter than I'd have liked.

Shit. Maybe I should've gone shopping for something else. The rumble of a truck engine sounds and my heart beats wildly. I rush to the spare bathroom to check my face one more time before slowing my pace to answer the door.

He knocks twice, and I take a deep breath to fake calm.

I swing open the door and lock my knees to keep from throwing myself into his arms. Wow, he's beautiful. "Hey."

He doesn't greet me, and rather than his usual easy smile, his expression is intense. He scrutinizes every inch of me, making me squirm as I feel the sweep of his gaze against my skin.

His blue button-up shirt offsets his cobalt eyes framed with shaggy blond hair that looks as if he tried to tame it. His jeans aren't tight, but they're not baggy. A dark denim hugs his long legs perfectly, giving a hint to the powerful muscle that lies underneath.

"Trix . . . I . . ." He clears his throat. "You're like . . ." He covers his mouth with his hand and shakes his head, his gaze giving away that he approves of my attire for the night.

Even with his admiration, I can't shake the feeling of inadequacy. My gold bangles jingle as I fidget with the short hem of my dress. "It's short, I know."

"Damn." He runs his hand through his hair, studying my legs. "I don't know what else to say." His eyes find me. "You look really pretty."

A giggle bubbles up from my chest, cooling the heat of my nerves. "Thank you. You clean up well too." I grab my purse off the small table in the foyer and lock the door before walking out and closing it behind me.

He offers me his elbow, and I blush at the kindness of his overly formal gesture.

"What do you have planned for me? More midnight four-wheeling?" I motion to my gold strappy heels. "Just want to make sure I'm wearing appropriate shoes."

He cocks his head and flashes a confident half-smile that stirs something deep in my belly.

"You'll just have to wait and see." He opens the passenger-side door of his truck. "Are you hungry?"

I climb inside his truck as gracefully as I can. He groans, but covers it with a fake cough. My face heats when I realize I'd most likely given him a peek at my modest nude-colored lace panties.

I try to ignore that and answer him. "I'm okay for now."

He nods and shuts me in, moving around the hood and climbing in the driver's side. "We'll hit up one stop, and then the rest of the night is all about us."

I turn and watch him as he studies the rearview mirror, backing out of the driveway. "All about us? So, the one stop involves someone else?"

He cringes slightly. "Eh . . . a few someones." His eyes find me, reassuring and kind. "But don't worry. It'll be fun."

"I trust you."

A shy grin curls his lips, and I have to look away to keep from leaning in to see if that smile tastes as good as it looks.

The cab of the truck swirls with the scent of fresh rain and honey, and I let the aroma soothe me.

We fall into a comfortable conversation about our day, mine being filled with sleep, some light cleaning, and then getting ready. His with training.

The summer heat is high, and we're still a couple hours away from sunset. Funny how different the city looks in the day compared to night. The dual-personality feel of Las Vegas is what draws people in with dreams of normal days and erotic nights. My stomach jumps as I consider normal, like now, being picked up for a date by a handsome gentleman. Basic and yet more exciting than stepping out on stage mostly naked.

We pull in to the parking lot of a restaurant that has a pig on the sign, and he opens the door for me to escort me inside.

"This was your big detour? A sports bar?" I lift one eyebrow at him, teasing, but also concerned that I'm overdressed.

"Don't worry. One drink and we're gone, cool?" He pulls my hand into the crook of his arm and leads me to the door. "I promised a few friends we'd stop by. They just got back from their honeymoon and wanted to catch up."

Sounds easy enough. A drink, some small talk, I can do that.

We push into the dark restaurant, and it takes a few seconds for my vision to adjust. The aroma of cooking meat, specifically pork, wafts toward me, and despite my best efforts to avoid it, my stomach growls and my mouth waters. What is it about bacon?

Mason leads me to a group of people that take up two large tables at the bar. I catch a flash of red hair, and my grip on his hand tightens. "Is that . . .?"

"It is. Rex and Gia are here." He pulls me close to throw an arm over my shoulder just as we approach the table.

Gia's eyes widen upon seeing us, and she rushes over. "I knew it!" Her gaze bounces between Mason and me just as Rex comes up behind her and wraps his big, colorful arms around her waist.

"Baywatch, you fuckin' punk." He leans forward and nips at Gia's ear. "Did you know about this?"

"No, I mean, I figured after . . ." She shakes her head then blinks as if she's snapped herself from her thoughts. "Well, come on, I'll introduce you to everyone."

She grabs my hand and I look up at Mason. He nods for me to go, but before releasing me drops a long soft closed-mouthed kiss against my lips. My insides tumble at his open show of affection, his public declaration of our being together.

Gia heads to the far end of the table where two women are sitting. The blonde is absently rocking an infant carrier, while the brunette stands, swaying slowly with a baby strapped to her chest.

"Layla and Raven, I want you to meet my friend." Gia pulls me up between the two. "This is Trix, my old roommate."

The blonde, who I assume is Layla, peers up at me with kind dark eyes and a welcoming smile. "Trix, nice to meet you. Here"—she motions to a chair next to her—"have a seat."

"Thanks." I sit and try to adjust my dress. These girls are wearing more casual attire, cute worn jeans and biker boots or sandals, and suddenly, I feel self-conscious.

I turn my head to the dark-haired girl, and although she's not purposefully looking unfriendly, her contemplative expression makes me uneasy.

She steps close, her hands braced on her baby, and I can't help but feel like I've seen her before. "Who are you here with?"

My eyes move through the crowd of men at the tables, all of them facing the television screens that are plastered on every wall surrounding the bar. I search out Mason, who, like the rest of them, has his back toward me, the man he's talking to nearly twice Mason's size with dark hair and full-sleeved tattoos. My heart flutters with an anxiety I can't shake, but I push it back and smile.

"She came with Mason." The high pitch of excitement in Gia's voice catches my attention.

"We're going out on a date tonight." I almost slap my forehead at how stupid I must sound, but I can't shake the unwelcome feeling that prickles beneath my skin.

Gia props a hip on the table, her big smile framed with all that orange hair. "How in the hell did you and Mase hook up? Did you meet him at the club?"

Embarrassment twists in my gut, and I do everything I can to keep a confident posture. "No, um . . . he had some friends in town, and Angel and I were hired to dance for them." I look between Raven and Layla, feeling more out of place than I've felt in a long time. I have nothing to be ashamed of.

The bar erupts in a mix of boos and groans, whatever happening on the television screen being some kind of disappointment.

"Oh my gosh . . . I know you." Raven's blue-green eyes flash with recognition. "You work at Zeus's."

"Trix, this is Raven, Rex's half-sister I told you about." Gia turns toward the guys. "The big guy over there? That's her husband, Jonah Slade."

Oh shit.

". . . baby Sadie." Gia finishes, but I'm crippled with panic as the pieces slide into place.

UFL guys. Rex, Jonah, and—

"Trix, I want you to meet the boys." Mason appears across the table, a big grin on his face. "This is . . ."

Blake "The Snake" Daniels. I remember.

Play it casual, Trix. Remember he's a total stranger to you.

Blake's eyes are narrowed for a few seconds, moving between Layla and me, before they widen and he swallows hard. "Trix." He nods.

"Blake." I nod back, but, as much as I wish I could cover up all the fear gurgling inside me, it's too late.

Tension settles in the air, and by the look on Layla's face, it didn't take her long to figure it out.

"Zeus's . . . do you and Blake know each other?" Her voice is barely a whisper, but the jagged edge of hurt is apparent.

"Mouse—"

"Shit." Jonah moves toward Raven, as if he's planning to hold her back once she figures it out.

Mason's smile fades. "What's going on?" He flicks his hand between Blake and me. "You two know each other?"

"Blake?" Layla stands and locks her hands around her stomach. "Do you know Trix? *Personally*?"

Everyone's eyes dart between Blake and me, and I feel Gia push in close, a silent but obvious show of support.

"Fuckin' A, Baywatch." Blake glares at Mason, who's staring intently at me.

"Blake? Tell me." Layla's a lot stronger than I am. Whereas she's inches from an angry tirade, I'm bordering on tears.

"Mouse, let's go talk out—"

"No, here."

"Fuck." He runs a hand over his cropped hair. "Valentine's Day, when I left, I went to Zeus's."

"I know that, Blake." She throws an arm out and points at me. "Tell me why you're looking at Trix like she's about to ruin your life."

"Nothing happened, baby. She danced for me. I had a private dance, but nothing happened."

"Don't you fucking lie to me, Blake Daniels. What did you do?"

He scrubs his face. "I thought you were leaving me for that asshole! You kicked me out!"

"So . . . did you guys . . . ?"

"No, Mouse. I love you." He moves closer to her, but doesn't touch her. "I love you."

"Would you just tell me what the hell—"

"I kissed him."

All eyes in the room swing to me, wide with shock.

"It's true. He hired me, and once we were in a private room, I kissed him."

Layla drops her chin to her chest and breathes deep. Blake moves in, pulling her to his chest and kissing the top of her head.

My gaze swings to Raven, who gives me a half smile, almost as if to say she's grateful I told the truth but even the kindness in her eyes isn't enough to erase the awkward tension in the air.

Gia and Rex are at my back, and although they're supporting me enough, they're arms are wrapped around each other. I suddenly feel like the odd man out, searching for an anchor, something to remind me that I'm not as horrible as I feel.

On instinct, my gaze swings to Mason. He's glaring at Blake, and I recoil at the disgust I see reflected in his eyes. I drop my gaze and slide away from the table. There should be something to say, some parting words that will give them some peace, but I can't think of what that would be.

The fact is I don't belong here.

This world of dating and romance and happily ever after isn't mine to have.

I'm a *stripper*. I'm the woman from a married man's past—the other woman, the temptation—and I'm staring boldly at my reality. Just my presence alone has managed to break up this entire event.

Yeah, this was a mistake. One I need to remind myself to never let happen again.

## MASON

I'm staring at Trix as if the power of my will alone could keep her here. I saw the second it happened, when the spark in her eye turned to fear and the urge to run. She forced her chin up, despite the awkward moment that would make a lesser woman hide behind her hair.

"Um . . . I should go." She scoots between chairs, extracting herself from the cluster of people and bar tables.

"Trix!" She doesn't turn around, but her shoulders hitch up at my call. "Wait up."

I move around to catch her before she gets too far, pulling her into my arms and holding her there. "Please, don't go."

"Mason, how can you say that? You know as well as I do I don't belong here."

"You belong with me, and if you don't belong here"—I survey my friends, all of them clutching their women, their expressions either that of pity or disappointment—"I don't belong here either."

Fuckin' hell! First Lane, now kissing Blake. This information should make me angry. Hell, at the very least, I should be jealous, but since I've gotten to know Trix, I see this shit doesn't mean anything to her. She said it herself that her body is nothing more than skin, bones, and nerves. She feels no attachment to the men she's hooked up with in the past, but it's me whose arms she's curled in now. Her tiny fingers are gripping my shirt for dear life, and fuck if it doesn't make me want to sweep her away and protect her from ever feeling the embarrassment she's suffering now.

After all, it's me who has the honor of taking her out on a date. She didn't throw on that sexy-as-sin dress, those mile-high shoes, and leave her hair and makeup simple the way she knows I like it, for them. She did it for me.

So fuck them. They reject her because Blake is a stupid piece of shit for walking out on his girl over a fucking year ago. That's on them. Trix doesn't deserve their judgment, and I'll be damned if I'm going to sit here and subject her to it.

"I'm getting Trix out of here." I glare at my team and shake my head, hoping they see the disappointment.

"Mason, you should stay," Trix whispers.

"No, don't go." Layla pushes back from Blake, a friendly smile on her face. "Could you give us a minute?"

I squeeze Trix to me. "No fuckin' way."

"It's okay, Mason." Trix peeks up at me with violet eyes. "I deserve it."

"The fuck you do." I turn my anger to Blake. "You treat her like she's the one who broke a damn vow, man. You walked out on your woman and showed up at a strip club."

Blake cringes. "You're right. It's not Trix's fault."

Jonah steps forward. "Told you this shit would come back and haunt you, Blake."

"We tried to tell him." Raven shrugs.

"Alright, I get it, assholes. Shit." Blake sets his eyes on Trix. "I'm sorry. This is my fault."

She looks up at me, shock registering on her gorgeous face. "Is he serious?"

I run a hand through her thick silky hair. "He fuckin' better be."

Layla approaches cautiously. "Hey, I'm sorry. I could've handled that better. If you had any idea how many times I've had to come face-to-face with someone my husband has seen naked . . ." She shakes her head, laughing, then sets apologetic eyes on Trix. "I blame the breastfeeding hormones."

The tension in the room dissipates and a couple of people even chuckle.

Raven steps up to us, grinning. "I saw you dance that night, when Jonah and I came to find Blake. You're really good."

Trix shrugs and I feel her skin heat against my arm. "Thanks."

"Can I just ask you one thing?" Raven says.

"Of course."

"Did you know a girl named Candy who used to work at Zeus's?"

Trix nods. "Yeah, I did. She was a real bitch. We used to put Tabasco sauce in her pasties."

Everyone bursts into laughter, and Raven pulls Trix in for a side hug. "Yeah, I knew I liked you."

Layla joins in, and Gia follows until Trix is tangled in the arms of three women.

"What the hell did we miss?" Cameron's voice commands our attention.

"Just me getting my ass chewed. Nothing new." Blake throws back a healthy gulp from his beer.

Eve's at Cam's side, her brows pinched in confusion as she takes in my woman, who has just won over Raven and Layla.

*My* woman.

# SIXTEEN

## MASON

"How is it?" I fork a piece of steak into my mouth and chew through my smile.

From the second we entered Patrico's, I've been captivated by her. At first, I could tell she was nervous, and when she whispered that she'd never been to a restaurant as nice as this one, I felt equal parts pride and anger. How a woman as beautiful and sweet as she is hasn't been wined and dined to the point of boredom is beyond me.

She closes her eyes as she chews, and my gaze fixes on her long slender throat when she swallows. "That's the best thing I've ever tasted."

I take a pull off my beer that's in some fancy-ass frosty glass. "I can't believe you've never had lobster before. Figured a San Jose girl would've at least given it a try."

Her cheeks pink and she ducks her chin. "We were more of a bologna and mayo family."

Dammit. I shove another bite of steak into my mouth to keep from reinserting my foot. Of course, she wouldn't have had lobster.

She takes a long sip of her white wine and sets her eyes on me. "What about you? I bet you were raised on expensive dinners."

I set down my fork and lean back in my chair, a little embarrassed that I'm that easy to read. "My dad's a plastic surgeon, and after the divorce, my mom moved us to Santa

Cruz. We lived more of a modest life there, but he was always good about making sure I didn't want for much."

"How old were you when your parents got divorced?"

"Four. Drake was barely walking." I shift in my chair, suddenly feeling suffocated by the conversation. "See . . . Drake and I don't have the same dad, but my own father didn't know that until well after D was born."

"Yikes, that must've been hard on your dad."

"I'm sure it was, but he made her suffer for it. Always took good care of me financially, while my mom and Drake were scraping by. Kind of a dick move if you ask me."

"Drake's dad didn't help out?"

"His dad is the reason my brother can't keep himself out of trouble, and no, he never sent money for Drake. I funneled my allowance to them when my dad gave me one, but between that and my mom's random part-time jobs, they struggled."

"Gosh, that's so sad." She pushes around some food on her plate. "So, Drake's dad and your mom didn't end up together. I wonder why she did it in the first place."

I grind my molars together. "Women can't resist the bad boy."

She nods and tilts her head, studying me. "Ya know, I've been around my share of bad boys, and they're not all they're cracked up to be." A shy smile curves her lips. "I prefer the sweet ones who might knock you on your butt in dark hallways, but know how to apologize."

My lips twitch with a goofy grin. "Yeah?"

"Yep." She stabs another meaty piece with her fork. "Okay, so you may've had lobster in the past." Her elbow propped on the table, she offers the bite to me. "But you've never had lobster fed to you by an exotic dancer, have you?"

I lean in, wanting so badly to knock the tiny table that stands between us away. "No, I never have."

Her pink tongue darts out to moisten her upper lip, and she pushes the juicy piece toward my lips.

I take it from her fork and groan as the rich buttery flavor bursts against my tongue. "Mmm." Delicious.

"Good, right?"

"Phenomenal, although it's not nearly as tasty as you."

Her lips part, and her chest rises and falls a little quicker.

"That spot." I tilt my head and nod in the direction of her throat. "Right there just below your earlobe. It's like nothing I've ever tasted in my life."

"Mason . . ."

"I'm hoping, for dessert, you'll let me—" We're interrupted by a man who strolls up to our table. He doesn't speak, but stares at Trix until she drops her gaze to her lap and shifts uncomfortably in her seat. "Is there something I can do for you?"

The guy is dressed in a suit, flashy watch, and if I had to guess, I'd say he's in his late forties. "Excuse me." His gaze finally swings to me. "I hate to interrupt."

Maybe he's a UFL fan? Someone in the business who recognizes me from my last fight?

I choose to ignore his greeting, because frankly, I don't excuse his interruption.

"I was having dinner across the restaurant with a colleague of mine and thought I recognized . . ."

Yep, UFL fan.

His head swivels to Trix. ". . . your date."

Trix's eyes are like saucers as she stares up at him.

"You're a dancer at Zeus's, right?"

She flicks a peek at me, and whatever she sees in my expression has her curling in on herself. "Yes, I am."

My muscles tense, pulse throbbing in my neck. I push out of my seat, snagging the guy's attention. "You mind stepping outside with me for a second, partner."

He looks confused for a second then holds up his hands in surrender. "No, I don't want any trouble. I just wanted to come by and introduce myself." He shoves his hand in my direction, almost every one of his meaty fingers ringed with gold. "Mitch Deeds. I'm the CEO of Fetish Television."

My fists clench. A fucking porn producer approaching my girl while we're on a date? Nope. Not happening.

I step up into his space and try like hell to say what needs to be said without embarrassing Trix any more than I need to. "Listen, fuckface. You're going to turn around right this motherfucking second and walk away, you hear me?"

"You misunderstand. I've seen her dance and she's got talent. With those moves, she could make millions on screen." He steps back and tries to look at Trix to address her, but I catch his chubby fucking chin in my hand.

"Don't fucking look at her."

"Mason, it's okay," Trix says, her voice shaky with emotion.

"If I could just leave my card—"

I grip the asshole by his suit jacket and drag him the few yards to the front of the restaurant. The hostess sees me coming and opens the tall glass door, probably to avoid me shattering it when I toss this fucker's body through it. Two steps outside and I shove the prick with enough force that he lands on his ass.

"Stay the fuck away from her," I growl and turn around, passing the slack-jawed hostess. "We'll take our check."

Once back at the table, I find Trix visibly shaken. Her gaze darts around the room, and her earlier confidence is non-existent. She looks terrified.

I move to her and pull her from her seat and into my arms. "I'm so sorry."

Her body melts into my hold. "It's not your fault, Mason." The defeat in her voice makes my chest tight. "I'm sorry I embarrassed you."

I release her enough to get her eyes. "You could never embarrass me, Trix. Ever. Nothing makes me feel more proud than to show up with you on my arm. I don't love what you do for work, but you deserve respect at all times and from all people, and what that fucker did tonight was unacceptable."

A few women pass by us, whispering something about purple hair. Trix watches them pass before peering up at me with watery eyes. "I'd like to go home now."

Fucking bitches. I glare at the women, silencing them immediately.

"Of course." I grab her purse, hook her around the shoulders and lead her to the hostess, who has our bill.

"Would you like me to box up your leftovers, Mr. Mahoney?" she says in true kiss-ass form.

"No." I shove cash at her and hold Trix close until the valet pulls up with my truck.

This night was supposed to be perfect for her, and instead of feeling like a damn queen on a throne, she was made to feel like she was wearing a big fat scarlet "A" on her chest.

That was not the plan.

I pull the truck from the restaurant, vowing to never go back there again. Trix is turned with her chin resting in the palm of her hand, staring out the window.

"Did you get enough to eat?" We'd only had a few bites of our food before that dickhead ruined it.

"Yeah, I'm fine." Her voice sounds almost robotic.

She's far from fine.

And I've seen the girl eat. No way two bites of lobster is going to fill her up. I pull onto the freeway on-ramp.

"This date stuff isn't as fun as I imagined it would be." Her voice is so quiet and directed toward the window, and I can barely figure out if what she said was for me or just her.

"It wasn't ideal, but being with you is all I care about."

She scoffs. "Welcome to the world of dating an exotic dancer."

Is that all she thinks of herself? That her worth is tied to her chosen career? "I'm not dating an exotic dancer. I'm dating you, Beatriks."

She sucks in a quick breath and turns to stare out the front window.

I exit the freeway and pull into a drive through.

She blinks up at the glowing red-and-yellow sign. "You're taking me to In-N-Out Burger?" The spark of a smile twitches her lips.

"I know you're hungry, and this is a date so . . . is that okay?"

"I love In-N-Out."

"Good." And I love doing things she loves. "And this time we're eating at my place where no one can bother you."

"Except you." She lifts one eyebrow.

"That's right. Except me."

## TRIX

As nice as that restaurant was, and damn, it was incredible, it wasn't anything compared to the prospect of a couch picnic with Mason. I can't help feeling like shit about the way the night has gone. That lobster cost a fortune, and we just left it all there.

That jerk from the porn company ruined it all. It's not that I haven't been approached with similar requests in the past, but it's only ever been done at the club. There's nothing worse than finally feeling like you belong, only to have the harsh reminder that you don't shoved right into your face.

And all in front of Mason.

God, even thinking about it now makes my face flame. He couldn't have been cooler about it. Even when confronted by Blake and Layla, his friends, he stuck up for me. I'm not sure I even deserved that, and yet he was there defending me.

I slip off my shoes and tuck my feet under me with a bag of greasy burgers and fries in my lap. We turn off a few main roads and into a newer part of town where all the strip malls and gas stations aren't more than a few years old.

"This is where you live, huh?" I scoot forward to peer out the front window at the rows of two and three-story condos, each boasting their own private garage. "These are really nice." They just don't seem like him. I don't know what I was expecting, but these places look uptown. I expected Mason to live somewhere with a big backyard, a garage full of tools, and a dog.

"Best the UFL has to offer." He turns down one of the winding roads and hits a button on his visor. A garage opens and he pulls the truck in. "Home sweet home."

I hook the straps of my shoes and grab my purse while Mason manages the food. He opens the door that leads to a staircase so narrow I wonder if he has to turn sideways to walk through it.

The top of the stairs opens to a sprawling living space, open kitchen and living room combo, and more stairs off to the side.

He drops a kiss on my head as he passes me. "Sit. I'll grab some plates."

I drop my shoes and purse by the stairs and sit on the large overstuffed couch. On the coffee table, there's an elongated tray that's covered in different-colored polished rocks. It's like something I'd see at one of those fancy décor stores in the mall or some doctor's office display that's meant to calm. None of this seems at all like the Mason I know.

"It came with the place." He watches me poke at the shiny stones. "I didn't pick out any of this." His hand motions to some framed art and a decorative mirror on the wall.

"How long have you lived here?" I call out to Mason, who's busy pulling plates and napkins out of the cupboards.

"It's been a year. I made enough from my last fight to get a place of my own, just haven't had the time to look." He's unwrapping burgers, and my chest swells with warmth.

It's such a simple gesture, plating up my food, but it communicates something so much more. He balances two plates in one hand and grabs my drink with the other.

"Need some help?"

"No, I got it." He slides down beside me on the couch, and I relieve him of my chocolate shake so he can set down our food.

I eyeball the burgers, stuffed with lettuce and tomato and dripping special sauce. My mouth waters. "Mm, this looks really good. Thank you."

"You gonna say grace for us, Miss Trixy?" He winks, and a playful grin pulls at his lips.

"I'd love to." I reach over and grab his hand then bow my head and close my eyes. "Dear Father in heaven, thank you for tonight, for Mason, and for this bounty of food you've provided for us. I pray, God, that you'll bless this food for our bodies. It's in your name we pray. Amen."

Mason squeezes my hand, and when I open my eyes, the look on his face would've knocked me off my feet if I'd been standing. It's as if he's seeing me for the first time or maybe seeing past this shell of a human body and into my soul. Like he's reading my thoughts, my secrets, even my heart.

I blink and focus on the food, hoping to shake this sudden vulnerability. "Please, don't look at me like that. Whatever it is that you think you see, it's . . . don't."

"What do you think I see, Beatriks?" His voice is thick and heavy with an emotion I can't name.

"You look at me like I'm bigger and more important than I am."

"Who's to say you're not?"

"I'm not."

"I'm pretty sure that's my call to make, not yours."

I peek up at him, and his lips are curved in a lazy smile. The moment has seemed to pass, and I relax and pop a few fries in my mouth, almost moaning at the greasy salty combo. In-N-Out fries might run a close second to lobster.

We eat and share childhood stories about Cowell Beach. I tell him about the time I was in high school and lost my bikini top while dipping under a wave. I had to sit out there in chest deep water until I got Lana's attention. When she'd finally realized what had happened, she'd laughed so hard I thought she'd bust. She was always so serious; it was rare to see her completely overtaken with laughter. The day she laughed so hard she cried is one of my fondest memories of her.

He countered my topless beach story with a similar one where Drake was depantsed in front of a group of girls he was trying to impress. I guess it was cold that day, and needless to say, the guy didn't impress them as he'd hoped.

I slurp down the last of my milkshake, still grinning. "It's hard to believe we'd both spent time on the same sand but it took us moving to Vegas to actually meet."

He grabs our plates and takes them to the kitchen. "Guess Fate had plans for us, yeah?"

"Hm." Fate. I'm not sure I believe in that anymore.

As a child, it's easy to trust that there's something bigger than yourself. That God is leading you on a path through life with your best interests in mind. Being adopted by American parents and rescued from the life of an orphan only proved that belief.

But my sister being brutally murdered squashed all that. After all, God could've saved her if he'd wanted to, right? If my best interests were of any concern to him at all, she'd still be alive today.

Guilt presses down on me, and I slump deep into Mason's couch.

"You tired?" He plops down on the couch next to me, his powerful arms spread wide across the back of the couch, and eyebrows lowered in concern.

"Not really. You?"

His gaze sweeps over my body. "No." He blinks and reaches for the television remote. "You up for a movie?"

The screen lights with a movie rental company that displays multiple movie options and a search box.

"Sure." I shift on the couch, trying to get comfortable despite my short dress.

"Wait." He hops from the couch and takes two stairs at a time up to a second floor loft.

I grab the abandoned remote and flip through screen pages of movies. A guy like Mason probably prefers something with blood and explosions; I'm more of a romantic comedy kind of girl. I chew my lip and flip to the horror movies. Would it be too obvious to pick something that would force me to curl close and bury my face in his chest?

"Here." He hands me two folded-up pieces of clothing, and I resist the urge to rub my face in them and inhale. "Thought you might want to get more comfortable."

I shake out the soft white T-shirt and light blue boxers. "Huh." I lift an eyebrow. "I didn't take you for a boxer man."

He shrugs one shoulder. "I'm not, but I have a few pairs lying around."

"Thank you. These are perfect." I scoot to the edge of the couch and pull off my bangle bracelets, earrings, and necklace to set them on the coffee table. Ah, I already feel lighter. I stand to pull my dress over my head and figure, while I'm at it, axing the strapless bra would restart proper circulation to my arms. I hate these damn things. Tossing it all to the table, I reach for the shirt only to have Mason grip my wrist.

"Trix . . ." The guttural sound of his voice calls my eyes. He's peeking up at me from beneath heavy eyelids, his eyebrows low and hunger radiating from his gaze. "What're you doing?"

I shake my head, not fully understanding his question. "I'm . . . I thought—"

He yanks my arm and grabs my hips, pulling me over to straddle his lap. "You thought you could strip naked and I'd just sit back and admire?"

Heat floods my cheeks. "I didn't realize—"

He flexes his hips, and a low groan falls from his lips. I gasp at the feeling of him hard between my legs.

"Realize it now?"

I nod quickly. "I'm sorry?" I've gotten naked in front of countless men and women, and never have I felt so exposed.

He cups the side of my neck, his thumb brushing against my jawline. "Don't apologize." He drops his hand slowly so the backs of his knuckles skate along the side of my breast. "You have nothing to be sorry about."

"I think . . ." God, what do I think? Feel? My head swirls with conflicting emotions, part of me wanting to hold on and the other terrified of acknowledging too much. "I'm so used to being naked."

"Mm, I get that." His hands make long and gentle passes up my sides, around my back and over my shoulders, avoiding my breasts completely.

I ache all over for him, wanting his touch to be firmer, secretly hoping he'll lose control and get rough. I want him to take from me because then I won't have to feel. I won't have to think and second guess. If he were like all the others, after me for one thing, this would be so much easier. But this tenderness, his touch against the inside of my elbow, the flare of my hips, and my collarbone, it's all too much.

"Mason, I—"

"I wanted to kill him," he says so softly I wonder if I misheard. "The night at the hotel room you were straddling Jayden like this, and he touched you." His eyes flash to mine with steely resolve as his hands continue to move over my skin. "I wanted to rip his arms off his body."

"Why? You hated me."

"I never hated you, baby." His fingers fork into my hair, and his lips are so close I can feel his heated breath. "I was a goner the second I laid eyes on you."

I push him back and tilt my head, lowering my mouth to his. He opens to me with a low growl that jacks my hips forward. His fingers dig into my scalp as his tongue lashes against mine.

My heart races with a desperation I've never felt before. The burning urge to get beneath him, to feel the weight of his body between my legs as he fills me, is overwhelming. I'll ask for it, beg for it, because in this moment, I need it more than air.

He takes control of the kiss, tilting my head in the opposite direction as if he wants to taste me from every angle, explore every inch of my mouth. He nips and sucks at my lips, as if doing so will produce more of what he wants as we drink from each other's mouths with gluttony.

I arch my back, pressing my breasts into his chest, searching for the friction that will surely detonate me. He moves, pushing me to my back on the couch and taking position between my legs. His hips move in a slow rolling rhythm that mimics love-making. Hard and long he rubs against me, the scrape of denim against my lace panties so good and yet so mind-numbingly frustrating.

He runs the tip of his hot tongue down my neck to my breast, sucking one nipple deep into his throat. A zap of pleasure shoots down my torso, and I cry out for more. More of him, more of everything.

I reach down and unbutton his shirt, my fingers fumbling as nerves and excitement race through my veins. He helps by sliding his arms from the sleeves and sitting up only long enough to rip his undershirt off over his head.

My mouth instantly floods as I adjust to the sight. Mason drops back down on top of me.

"Wait."

His body freezes, and his lips still at my neck. "What? Did I—?"

"Get up." I wiggle to get out from under him, but it doesn't take much because he pushes back with his hands held up and sits back on his heels.

His chest is rising and falling faster than I've ever seen it and his blue eyes are dark with lust. "I'm sorry, is this too fast?"

Ha! If he only knew, not fast enough. "No, not at all. I just . . ." I push up to my knees on the couch and move to him. I place my palm flat over his heart and soak in the furious pounding of his heart behind warm smooth skin. "I just want to take a second to see you."

He lets out a long breath and drops his chin, his hand coming over mine. "Fuck, I thought I'd done something wrong and you were about to bolt."

Relief washes over his face as I run my hand over the swollen muscles of his abdomen and chest. So soft and yet incredibly powerful. "I've never seen you with your shirt off. I wanted to get the hands-on experience."

He cocks his head, and a tiny grin tilts his lips. "If you let me take you to bed, I'll give you the all-night experience."

I scrape a nail over his nipple, and he groans then scoops me up off the couch. My arms hold tight around his neck as he crosses the living space to the stairs and carries me up as though I weigh nothing. Once there, he lays me on the bed then clicks on the lamp at his nightstand.

The single light in the dark room plays against his massive form, making him look dangerous. Even when I know he's anything but.

# SEVENTEEN

## MASON

She's here. Trix, my woman, is sprawled out on my bed in nothing but a pair of panties and smiling at me like I own every fucking inch of her body and she's begging me to take it.

I want, more than anything, to lose myself inside her, burrow so deep into her soul she'll never be able to get rid of me. I told myself I'd take it slow: prove to her that I'm not like Lane and fucking Talon. She's so much more than a piece of ass, and her body is a damn treasure. Any man lucky enough to have it should have to spend a lifetime searching, slowly digging away with patience for the pleasure of making love to her.

She pushes up to her knees and scoots to the end of the bed. I don't have to think as my feet carry me to her on instinct; the basest most primal need to claim her rides me hard. Her hands go to my waistband, but her violet eyes are on me. She pops the button on my jeans, and the heat of her fingers runs the length of my dick as she slides down the zipper.

I grip her by the hair, pulling her mouth to mine roughly for a quick deep kiss. My forehead rests against hers, and I hold on to barely controlled restraint. "Trix, I want this, you, right now."

Her hand dips beneath my boxer briefs, and my legs almost give. "Me too. More than anything." She strokes me, and I grind my teeth together to keep from pumping my hips into her hand.

"Are you sure? I don't want to push you." And there're other reasons why we should slow down, but fuck if I can think of a single one.

Her other hand runs along my hip, around to my ass, and she slides my pants and briefs down my legs. "Then let me push you."

"Done." I put a knee on the bed, she falls back with a giggle, and I take my place between her legs. "I want to go easy, but I'm barely hanging on as it is."

"I don't want you to go easy, Mase." She rips her fingers through my hair and pulls my mouth to hers.

We kiss long and hard until I drop to an elbow to free up my hand. Her skin is like silk beneath my fingers as they trace down her belly. I run them slowly back and forth along the hem of her panties, and she nips at my lip in frustration.

A low chuckle vibrates in my throat. "Patience, Beatriks."

"I've never been good at delayed gratification." Her hips jack up off the bed with a whimper. "Please."

"Shh . . . I've got you." I tug her panties down, and she makes quick work of kicking them to the floor. The air in my lungs leaves on a whoosh as I take in her naked body. "Fuckin' hell."

I run a hand up her thigh, between her legs and—Shit, I'm never gonna make it to sex at this rate. She grips my wrist and holds my hand to her, biting her lip. Her desperation is addicting. I bring her to the edge, playing with her just enough to have her quivering beneath me and rocking against my palm. Warm, wet, and delicate. What I wouldn't do to feel her against my tongue.

"Hold on." I reach over to the bedside table and pull a condom from the drawer. Since I moved to Vegas, I've only had two women in my bed: drunken one-night stands that left nothing more than hazy memories and guilt in their wake.

Trix watches with wide eyes and parted lips as I roll on the condom, and I hope she's not thinking about why I have condoms on hand. I want her to feel like she's the only woman I've ever had.

She crawls to her hands and knees, giving me a visual that I know I'll carry to my grave. "Lie back." She throws a leg over my hips and straddles me, all her long bi-colored hair falling to brush the tips of her breasts.

With a lift of her ass, she takes me into her body. A low groan slides from her parted lips as she slowly and deliberately welcomes me inch by inch. A vise grip of heat wraps me tight and my abdomen flexes in response.

"Never seen anything so beautiful in my life." I force myself to loosen my hold on her thighs, will my muscles to relax, and avoid being too rough.

Her palms flatten on my pecs, and she rolls her hips just as I've seen her do on stage. Tingles shoot from my dick straight up my spine and make my head swim. She moves again, this time leaning to one side then the other. Like some kind of sexual goddess, she hits every angle with the swivel of her narrow hips.

"Fuck, baby . . ." I want her to stop. The sensations are too much, everything hypersensitive and jacked-up on overdrive. "You need to slow that shit down or—"

"Or what?" She grinds down hard, groaning and tossing her head back.

"Fuck it." I flip her to her back. "My turn."

I pull out completely before filling her so deeply her neck arches off the bed. "Oh my . . ."

Again, I slide out and in, allowing her to feel every inch as I press against her. She sucks in a breath, her eyes wide and lost in the sensation. Over and over I move with force but at a pace that'll keep her wanting. Firm, deep, and slow.

"I could do this all night, baby." I pull out and glide back in. "All fucking night inside you." I bend my knee, angle my hips, and grind in deep.

"Oh, Mase…it's—" She gasps, her legs clamp against my hips, and she throws her head back. My name falls from her lips with the guttural groan of release as she pulsates beneath me. I cushion the top of her head to keep it from banging against the headboard as I power into her, easing her back from her orgasm.

"Whoa." She sighs with a scratchy voice. Her legs drop from being wrapped around me, and her breathing is labored as I rock into her slowly.

I drop soft kisses on her eyelids, her forehead, and the tip of her nose. "You good?"

A lazy and sexy-as-hell smile pulls at her lips. "So much better than good."

"Mmm . . . I like hearing that." I move again, testing her to see if she's open to more. As much as I'd hate to be done, I'd rather suffer through the blue balls than push her too far.

"Don't stop." Her feet hit the bed, and she meets me thrust for thrust.

I hook one of her legs with my arm, getting deeper than I had before and almost coming right then. I don't want to stop. Ever. Not with Trix.

The powerful need to keep her rides me harder and my pace quickens.

"Yes!" She digs her nails into my arms, scraping down my biceps, and intensifying the tingling at the base of my spine. "Mason, you're so good, perfect, and mine . . ."

I ignite.

Stars burst behind my eyes, and I bury my face in her neck. My hips jackhammer into her body while my head spins from the euphoric high of her words.

I'm hers.

Fuck, but no truer words have ever been spoken.

I kiss her long and deep, unable to look into her eyes out of fear that I'll see her regret. "Let me get rid of this." Pushing up from the bed, I toss one side of the comforter over her and she giggles.

Moving to the bathroom, I blink into the bright light and trash the condom.

Does she mean it? Or is that like telling someone you love them while having sex? I'm almost afraid to ask.

Fuck it. It doesn't matter. I know she's it for me.

—

## TRIX

Curled up in Mason's thick down comforter, surrounded by his scent, and with a delicious ache between my legs, I'm grinning like an idiot.

I really, really like this guy. More than I should, but I don't care.

A tiny voice in my head reminds me that I'm getting sidetracked. I'm not supposed to be dating or having mind-blowing sex with handsome fighters. I'm supposed to be searching for Lana's killer.

After her body was discovered, the crime scene investigators swept the entire area for clues, but there were none. No fingerprints or DNA on her body or clothes. The only tire tracks were from her car. Best evidence they had to go on was an eyewitness who said they saw Lana's car pull over to help a motorcyclist. And a card found at the scene.

One card was buried beneath rotting leaves and Lana's blood.

A VIP card to Zeus's.

Every decision I've made in these last four years has been because of those two things: bikers and Zeus's.

Every decision, except the one I'm currently basking in the glow of.

Dating and sleeping with Mason is the first thing I've wanted to do for me. It's a little reminder that, under all this revenge and anger, I'm still a person with a beating heart and desires of her own.

And as much as I'd love to set her free, I'd never forgive myself for giving up on Lana.

"Don't think so hard. It'll give you a headache." Mason stalks toward me from the bathroom, and my mind short-circuits as I take in his masculine naked body.

Wide shoulders, bulky arms, and a narrow waist flow into powerful hips. He's a Michelangelo sculpture. A flash of ink catches my eye. I caught a glimpse of it earlier, but in the heat of it all didn't think to study it.

On his hip, riding just below where the waistline of his pants would fall, is a tattoo of a wave. Its base is low, touching the outside of his upper thigh, and it curves up to just over his hipbone.

He catches me staring and groans. "Don't ask."

"How can I not?" I crawl from my comforter cocoon and meet him at the edge of the bed. "Turn."

He rolls his eyes, but shifts to the side so I can study it further. On closer inspection, it's more than a wave. There's the letter "B," and the fingers of the wave crashing over it make the number three. "B3."

"Yeah." He gathers my body to his and slips us both beneath the covers. "It's stupid. We were kids at the time and thought it was so badass. I've been meaning to get it covered."

"What is it?"

"The Bone Breaker Brotherhood."

"Bone Breaker? As in Bone Breaker Alley?"

"Same one. We claimed that break a long time ago. Kept the local surfers protected from the tourists that would come and disrespect them."

"Howlies?"

He chuckles and kisses the top of my head. "Yeah, howlies."

"Do all the guys have the same tattoo?"

"Yeah, but most of them have it on a more visible part of their body. I knew I wanted to go to college and wrestle, so I made sure I could keep mine covered. Not a lot of hiding places under a wrestling singlet."

"Mmm." I run my hand over his hip. "I like the location. It's sexy."

"Fuck it, then. It stays."

We laugh, and I fight to keep my eyes open. I have no idea what time it is, but this night has exhausted me as much as the stress has probably aged me.

"Trix, baby?"

My eyelids flutter open. "Hmm?"

"I want to take you out of Vegas, just for a couple days."

"What?" A yawn rips from my throat. "Why?"

"After what happened tonight, it feels like we can't go anywhere without someone giving us shit."

"Who says we have to go anywhere? I'm happy right here."

His fingers draw lazy patterns on my back. "I am too, and we'll do that as well. Starting this weekend."

Disappointment settles in my gut. "I can't this weekend. I'm going home for a few days."

"Oh yeah?"

"It's my dad's birthday, and I try not to miss it."

"That's perfect. I need to take care of some shit with my brother. Let's head up together."

I tilt my head back, resting my chin on his chest. "Are you serious? You'd do that?"

"Of course. You can do your dad's birthday, and then we'll have a couple extra days to hang out. We can go to Cowell."

"That would be great, except my dad is . . . Well, he's a pastor, so you can't stay with me."

He laughs hard, his body shaking with the force of it. "No shit, Beatriks. I'll stay with my mom."

"Okay, but I already got my plane ticket."

"It's cool. You give me your flight info, and I'll see what I can do."

"Wow, we went from first-time sex to meeting my parents."

"No, we went from sex, to a sleepover, to meeting your parents."

My chest warms with the gentleness of his voice, as if everything we've experienced so far and will experience in the future means something to him. "Sleepover?"

"Stay with me." He rolls to his side, positioning my back to his front. "I want to hold you a little longer."

"Okay, Mason." I relax, and this time I don't fight the comfort that consumes me. I don't try to talk myself out of how right this feels. Being with Mason is as easy as breathing. I don't allow the guilt to penetrate, and I ignore the voice that tells me I'm selfish.

With a smile on my face, I hold him to me while sleep takes me under, and dreams of a life I never imagined skate through my mind.

# EIGHTEEN

## MASON

Getting out of training on a Friday wasn't as hard as I thought it would be. After getting an earful of shit from Blake and only mild dirty looks from Cameron, I managed to convince my team that one day off wouldn't kill me. Or them. Upon receiving their grumbled agreements, I made a phone call and was able to book the same flights as Trix for our trip back home.

We're waiting outside on the curb of San Jose International Airport, my duffle slung over one shoulder and Trix's hot pink roller bag in hand. She tilts her head up, and a slight breeze tosses her loose blond and purple locks around her face. Her lips curl in a smile, and I can't see behind her sunglasses, but I'd be willing to bet her eyes are shining with humor.

She hikes her purse higher on her bare shoulder, tugging on the skinny strap of her tank. "You look good in pink."

I cock a shoulder and swing my gaze to the row of cars trickling down the terminal as they wait for their passengers to appear. "I look good in everything, baby." I squint, searching for my brother's Cadillac.

Since our flight took us to San Jose, I called up Drake and guilted his ass into picking us up from the airport. Trix assured me that her parents could get her, but knowing I'd have to let her go eventually, I'd rather milk every last second of our time together.

She giggles. "I can't argue with that."

Damn, I dig this girl.

"Come here." I throw my arm over her shoulder and pull her to me, maneuvering her around my bag so I can get to her lips. Aware we'll have to keep all public affection to a minimum when around her family, I refuse to pass up the chance to steal a kiss. Tilting my head to avoid bashing her forehead with the bill of my baseball hat, I press a long close-mouthed kiss to her soft lips.

A slow hum vibrates our connection as she gives her weight over to me. I should stop, pull away to avoid making a scene, but the way her hands grip my tee at my belly, her sweet floral scent whirling through my senses . . . I part my lips. She takes my cue and wraps her arms around my neck, pushing up on tiptoes and pressing her tits into my chest.

My pulse rockets through my veins, and I slide my hand down her back to the base of her spine. Don't grab her ass in front of all these people. Do NOT grab her ass—

A horn honks. "You gonna fuck her out there, or do you two horny bastards wanna get in the damn car!"

We grin against each other's lips, before turning to see Drake leaning over into the passenger side of his ride, windows down, and scowling.

"Have some fucking respect, you little shit!" I motion to the back of his car. "Pop the trunk."

I open the back door for Trix to get in before I take our bags and secure them in the trunk.

I hop in the front seat and pull on my seatbelt. The smell of Drake's cologne mixes with the stale scent of weed. My stomach twists with worry. "Thanks for the ride."

"Sure thing." Drake has on his sunglasses, but I can tell by the slight lift of his chin that he's checking Trix out in the backseat through the rearview mirror.

"Eyes on the road, bro."

He shoots me a look and a cocky grin then merges with traffic. "Where to, sweetheart?"

"Drake." Fuckin' thinking he's a damn baller. Idiot.

He laughs and sits deeper into his seat.

"I-17 south to Los Gatos." There's a hesitant sound in her voice that makes me wish I was in the backseat so I could touch her in some way to calm her nerves.

Silence descends on the three of us. Drake and I have plenty to talk about, but none of it I'll say in front of Trix. And there are a million things I'd like to say to my girl but don't want Drake to hear.

He pulls onto the long stretch of highway and settles into the fast lane. "So you guys are dating, yeah?"

I cock my head to glare at my little brother. "Are you stupid?"

He shrugs. "What? It's an obvious question. She's a stripper, dude. For all I know, she's just *escorting* you home for the right price."

I grit my teeth, fists clenched as I contemplate the cost-reward of knocking Drake out while he's flying down the highway with the girl I care for most in the entire world sitting in the back. Fuck!

The soft sound of Trix's laughter filters from the backseat. "You're so right, Drake. Mason's paying me for full service all weekend long." She pushes up to place her face right between Drake and me. "You should've seen the expression on the stewardess's face when I sucked your brother off under a blanket on the plane." She licks her lips and moans and Drake shifts in his seat. She leans in closer to him. "Your brother's a big boy, and I mean *big* in every way. I have bruises all over my ass after we fucked like monkeys in the airplane bathroom."

Damn, she's good at this seduction shit. Drake's practically drooling, and I'm doing everything to keep my dick from responding to her tease.

"You lucky son of a bitch!"

I turn and grip my fingers into Trix's hair, pulling her to me for a hard kiss while she giggles against my lips.

She flicks Drake's ear. "Sucka."

"Wait, so you're kidding . . . or . . . ?"

I punch him in the shoulder, eliciting a bitch-ass squeal from his wanna-be gangster lips. "Why don't you mind your own business?"

"Fuck, man." He rubs his arm. "Fine. Shit."

I shake my head and consider a rental car or even a few hundred dollars to get a cab to take us back to the airport at the end of the weekend.

"Trix, baby, your dad's birthday is Sunday afternoon, right?"

"Yeah. It's at one, so we can hang for a few hours, and then Isaac will take us to the airport. You're still going to come, right?"

"Yeah, yeah, but I was thinking . . . You wanna bring the kids to Cowell tomorrow? Figure we could give your mom and dad a break from the kids, hang out at the beach all day, maybe a bonfire that night?"

"Really?" The high-pitched sound of excitement from her lips makes my chest pound. "That would be awesome!"

"Great, let's do it. We'll figure out all the details tonight after you settle in."

"The kids are going to shit, they'll be so excited," she mumbles to herself.

Drake laughs, low and shitty sounding. What the hell is his problem? "Look at you getting all domesticated." He shoves me. "No more back in town for hanging with your boys and fucking bitches, huh?"

What the fuck? I've come back in town and hung at the bars with The Brotherhood, but fucking bitches? That's never been me. Not that the occasional one-nighter didn't sneak up on me, but it was rare. "Are you high?"

He ignores me, and I make a mental note to talk to Trix about this later. I know she wouldn't care even if what Drake said was the truth—after all, she's been honest about her past conquests—but I need her to know that it's bullshit.

The rolling hills of San Jose fade into the distance as we approach the Santa Cruz Mountains with their towering redwoods and evergreens. With a few more instructions and forty minutes later, we pull up to an older homestead-style house in a remote area of Los Gatos. The home is tucked deep into the woods on a dirt road. Even though only a few miles from multi-million dollar homes, new developments, and middle class homes, it's so hidden in the trees I wonder if the city even knows they're still here.

"Is this it?" Drake says with a hint of disgust in his voice.

"Yep. Home sweet home."

The second the last word is out of her mouth, the front door flies open, and kids pour out of the tiny home like circus clowns. Trix squeals with excitement and barrels out of the backseat. She runs, kicking up dirt with her flip-flops, and catches the fastest of her brothers and sisters as a little boy leaps into her arms.

"Dude, what the fuck . . .?" Drake whispers and I know he's confused about the myriad of ethnicities and ages of all the children now piled around Trix.

"Big family. Stay in here." I push out of the car just as an older man steps out of the door.

He's bigger than I expected, full beard and overgrown hair, but dressed well in a long-sleeved collared shirt tucked into jeans. That must be Pastor Langley, Trix's Dad. A small, thin woman with short dark hair pushes past the man and races toward the kids' squealing, and it doesn't take a genius to realize it's Trix's Mom.

I'm transfixed on this family reunion. Hell, I don't even remember the last time I hugged my mom. Trix closes her eyes as her mom kisses every inch of her face. It isn't until I feel the prickle of being watched that I peek up to find a set of dark brown eyes on me.

Trix's dad looks curious as he moves off the front porch towards his family. His daughter breaks away from her siblings and meets her dad with a hug and a kiss on the cheek. They say a few words to each other then look in my direction. I take my cue and head over to introduce myself.

My muscles are tense as I approach, uneasy about being the odd man out to this welcoming home.

Trix grabs my hand, her sunglasses up on her head, wide grin across her face, and if I weren't so concerned about honoring her father's wishes, I'd plant a mind-scrambling kiss against those lips.

"Dad, this is Mason, the guy I told you about."

I reach out my hand to the older man. "Mr. Langley, it's a pleasure to meet you."

"Please, call me Jerome." He reaches forward, exposing a heavily tattooed forearm, and grips my hand in a firm shake. "It's nice to meet you. I wish I could say I've heard so much about you, but I've only heard of you over the last couple days."

"Sir, your daughter talks plenty of you, so I feel I've known you for a while now."

His gaze moves between Trix and me. "Thank you for making sure she got home safely. I would've been happy to pick her up."

"No need. We're passing through to Santa Cruz anyway. I'm happy to do it."

"Oh, this must be Mason." The woman I assumed was Trix's mother approaches, a warm and welcoming grin on her face. She wraps me in a hug. "I'm Aggie. It's so nice to meet you. Will you be coming to the party on Sunday?"

"Yes, I'd planned on it. Thank you for the invite."

"Whoa, Bee-ee-ah. He's hu-u-mong-u-us!" A tiny little girl whose hair, eyes, and skin all seem to be the exact same shade of bronze, tugs Trix's hand.

"Leah, honey," Aggie whispers.

"You play football?" The tallest of the kids with thick black hair, light skin, and almond-shaped eyes joins the conversation.

"I did in high school, but not anymore."

"Mason fights for the UFL." Pride shines in her eyes as she looks up at her little brother. "Mason, this is my brother Isaac." Trix looks around and continues. "My other brothers, Josiah, Zane, and Aaron." She scoops up the squealing little girl and props her on a hip. "This little rug rat is Leah." She rubs the head of a tiny Asian girl who is clinging to Trix's leg, looking up at her big sister. "And finally, this is Zoe." Her bright eyes flash back to me. "And, everyone, this is Mason."

The little ones wave shyly, and the older ones stand back, studying me with speculative glances.

"It's nice to meet you all." The kids explode in a flurry of chatter, and Trix's face lights with love for her siblings. I run my knuckles down her upper arm to get her attention. "I better take off."

"Oh, yeah." Her smile falls and she nods. "Guess so."

I say good-bye to her family and move back to the car with Trix. With the trunk of the car open, no one can see us, and I lean in to place a small kiss to her forehead. "I'll call you tonight."

"I hate this." Her eyebrows are pinched together. "We've spend the last three days together, and saying good-bye to you just feels wrong."

I tuck a piece of hair behind her ear. "We have all day tomorrow at the beach. I can't wait to see you in your bikini—"

"Dad wants me to help you with your bags." Isaac's there with his arms crossed at his chest.

Trix rolls her eyes and takes a step back to create distance between us.

"Sounds good, man." I pull her bright pink suitcase from the trunk and set it down for Isaac. "See you guys tomorrow."

"Bye." She gives me a small, sad wave and heads toward the house with her brother, who I hear say, "What's going on tomorrow?" a few seconds before he shouts, "Awesome!"

My chest is heavy when I watch the door close behind Trix and fold back into Drake's car.

"Holy shit, bro. You're buyin' the cow too?"

This time I unleash all my frustration and knock the asshole in the chest. He doubles over the steering wheel, gasping.

"That's your final warning."

"Jeez, you didn't have to knock the wind outta me, dick."

"Talk about my woman again, and I'll knock the fuckin' life out of you."

Not that I blame him for being surprised. As soon as the words come from my lips, I realize I'm telling the God's honest truth.

# NINETEEN

## TRIX

The sun is dipping behind the Santa Cruz Mountains by the time we get the kitchen cleaned up after supper. Mom went all out for my homecoming, making a slow-cooked roast with all the trimmings. I can't imagine how much the meal cost them, and they dished it out, helping after helping to all of us kids with leftovers to spare.

I shove a few more plastic containers of our dinner into the fridge and move to the back porch where my mom and dad are lounging on a swing. My mom's eyes find mine and she grins. Even through her smile, I can tell she's worn out. "You didn't have to do that, Bea." She scoots to put a spot between her and my dad.

I plop down between them, the three of us now crammed into the loveseat-sized swing. "I know, but you work too hard, Mama."

"Taking care of my babies is never work." A yawn falls from her lips. "Sheesh, maybe I'm more tired than I thought."

"Honey, why don't you go to bed? Bea and I will put the little ones down." My dad nods toward the outdated metal swing set and slide out in the yard. It's more like a stretch of dirt fenced in by towering redwoods. Leah, Aaron, and Zoe are laughing and arguing as they play Marco Polo.

"Yeah, Mom"—I grab her hand and squeeze it—"go take a hot bath before they all start fighting over the bathroom before bedtime."

"Oh, a hot bath does sound nice." She flashes a tired smile. "We can catch up some more in the morning?"

I already updated the family at dinner, sharing with them about some of the kids at the Youth Club, my new roommate, and an update on Gia. I left out talking about my job, but I always do, and they don't seem to mind.

"Sure, but there's really nothing more to talk about."

She hoists herself off the swing and drops a kiss to my forehead. "So you're saying that handsome boy who dropped you off is nothing?"

"Aggie, don't go snooping." The low rumble of my dad's chuckle makes my mom gape.

"I'm not snooping. I just want to learn more about a man who would travel all the way from Las Vegas to San Jose just to escort our daughter home." She unties her apron that I'm sure she forgot she was wearing until now, and folds it up.

"He came home to see his family too, Mama. It's no biggie." The words sour in my mouth. It's a huge biggie. I like Mason more than I should, and I'm pretty sure he feels the same. The thought makes my tummy tumble and my chest flutter.

"Bea, sweetheart"—my dad turns his dark brown eyes to me—"that boy is crazy about you."

I blink up at my dad. "How do you know?"

He shrugs and turns out to watch the kids as they launch off the swings in a contest to see who can jump farthest. "Because he'd be stupid not to be. He doesn't look stupid to me."

My mom rolls her eyes. "I better grab that bath while I can. And Bea, I'm sorry you're stuck on the bunk beds with Leah and Zoe. We moved Isaac into your and Lana's old room."

Sadness pierces my chest, but I push it back and focus on the kids, pretending that speaking her name in this place doesn't bring me to my emotional knees. "No problem. I'm happy to stay with the girls."

She leans down and kisses my head. "I'm so happy you're home."

"Good night—oh! I forgot, I thought I'd take everyone to the beach tomorrow, if that's alright with you guys."

My parents share a lingering glance.

"I thought you could use a quiet day at home."

"Sure, honey. That would be great." My mom heads back inside. "And tell Mason he's welcome to come over for dinner after the beach."

I whip around just in time to see her disappear behind the closed door. How did she know?

My dad chuckles, apparently reading my shock. "She's an observant woman, Bea." He scratches his bearded cheek. "The Good Lord has blessed her with discernment like I've never seen."

"It's freaky."

He chuckles and throws an arm over my shoulder. "It can be."

We swing in silence for a few minutes, and the sun dips further behind the mountains. The air cools slightly, and the scent of pine soothes me along with the gentle sway of the swing and the safety of my dad's arm.

"So . . ."

I know that tone and exactly where it's going. Steeling my resolve, I blow out a long breath, and the sense of what's coming weighs heavy in the air.

"Vegas is treating you well?"

Not again. "It's alright, Daddy."

"You find a church over there yet?"

"You know I haven't stepped inside a church since the funeral."

"Hmm . . ." The squeak of the swing fills the silence and mimics a countdown.

In five . . . four . . . three . . .

I squeeze closed my eyes. Please don't ask, please don't ask—

"Still dancing . . ." *Blastoff!* "I assume?" There's no judgment in his voice, but there's the unmistakable twang of disappointment, which is worse.

I don't answer and keep my eyes forward. I can't tell him the reasons why I'm there. He'll tell me that I'm wasting my time, that Svetlana's killers can't run forever and eventually they'll have to face the ultimate judgment and that alone will be enough.

I disagree.

I want whoever tortured and mutilated my sister to spend the rest of their breathing days in prison *before* they get to spend an eternity in hell.

But that's me. I'm not nearly as forgiving as my dad.

"Beatriks . . . no one can worship both God and money." He quotes the Bible in such an everyday way that proves he really lives by the word.

"I don't do it for the money." I do it for Svetlana.

He groans and squeezes me tighter in a way that feels like reassurance or possibly worry. "The Bible says our body is a temple for The Holy Spirit—"

"I know that, Dad." The words come out harsher than I intend, but the fact that he insists on repeating things we've been over a hundred times is infuriating. Not to mention, he's absolutely right. I focus on steady breathing and hope my voice doesn't shake. "It's just a job."

"To you, it's just a job. But there are men you dance for who are struggling in their marriages, dipping into pornography. You have to consider the stumbling block that your dancing is to—"

"That's not my problem. Grown men are capable of making decisions for themselves." I turn and look at him. "Free will, right? They want to screw their lives up, destroy their marriages; they have the right to do that. Don't blame me for it."

He nods and takes my hand in a gentle hold. "I don't blame you. I just don't want you to look back and wish you'd spent time doing something more with your life. Something that involves serving and helping others. That's where true joy lives."

Bitterness wells up in my gut and turns my stomach. Serving others. That's what my parents have always preached to us. The joy in giving. The blessing in selflessness. But it doesn't always work out for everyone, now does it?

"True joy?" I sit up and put down a foot to stop the swing. "Dad, it was Lana's selflessness that got her killed."

He blanches but recovers quickly. "No, it was the sin and the brokenness of man that killed your sister. It—"

"She pulled her car over to help. It was dark, and she knew if she drove by a person in need without stopping she'd be letting you down, letting God down. She'd never be able to look at herself in the mirror. That was Lana, Dad."

"Honey—"

"She never should've stopped. If she never stopped, she'd be here." *And I wouldn't be stripping!* "She'd be sitting right here with us, but she's not." I push up from the swing.

"No, but she's with our Father in heaven, and that's better than—"

"Don't." I hold up my hand. "Please, don't tell me that her being in heaven is better than her being here with us."

He stands and studies me with a compassion that wrecks me. "I love you, Beatriks. You and Svetlana were the first children that God brought to us. You two were a package deal. Your sister refused to leave you even at a young age. I can only imagine how her death—"

"Murder."

"Murder . . . must've affected you. Still affects you." He steps forward and places a comforting hand on my shoulder. "You've got to let her go, Bea."

"I can't." Not until whoever killed her pays for what he's taken from me. "She refused to let me go, Dad. I'm doing the same."

"She held onto you to keep you safe. Your holding onto her is poisoning the life you could have. The life you were fated to have." He squints up at the sky and then back down at me. "Don't you see, Bea? Her life's purpose was your safety. Your happiness. Everything she did revolved around her protection of you. Honor her life and all she sacrificed by becoming all you can be. Don't settle for simply being an"—he clears his throat—"exotic dancer."

I swallow past the lump in my throat. "You don't understand."

"That's probably true, but know this. There is nothing, and I mean nothing, you could do that would change my love for you. I don't think any father dreams that his daughter becomes a dancer in Vegas, but if this is truly what makes you happy, that's all I want for you." As painful as the words must've been to say, I truly believe he means it.

The truth is it doesn't make me happy. It hasn't made me happy in a long time. Ever since my best lead took off to Mexico, everything else has led me to a dead end. Sure, I like to dance, but I get plenty of that at the Youth Club.

He pulls me in and wraps his arms around my shoulders. "I love you, sweetheart."

I bury my face into his shoulder, fighting tears. "I love you too, Daddy."

"Now, we better get these kids ready for bed." He yells into the yard for the kids to come in. "Shouldn't take longer than just a few minutes."

Two hours and thirty-seven minutes later I'm lying on the top bunk bed in my little sisters' room, my nose about a foot from the ceiling and the sound of two little girl snores coming from the bed below mine.

I can't stop thinking about what my dad said earlier tonight. I've given up almost four years of my life to stripping, all in the hope of finding something that even the police were unable to find. What seemed so possible at one time now seems as impossible as lassoing the fog. How many more years of my life will I give up for my dead sister? One? Ten? Would I give up my life? If Svetlana were here right now, she'd tell me I'd already wasted too much time. Her interests were always me first, everything else second, and all I ever wanted was to give that back to her.

But she's gone.

Dead.

I'm fighting for nothing more than a memory.

The last few years have been filled with sacrifice, and it never bothered me. At least, it never bothered me until Mason.

He's the only person who has ever made me wonder what it would be like to leave all this behind. To hang up my search for revenge and go after a life worth living. A life of honor and respect. One my parents could be proud of.

One Svetlana would be proud of.

On a heavy sigh, I power up my phone. I scroll to Mason's number and punch out a quick text.

**In bed. Missing you. Can't wait for tomorrow.**

I stare at my phone, waiting. Nothing.

I scroll through my social media sites, watch a few funny cat videos without sound, and then check my text messages again.

Huh, still nothing.

Maybe he's out with his mom?

I type out one more text.

**We'll be at Cowell bright and early. G'night.**

Rather than turn my phone off, I tuck it under my pillow so I'll feel it vibrate when he texts me back.

# TWENTY

## MASON

"Have you lost your fucking mind?" I spit through clenched teeth and an aching jaw at the back of Drake's head.

I'd rather be in his face, but it's impossible to do when he's nose first in a pile of white powder.

"Dude, calm down, Mase." Birdman's eyes are practically slits as he pulls a heavy lungful of smoke from the bong wedged between his ankles. He holds the shit in until it makes him cough and then exhales. "It's a fucking party, man."

A party? Just last week my brother was hiding out, and now he's snorting the shit that got him in trouble in the first place.

After dropping Trix off with her family, Drake took me to my mom's place, where I unloaded my stuff. She wasn't home, and according to Drake, she rarely is. A new boyfriend with a yacht is her latest diversion. We'll see how long that lasts.

I avoided calling Trix all night, knowing she was catching up with her family, and finally accepted Drake's invitation to go hang out with The Brotherhood to avoid staring at my phone like a love-sick pansy.

It took all of ten minutes to realize I would've been better off at my mom's in front of the TV.

"Give me your keys." I hold out my hand, and Drake glares at it like it's dipped in dog shit.

"No way. Besides, I told Jessica I'd meet her here." He gives the room a once over with glazed eyes.

I do the same, although I'm completely sober. The small beach-style bungalow is no more than a thousand square feet, and it's filled with local surfers. I can spot them from a mile away. Trucker hat, surf brand tee, long shorts held to their hips by a belt, and flip-flops or skate shoes.

"Mase, man"—Jayden slaps me on the shoulder, his big grin showing off his gold tooth—"welcome home."

Home. Yeah right. This is not home.

"As soon as Jessica gets here, we're leaving."

"Jessica's here, man." Harrison has a big grin on his face too. All of them are as high as airliners. "Saw her with J.P. when I came in."

That asshole's here? He graduated ten years before us, and even now that he's in his thirties, he still hangs with Drake and his crew. From what I understand, he's weaseled his way in with Drake's dad, pushing my brother out of the way to get close to the criminals they run with. Fucking loser.

Drake's jaw gets hard and he scowls. "With J.P.? *Where*?"

Harrison cackles with unrestrained laughter, sending Drake to his feet.

I hook my brother's bicep. "Whoa . . . what's going on?"

Drake jerks his arm out of my grip, his eyes bloodshot and crazed. "Nothin'. I'll be right back." He turns his trucker hat forward and storms from the room.

Shit. This isn't good.

I follow behind Drake as he heads to the short hallway and starts pushing open doors. "Jessica, where the fuck are you?" He throws open another door and finally gets to one that's locked. He bangs with a closed fist. "Jess, you in there? Jess!" He kicks the door, making it splinter.

I stand back, close enough to jump in if something happens, but far enough away so that I'm not breathing down my brother's neck, only further pissing him off.

The lock clicks and the door opens.

J.P., over six feet of asshole and looking like he's jacked up on 'roids, comes out of the bathroom, making a show of zipping up his fly. "Drake, you piece of shit. Way you were banging on this door I thought the cops were busting in."

Drake pushes past him into the bathroom then comes out with a staggering Jess in his arms. Her hair is tangled around her face, and if it weren't for my brother's arms bracing her weight, she wouldn't be standing. Her head lulls on her shoulders, and she mumbles something incoherent.

"What the fuck happened in there?" Drake's question isn't directed at anyone in particular, but the way he's asking demands someone answer.

Jessica's legs give out, and he hefts her up to his chest.

"We were just having a little fun. Don't sweat it." J.P. reaches to Jessica, but Drake knocks his hand away.

"Don't fucking touch her, man."

My mind spins with sick irony. Drake's not ideal, but he's better than this piece of shit.

Jessica was my girlfriend, but I knew Drake always had a thing for her. The second I wasn't looking, he made his move. It sucked at first. I really thought we'd end up together, but I was wrong. Drake has never been faithful to Jess, and now that this J.P. guy is moving in on his girl, he's decided to stake his claim? Fucking ridiculous.

What's most disturbing about all this is the fact that Jess is clearly out of her mind either on booze or drugs or a combo of the two and neither of these guys has the right to lay a finger on her body when she's this fucked up.

I step closer. "Drake. Give me your keys. I'm taking Jessica home."

"No way. I've got her—"

"Now."

J.P. steps up, his jaw hard. “Well look who we have here? College boy.”

“Always knew you were a fuckup, J.P. Never took you for a rapist.”

He shrugs, his lips curling back over his teeth. “I was just takin’ a piss. Not my fault she followed me in, beggin’ for my dick.”

Drake tries to lunge. “You motherfu—”

I hold my hand up to keep Drake back, noticing briefly that Jessica is completely slumped over in his arms. “Take her to the car, Drake. I’ll be right there. Don’t drive, understand?”

My brother’s eyes are buggin’ out of his head, clearly the high from all the coke he snorted in full force and intensified by adrenaline.

“Drake!” His eyes come to mine. “Now. Get her to the car.”

He shifts his gaze between J.P. and me, not moving.

Jessica sucks in a breath and coughs then vomits all over Drake’s leg.

He blinks down. “Shit.”

Her back arches with a dry heave.

“Take her outside, D.”

This time he doesn’t stall and guides her down the hallway to the front door. “Hang in there, baby. You’re okay.”

How he can be so damn sweet to her now and such an asshole at other times, I’ll never understand.

I turn my attention back to J.P. “We need to talk.”

“I’m listening.”

“What will it take to get my brother out of his dad’s business?”

His face registers nothing, and I wonder if he didn’t hear me, but when he throws his head back in booming laughter, I realize he most certainly did.

“I’m serious, J.P.”

"Oh, I know you're serious." He sniffs and wipes at his eye. "But there's no fucking way Drake gets to walk away. Not after the shit he pulled."

"He replaced that. He should be square."

"He's not."

"You just fucked his girlfriend." Sickness stirs my gut, managing to just piss me off more. "What more do you want?"

He scratches his jaw, which is covered in a week old beard. "Simple. They want what he promised them: his life."

"His life? You can't be fucking serious?"

"As a damn heart attack," he growls.

"He's twenty-one. You can't expect him to run drugs for you guys until he's an old man."

"Who're you kidding? No one in this business ever lives that long."

"So that's it? He takes orders until he's dead."

He shrugs. "It was his choice."

"How much will it take to buy him back from you?"

He casts a glance over my shoulder and gives someone just beyond me a head nod. "I'll be right there." His eyes come back to mine, and he grins before pushing past me. "He's not for sale."

I grip his shoulder, stopping him in his tracks. His narrowed eyes go to my hand and then to me.

"Everything has a price, J.P."

The tension between us pulls tight, and I ball my fist prepared for his attack, but he doesn't hit.

"Drake knows what it takes to get out. Blood for blood," he says.

And with that, he delivers a blow more painful than any punch. In order for Drake to be free, someone needs to get hurt. Fuck, what will they do to him?

"You guys okay back there?" I dart my eyes to the rearview mirror to see Jess passed out against Drake's chest, his arms holding her to him.

We pulled over twice so she could throw up, and each time I was surprised to see how gentle Drake was with her. He held her up with one hand, had her hair off her face with the other, and whispered soothing words to her while she tossed up God knows what.

"I fuckin' hope so. I don't think she has much left in her." There's unease in his voice.

"You get her to talk at all?"

"Yeah. She said she's just drunk. Guess she got dropped off by some friends and felt sick, so she rushed to the bathroom. J.P., that fucking prick, followed her in there."

I swallow past my urge to rip into my brother about how this is all his fault, about how exposing a woman like Jessica to this world was a huge fucking mistake, but I can tell by the worry and guilt in his voice that he's suffering enough. "She tell you what happened back there?"

"I don't want to talk about it."

Damn. That's what I was afraid of. "Did he force her?"

"I told you I don't want to fucking talk about it."

"If he raped her, we go back and feed him his own dick."

He shakes his head. "He didn't, alright. She says she sucked him off, but she lies about shit like this just to piss me off."

"It work?"

"Shut the fuck up."

Petty game to play, but if anyone deserves a little of what he dishes out, it's Drake.

We pull up to my brother's house. It's bigger than my mom's, and I'm sick at the thought of what he's had to do to pay for his pad and the brand new Caddy ATS-V I'm driving. I pull into the long driveway that leads to a two-car garage and is bordered by a professionally manicured lawn.

I grip the passenger seat and twist my neck to see my brother. "I'm dropping you guys off and taking the car. You can come pick it up from Mom's in the morning."

"Fine. Whatever." He pops open the back door. "Jess, baby . . . we're home." Maneuvering himself to the edge of the seat, he pulls her tiny body into the cradle of his arms and stands.

"Yo, Drake."

He pauses at the open door, but doesn't say shit.

"Nothing but water and some food tonight, yeah?"

His head drops. Whether he's looking down at Jess or just staring at the ground, I don't know.

"Drake, man—"

"Yeah, I know. I got it." He knocks the door shut with his hip, and I wait until he's inside before pulling out and heading to my mom's.

Things are so much worse than I thought. Drake's in deep and Jessica's whoring—or pretending to whore—herself just to get my brother's attention. They should be in college, filling their days with classes and stupid jokes with the occasional weekend debauchery. Instead, they're tied up in God knows what, and the only way out is a life for a life. Blood for blood.

Confusion and frustration swirl behind my eyes, bringing on the beginnings of a massive headache. What a fucking mess.

I pull up to the curb in front of my mom's house and think maybe I should've left his car at Drake's and taken a cab home. The house we grew up in is one of the roughest parts of town, just outside of Garfield Park. I shrug and pop the keys from the ignition. If the thing gets fucked with, serves Drake right.

At this point, his world needs a little shaking up.

Headed to the front door, I hit the fob to engage the alarm on the car. The front light in the living room clicks on.

Mom must be home. I pull out my house key and let myself in.

"Mom? It's me. You home? *Oh shit!*" I turn around and throw my hand over my eyes for good measure because no amount of eye blocking can erase what I've just seen, but I wish like hell it would.

"Omigod, Mason!" My mom's voice, laced with panic, mixes with the sound of frantic redressing. "What are you doing here?"

"Um . . . I'll go. I . . . I'm in town, but I'll give you guys a minute to get—"

"No, honey, it's okay. Tom was just leaving." Her hand grips my shoulder before she moves around to pull my hand from my eyes. "Hey, you can open your eyes now."

I squint open one eye to see my mom, her face youthful and betraying her real age despite the lifestyle she's subjected herself to. Her shoulder-length blond hair is tossed around like—ugh, my stomach roils at the thought. She blinks bright blue eyes up at me.

"Hey, Mom, I'm really sorry."

"Don't be silly." She swats me playfully on the shoulder. "We're all adults."

Maybe we're all technically adults, but that doesn't mean I should be okay with seeing my mom on her knees in front of—no, bleaching my brain of that memory ASAP.

"Tom, this is my son Mason. He's the one I was telling you about. The fighter in Las Vegas." The pride in her voice and the way she beams settles me a little after that terrifying entrance.

"Ah, right." Tom, an older guy with dark hair and an athletic build, reaches out to shake my hand. His flashy gold watch catches my eye along with his not-so-flashy gold wedding band. "It's nice to meet you. Your mom's told me a lot about you."

I shake his hand, but can't take my eyes off his wedding ring. He must notice as he shifts uncomfortably before releasing my hand to pull my mom to his side.

"Tom's in the middle of a divorce," she says by way of explanation.

I turn my gaze to Tom and wonder why the fuck he's still wearing his damn wedding ring if he's going through a divorce. "Is that right?"

"I caught your fight a few months ago. You're good. Really good."

Avoiding my question by kissing ass? Not only is he pathetic, but he's also a spineless douchebag. Fatigue washes over me at the thought of fighting my mom's battles after I just got done saving my brother from being blown away by his own shit storm.

"It's been a long day." I set my eyes on Tom. "Would you like me to walk you out before I hit the sack?"

My mom's uncomfortable giggle fills the room. "Don't worry about him, Tom. He's just overprotective." She pinches my cheek like I'm still five years old. "Always has been."

Tom grabs his sports coat off the back of the dining room chair. "No, I believe I can walk myself out. Good to meet you, Mason."

Suuure, dude.

"Oh, I'll come with you." My mom wiggles her eyebrows, and I almost vomit in my throat.

Why did I think coming home would be a good idea?

Trix.

Shit. I check the glowing numbers on the digital DVD clock. It's after midnight. Motherfuck.

"Right, I'm off to bed."

"Okay, honey." My mom pushes up on her tiptoes and kisses me on the cheek, practically running after Tom who's made it halfway to the door. "I'm glad you're home."

She chases after Tom, and I head for my old room, pulling out my phone before I close the bedroom door behind me.

Two texts from earlier tonight, both from Trix. I'm smiling before I even read them, and just seeing her name light up on my phone makes tonight feel like a distant memory.

I drop back on the bed and kick my shoes off, my feet hanging off the end. She was thinking about me before she went to bed. I contemplate calling her, but this was hours ago. Damn, I'd love to hear her voice right now, but it'd be a dick move to call and wake her up.

I head to the hall bathroom where I dumped my toothbrush earlier. After I take a leak and brush my teeth, I head back to bed with heavy steps. I've lived in this house since I was seven years old, and it's never *not* felt like home. But something about it now feels foreign.

"Mason?" My mom strolls down the hall from the front door, chin high as if she's not broke, living in a rundown house alone, and sleeping with a married man. She tilts her head and smiles. "Is everything okay back in Las Vegas?"

"Yeah."

Her eyebrows pinch together. "You haven't been home in a while, so . . . why now?"

I shrug, trying to make my reason for coming to Santa Cruz seem like a casual visit when it sure as fuck is not. "There's a girl I'm—"

"A girl?" Her eyes grow as wide as her grin. "Here? Do I know her?"

"Mom, calm down. No, you don't know her. She's from San Jose, lives in Vegas now. She came home to visit family. I tagged along to spend some time with her."

Her face contorts with disapproval. "You 'tagged along'? No." She wags a finger at me. "No, no, no. You don't want to do that, honey. It makes you seem desperate. Women like a man who's hard to get."

*And what man's harder to get than the married kind.* I fight the urge to roll my eyes. "She's not like most women."

"All women like the chase." She props a hand on her narrow hip. "Trust me. I know."

I bite my tongue to avoid the outpouring of angry words that force their way to my lips. Taking relationship advice from a liar, cheater, and a woman who has always been looking for lust in reprehensible places? No thanks.

"I'm serious. Make sure you hang out with your friends while you're here; see if your brother can take you out. You know he's made quite the turnaround." Her eyes flash with pride. "His car is worth more than my house!"

Bought with drug money, not that she'd care. If she only knew how close he came to being killed in that alley, and that's only one time that I know of.

"You still talk to D's dad?"

Her expression sobers. "I see him around town, hear his bike coming, and try to duck out of his way. I ran into him at a bar about six months ago, but I left right after he got there. He doesn't need me anymore. Ever since Drake turned eighteen, they have a relationship of their own."

"A *relationship*? Mom, Drake works for the guy."

She shrugs. "I figured he did. Makes sense, I guess. Keeping it in the family."

Keeping drug dealing, gun smuggling, and God knows what else *in the family*? Nothing has changed. Not a single fuckin' thing.

I throw my thumb over my shoulder, motioning to my room. "I'm gonna hit the sack." And I can't stand to hear another word of her cluelessness.

"Okay, sure. Sleep tight." She pats me on the arm. "I'm glad you're home."

This isn't my home.

My thoughts crank back to a few nights ago, in my apartment, tangled up in bed with Trix, her purple and blond hair tossed around my chest and neck.

That's home.

I've been in Vegas for a year and never felt like I totally belonged. Until her.

I grin as I step out of my jeans, crawl into bed, and hit the light. I pull my phone off the bedside table to plug it into the charger. Damn, I miss her. Maybe a quick text. Even if she's sleeping, she'll see it in the morning and know I didn't forget about her.

**Just got home. Miss you too. Seeing you bright and early doesn't seem soon enough.**

I lean over to hook up my charger when the phone vibrates in my hand.

New text.

**I can be there in an hour.**

I grin so big my cheeks hurt.

**I'll be here waiting. Don't forget your bikini.**

I hit "send" and stare at the screen, willing her to write back.

**Oops! I didn't bring one. Nude beach?**

A low groan rolls around in my chest at the thought of Trix fully naked on a secluded beach with no one around for miles. Just the two of us, the contrast of the coarse sand against her silky skin beneath me as—my phone vibrates.

**Hello? Did I scare you?**

I run my hand through my hair, taking note of the tent I've created in my boxer briefs, and contemplate how to respond.

**Got lost on a nude beach alone with you for a sec. I'm back now.**

I press "send" and wait.

**That didn't take long. Should I be worried?**

I type back.

**We stay on this topic, the next time I get you naked beneath me I won't be responsible for what happens.**

My phone vibrates almost immediately.

**Promises . . .**

Seconds pass and I want to tell her how much I miss her, I want to smother her with fancy words and flirty innuendos, but everything seems like too much and never enough.

**Mason?**

**Beatriks?**

**I want you. More than I should.**

I blink at the text and then type back.

**You've got me. Whether you should or not, you have me, baby.**

My phone vibrates.

**I'm smiling.**

I type back.

**Get some sleep. I'll see you in the morning.**

Minutes pass and stretch into longer minutes, and I wonder if she fell asleep when my phone vibrates in my hand.

**Goodnight, Mase.**

I smile through a small wave of disappointment. I don't know what I was expecting, but something felt like there was more to say.

I close my eyes and go back to a deserted beach with nothing but the warm body of my woman and the waves crashing around us.

# TWENTY-ONE

## TRIX

I squint into the sun that just came up minutes ago as we cover the last few miles from the highway to the beach. The weather report said it's supposed to be a perfect day, sunny and seventy-five degrees. Although the water is cooler up here than in Southern California, when the sun's out, it's heaven.

I shake Isaac, who's in the passenger seat next to me. "Wake up! I can see the water!"

He jerks awake and pops on his aviator sunglasses, his black, board-straight hair sticking up at all angles. "Sweet, we got here before the crowds."

"Yeah, that's because we basically left last night," Josiah pipes up from the back of the van followed by a yawn.

"Bee-a-ah, are we the-r-r-e?" Leah's scratchy, sleepy, little-girl voice quakes with excitement.

"We are, Leah-bear. Now remember . . . whoever sees the sand first wins."

The entire van explodes in voices saying "I see it!" at the same time.

"Guess we all win," Zoe says and then squeals.

After I texted Mason last night, I was so excited to see him I barely slept. I didn't even need to set an alarm to get up at five a.m. and make a ton of peanut-butter sandwiches to pack in the ice chest. I hope Mason likes peanut butter.

My stomach flutters with nerves as I pull into the lot, not sure what I'm expecting to find, but I'll know when I find it.

I'm not even sure what to look for, but knowing Mase, he won't make me search.

There are about a dozen cars scattered in the lot, and I maneuver to get to the few spaces close to the sand.

"That your man there?" Isaac points to an older pick-up truck right up front, the tailgate down and, simply put, a god of the male form propped up on the back.

I swallow and try to calm my racing heart. "Yep, that's him." Yeah, that sounded good. Not at all shaky like I feel inside.

"He brought boards!" Josiah has the back doors sliding open before the van is even to a complete stop.

"Whoa, awesome!" Aaron pushes past Zoe and they all start to tumble out, two at a time.

I pull the keys and toss them into my beach bag. I want to fluff my hair or check my face one more time, but it's too late. My door swings open, and I'm scooped up by Mason and slammed against his chest.

"God, I missed you," he says into my neck, his grip so tight that I believe he really did miss me as much as I missed him.

I wrap my arms around his middle and hold on, breathing in the clean cotton scent of his shirt that's now mixed with the nutty and tropical smell of sunscreen. "Mmm, you too."

"I wanna kiss you so bad, but I don't want your brothers to kick my ass." He drops a hidden and lingering kiss against my neck.

As much as I want to laugh, thc tiny brush of his lips has robbed me of the ability to speak and infused me with pure need. Dammit, if this is how cranked up we are just from being separated for twelve hours, what will we be like at the end of weekend when we finally get back to Vegas?

"Mr. M-m-ason?" Leah tugs on his shirt, and he releases me quickly as if being caught hugging by a six-year-old is a felony. "Are you g-gonna teach us h-h-ow to surf?"

He squats down to her eye level and my heart melts. It's now I notice his hair is a little damp and his strong jaw is covered in stubble. With his hand braced on the truck tire, his bare arms, which are exposed by his sleeveless shirt, flex in the sun.

"Would you like to learn how to surf?" His voice has taken on a softness that I don't even know if he's realized, but Leah responds immediately by grabbing his hand.

"Yeah, I wa-a-ant to be like Be-th-th-thany Hamilton when I grow up." She tugs him to the back of the truck, and I lock up the van then follow.

"Except maybe avoid the shark thing, yeah?" Josiah says, his tanned twelve-year-old-boy arms crossed at his chest.

"Oh, yeah." Leah blushes. "No shark."

Mason reaches into the back of the truck and pulls out a long surfboard that looks like it's made out of foam. "I brought this for whoever wants to learn. The waves here are pretty mellow. Good for first-timers."

Isaac points to the other board in the back. "What's that one for?"

Mason props the long board against the tailgate and grabs the short, stealthy looking one. It's white with blue-and-green flames. "This one's mine. It's better for doing airs, trick riding."

Zoe peeks up from under the brim of her wide sun hat. Dark eyes peer up in wonder. "Can you show us some tricks, Mr. Mason?"

His deep blue eyes find mine. "Tricks? I'd love to."

My cheeks get hot and I tug at my cover up.

"You guys think I can get your big sister to surf with me today?"

They all respond in some form of "good luck with that."

He stares at me. "Well, what do you think? You up for a little surfing, baby?"

I nod. Yes. Of course. With him, I'd do just about anything.

—

## MASON

Cold water. Lots and *lots* of cold water.

That's the only way I'm going to get through a day of being around Trix in her bikini without embarrassing myself. Sitting on the sand, I thought the distance would help. It doesn't.

My gaze stays locked on her at the water's edge; she's holding Zoe's and Leah's hands, jumping little waves and laughing so hard it drops her head back. The older kids are a little deeper in the water, doing the same. Trix splashes Leah, and the little girl runs away squealing before coming back to crash into her big sister's arms. Trix's smooth bronze skin warms beneath the sun, and the swells, dips, and gentle flares of her curves call to be touched. Kissed.

Kids! Kids . . . focus on the kids.

I blink away from my woman in her bright green string bikini and focus on Isaac. He's tossing a football from hand to hand, staring out at the breaking waves.

"Isaac, man."

He turns toward me, his gaze not unfriendly, but I can see he's protective of his older sister and he won't be won over easily.

"You wanna throw?" I nod to his football.

He assesses me for a second longer then shrugs. "Sure."

I hop up from the big sheet that Trix laid out for everyone right before she slathered them in sunblock and took the younger kids to put their feet in the water. She asked me to come with her, but the vision of her in that tiny bikini had me benched.

Even thinking about it now—football. Focus on football.

I jog out to give the kid a decent distance, but not too far that he can't get the ball to me. I lift my hands, signaling I'm ready. He tilts his head then shakes it a few times before taking two steps back. He cocks his arm then fires the ball. It spins and arcs high, higher, and sails over my head to land a good fifteen yards behind me.

"Holy shit." I stare at him, unbelieving, only to get another shrug. "Sixteen years old? Damn." I jog to get the ball.

After scooping up the football, I slap it between two hands and torpedo the thing back to him. He catches it easily then throws it back.

Seems like I may've underestimated the kid. We play like this until we're both sweaty and my right arm is burning like a motherfucker. Trix and the kids have been working on a sandcastle, and other than the few times I've caught her watching and stolen a smile, I haven't spent any time with her.

I flag Isaac and we jog to meet in the middle. He's breathing heavy, thankfully just as exhausted. "Damn, you've got some serious talent."

His eyebrows pop up behind his shades. "Yeah?"

"Hell yeah! You kidding? I've never seen a kid your age throw like that." I hold out my fist and he bumps it.

"Thanks, bro." He wipes his forehead.

"Why don't you take a dip, cool off a bit." I grab the football to deposit it with our stuff.

"I think I will."

"You mind watching the little kids for a bit so I can take your sister out on the long board?"

He watches me for a few seconds then nods. "Sure thing, man. Just give me a sec to get wet."

He takes off to the water, and I grab the long board, hoisting it up under my arm, and head for Trix. Little-girl voices go back and forth about building a tower high enough so that the prince has to work to get his princess, and the younger boys are deep in the process of moat construction.

I stand over Trix, blocking the sun, and she regards me from behind long strands of her wind-whipped hair. "You up for a surf lesson?"

She shakes gloppy sand off her fingers and stands up, raking her sunglasses up on her head. Her violet eyes flash with excitement, and even without a hint of makeup, they stand out against her sun-kissed skin. "Right now?"

"Sure. Why not?" My fingers itch to push her hair behind her ear.

She stares out at the waves just as Isaac comes in shaking his head to spray the little kids with water. They all squeal.

"Go for it, Bea. I've got the kids." Isaac ruffles Zoe's hair. "What're we building here, Zee?"

Josiah jumps up, his face covered in sand. "We've got a moat with an alligator-great-white-shark hybrid that feeds on the princes that fail to rescue the princess!"

"Of course you do." Isaac grins then drops to his knees to help out.

"Let me put my sunglasses away." Trix moves to our stuff.

"Oh, wait." I set down the long board and pull my sleeveless shirt off over my head. "Can you drop this up with your sunglasses?" I toss my shirt to her, but it hits her flat belly then drops to the sand.

She eyeballs my chest, her lips parted as her gaze slides down my abdomen to settle below my belly button. My dick jumps behind my board shorts at her open appreciation.

"Trix." It's not a command, more like a plea. As if this isn't hard enough without her eyeballs molesting me, I groan, and her gaze slides to my hip where a few fingers of my tattoo peek out from the waistband of my shorts. Damn, if looks could stroke . . . I clear my throat.

Her eyelids flutter, and then a bright blush paints her cheeks. "Uh." She blinks. "Okay, right. I'll, um, be right . . ." She doesn't attempt to finish her sentence, but turns on her heel, throws our stuff on the sheet, then runs back to me.

Runs.

Back.

I rip my eyes from her bouncing body and pick up the long board to create a barrier between the castle builders and the swelling in my shorts. She comes alongside me and grabs my free hand.

"You ready?" I find a mellow break and pull her down the beach to the spot that will be easier for paddling out.

"I'm a little nervous, but ready. Yeah."

We head out into a few feet of water.

She squeaks. "Holy crap, it's cold."

I try and fail to keep my eyes off the goose bumps that break out across her chest and her firm nipples that tighten behind the tiny triangles of her top. "Should've brought her a wetsuit," I mumble.

"What?" Her bright eyes catch mine.

"Nothing." I drop the long board onto the glassy surface. "Alright, Bea." I wink. "Climb on."

It's going to take a damn miracle to keep my hands to myself.

# TWENTY-TWO

## TRIX

Mason grips the long yellow foam board to keep it steady as I put one knee up to climb on.

"Straddle it first then lie flat on your belly." His voice is gravelly, and the sound shoots straight between my legs.

I bite my lip and do as he instructs, straddling the wide board before bracing my weight with my arms and lying flat on my belly with my legs out of the water.

"Good." He walks us out into the waves, pushing the board up and over the smaller waves. His crystal-blue eyes are scanning, as if every surge and splash of the surf is giving away some secret information that only he understands. "Open your legs."

I jerk so hard I practically fall off the board. "Wh-what?"

He flashes a confident smile and runs his big hand up the back of my thigh, prying it open. "Trust me."

Propped up on my elbows, I drop my forehead and allow him to manipulate my legs. Having to watch him on the beach, all that messy blond hair and muscles that caught the attention of every woman within eyeshot, it was impossible to not get turned on. And now, with his shirt off and his board shorts hanging low on his hips to expose the "V" of his lower abdomen, it's enough to have me drooling and ravenous. I need him to touch me, as if I'm sinking and his touch will keep me afloat.

The tail end of the board dips, and the heat of his body hits the insides of my thighs. I squirm to look behind me, but a firm hand at my hip stills me.

"Steady, babe. Don't wiggle." A wave comes toward us. "Paddle."

His shoulders and chest press between my legs and keep me steady as I push with my arms. One then the other, I thrust my hands through the water. When the wave comes, the power of Mason's stroke propels us up and over. A thrill of adrenaline races through my muscles, and I push harder, up and over, wave after wave.

"Atta girl, Trix. Keep it up!" His encouragement spurs me on, salt water splashes into my eyes, and I squint past the burn and continue to paddle.

Briny ocean water sprays my teeth, alerting me to the fact that I'm grinning wide, but damn if I can help it.

My chest feels light and my arms weaken, but the weight of Mason at my back combined with the power of his body pushes me harder. Finally, we make it out past the breakers, and I holler out in victory.

The vibration of his laughter rumbles against my backside, and I swear if it were possible to have a full-body orgasm, I just had one.

A pinching sting against my ass makes me jump, and I whirl around to catch the tail end of a wicked smile. "Did you bite me?"

He shrugs unapologetically. "Can't have your ass in my face and not take a bite, baby."

I giggle, but it dies the second I lose the heat of his body as he pushes up to sit, straddling the board. "Steady." He holds my hips in a firm grip. "Now sit up."

Doing as I'm told, I gasp as I see the entire ocean laid out before me in a vast stretch of dark blue with dancing flecks of yellow from the sun.

"Wow."

"Amazing, right?"

"It's incredible." Maybe it's the kiss of salt against my skin combined with the cool water and warm sun, but I'm tingling. Or maybe it's the man at my back. "I've never felt so tiny or insignificant. It's like a different world out here, ya know?" I'm glad he can't see my face as embarrassment overcomes me.

"That's what I love about it. Out here there's no judgment, no expectations. It's just you and eighty-two million billion gallons of salt water."

"That's a lot of water." I breathe deep, taking in the damp ocean air, and close my eyes. The crashing waves and cawing seagulls lull me to a place where I'm only a girl with a boy. I don't hear the cries of my sister, don't see her mutilated face, or feel the pain of her loss. As my legs dangle off the board, I'm free to bob with the ebb and flow of the tide. Not anchored to my promises, obligations, but completely unburdened. And for a moment, I pretend I'm who I want to be, not who I need to be.

His hand runs down my bare arm, leaving goose bumps in its wake. He shuffles forward, and the heat of his chest hits my back, his strong thighs framing my smaller ones. Big hands run over my hips, around my belly, and his breath is hot on my shoulder.

*Just a girl . . .*

His lips trace an invisible path to my neck.

*And a boy.*

I drop my head back and relax into his embrace. He moans and slides his hands up to my breasts, cupping them gently before running his thumbs back and forth over my peaked nipples.

"Torture not being able to touch you." Squeezing my breasts, he bites my shoulder as a delicious combination of sensations rack my body.

I shift my gaze left then right and find the closest people are surfers, but they're at least fifty yards away and closer to the beach. Perfect.

Slow and carefully, I press forward and pivot around, reversing my position so that I'm now facing him. His eyes flare, and his wet hair is dark blond now as it sticks to his forehead, making his eyes appear brighter. He lifts my knees and pulls my thighs over his. I suck in a breath as his hands go to my face, tilting my head to dip in for a long deep kiss. Salt, coconut sunscreen, and mint flood my mouth in a delicious combination that has me moaning into his mouth. His grip tightens, and my head swims as his tongue lashes against mine. I hook my arms around his neck in an attempt to get closer. Our damp bodies slide easily and he groans, fisting my hair as the centers of our bodies make contact. One hand on my ass, he tugs me up and onto his hips. I wrap my legs around his waist and grind down against his hardness, searching for much-needed relief.

He rips his mouth from mine, panting. "Shit . . . I need you."

"Shhh, babe. This time," I whisper against his lips, "*I* got *you.*"

I slide my hand between us and unlace his board shorts, dipping my hand inside and taking him in a strong grip.

A growl rumbles in his throat and power surges through my veins.

He leans back, propping his weight against the board behind him with one hand while the other is still threaded in my wet, salty hair. He watches my hand wrapped tightly around him, stroking, and rolls his bottom lip between his teeth.

My heart races, and my legs quiver at the visual of him watching me pleasure him. How could something so seemingly innocent feel so weighted with meaning?

"Feels so good, baby." His grip in my hair gets tighter. "Don't stop."

I lick my lips, wishing we were somewhere more private where I could get away with more. I quicken my pace, and his abdomen flexes. The fly of his shorts loosens more to have him almost completely exposed but hidden between our bodies.

He pushes up, and I drop back off his lap and onto the board. His hand dives between my legs, and pushing the thin fabric of my bikini aside, he buries two fingers inside me. I cry out at the intrusion, forcing my eyes to stay focused and avoid rolling back into my head as he meets every stroke with a thrust of his hand. I hold onto him with a hand gripped into his hair behind his neck, and we chase down our orgasms with a primal force that I've only felt around Mason.

Needing so badly to bring him pleasure with my hand while showing him how good he makes me feel is a heady mixture. Our lips crash together, hungry, uncoordinated, but beautiful in their untamed passion.

His body tenses seconds before mine implodes. Stars dance behind my eyes as I slam them shut and bite down on his lip to muffle my whimper. He pants heavily against my mouth; our chests touch with the force of each inhale.

"You okay?" He massages the spot on my scalp now warm from where he was fisting my hair.

"Yeah, I am." I'm grinning so wide he has to hear it in my voice. "Are you?"

I sit back, as he rights my bikini bottoms and tucks himself back into his shorts.

"Baby, I'm way fucking okay." He flashes a smile that promises a thousand kinds of dirty then grips the board and throws his weight to one side, capsizing our little love canoe.

The cool water against my heated skin refreshes me and draws me from the lazy post-orgasmic slumber. When he comes to the surface, he shakes out his hair and pulls me to him, holding to the board to keep us afloat.

His lips run along my hairline, and he inhales deep. "I probably shouldn't have done that, but honest to God, I can't control myself when we're together."

With miles of ocean at our backs and far away from the breaking waves, too distant for anyone on the beach to see what we're doing, I can't think of anything better to do out here than what we just did. Oh, well maybe one thing.

"I'm glad you did. I've been wondering how I would get through the rest of the weekend without touching you."

He leans his forehead against mine. "Who thought bringing the kids to the beach would be a good idea again?"

I laugh and drop a quick kiss on his lips. "You did, remember?"

"Changed my mind." He drops his eyebrows low, his voice serious. "I'm ready to take you home."

"We are home."

His eyes dart to the side, and a slight grimace twists his lips.

I cup his jaw. "Hey, what is it?"

He recovers immediately, as if he didn't even realize how much his expression gave away. "Nothing." He kisses the inside of my palm. "Now, are you ready for your surf lesson?"

Almost as if on cue, a large wave breaks just ahead of us. "Out here?"

"No. We'll go to the baby waves closer to shore. I just brought you out here for privacy."

I lift an eyebrow. "Smart man."

He grips my thigh, and with one more kiss, he hoists me back up onto the board. We resume the same positions and paddle closer to shore. At one point, a large wave swells up behind us, and Mason tells me to hold on. He paddles hard and then stands up between my legs. His powerful legs work to steady us as we ride the wave in. Flat on my belly I laugh as salt water splashes my face, cooling and reviving.

"Alright, surfer girl." Once the wave dies, he hops off the board in shallow water. "Let's see what you got."

My belly flutters with nerves, or maybe it's the sweet way he called me surfer girl.

"I'm ready." I push back to center myself on the board. He keeps it steady in the waist-deep water, and his eyes cast back toward the incoming, but manageable, waves.

The sun shimmers off his wet abs, and my lips tingle to lean in for one taste.

"When I say go, paddle hard." His gaze stays back as if he's reading the tide. "When you feel the board catch, you wanna pop up."

"Pop up?"

He nods and fixes his eyes on me, the blue seeming brighter surrounded by thick dark, wet lashes. "Stay centered on the board. Keep your feet at the back, here." He slaps the tail end. "The sweet spot. Once you feel the board catch, push up on your hands." He shows me by locking out his elbows in front of him. I nod. "Then push back on your knees. From all fours, bring one foot forward, but keep the other one where it is, then stand."

Hands, knees, all fours to a lunge, stand. "Got it."

"Always keep your feet centered and don't forget to bend your knees." He swings his gaze back to the incoming waves.

"Paddle, catch, pop. Okay, I can do that." I crank my head around and follow his gaze to incoming white water. "This one?"

"No." His triceps flex under the pressure of the wave that pummels me and the board, but his grip keeps us in place. "Okay, this next one." He squints for a second before swinging excited eyes to mine. "Ready, surfer girl?" His lips tilt and salt water drips off the tips of his hair.

I blink and turn forward. "Ready."

He angles the board just right. "Paddle as hard as you can. You'll know when it catches."

I nod, my belly flip-flopping like crazy.

"'Kay, babe, here ya go." He shoves the board just as a swell builds behind me. "Paddle!"

My hands dig into the water, one after the other. Hard and fast, I push through the ocean until my shoulders burn.

"Shit, shit, shit, I'm gonna miss it." I groan and throw every last bit of my strength into pushing myself ahead of the wave.

Then it happens. The board thrusts forward on its own.

"I did it!"

"Atta girl!" Mason's voice is laced with pride. "Now pop up!"

Pop, right! I push up to my hands and knees then wobble. Stay centered. Bringing one foot forward, I pop up. The board tilts, almost tossing me off, but I regain my balance. I did it! I'm not going nearly as fast as Mason and I did on the bigger waves, but I'm still moving.

"Go, Bea!" My siblings cheer me from the beach, and I sway but manage to stay up on two feet.

"Yeah, baby!" Mason yells.

*Holy shit! I'm surfing!*

"Woo hoo!" My holler is mixed with my laughter as the power of the ocean propels me forward.

And for the first time since before Svetlana died, I feel free.

# TWENTY-THREE

## MASON

The sun is getting lower, and our little group of ragtag beach-goers is running out of steam.

After we ate the peanut-butter sandwiches and grapes that Trix brought for everyone, I busted out my ice chest full of mini-mart snacks, including chips, candy bars, and flavored sports drinks. The kids went nuts, and for a second, I felt guilty like maybe their parents wouldn't want them gorging on crap, but when I caught the soft look on Trix's face while the kids gobbled up chocolate bars and cheese puffs like it was their job, I knew it was something more.

My guess is they don't get the opportunity to indulge in shitty food while living on a budget. After watching Isaac power down four sandwiches and having been a sixteen-year-old athlete myself, I'd be willing to bet it takes every cent they have to keep him fed, and that's only one of the six kids living at home.

I pop my shades up, squinting into the lowering sun as Isaac carves into a wave on my short board. Is there any sport this kid doesn't dominate?

Isaac picked up on surfing the long board quickly and had asked if he could take mine out. I went with him, showing him the basics, the differences in how it moves, and gave him some pointers on a few waves.

"He's getting really good, Mason!" Trix is lounging back on the sheet. Thankfully, her gorgeous bikini-clad body is wrapped in a sweatshirt, as Leah dozes off in her lap.

I rip my gaze away to follow the direction of her pointing finger. Isaac's still holding his own against the sunset break. I scan the horizon for surfers, who appear like black dots, noticing it's gotten more crowded since the sun started to set. Usually, this beach doesn't attract the surf locals as much as some of the heavier breaks in the area. Cowell is a great place to learn to surf, but the seasoned shredders prefer a more challenging wave.

However, with some recent big open-ocean storms and El Niño, the waves at Cowell are a wild card and predictions are high.

I shake off the edginess that pricks against my skin, but maintain a visual on Isaac. Truth is, when the local surfers come out, not a single outsider is safe.

The bump of a swell rolls in from the distance, and all the little black dots paddle into position. My eyes stay fixed on Isaac. I stand up, trying to gain a better vantage point, blocking the glare with my hand.

"Mason?" Trix is up and next to me. "What is it?"

"Nothing, he's fine." For now.

I watch as the wave builds, and little does Isaac even realize, he's in the optimum position, but not in the right order of the line up to catch this one.

Bottom line, this wave doesn't belong to him.

If he catches this wave, he's going to get his ass kicked.

The swell builds, barreling in, and I see the exact moment that he realizes where he's at. He turns his board around, paddling in front of a group of black dots.

"Fuck," I hiss under my breath.

"What?" She grabs my hand.

Isaac moves, completely unaware that he's thrown down a challenge and is shit deep in a paddle battle. My jaw locks down and I grit my teeth. Lose, Isaac. Don't out paddle these guys.

He hits the lip of the wave at full force. It catches, grabbing Isaac along with one other guy on his outside. Shit. I move, headed for the waterline, dread heavy in my gut.

The guy catches up to him. Fuck. He dives off his board and takes Isaac down.

Trix gasps. "That guy went after him!"

Motherfucker. "Yeah, your brother dropped in on his wave."

Now let's just hope the dude's not a local.

"What does that mean?" I don't look, but I know Trix is scanning the water just as I am, waiting for her brother to resurface.

"Isaac was in the wrong, but . . ." I squint as two black dots surface only to be surrounded by four more. "Fuck. Stay here."

"Mason . . ." Fear and worry lace her voice.

I kiss the top of her head. "It'll be okay; just stay with the kids."

I run into the water, hopping small waves until it's easier to swim. I break the surface with a dive, powering through waves with urgency. Surf conflicts escalate quickly and under no fucking circumstances will I allow Isaac to learn this lesson the hard way. I make it to the group of guys who are chest deep and bobbing in the current.

"Hey." I barely get the word out when Isaac takes a fist to his jaw. "Fuck."

Fights are bad enough, but fights in water while waves thrash all around are almost impossible to win. I make it to Isaac just as he's about to swing on the guy, wrapping my arm around his chest.

"Let me go, man!" Isaac tries to kick from my hold, and I, again, give the kid credit for his strength. "That fucker hit me out of nowhere!"

"Yeah, I know." I drag him toward shore. "Don't worry." I look back to see that, sure enough, they're following us in. "It's not over yet."

As soon as our feet hit solid ground, the group of guys descends. Trix moves toward us, but I hold a hand up to keep her far enough back so that she can hear what's going on, but she's not close enough to get hit.

"Fucking, kook." The guy shoves Isaac, who at sixteen stands eye to eye with the dude that could be twice his age. "Go back to your island, chink."

Isaac rushes the guy. I hook him around the waist before he makes contact and toss him behind me. "Enough. He's new to Cowell, doesn't know the rules yet."

"No shit, asshole. That's what I'm here to teach him." The guy puffs out his chest, and his crew backs him up. They're all tense, flexed, and I know from experience they won't walk away until Isaac bleeds.

"Listen. Give him a pass just this—"

They all burst into laughter, but quickly sober and step into my space. "Maybe you'd like to take the beating for him. Break our rules; pay our fines."

I hate to play this card, but I grew up in this area and know for a fact that it's my only chance to save Isaac from an ass-kicking. "This ain't your break," I say low enough to avoid drawing attention.

A short bulky dude with a shaved head and wild eyes shoves my shoulder. "What the fuck you know about it, *kook*?"

A growl bubbles up from my throat, and I swear if there weren't the eyes of little kids on me, I'd destroy this cocky fuck.

"B3 protects this break." I know it, they know it, and even though I'm no longer an active participant in the local surf gang, these guys understand me.

They each blink, pass a guarded look to each other, and glare at me. "Whatchu know 'bout B3?"

"Emery, dude . . ." Dickhead number two whispers something that sends Emery's eyes to my hip. He tilts his head, and his eyes widen. "No shit?"

My tattoo isn't obvious, but anyone familiar with B3 and everyone local is more than familiar with, if not terrified of, The Brotherhood. They see the waves of the B3 emblem curling up from my hip.

They visibly tense.

"I think it's time you guys move on, yeah?"

They flash looks to each other, trying to hide their concern or fear with the nonchalance of gangster badasses and failing. "Keep your friend safe. Guarantee if he dropped in on one of your brothers he'd never live to talk about it."

That's probably true.

They strut to their boards and head back into the water. With my hands propped on my hips, I feel the unexpected release of tension in my muscles. That could've been so much worse.

"Mason?" I turn to see Trix holding the little kids to her body while the bigger ones crowd around her.

I turn to Isaac, who looks like a ticking time bomb. His fists are clenched, jaw hard, and back rigid. "Go for a run, man. Blow it off. Letting that shit fester will do you no good, understand?"

He's scowling at the guys who are back to being black dots on the horizon. "I could've taken him."

"I don't doubt that. But those guys don't fight fair. It would've been six of them against two of us, and your brothers and sisters would've witnessed it." I slap him on the back. "Now go. Run the beach and blow it off. Trust me."

He drops his eyes to the sand and nods, his shoulders relaxing. "Yeah." He blows out a long breath. "Okay."

"Alright."

He takes off running down the beach, and I turn to Trix, who's chewing her bottom lip and pulling at the skin on her throat.

"Where's he going? Is he okay?"

"He's burning it off. He'll be okay." I motion to a concrete fire ring in the sand. "You guys up for a fire and s'mores before you head back?"

The kids jump with excitement, the mere mention of more junk food erasing what just happened from the forefront of their minds, but Trix doesn't look at ease.

I pull her to my chest. "Babe, what's wrong?"

She curls into me easily, not seeming to care that I'm wet. "He's my baby brother, Mase."

"I know and he'll be okay."

"I guess B3 is a bigger deal than what you told me. 'Just kids' my ass."

I fumble with how to tell her this and have it make sense, or better yet not freak her the fuck out. "B3's a big deal around here. It's a big deal to a lot of people. It means very little to me anymore. If my brother weren't neck deep in it, and if I didn't need to use it to keep your brother from getting sand in his blood, I'd never think about it again."

"Your brother and all those guys who came to Vegas, are they . . .?"

I nod into her hair. "They are."

"So, B3's a real gang."

I run my hands up and down her back with a soft pressure and feel her melt deeper into me. "Started off as a way to protect the locals here, but greed led them to hook up with some bad dudes, and things went downhill from there."

"That's what your brother's involved in now, all the stuff they had lying around the hotel that first night?"

"Yes, and no matter how many times I try to fix this shit for Drake, he just keeps running back to it because of his dad."

She pushes back enough to peer up at me. "I guess any relationship with his dad, even an unhealthy one, feels better than none at all."

I nod and lock my hands together behind her back. "Let's not waste the rest of our time together, focusing on that shit. I'm going to blow my surfer girl's mind with the best s'mores she's ever tasted, and then we're going to get these kids home before they all pass out on the beach and we're carrying sleeping bodies back to your van. Sound good?"

The dark shadows from her eyes clear and she grins. "Sounds perfect."

---

It's been a couple of hours since the sun dipped below the horizon, and our fire is burning the last piece of wood we have. Leah and Aaron are sound asleep on Trix's lap, their mouths caked with a mixture of sticky marshmallow and sand.

Trix's hair is pulled away from her face, the flicker of fire light highlighting her cheekbones and full lips. She looks focused, but somehow vacant at the same time as she watches the flames dance.

I wish I knew what she was thinking, could see inside that pretty head of hers, and carry the burden of whatever makes her drift off like this. Other than the run-in with those locals, today couldn't have been any better.

After Isaac got back from his run and we stuffed ourselves with s'mores, we sat around while everyone shared stories about growing up on this beach. They all lit up with stories about Lana, their sister, all except for Aaron and Leah, who were too young to remember much of her.

As quiet as Isaac and Trix are now, I have to think they're lost in memories of her life or her death.

"Thank you for this." Trix slides her hand into mine. "We needed this day."

Her face is free of makeup and a little sunburnt and reveals so much more than her beauty, something heavy. It's the softness in her eyes, the transparency of a day without guards up, and the vulnerability of being herself rather than Trix the Vegas stripper. It's as if I'm seeing *her*.

I pick up her hand and press her knuckles to my lips. "I needed you like this today."

Her mouth tilts in a shy smile.

"Feels good to get you away from Vegas. Here you're Bea, the greatest big sister ever." My thumb traces circles against her wrist. "Not Trix, the . . ." *Stripper*.

Her smile falls. "Yeah."

I don't mean to upset her, but after these last few days, having her in my bed in Vegas, spending time with her at my beach, and watching her with her family, I don't want to give her back. The thought of her dancing for strangers, using a body that I've watched comfort her young siblings, a body I've claimed for myself, it's enough to make me want to pop the eyes from every man who steps foot inside Zeus's.

I place one last lingering kiss against her hand. "It's getting late. I don't want your parents to worry."

"Sucks, but . . ." She nods and shifts, waking the sleeping kids sprawled on her lap. "Wake up, guys." She runs her fingers through their hair. "Time to go."

Life returns to their faces and their limbs as they yawn and stretch. After a few protests, they get up, and we pack up our day-long campsite and head to the parking lot.

"Whose truck is this?" Trix brings over a stack of towels she's folded and places them on the tailgate while I slide the surfboards into the bed.

"It's mine." I shove the towels in the back and take the ice chest from Isaac to load it up. "Drove it in high school."

She runs her hands along the faded blue paint. "I can see you in this. It's"—she shrugs one shoulder—"you."

I slam closed the tailgate. "Thanks. I think?" I nod toward the big white van that is now filled with sandy kids. "Hate to see you go, but I don't want you on the road too late."

"Okay." She knots her hands together and chews her lip.

I stare at her, licking my lips, so desperate to kiss her but knowing I can't, not with the six sets of eyes that are peering out of the van windows. "I'll see you tomorrow."

"Tomorrow." She throws her arms around my neck in a tight hug, her lips finding my neck where she drops a kiss, hidden from prying eyes. "Text me later."

"Drive safe," I say into her hair, making sure to draw in one long breath before releasing her. Trix always smells amazing, but her scent mixed with salt water and suntan oil is fucking euphoric.

My eyes devour her legs as she climbs into the van. Twenty-four hours and those'll be wrapped around my hips. *Hang in there, man.* I adjust my board shorts to accommodate the raging hard-on that seemed to rise up instantly.

Trix waves at me from the window before reversing out of her spot.

I stand in the lot, watching until the red glow of her tail lights disappears around the corner.

"Things are going to change when we get back to Vegas, Surfer Girl. I just hope you're ready for it."

# TWENTY-FOUR

## TRIX

My dad's birthday party is in full swing. A yard full of kids and a few dozen friends from church all huddle around, laughing and eating cake. Mason showed up about an hour ago and was nearly tackled by my brothers and sisters the second his feet hit the front porch. Even Isaac seemed eager to get Mason outside to throw the football. With a quick hug and kiss to my forehead, he indulged my siblings.

It's selfish, but part of me is ready to get back to Vegas so I can have him all to myself again. I plop down on an old swing my dad hung from a tree back when he brought Svetlana and me home for the first time. My fingers absently trace the letters "S&B" that we carved into the edge after they brought Isaac home from Thailand. We'd never had anything that was just ours before and wanted our new brother to know it was off limits.

What we didn't expect was how much we'd love him. We mothered that poor kid every chance we got and continued with every other child that my parents welcomed into our family.

Mason runs across the yard, the football tucked under his arm, as at least ten kids descend and wrap around his legs. He drags them along, taking big wide slow steps while they squeal and giggle themselves silly.

"Lana, what should I do?" I whisper to no one, but hope she can hear me. "Everything is so confusing."

Before, finding Lana's killer was all that mattered. Now, my plight seems completely pointless.

It's only been weeks since I met Mason, but he's fallen right into my life and clicked into place like a missing puzzle piece.

Lana is gone. Nothing done on this earth is going to bring her any peace. It's me. I'm the one who's been searching for something that I thought I'd find in my quest for vengeance.

But now, that empty place in my heart, the hole I've been so desperate to fill after Lana died, doesn't feel so empty anymore.

Maybe my dad was right, and I should just leave Lana's case unsolved and allow God to sort out the rest.

"That was a sick pass!" Isaac high-fives Mason, both men laughing as the team of little football players tries to take out their legs.

"He's a really good guy, Svetlana." I breathe in deep, taking in the cool mountain air and desperately searching for my sister's presence. "Tell me it's okay to move on. That I'm not letting you down." I cast my gaze toward the sun and close my eyes, needing her guidance now more than ever. "Please . . . tell me what to do." A sign, something. Anything.

A twig snaps and my eyes dart open.

Mason.

His hand extends toward me. "You ready?"

I blink up, taking in his peaceful smile, soft eyes, and the sun shining behind all that blond hair that makes him look like an angel. "Is it time?" *To move on?*

"Yeah, baby," he whispers.

I suck in a shaky breath and grip the big wooden seat. "I think I am." I brush my fingers along our carved initials. *I'm scared.*

The warmth of his hand slides behind my neck, coaxing me off the swing and into the solid strength of his chest. "I know it's hard to say good-bye."

He has no idea.

I sniff back tears that threaten to spill and simply nod.

"Bea, we gotta go or you'll be late," Isaac calls.

Mason looks over at Isaac, and whatever my brother reads in Mason's expression softens his face and he nods. "I'll load up your stuff." He walks away, leaving me in the capable arms of my boyfriend.

"Do you want to stay for a few more days?" His hands sift through my hair, and the caress soothes my aching heart.

"No, I'm ready to go back to Vegas."

"Want to talk about what's got you so upset?"

I shake my head and peek up at him. The truth is I'm not upset as much as I'm feeling the weight of defeat. His blue eyes, heavy with concern and worry, fix on mine.

"I'm okay, just"—I pick at the neck of his tee—"ready to make some changes when we get back."

Like giving up looking for my sister's killer and starting fresh, fighting for a life of my own. With him. If he'll have me.

His eyebrows pop. "Changes? Mind sharing?"

"I want to quit dancing. I don't know . . ." I shrug. "Maybe take some classes, pick up more hours at the Youth Center. I think Sylvia—"

The wind rushes from my lungs as Mason lifts me into his arms and spins me around. "Yes!"

I wrap my arms tighter around his shoulders, giggling into his neck as he yelps in excitement before dropping me back to my feet. "Are you serious?"

"Safe to say you approve?"

"Approve? Fuc—er—heck yeah! Are you kidding?" His gaze sweeps along my face, my eyes, cheeks, settling on my lips. "I want to kiss you so badly right now," he whispers.

"Your dad would probably shoot me; all these church people would, for sure, think we were going to hell."

I tilt to the side and see the yard full of people, and after Mason's outburst, most of them have their eyes on us. "Mase? I don't really care what they think." Pushing up on my toes, I drag my lips along his, and he flinches slightly before his eyelids close and he sinks into a sweet and tender kiss.

It's open-lipped, but no tongue and filled with more meaning than any sexual encounter we've had before. It's a promise, a vow that whatever these changes bring he'll be there.

He rests his forehead against mine, his eyes still closed. "Let me take you home, Surfer Girl."

The tenderness in his voice makes my chest feel like it could explode. I drag in a shaky breath. "Yes, please."

# TWENTY-FIVE

## MASON

"Good morning, gentlemen!" I hold my arms out wide, gloved hands, ready to train.

Blake jerks to a stop and glares at me. "Baywatch? How long have you been here?"

He and Jonah, who just entered the training center, stroll over to the octagon where I've been waiting since seven a.m. Waiting and training.

"Couple of hours." I roll my head around, keeping my muscles loose. "Getting an early start." I squint at Blake. "Hey, did you just wake up?"

"Fuck off." He turns to head toward the locker room. "I'll be right back to kick your morning-glory pansy ass."

I cup my mouth. "Take your time!"

"Eat a dick!" He gives me the finger over his shoulder.

"Man, that guy is grumpy in the morning." I shake my head, unable to wipe the shit-eating grin off my face.

Coming off an epic few days with Trix, I'm a damn circus clown. Our plane got in just in time for us to grab a quick dinner and head to my place. We showered together and stayed naked as long as we could, that is, until she had to head home and start her plan for making changes. I was so pumped up with excitement over where our relationship is heading I came straight to work to train.

She's not going to strip anymore. Even thinking the words makes me fuckin' giddy.

"Alright, Baywatch." Jonah crosses his arms over his chest, his eyebrows dropped low as he assesses my practically dancing ass. "What gives?"

"Can't a guy just start the week out with a smile?"

"Sure he can, but there's always a reason and nine and a half times out of ten that reason is a woman."

I try to hide what I'm sure looks like a ridiculously goofy smile.

"Fuck." He shakes his head. "Trix did a number on your ass, huh?"

"Is it that obvious?"

"You're wearing it like skin, brother."

"She's pretty amazing."

"Who?" Blake jogs up, wearing his training gear and slipping on his gloves. "The stripper?"

"*Ex*-stripper." And that fucking grin is back. "She's quitting."

Blake's eyebrows jump. "No shit? Good for you, man. Must have some kind of King Kong dick to get her to give up all that cash for you. Those girls make bank."

My smile falls a little. "She'll get another job. It's no big deal." We move to the heavy bags on the far end of the training center. "But yeah, I do have a King Kong dick, so that helps."

Blake cringes. "Little slow on the uptake there, Baywatch." He leans against the wall, studying me. "I'm serious though. She gives up that kind of green; you better be worth it."

Am I worth it? Maybe not, but we're worth it.

I'll make damn sure we're worth it.

He pulls an arm across his chest, stretching. "Can she afford her house, all her expenses, if she quits?"

"Um . . ." Shit, I didn't really consider that.

"You sure pushing her to quit stripping without figuring this shit out first is the smartest thing to do?"

*Adios* good mood. Fucker.

"It's her call. I didn't ask her to quit."

"Right." Blake shakes his head. "I'm sure you have zero to do with her quitting." He practically rolls his eyes.

"So, you're saying she should just keep getting naked for dickheads like you while I just sit on the couch and wait for her to come home and wash the smell of a dozen different men's colognes from her body, *my* body."

"No, just stop thinking with your damn pride." He smacks the side of my head.

"Ow!"

"Start using your brain, Baywatch."

Shit. So maybe quitting tomorrow isn't possible.

If money is the issue, she can move in with me. My chest lightens at the thought of waking up to Trix every day. Having her body warming mine every night. If things keep going the way they have, I can see making this woman my wife.

---

## TRIX

"Hold the door!" I race from my car to the back door of Zeus's, my arms overloaded.

"Here, let me help you." Kayla, one of the other dancers, grabs my bag and a few loose papers that slip from my grip.

"Thank you." I blow hair from my face, spitting it from my mouth.

She props open the door with her foot while eyeballing all my crap. "You movin' in?"

I pass her into the hallway that leads to the dressing rooms. "Oh no, definitely not."

She follows me to my dressing table and drops my bag on the floor and papers on the table.

"Thanks, Kayla."

"Sure thing." She moves to her station across the room while I try to organize the mess I brought in.

"What the hell is all that stuff?" Angel perks up from her gossip magazine and glares.

"Just some outfits I thought I'd try out. Changing things up." More like covering things up. It seems stupid, but I have a boyfriend now. First boyfriend in my entire adult life and I don't want to mess things up.

Mason has made it abundantly clear that he hates me getting naked for a room full of men, so until my two weeks' notice is up—which I've yet to give—I don't feel as comfortable in nothing but a G-string.

Angel bends over and picks through my bag of clothes, pulling out one-piece corsets and lingerie. All of them sexy, just not showcasing as much skin.

She lifts an eyebrow and drops a satin number back into the bag. "There's no way this shit is gonna fly, Trix. This is a titty bar, not a burlesque club. You'll get booed off stage and then fired."

I slam a stack of papers down on my dressing table harder than I intended. "What are you talking about?" I reach in and pull out a strappy one-piece that has cutouts across the stomach and back. "This is sexy."

She flinches away from the offending lingerie and points. "*That* is a bathing suit."

Whatever. I drop the thing back into the bag, feeling irritated at how right she really is. No one pays to get into a club to see what they can find at any public beach.

"Trix, what's going on?"

I dig through my purse to find a pen. "Nothing." At least nothing I want to talk about.

"These are job applications."

My eyes slide to her as she sorts through all the papers I had on my table. "Yeah, they are." I continue to search for a pen, avoiding her eyes.

"Are you getting a second job?" Her question is tentative, like she already knows the answer to the question she's asking.

Frustrated, I drop my purse and grab the applications from her hands. She doesn't seem to get the hint and pulls the folded up newspaper from my purse. The classified section.

Can't really lie my way out of this one. "I think my time here has run its course, that's all."

"So you're quitting." Not a question, obviously.

"I think so. Yeah." My scalp prickles as I anticipate Angel's reaction.

"No!" She pulls up a stool to sit next to me, her eyes searching mine. "You can't! I can't do this if you're not here."

I'm moved by the emotion shining through her dark eyes, but cringe because I'm letting her down. I return to my applications, pulling out the one for the Youth Center which is hiring for a camp counselor. The pay sucks, and it's only part time, but it's a sure thing, and Sylvia said the second something full time opens up I'm in.

"Trix, why?"

"My heart's just not in it anymore." And sometimes when someone great comes along, a girl is forced to decide what's more important: living for a dead sister or living for herself.

"Well shit." Angel slumps back against the wall. "This sucks so bad. Santos is going to cry. You know that, right?"

"Please, don't say anything until I put in my official two weeks in tonight after my shift. And quit with the pouty face. I'll come in and visit. I promise."

She frowns and moves back to her table. "No, you won't. Everyone knows once a stripper leaves the life she never comes back."

God, hope she's right.

"Let's give her a welcome worthy of the gods." The DJ's voice powers through the speakers, and I will my body into action, knowing this is my last dance of the night before I get to go home to Mason.

Warmth fills my chest, beating out the hungry roar of the crowd. I smooth my hands down the black satin of my corset to the clips of my garters.

"Put your hands together for our own . . . Trix!"

The bass throbs all around me, and I force my stiletto-tipped feet to move. I focus on the fact that after I speak with the club manager tonight I'll be able to share with Mason that I've given my notice. I expect to be naked shortly after sharing that with him, and he'll undoubtedly want to show his appreciation with his hands and mouth.

My hips sway to the music when I imagine Mason's soft lips, his slick tongue as it glides down my neck and over my breasts. My joints turn to liquid as I think about all the wicked things he does with his tongue, and excitement builds in my chest.

I've shared my body for way too long. Anyone who has had enough cash to pay a cover charge has seen me naked, felt every curve of my body, and some even tasted my skin and mouth.

I drop my clothes piece by piece, refusing to allow the strange betrayal I feel over my past to penetrate my mind. Soon enough, I'll be able to leave this life behind and move forward with Mason. Two more weeks at Zeus's is an easy sacrifice for a future with my fighter.

The thought alone brings me peace. I can't pinpoint the time and place where my desire for revenge died, but it was somewhere between running into Mason at Caesars and yesterday, sitting on the swing at my parents'.

The music picks up, and I run though one of my go-to routines. I could dance it in my sleep.

"Hey, over here!" I turn toward a table of guys no older than I am. They wave money at me, and I smile and slink over on my hands and knees with a swing to my hips that I've perfected over the years.

I toss my hair around and shove my hip out for them to stuff wads of their parents' money into my lingerie. Then suddenly, it's as if the air around me becomes electrified. There's no sound out of the ordinary, but it feels like I'm surrounded by violence. Like a silent war is waging right in front of me, but I can't see it. I continue to dance, but my heart picks up a frantic pace. My skin pricks as I scan my surroundings.

And then I see why.

Black eyes fix on me. Desperation rolls from them in waves. I freeze, staring straight at him. A face that used to bring hope now shatters my soul. My stomach churns and dizziness throws me off balance. The corner of his mouth lifts.

And just like that, with one look, my future plans are forgotten.

# TWENTY-SIX

## MASON

"Bea, it's me again." I check my kitchen clock as I pace. "It's two thirty. I'm sorry to keep bothering you, but . . . did I do something or say something?" My fingers fist into my hair. "Please, call me back. I'm starting to worry."

I hit "end" and shove my phone into my pocket. She told me she had to work until one a.m. but that she would come straight to my place after. Now it's almost three in the morning and still no word. I've called, texted, left messages, even called Zeus's, but got nowhere.

She was quiet when she left this morning, but I just thought it was because she had a lot on her mind. I've spent the last hour going over everything I said. Maybe I pushed her too hard?

Maybe Blake was right and she's having second thoughts about quitting her job? Second thoughts about us?

No. That can't be it, not after the weekend we had. She was excited about us, about our future, wasn't she?

Shit. I grab my keys and jog down to the truck. If she won't come to me, I'll go to her. Not a chance in hell I'll get any sleep tonight wondering if she's okay.

My phone chimes in my hand. A text from Trix.

**Sorry about tonight. I came down with a fever out of nowhere. Got sent home early and fell right to sleep.**

Oh, shit. Now I feel like a dick.

**I'm sorry, baby. Do you need me to bring you anything?**

I hit "send" and wait nervously, hating that she's sick and I'm not there to take care of her.

**No, I just need to sleep. Call you tomorrow.**

Well, fuck. I frown and my stomach clenches. I'd like her to run to me when she feels sick. Want me to take care of her. But maybe it's too soon to expect that kind of thing.

**Of course. Get some rest. If you need anything, I'm a phone call away.**

I hit "send" and wait for a text back that never comes.

---

## TRIX

I squint my eyes to focus, the booze doing a number on my vision, as I punch out another text to Mason. My fingers hit all the wrong buttons, and I teeter on the edge of typing "I love you." No. I need to tell him that in person. He needs to hear it from my lips and believe me. That's the only way he'll understand the reasons why I have to break both our hearts.

I erase the garbled words and toss my cell onto the patio table in front of me. I'm not sick, at least not physically. Mentally is another story. I stare at the roughed-up man across from me in my own backyard, and a shiver skates down my spine.

Hatch is back.

Lingering in the shadows at Zeus's all night, he waited until I finally approached him. Buying me shots to celebrate his return morphed into a party of two at my place. And here we are, almost as if no time has passed at all, except for the subtle changes in his face. Whatever he's been up to this last year has given him an edge, a darkness in his gaze that speaks of violence and rage.

"Why are you here?" I force my lips to enunciate the words, not wanting to give away how buzzed I am. Expose any weaknesses.

He takes a long drag of his cigarette, his jaw now covered in a full beard and his hair longer than it was the last time I saw him. "Some dumb fuck turned himself in, went down for the shit the cops were trying to pin on me. I'm off the hook."

"How long have you been back?" My guess is he didn't just breeze into town today after being on the run for a year.

"Few weeks. Had some business to take care of before heading back to Denver." He puts out his smoke and throws back a shot of whiskey. "Figured I'd stop in, say hi, grab a quick fuck." Lust coats his expression and my stomach roils in response.

"Not tonight, Hatch. I know what we used to have, but it's going to take me some time to warm back up to that." Understatement of the year.

His eyebrows drop low over his eyes. "Used to like how uncomplicated you were, Trix. You'd hear my bike pull up and your legs would fall right open." He scratches his hairy jaw. "Gone a year, come back to an uptight bitch I gotta warm up to?" He laughs, low and garbled. "Fuck that."

I wish I could watch him walk away, shove his ass out my door, and never see him again, but I can't.

The second I saw him at Zeus's my whole world, my plan to move on, all my dreams of a future with Mason, crumbled in an instant. God dropped the opportunity in my lap, or rather in a strip club, and I can't pass it up. No matter how much I'd like to. This is my second chance.

"I just need . . ." *To talk to Mason.* I pour myself a shot. "A day to adjust to you being back."

Hatch's dark eyebrows drop low over menacing eyes. "What's up with you?" He's thinner now. Time on the run obviously doesn't pay well, or he's been living on tequila.

I throw back my shot and grunt through the burn. "Well, let's see. You kidnapped my best friend, got her hooked on drugs, and then left her to die so you could save your own ass."

"Ah, so that's why you're not givin' it up," he says with a frustrated tone. "First off, I didn't fucking kidnap anyone. She came willingly." A lecherous smile pulls at his lips. "You're pissed about Annie—"

"Don't you fucking call her that!"

"Trix, calm your shit down."

Fuck him! I pour myself another shot of whiskey and can't help but feel like I'm partying with the devil. Is this even worth it? Even if he does end up telling me who killed Svetlana, is it worth it when I have to betray Mason and Gia, the two people outside of my family who mean the most to me in the world?

I set my eyes on him, knowing the girl he sees now is Trix. Cold and dead inside. Mason brought Beatriks back, the real me. After our trip, I felt more like myself than I had since before Lana died, but setting eyes on Hatch in the club brought Trix back in the span of a breath.

"Before you left, you told me a story."

"Told you a lotta shit." He leans back in his chair and sips from his beer. "Shit I never told anyone."

"This story was about a guy who picked up a young girl. She thought his bike broke down, stopped to help. Do you remember that?"

He shrugs but purses his lips. "Probably fucked up, makin' up stories."

"You weren't making it up, Hatch. I remember."

"Trix—"

"Finish the story."

"Don't—"

I chuck the full shot glass across the back patio in an arch of amber liquid and glass shatters on the deck. "Finish the fucking story!"

Tears burn my eyes and I'm shaking.

He sets thoughtful eyes on me and registers my extreme reaction. I'm fucking this up. I know I'm fucking this up! I can't push him. If he spooks, I'll never get him to tell me. Never.

I breathe deeply and focus on relaxing my muscles.

He pushes up from his chair, slamming his beer bottle onto the table so hard it makes me jump. "I'm out."

"What?" I hop to my feet, but his legs are carrying him through the house and into the garage where I had him park his bike.

"Later, Trix." The door slams behind him, and shortly after, I hear his bike roar to life.

"Fuck!" My head spins and tears drip from my eyes. "I need a plan. I need a plan."

---

## MASON

I don't know what woke me up, but I'm up. Staring at the ceiling, I'm wide awake. I rub my eyes and check my phone.

It's almost five o'clock in the morning.

Either the sun is just starting to rise, or it's a full moon because my condo is already tinted in muted light. I need to check in on Trix, but it's too early. She needs her sleep. Not too early for a run—*Knock-knock-knock!*

A frantic pounding on my front door tenses my muscles. Just the sound alone radiates panic. What the hell?

I rip off my comforter and charge down the steps, whirling around the corner and flinging open the door.

"Trix?"

She rushes into my arms, her body going almost completely slack once I grip her to me.

"Trix, baby, what's wrong?"

Her hair is pulled back in a messy ponytail, and the smell of liquor is all over her. She shakes her head and squeezes me tighter. Something's not right. Fear floods my veins.

Shutting the door, I hook her beneath the legs to scoop her into my arms and take her to the couch.

"I'm sorry." She buries her face in my neck, her forehead cool against my skin. No fever. "I'm so sorry."

My gut clenches and I hold her tighter. "Shh, it's okay, what are you sorry for?"

She shakes her head, her nose brushing against my neck. "I lied to you. I should've told you the truth from the beginning." She continues to whisper a mumbled "I'm sorry."

My hold on her lets up at the sudden need to see her face. Sliding her off my lap, I release her to pull back enough to see her. "Lied about what?"

Her face, still heavily made up from her shift at the club but smeared with dripping mascara, bunches with a cringe. "I'm not sick. I'm a little drunk though."

Okay, that explains the booze smell. "Didn't drive, did you?"

"Cab."

Good. "So you lied about being sick?"

"Yes, and . . ." She dips her chin for a minute before her eyes search mine; fear and worry shadow her expression. "He's back."

My stomach drops with a sickening thud, and my fists clench. "*Who* is back?"

"I'm sorry. I'm so, so sorry, Mason." She shakes her head as tears roll down her face. I've seen this look on a woman before, the struggle between what she needs and what she wants. The war behind her eyes says she's about to crush the soul of a man who cares for her more than she can return. If memory serves, I'd say history is about to repeat itself.

I straighten and stalk to the other side of the room, fisting my hands in my hair and wishing I could turn off my feelings. Shield myself from what's about to happen and fall into numbness. Pain slices through my chest, and I force my mouth to ask the question. I need to hear it from her lips, but pray, by some miracle, it's not what I think. "You're leaving me."

"I . . . need to explain," she whispers. "I don't have a choice."

There. She said it. It's done.

A numbing heat envelops me, and I glare at her. "So that's it? Just like that."

Blackened splatters of mascara-soaked tears drip from her eyes and dot her white shirt. "I thought he was gone for good."

Son of a bitch! An ex-boyfriend.

". . . but he showed up tonight. I—"

"Fine. You said what you had to say. Now you can leave." Unable to look at her for another second, I storm upstairs to my room and straight into the bathroom.

I practically punch on the shower and rip off my shorts, ducking under the spray, needing to be wet and naked to avoid chasing after her. This can't be happening. I wasn't wrong about this girl. Jessica and Eve, yes.

But not her. Not Trix.

Bracing my weight, I force my hands to stay planted against the tiled wall, fighting the urge to run back downstairs and beg her to stay. I've chased after women in the past and it got me nowhere but alone without even a sliver of pride to call my own. I won't do that again. I allow the hot water to beat down on my neck and shoulders in hopes that it'll calm my racing heart.

Her words run through my head on a loop—over and over again until I'm no longer pressing against the tile with my palms, but with my fists.

"Mason?"

I jerk toward the sound of her voice, strands of my hair hanging wet and heavy in my eyes. She's standing on the other side of the glass shower door, totally and completely naked. My eyes rake over her body, and again, I'm struck by her beauty. She reaches a shaking hand to the door, but her gaze locks on mine, waiting for permission.

What is this? One last fuck before she runs back to her boyfriend? If that is what's going on, I don't have the strength to tell her no. I'm too weak, too sold out for her to turn her down. Pussy-whipped and fucking drunk on her to push her away.

I keep my gaze on hers and she pulls open the glass. Stepping one delicate foot at a time onto the heated tile, she closes the door behind her and stares up at me. Her eyes communicate a pain that she hasn't given a voice to. God, I wish she would. Is she hurting as much as I am?

A war wages within, the fight to run from the pain, but the draw that demands I soothe her. My fingers itch to touch her and before I can contemplate the consequences, they move.

I cup her jaw, wiping the dark smudges beneath her eyes with my thumbs. "Why are you crying?" Steam rolls around us, leaving a sheer mist upon her skin that calls for my lips. This is wrong. I should let her go, but—

A sob rips from her throat.

"Stop holding back from me."

With a gentle tug, I pull her to me. Her breasts press against my ribcage and my hard-on to her stomach. Disgust rolls in my gut at how I can be so fucking hard for a woman who's ripping my heart from my chest.

"Mason, I . . ." She shakes her head and her gaze drops away from mine.

"Talk to me." It's all I can get out before my lips crash against hers. Hunger fuels my body as my arms wrap tightly around her. Our tongues tangle together in a cocktail of fury and possession. She groans and hitches her leg to my hip and I drive my hands to her ass, gripping hard until she whimpers. Adrenaline bursts through my veins at the satisfaction that comes with her pain. I lift her up, slamming her back against the wall while I delve deeper into her sweet mouth.

Her heels press against my ass, her body begging for me to enter her, to take what, after tonight, will belong to another man. I growl into her mouth as anger rips through my body. She wants one last good-bye fuck, a pity party for the poor schmuck who lost the girl. I want to. My dick and the drive to punish her tell me to fuck her hard and walk away. Leave her with an ache between her legs, matching the ache she'll leave in my chest.

She claws at my arms. "Please, I need you." She said herself that she uses her body as a tool, which is exactly what she's doing now. As angry as I am, I'm incapable of using her. She's worth more than that, even if she doesn't realize it.

I force my lips from hers, and her eyes pop wide with shock. Reluctantly, I unhook her legs to place her gently to the ground. I put as much distance between us as possible in the confined space.

"I can't do this." I run a hand through my wet hair. "I won't."

"Why?" Her voice threatens to unman me. "Will you look at me?"

I contemplate saying no, telling her that looking at her will only remind me of all I'm about to lose. I can't bear to see her regard me like I'm just *some* guy rather than her *only* guy.

"Please."

I shake my head, but peek up at her. "What?"

She's covering her breasts with her arms; her lip quivers. "I love you."

The words hit me like a roundhouse kick to the head. "What? How . . . what?" I blink and lean closer, sure I misheard.

"I know this is soon and sounds crazy, but I'm in love with you, Mason. The head-over-heels kind, the making-big-changes kind, the forever-and-ever kind."

"How drunk are you?"

"Not drunk enough that I don't know how I feel."

This is bullshit! All of it.

My thoughts spin with confusion. "What do you want from me, Trix?" My hands shake as I step closer to her, not sure if I want to grab her into my arms or wrap my hands around her neck.

She stands tall, confident. "I want to be a better woman for you, wake up every morning with you. I want you to wonder what kind of mother I'll be and dream about the future we'll have together. I want you to want to marry me, spend the rest of your life with me, and be proud to do it. That's what I want from you."

A low growl rumbles in my chest. "That's a lot to ask seeing as you just told me you're leaving me for someone else."

Her gaze sinks to the floor. "I know. But there's a lot you don't know. If you'd give me time to explain, I think you'll understand. I *hope* you'll understand."

"Start fucking talking."

# TWENTY-SEVEN

## TRIX

I take a shaky breath and wipe my eyes with the hem of the T-shirt Mason gave me to wear. Sitting cross-legged on his bed, I want so badly for him to hold me in his arms, but he's all the way across the room. His back is to the wall, elbows on his knees, with his head in his hands.

"It took me two years of working at Zeus's, trying to get close enough to every biker who came in and hope beyond hope they knew something." Every word that leaves my lips seems to deliver Mason physical pain, but he needs to know. He needs to hear it all. "When I met Hatch, he warmed up to me, and it was easy to get him talking. Found out he had ties to Northern California."

Mason's eyes stay downcast, his fingers fisting in his hair.

"When he got drunk, he was like an open book, treated me like his confessional. The things he told me . . ." I shake my head at the memory of his admission.

*No one messes with us, sunshine. Gotta guy who gets off on cuttin' up people. Even killed a girl doin' it.*

"Fuckin' hell," he mumbles beneath his breath.

"He took off for a year, and I thought it was over—that he was dead and that everything he knows died with him—but he's back now."

I wait, for something, anything. Silence thickens the air between us.

"Say something." I'd go to him, but his body language is screaming to be left alone.

He rips his hands through his hair, and he spears me with an icy-blue glare. "You're asking me to do the impossible!"

My body jerks to touch him, but I sit back, refusing to take away the space he needs to process. "Is it? Is it impossible?"

"To sit back while you date someone else? Someone with ties to a murderer? Yes. It's motherfucking impossible."

"I don't want him. I want you. Forever. After this is over, after I get the name of the man—"

"And if you don't?" He shrugs. "What then, huh? How long will you be fucking this guy before you finally give up?"

*I don't know. Can a time limit be put on this kind of thing?* I shake my head. "It took me years to get him to open up, years of living a life I hate, doing things that make me sick, knowing every day I'm disappointing my family because they think I actually like the person I've become."

Mason's face twists in disgust. "Exactly. So why go through it? There's no guarantee you'll find what you're looking for. That guy could be full of shit. Why not just walk away now? You said it yourself you were going to quit stripping. Leave this vigilante mission behind, for us." He implores me with his eyes. "Please, do that. Walk away and I promise I'll give you a life you'll never regret leaving that shit behind for."

I swallow the lump forming in my throat. "You're asking me to turn my back on Svetlana when I'm finally so close to figuring out who killed her."

"Yes. But it's for us, for your safety. Fuck, Trix, just think about all the things that could go wrong here."

I blink up at him. "You're asking me to choose you over her. If I walk away, I'll always wonder."

"No, you won't—"

"And I'll hate you for making me choose."

He flinches at my words, but understanding comes over his face.

"My parents told me that they wanted to adopt Svetlana because she was older. Young children have a much better chance at finding a family. It took them years of legal shit and paperwork until they finally made it to Russia to pick up their little girl. When they got to the orphanage, they said she refused to go. She didn't cry or throw a fit, but just kept saying over and over, '*Moya sestra. Moye serdtse.*' They said she wouldn't stop, just kept chanting it."

"What does it mean?"

"My sister. My heart." Pain slices through my chest at the memory of her words. "My dad told me I was like a growth holding on to her leg: screaming, crying, and kicking up a huge fuss. They knew then there was no way Svetlana would leave me and if they wanted her they'd have to take me too."

"I don't understand why—"

"Don't you see? She saved me. She fought for me and refused to give up until she knew I'd be in the safest place possible, and that place was with her."

He shakes his head, almost as if he's battling against my words, trying to physically push them from his ears.

"Even in her death, she saved me."

His gaze jumps to mine, jaw slack.

"Her death brought me to you."

"If you believe that, then stay with me." He leans forward. "Don't do this. It's not worth it."

He doesn't get it. I crawl off the bed to the floor in front of him. His eyes watch me warily as I push to sit on my knees between his open feet. "She was sliced from here"—I turn my head and run my finger from my ear to the corner of my mouth—"to here. Like they were trying to cut her jaw from her face."

He turns away. "Stop, I don't—"

"Look at me."

His eyes dart back to mine then follow my finger to my neck.

"Then to here." I trace my fingertip down the side of my breast, making X's at my nipples. "Here." I slide my finger down my sternum and across my stomach. "Here he criss-crossed." Back and forth I drag my finger across my bellybutton, lower to between my legs. "All the way down." I lower my hand until—

He catches my wrist hard and tosses my hand away. "Fuckin' enough! I got it." He rubs his eyes, as if the visual is playing in his head. "So, what? You plan on seducing this man to get him to spill?"

The simple answer is yes. It's worked before. The right combination of liquor and my body has loosened Hatchet's lips in the past. I know I can do it again. I have to. "It works." My cheeks heat with shame.

"Men aren't that stupid." He grimaces as if he hears the lie in his own words.

"Women have been using their bodies to get what they want since the beginning of time."

He doesn't respond.

"I'm begging you, Mason, to let me do this for her. I'm asking you to wait for me. Please, don't let this be good-bye."

"I can't. I . . ." He drops his head back and closes his eyes. "Knowing that you're giving your body to someone else, sharing yourself with another man, is more than I can handle, Trix."

"My body is just a shell. It's—"

"Nothing but skin and nerves. I know. You've made that clear." He laces his fingers behind his neck and drops his chin. "Fuck!"

"*Except* when I'm with you." I place my hand on his knee, and when he doesn't flinch away, I run it down the length of his thigh, scooting myself closer so that I'm between his cocked legs. "Every time, from our first kiss until now, my body has been yours. My heart, mind. God, Mase, it's like my very soul has belonged to you since day one." I run my palms up his bare chest to his shoulders until he finally looks at me. "You've seen me dance. You know what everyone else is seeing isn't really me. Only you have seen the real me, and I need you to know that you're the only man who ever will."

A long desperate sigh falls from his lips.

"I'm in love with you, Mason. You're the one I want. Forever." I slide my hands to his, which are fisted at his side. "Let me prove it to you."

His eyebrows drop low and he cocks his head. Pushing to stand, I pull him to his feet and lead him to stand at the foot of the bed. Without a doubt in my mind, I pull off the T-shirt and let it fall to the floor.

"I told you I was saving a part of me, a very private part of me for the man I wanted to spend the rest of my life with." I sit onto the bed, and he tracks every movement with flawless concentration. "This is my commitment to you."

I drop to my back and take a shuddered breath as I lay myself out before him and pray he doesn't reject me.

He's silent for a minute that slowly ticks into two. I squirm as his gaze glides over every inch of my body.

And here is the deciding moment, the choice I've laid out before him.

Choose me or walk away.

—

## MASON

It's so close to everything I've ever wanted. I have her love, her distant future, but not her loyalty. Not her body. Not her heart, at least, not completely.

Her desire to solve her sister's murder isn't what shocks me most; it's the irrational idea that she'll be able to do it on her own. And if she thinks I'm going to sit on the sidelines twiddling my thumbs while she throws herself and her naked body in front of a man who's not only unsafe but tied to a murderer, she's out of her motherfucking mind.

I put a knee to the bed between her open legs, their golden length spread out before me as a runway to the heaven that waits between them. My hands smooth over her ankles, up the thin contours of her shins to her knees. She takes a shaky breath and chews her lip.

"Are you scared?" My voice is low and harsh.

"Yes, only scared that you'll take what you want and walk away."

What I want. Ha. It's almost laughable. What I want is her heart, the one thing she doesn't seem able to give until she finishes what she started. "Do you trust me?"

"I love you. But I don't know if you love me, and that makes this scary."

Ah, so she thinks I'll take the one thing she's saved of herself and throw her away right after. *Trix, you don't know me at all.*

Rather than set her mind at ease, I continue to run my palms up her smooth thighs, pressing them apart farther and farther with each stroke until her knees are bent and her feet are flat on the bed.

My breath catches in my throat at the view before me: her lush little body open and practically trembling with anticipation while her chest rises and falls with quickened breath.

I lean over her, making sure to keep my hips high. I know how badly she needs to be touched, but by the time I get my mouth between her legs, I want her begging, desperate to be reminded of what we have.

"This"—I dip down to suck one firm nipple deep into my mouth—"and this"—I move to the other and do the same, this time clamping down with my teeth and leaving a mark—"are mine." It's animalistic, barbaric, but I need to mark her.

I dip to the hidden cavern beneath her breast and suck the tender flesh deep into my throat. She gasps, arching into my mouth. I suck her deeper and groan when she lifts her hips to rub against my dick. With a firm grip, I press her hips to the bed and release her to find a dark purple spot where my mouth once was.

"Tell me you're mine." I need to hear her confirmation.

She nods, her lips parted with her panting breath. "All yours."

I move to her face and drop a kiss to her forehead. "I want your mind"—I kiss her eyelids—"your dreams." I lick at the seam of her mouth. "No secrets between us."

"Mm-hmm." Her hands fist into my hair, but I pull them free and press them above her head with one hand.

I continue to kiss down her body, only freeing my hold on her hands when I'm at her ribcage. She keeps them high above her head as I explore the dips of her abdomen, the peaks of her hipbones, and the soft cushion of her inner thighs.

"Beatriks," I call up to her from my position between her legs.

She fidgets before me; her hips jack off the bed searching for contact.

"I want you to watch every fucking second. Don't take your eyes off me, understand?" Fire rages through my veins, and as much as I want to please her, I want to torture her for what she's asking of me. Push her to the brink of insanity so that she can get a sliver of an idea of how crazy she's making me.

She pushes up to her elbows, her eyes heavy with hunger as she pores over the view.

"Tell me you want this." I run my tongue along her inner thigh, moaning at the sweet scent of her skin. "Beg me for it." I switch to the other thigh, alternating between long drags of my tongue and deep bites that leave indentations. A roar threatens to burst from my chest at marking her skin, even if only temporarily. “I can’t hear you.” It’s the last chance she’ll get because after I take this from her there will be no turning back for me.

She whimpers as my lips inch closer to where she wants me. “I want this,” she says around a moan. “Please, I need you.”

With that, I incline my head and take the first sweet taste of her. I groan deep in my throat at the honeyed tang of her tender flesh. Her loud gasp is followed by a low rumble of satisfaction as she rolls her hips into my mouth.

My tongue floods with the luscious flavor so unique to Trix I can’t help but feel in this moment that it was created only for me. I nip at her most sensitive parts, alternating between short flicks of my tongue and long, deep swipes.

Time passes and I’m completely lost to her body. Every sound, every muscle that tenses I can see and feel beneath my hands. I say a silent prayer, knowing I’m the luckiest bastard alive to have this, accepting this gift from a woman who’s held onto it for so long. And now it’s mine. She’s offered it to me along with her love, and I will hoard it as long as she’ll allow.

“This is . . . I’m . . .” She shakes her head, unable to complete a sentence before I sense the pulsing of her impending orgasm.

I add two fingers, and she drops back to the bed. Her back bows as she presses harder into my mouth and cries out my name.

So fucking perfect.

A guttural sigh rolls from what seems like her toes to her lips, and she throbs against my mouth. I lap my tongue over her, sucking and licking until her legs fall open and her muscles loosen.

“Mase, I’m . . .” She shakes her head again.

I move from between her legs up her body, this time allowing my weight to press down on her so she can feel the full extent of what she does to me.

Before I kiss her, I notice a small tear escape her eye.

Please, tell me she doesn't regret what she's given me. "Baby, why?"

She wipes it away and flashes a tiny grin. "I'm fine. I just . . . I love you."

I dip down and place a kiss on her lips, loving the way she darts out her tongue to taste herself from my mouth. My hips flex, and she pulls her mouth from mine before lifting her leg to hook her toes into the elastic of my shorts.

"Off."

Together we push my shorts down my legs, and I kick them to the floor, re-settling myself between her warm and welcoming thighs.

I take in her face, cheeks pink, lips plump, and eyelids heavy. My fingers trace her hairline down to her jaw and over her lower lip. "You're so beautiful, Beatriks."

She grips my biceps and wiggles beneath me to take me into her body.

"Wait, baby." I lean over to the bedside table, but her legs wrap around my waist.

"No, don't. I'm on the pill." Her gaze falls to my neck and she blushes. "I'm clean, I promise. I know you have no reason to trust me, but—"

My mouth covers hers and she sucks my tongue so hard I almost explode. "I'm clean too." I breathe before she takes my mouth again. "I trust you."

I push up on my elbows and align our bodies, dizzy from my racing pulse. I groan and drop my forehead to hers at the wet warmth that envelops me. My chest throbs with all the things I'm feeling; all the conflicting emotions do battle within my head.

Whether I agree to her ridiculous plan or not, she's going to move forward and I'll have to live knowing she's giving this to someone else. Sharing what I've claimed as my own with a man who'll never love her as much as I do.

My blood fires with the unfairness of it all, and I thrust hard into her. She cries out and presses her head back into the pillow. If she loves me, really loves me, how can she expect this of me? I power into her again and her body lurches beneath me. No male in his right mind would knowingly allow his woman to be with someone else. My hips flex hard, fast, half loving and half hate-fucking. Her mouth drops open with the power of my thrusts. I want her to feel me between her legs every time she looks at another man, remember that I'm the only one who owns her heart, the only man she's ever given every part of her body to.

I want her to hurt as bad as she's hurting me.

I pull back and flip her to her belly then grip her hips to pull her ass up to take me again. A growl rips from my chest as I enter her from behind, deeper this time, and she moans into the sheets.

Over and over I slam into her body, punishing her and hating myself for it. Hating her for making me love her and then taking herself away. Fury and lust shred through my veins until my muscles tense. My thighs tighten as every plunge seems to bring me deeper. Fuck, this woman, I despise what she's doing and love every square inch of her.

She's loyal to a fault, honest, viciously protective, and fuck, but I love her fight.

Love her.

So balls deep in love with her.

Blinding white light flashes behind my eyelids. I drop to her back, crushing her beneath my weight as my orgasm overtakes me. My teeth sink softly into her shoulder and an almost inhuman sound vibrates in the back of my throat. Sweat covers my body as my release seems unending. I fight to catch my breath, the muscles in my back uncoil, and I drift in a post-orgasmic haze.

I roll to my back, my mind replaying what just happened in agonizing detail. It was too rough, too angry. I'd lost control. I throw my forearm over my eyes. I can't look at her, can't stand to see the disappointment in—

Her soft body curls up to my side.

What?

Her hand pushes my forearm off my face until my view is filled with her pinched expression. "What are you thinking about?"

I exhale hard and shake my head. "I'm sorry. I shouldn't have . . ." Fucked you like that. I'm an asshole.

She pushes a few strands of hair off my forehead. "I understand." Her eyes drop to my chest. "I knew by telling you how I felt, giving you the only piece of me I had left to give, I was taking a chance. If you don't feel the same w—"

I shove my fingers into her hair and fist hard enough to sting. Her eyes widen and dart to mine.

"Listen and listen fucking good, Beatriks Langley."

She blinks, and I can see fear flicker behind her eyes.

I pull her face so close to mine that I can feel her breath. "I'm so in love with you I don't know my own fuckin' name anymore. There's not a thing in the world I wouldn't break my back to give you. If it meant making you happy, I'd give up everything I have, everything I've worked for. You name it; it's yours."

She attempts to shake her head, but my firm hold doesn't allow her much movement. "Do you . . .? Are you saying you'll—?"

"I'm pissed as hell. Madder than I've ever been in my entire life about what you're asking me to do, but there's no way I can say no to you. I'm angry, hell, I'm fucking furious at you, but I love you more."

A single tear drips from her eye and lands on my lip. I lick it off, tasting the salt of her revenge, the bitterness of the hard decisions she's had to make, the heat of her sacrifices. I'll be damned if I'm capable of letting her go now.

She sniffs. "I love you." Another tear threatens to fall, but before it can, I pull her to my lips and kiss it away, along with every one that comes after.

"Love you too, baby." Even though loving her is probably going to kill me.

# TWENTY-EIGHT

## TRIX

"Mmmm." The sound of my own pleasure wakes me from a deep sleep. I blink open my eyes against the force of arousal that demands they slam shut.

I dip my chin, peering between my breasts and down my belly to see a mop of blond hair between my legs and two strong hands gripping my thighs.

Mason.

My eyes burn with unshed tears as I watch him devour me. Slow and deliberate swirls of his tongue and strong lips pull against my overheated flesh.

I should've known this would happen: that giving him this part of me would only open me up to falling even deeper in love with him.

I gasp as he buries his fingers inside me, growling against me in a way that vibrates my most sensitive parts. My fingers dig into the bed, searching for something to hold onto so this orgasm doesn't launch me through the air. As hard as I try to stay grounded, the wave hits with a force that sends my head to the pillow and my back bowing. Stars explode in my vision as he continues to feed and not let up even after my pulsing orgasm fades.

It's too much and not enough. I pull against his hair, rolling my hips in an attempt to get free or maybe get more. My head scrambles until it feels like it might combust.

"Mason."

Drunk with need, I roll my hips. He climbs up my body, placing his very naked and aroused self between my legs.

"Good morning."

"'Morning." I suck in a long breath as he enters me slowly until he's firmly seated inside me.

He offers his lips to me, and I greedily kiss him, tasting myself on his mouth. It doesn't seem like much, but it's as if the gesture is meant to remind me whom I belong to. "I think I like waking you up."

I nip at his bottom lip. "I think I like you waking me up."

He pulls almost all the way out, before moving back in, each time circling his hips to rub against me. I'm already so close and we've barely begun. Again, he continues in torturously slow glides back and forth, around and back, until I'm moving beneath him to go faster.

"Last night, I was too rough with you." His eyes never leave mine, and I don't miss the flicker of pain that passes behind them.

"No, you weren't. I want you to do it again." My cheeks heat at my honesty. The truth is I loved his anger. It felt similar to my own, something I could relate to.

"There'll be times for that"—he traces the line of my jaw to my lips with his own—"but now I want to make love to you."

"I've never been made love to before."

Don't cry, don't cry.

The corner of his mouth lifts, but only slightly. "You have, we just didn't have a name for it then."

I don't know who kissed whom first, but our mouths came together in perfect time as he loved me with his body. He took his time, making sure to hit every single spot that sent sparks across my skin. Just like the roll of the waves while sitting on the long board, he works himself over me in a steady but constant rhythm. Not sex or fucking, but a combining of souls for the singular purpose of communicating a tender adoration. Unconditional love.

A forever kind of love.

His jaw hardens, and his neck tenses as we slowly crawl towards release, together. Neither of us in a rush, we climb gradually, every deliberate stroke a step closer to what's sure to be an earth-shattering orgasm. Tenderness shines through his eyes as he watches me, and my throat swells as I fight back the tears.

It doesn't take a mind reader to know his thoughts are on us, on all that's going to happen once we leave the safety of this bed. The protection of this moment. With a force unequal to any I've felt before, my body detonates. My nails bite into his biceps as I soundlessly cry out his name. My head swirls in a fog, and I grip him tighter through the aftershocks that wrack my limbs. He growls into my neck, his strokes still constant and controlled, but the sting of his teeth and heat that pours from his body, signal his release. He drops on top of me, not bothering to hold himself up and shield me from his weight.

I'm breathless, pressed deep into the mattress while he's buried inside me, and I've never felt safer or more taken care of, more connected to another human being.

He rolls off me, and I'm instantly slapped in the face with the loss of his presence and the harsh reality of what's to come.

This is good-bye. For now.

Fear grips me from within, and my muscles shake uncontrollably.

"Come here, baby. It's okay." He pulls me close, rolling to his side so that we're face-to-face. His glare burns into mine. "One day at a time. One minute at a time if you have to." He pulls my hands to his chest, holding them to his pounding heart. "No decision is permanent, except this one."

I nod and focus on how clear and determined he looks now. Nothing like the man I saw last night who was filled with doubt and anger.

"Whatever happens, you keep in contact with me at all times, understand? If I don't hear from you, I'm going after you."

"But—"

He shakes his head. "Nope. No buts. You're not in this alone. Not anymore."

Warmth overtakes me and I suck in a deep breath. All I've ever been in this is alone. But not now.

"Stay public. As much as you can, try to stay public. If you're forced to be alone with him, always have your phone."

I nod. "Okay."

He nods too. "Good." His eyes slam shut, and he brings my bunched hands to his mouth, kisses my knuckles then drops them back to press against his chest. When he opens his eyes, I cringe against the worry and pain reflected in them. "And please, if you can get out of, you know, if you can avoid—fuck!" He groans and shakes his head.

Sex. I get it.

I won't make him say it. "I will. I promise. Headache, period, whatever I have to do to get out of it, I promise I will."

He shakes his head, mouth twisted in a disgusted frown.

"Mason." I rest my forehead against his. "God, I'm going to hate every second of this. Being away from you will kill me. I'll do this quickly. Knowing that Lana's vindication and you, the two most important things to me in this entire world, are waiting for me on the other end, I'll make the most of every second and see this through. I promise."

He rolls his head back and forth against mine, growling. "I can't fucking believe I'm letting this happen."

"I can."

He blinks open his eyes.

"You have a good heart, Mase."

"Fuck, don't say that. I'm allowing the woman I love to be in the arms of some sick fuck. I deserve to be castrated for that!"

"Stop it. No more looking back. It's only forward for us. Forward and forever." I grip his face, forcing him to look at me. "Promise me we're never saying good-bye."

I nods. "I promise."

"Say it." I need to hear it.

"I'll never say good-bye."

"And neither will I. Never. No good-byes. Forward and forever."

A weak smile touches his lips. "The two effs."

"Well, for us there will be three." I wink with the hope of lightening his mood.

"You have a dirty mind, Miss Trixy." He pulls at my lower lip with his thumb, and I suck it deep into my mouth, eliciting a growl from his chest.

"We have a few more hours before I need to head home. I'll show you how dirty my mind is."

His expression sobers, and he places a small kiss on my lips. "Promise me you'll stay safe."

"For you? Always."

# TWENTY-NINE

## MASON

Three days feels like three months.

So far, Trix is no closer to finding her sister's killer. She's kept me informed through short phone calls and texts, even managed to come over for a few hours before she went to work yesterday, and for that I'm grateful. This guy she calls Hatchet has been MIA since the night Trix showed up drunk on my doorstep.

Although it would break her heart, I'm praying the fucker never shows his face again.

I flex my sore fists, reveling in the ache of my joints as I gear up for a session with the heavy bags. There's something to be said for being hate-fueled and resentful. These last few days in the gym have been some of my best. Amazing what happens when I paint a faceless man who'll have his hands all over my woman on every fucking thing I punch.

After five minutes of jump rope, I throw my first punch, feeling stronger than I did even yesterday. Blow after blow, I imagine the man who will be seduced into giving up information by *my* woman.

Fuck, fuck, fuck!

NOFX's "Stickin' in my Eye" bleeds in my ears; the beat pushes me harder as I throw all my weight behind each hit. Sweat blurs my vision, but doesn't slow my pace. With every strike, I throw up a silent prayer that Trix's mission goes down in flames and we can return to where we were the night we got came back from San Jose. I throttle the bag with a series of jabs when NOFX fades to the pinging of my ringtone.

I rip my phone from the elastic case at my bicep. Drake's name flashes on the screen.

Dammit.

I hit "accept," panting into the speaker hanging from my earbuds. "Drake, man . . . what's up?"

"Whoa . . ." He chuckles. "You fuckin'?"

I work to catch my breath. "Shut up, asshole."

"Needta' finish up? Call me back?" He laughs. "Hate to be the cause of a nasty case of blue balls, brother."

Dumbass.

"I'm *training*." I pull my bandana off my head and wipe my face. "You call for a reason?"

"I did. I'll be in town this weekend. My dad's putting us up at Caesars again."

My pulse pounds in my ears and my muscles tense. "Business?"

He's silent for a few seconds then clears his throat. "Yeah."

I drop my chin and dig my fingers into my eyes. "Drake."

"It's not what you think."

Like I don't have enough shit to deal with right now, Trix and her renegade mission, and now my hard-headed brother.

"Not bailing you out again. I'm done. This last time could've totally fucked me."

"I know. I know. Listen. I need you to come by Saturday night."

"*No*. Wait. Scratch that. *Fuck* no." I pace and run a hand through my sweaty hair.

"It's not me, man; it's my dad. He's asking for you."

"Yeah, well you can tell him to kiss my ass." I've been more of a father to D than his biological father ever was. "He thinks he can snap and have me jumping, he's out of his motherfucking mind."

Drake blows out a long, frustrated-sounding breath. "Don't make him come after you, Mase. Puts me in a shitty-ass position. Just come by, see what he has to say."

"No, I told you—"

"He knows I want out."

I freeze my pacing and stare blindly at the heavy bag. "You told him you're done?"

"Yeah. Thing is . . . fuck . . . Jessica's pregnant."

I drop to the bench and lean back against the concrete wall. "Oh shit."

"Exactly, oh shit."

"Are you . . .? I mean, is it—"

"Mine?"

I didn't want to just come out and ask, but after what I saw last weekend I have to wonder.

"She messes with me, but she's a good girl. I don't think she'd fuck anyone else." He groans. "Hell, I don't know what I know. No way I'm asking her now though. She hasn't stopped crying in days."

"So you're pulling out of your dad's shit to . . . what?"

"What do you mean to what? Take care of my kid, my woman, what the fuck you think?" It's only natural for me to doubt his intentions. The guy fucks up things without even trying.

"Good to hear, D. Really. So, this Vegas thing, is it like a one last hurrah and then you're out?"

"Something like that." He mumbles something I can't make out. "Shit. I gotta run. Saturday night. I'll see you there."

"I can't guarantee—" The line goes dead.

Fuck.

I pop my phone back into my armband and take a swig of water. This is good. Drake's moving towards cutting ties with his dad, and although getting his girl pregnant wasn't in the plan, it's helping him to man up. Can't be angry about that.

I'll go to Caesars Saturday night and see what his dickhead dad has to say; then hopefully Drake can put all this shit behind him for good.

---

## TRIX

Midnight.

Officially five days now since Hatch walked out of my life. Again.

Every day that comes and goes feels like fingernails slowly raking across my skin, digging deeper each pass they make, elevating my irritation. Hours, minutes, seconds tick by and all of it is wasted time. Time I could be spending with Mason.

A pathetic growl gurgles in my throat as I toss the contents of my dresser drawers onto my bed. Organizing has always managed to calm me when I'm angry. Sorting through my belongings, tossing the old shit, and arranging the still wearable.

I separate my shorts between casual and dress-up, throwing some of the worn pairs to the floor with more force than necessary.

How long will I wait before I give up and resume my life?

I told myself a few weeks, but here I am almost a week into it, and I'm ready to give up and launch myself into Mason's arms for good.

Svetlana's gone and Mason's here, alive and wanting me, just as much as I want him. Neither of us deserves this torture.

As if summoned from my thoughts, I find a photo beneath my clothes pile. Bright shining eyes and her barely there smile. Svetlana.

I flip it over in my hand. It's her passport photo.

She had plans to do missionary work with my dad at the orphanage we were adopted from in Russia. She'd had her photo taken, and days after she died, it was delivered in the mail.

Giving hope to all those children in the orphanage who feel completely forgotten was something she'd talked about for years. The last known picture of her is a sick stab to the heart.

Dammit. The senselessness of it all racks my body, and I drop to my knees at my bedside, resting my forehead against the mattress and pressing the photo to my chest.

"Why, God? Why did you have to take her? You had plans for her, plans that were bigger and better. I know you're capable of using even the worst tragedies for good, but how, God? How can this ever be made good?"

I wait, listening with not my ears but with my heart. Waiting for an answer, a divine intercession that would throw me back and help me to see the purpose to it all.

But I get nothing.

"So that's it, huh? Maybe some people aren't worth your help." Anger boils deep in my chest. I push up off the ground with my fists balled, crunching Lana's picture in my palm. Not that it matters. She wasn't important enough to God for him to save her. I'm not important enough for him to give me direction in all this.

With a primal roar, I lash out, sweeping my arm over my bed and sending my neat piles of clothes sailing across the room. Why can't this just be over? A deep sob forms in my chest, but I refuse to give into my weakness. Sadness is pointless. Anger is motivating.

The low growl of a motorcycle filters in from my open bedroom window. Listening hard, I concentrate as the rumble grows louder and louder. I wait for the sound to reach my driveway, fully expecting it to continue by as the rest of them have these last five days.

But this one doesn't.

Holy shit, he's here.

Panicked, I race to the mirror, pinch my cheeks, and practice my fake look of indifference. Good enough.

I race to the front door just as I hear the motorcycle engine cut off. Crap, I can't fling the door open right when he walks up. I scurry to my couch, flipping on the TV and trying to look casual just as the knock comes at the front door.

"Hold on." With a deep breath, I force my feet to drag. "I'm coming."

When I open the door, my heart jumps and quickly sinks. It's Hatch.

I yawn and try to act casual. "Hey, you're in town."

His hair is pulled back in a low ponytail, and he leans against the doorframe. "You done bein' a bitch?" His voice sounds like jagged rocks over broken glass, but he flashes a teasing smile.

I cock my head and force myself to smile. "Am I ever done being a bitch?"

"Good point." He doesn't wait to be invited in, just moves past me and into the kitchen. "I need a beer."

Hoping he'd show up eventually, I've kept my fridge stocked with his favorite all-American brand, bottles, extra cold the way he likes it. I close the door and move to the couch, trying to remember how the old me—the me who hadn't completely given her heart away to another man—would've acted.

He's right behind me and drops to the couch, popping off the cap to his beer and tossing it to the coffee table. The familiar smell of Hatch—wind, desert dirt, leather, and a hint of sweat—permeates the air. His heavy boots clunk hard to the table as he reclines and the creaking of his cut as he makes himself comfortable are so opposite of Mason.

My Mason is smooth. Everything he does is like liquid, clean and fresh, powerful, beautiful, and peaceful on the surface that covers the raw danger that stirs underneath. Just like the ocean.

"The fuck you watchin' here, Trix?"

My eyes dart to Hatch, who has his glare aimed at the television. "Oh, this?" I grab the remote, hit a few buttons to turn off the DVD player, and put on the racy cable TV network Hatch loves. "The Lion King. There was nothing on, so . . ."

Fuck. The old me never would watch Disney movies with Hatch around. The last thing I need is for him to get inside my head, and even though the DVDs are on display, he's never taken an interest in them.

Never taken an interest in me outside of blow jobs and sex.

Unlike Mason.

My chest warms, and a tiny grin curls my lips before I can wipe it away.

The sooner I get down to it, the sooner I can get back to him. I turn to face Hatch and fold my legs beneath me. "So, how long are you in town for?"

His eyes dart to me, rake over my bare legs to my cut offs and then to my chest. I rejoice in silent victory that I'm wearing a bra beneath the threadbare tank. Hatch seems to notice then slides his intrusive gaze back to the TV and shrugs. "Got a little business here this weekend. Then I'll be gone."

I chew my bottom lip, wondering how to bring up some deeper conversation without being completely obvious. I'm about to open my mouth when he turns his eyes to me.

"You busy this weekend? I might be able to use you and a couple of the girls tomorrow night."

"Maybe." I shrug one shoulder. "You have *associates*"—I use air quotes and lift a brow—"who need entertaining?"

He reaches out and fists a handful of my hair, tugging my face to his. "Fuck, you're cute."

I do my best to bat my eyelashes and play coy even though I'd rather spit in his face.

He presses a quick and bristly kiss to my lips. "Yeah, babe. *Associates.* Important ones. You game? They pay well."

I swallow hard, my eyes burning with the realization that I've just officially cheated on Mason with that kiss, but I force all that back. "Saturday nights at the club are busy. I have to work."

"I'll make a call. Your boss has never been able to say no to cold hard cash."

His grip is still tight in my hair. I pull against him, only to get a tug back, reminding me who's in charge.

"Sounds fun. You know I've never been one to turn down a well-paying job." I lick my lips as my nerves get the best of me. It's not that I think Hatch will hurt me. God knows he's had plenty of opportunity to do so and hasn't. But a game that was once easy for me to play has now become complicated as every choice I make revolves around Mason.

He releases my hair and runs the rough pad of his thumb along my jaw. "Been a long time since I've had that mouth."

Fuck! No, no, no. I roll my lips between my teeth in an attempt to keep them away from him, but his eyes flare with hunger.

My body revolts and I sit back, putting distance between us. He glares, suspicion registering in his expression. Dammit, I'm losing him!

"It's been a long week. I could use a few drinks." I give him my most seductive smile, and his wariness morphs back to desire.

"Grab the six-pack and the Jager. I like how your mouth gets sloppy when you're drunk on that shit."

My stomach twists, but I wink and move toward the kitchen as a plan forms in my head. Jager will be perfect. I'll be puking before the night's through and sleeping in the bathroom.

With the door locked.

# THIRTY

## MASON

I got out of bed on edge. My skin too tight, muscles coiled, and my head screaming.

Last night was the first night I didn't hear from Trix.

I checked my phone every fucking hour, only dozing off in thirty-minute sessions before jerking awake to check it again. And every time . . . nothing.

She warned me that this would happen. One day that fucker would roll back into town, and she'd text me to let me know, that is, unless he showed up unexpectedly and she couldn't. I've contemplated calling, blowing up her phone with messages, driving by her house, all the things I promised her I'd never do in this situation. I gave her my word that I wouldn't be a complication to her plan, a chink in her iron-clad mission. I'm re-thinking that. Big time.

I throw down the dregs of my protein shake and force myself to swallow, worry and anxiety taking up most of the space in my stomach.

She better fucking be okay.

I check my phone again and still nothing. It's six-thirty a.m. Maybe a quick drive by her house on the way to the training center will help to calm my nerves. Chances are I won't be able to tell if either of them is there, but it's worth a try if it means setting my nerves at ease. Hell, it's all I've got!

Today is Friday and she works tonight, so there's always a swing by Zeus's later to make sure her ass is safe there. I brace my weight on the counter in my kitchen and blow out a long breath. Never thought I'd see the day where I'd be hoping my girl showed up for her shift at the strip club.

Never thought I'd all but give her permission to date another guy either.

Fuckin' hell. Why did I do that?

As soon as the question filters though my head, so does the answer.

She gave me no choice.

In order to be with her, I had to agree to this. Otherwise, I'd be standing here doing the exact same fucking thing, but she wouldn't be keeping me in the know.

Lose-fucking-lose situation if I've ever seen one.

My phone rings, and the speed in which I grab that shit, press "accept" and press it to my ear shocks even me.

"Hello?"

"Hey, bro."

"Drake." Disappointment settles in my gut, heavy and annoying. "What's up?"

"Listen, man . . . I have a favor to ask."

"No."

"Dude, fuck off. I haven't even asked yet."

"Don't need to. I'm sure the answer's no."

"Whatever. Listen. I need you to let us crash with you this weekend."

"What? Okay, you're right. I take back my 'no' because the answer to that is 'hell motherfuckin' no.' No way. Uh-uh." I shake my head as if he can see me. "Nope. No."

"You finished?" He sounds bored.

"If you heard me say no and don't plan on driving that shit home a hundred million times until I concede, then, yeah, I'm finished."

"It's only for two nights."

"I don't have a spare bedroom, Drake. You think I want six fuckin' guys crashed all over my place? This isn't a damn hostel. No."

"It's for Jess."

Oh . . . well, fuck.

"I don't want to leave her in Santa Cruz. She's been . . . upset, and . . . I'm not headed to Vegas to party. I'm just going to meet with my dad and some of his crew, talk about getting out. I need to put Jess up somewhere she feels safe, and shoving her in a damn hotel room in Vegas ain't it."

"Gotta say I'm semi-impressed that you're finally takin' care of your girl."

"So that's a yes?"

"Yeah, you two can have the bedroom. I'll crash on the couch. Only two nights, right? No plans on an extended stay?"

"Nah, we have a doctor's appointment on Monday for the baby."

Damn, I almost want to make some wisecrack about the grown-up on the phone, but something about the tension in his voice tells me he's probably not in the best mood for jokes.

"Alright. I'll leave a key under the mat. You remember where my place is?"

"Yeah."

"I'm training 'til late. Have something I need to do tonight. Tell Jess to make herself at home."

"Sweet, bro. Thanks."

We disconnect after grunted good-byes, and I throw some clean sheets on the bed and pull out some fresh towels before snagging my keys to head out.

There's a little part of me that's looking forward to Drake and Jess staying for the weekend. At least it'll distract me from worrying about Trix. Ah, who the fuck am I kidding?

—

## TRIX

A firm grip on my shoulder shakes my body. "Trix." Another shake. "Babe, wake the fuck up." There's tension or anger in the voice that I immediately identify as male.

And not Mason.

Sadness washes over my body, leaving me heavy with an ache in my chest. I groan and bat at the hand that will not let up its grip. My mind settles back into my head, and I instantly regret it as the throbbing pain between my temples roars.

Hatch.

Did we . . .? I take quick stock of my clothes, the aches and pains in my body being in my stomach, neck, and head. If it didn't hurt so bad to do so, I'd smile at how well my plan to get drunk and pass out in the bathroom worked.

"Trix, come on. Wake—"

"Stop—*aargh!*" I grip the sides of my head and curl into the fetal position on the hard floor. "My head. Shhh."

"I'm outta here. I left the shit about tomorrow night on your dresser." His voice is farther away, as if he went from crouching beside me to standing up. "Bring Angel and that other chick, the redhead." The sound of a fast-flowing stream of liquid hitting water permeates the air. "These guys have cash, high-roller types. Dress to impress. They don't—"

"Are you *peeing!*?" I curl up into a tighter ball, as if the act could protect me from Hatch's lack of respect for my personal space.

He groans, low and raspy. "Didn't give me much choice, babe. Tried to get you up."

"Ewww, get out—*ugh!* Stop making me yell." I dig my fists into my eyes and whimper. "Fuck."

He zips up his fly and the toilet flushes. "You strapped one on last night. Not shocked you feel like shit today."

"Stop. Talking."

He grips my shoulders, rolling me to my back, and sets me on my butt. My brain feels like it should leak out my ears at any minute, and I groan as the room sways. He dips to meet my gaze. "Anything you wanna tell me, Trix?"

What a strange thing to ask? I blink, trying to figure out what the hell he's getting at. "Um . . . no?"

"You sure 'bout that? I'm giving you a chance to come clean." He holds up a finger. "One chance."

Oh shit, he must know about Mason. I stretch my legs out, feeling for my phone without making it too obvious. No phone. Dammit. "I don't know, Hatch. I mean . . . I'm sure there's a lot we haven't talked about."

"You stickin' with that?" He lifts his eyebrows, giving me a chance to fess up.

"You do realize making me think this hard is excruciatingly painful, right?" I close one eye and look at him. "Are you trying to hurt me?"

I expect him to laugh or at the very least crack a smile, but he doesn't. He stands and walks away. "See ya tomorrow," he calls out just before the sound of the front door closes.

What the hell brought that on? I deleted all Mason's messages on my phone, so if Hatch did snoop, he'd only read one that must've come in recently. I drop my head into my hands. If that's what all this is about, Hatch can get over it. We've always had a no-strings relationship that's gone both ways. No way he's allowed to get jealous now.

Pushing up to standing, I stumble off-balance, bracing myself with my elbows on the sink. My mouth is dry, and as much as I want water, just the thought of drinking has my stomach protesting. I breathe through a fresh wave of nausea, remembering that I never did end up tossing up my liquor last night. Too bad. Probably would've felt better if I had.

Hatch and I drank until . . . fuck, I have no idea. We talked, and with the exception of a few stolen kisses, I managed to get too drunk and avoided having to cheat on Mason.

Memories from the night trickle back, one at a time. He told me about Mexico, that he was on the run for killing a couple of guys who got too deep in MC business. He swears he didn't do it, not that it matters now. A rival MC wasn't happy about Hatch's men offing their members and went after Hatch. I guess the rival MC ended up with an indictment and several mysterious deaths. So things mellowed out. Hatch came home.

I'd brought up the man he started to tell me about before he left—the one who he said, "cut women up for fun." He'd remembered telling me about him, admitted the dude is bad news, but didn't give me anything else.

At least he's back to talking, and I seem to be on the right track. Getting in with Hatch and his associates can only bring me closer to finding out who this guy is, and tonight's party is the perfect opportunity to do that.

I splash some cold water on my face and pull two pain relievers from the cabinet, washing them down with a palm full of tap water. I never did text Mason last night, but by the time Hatch showed up, I'm sure Mase was already sound asleep. If he tried to contact me this morning . . . A red flag fires in my head. That would explain Hatch's interrogation. What did Mason say that Hatch read?

Unease crawls through me as I search out my phone. Last time I had it . . . I close my eyes and concentrate, pushing through my painful headache and focusing on what I was doing when Hatch showed up.

Sorting my drawers. I push from the sink and head to my room.

My bed is still strewn with clothes, Hatch most likely slept on the couch. I run my hands through and beneath everything, searching for my phone, when my fingers brush across a photo, slicing into my skin.

"Ouch!" I pull my hand out, sucking on the thin line of blood from the paper cut. Damn, that hurts.

I shove my uninjured hand into the pile and pull out the photo of my brothers and sisters and me. I grin at my Mickey Mouse sweatshirt and Mason's response to my Disney obsession.

Right, Mason. I need to find my phone. I search my pocket. "Swore it was there . . ."

I race out to the living room, the back patio, and even pull all the cushions off the couch, but it's gone. Nowhere to be found.

What the fuck? Where is it?

I find my charger in the kitchen and head back to my room. Sitting on my dresser is my phone with a slip of paper beneath it. Scrawled in barely legible writing is *Car will pick you up at nine. Dress fuckable.*

Charming. I shake my head and go to read whatever is on my phone that got Hatch's hackles up. Dead battery. I move to the kitchen, plug in my phone, and wait for it to get enough juice to power up.

No new texts. Hm . . . then what the hell did Hatch mean?

I hit Mason's contact.

It rings and I check the clock. It's almost noon. I'm sure he's working. His voicemail picks up, and I close my eyes, allowing the sound of his recorded voice to soothe my racing heart and aching head.

*Beeeeeeep!*

"Hey, Mase, it's me. Sorry I didn't text you last night, but . . . he's back." My lips pinch together, almost as if I'm waiting for him to get angry, even knowing this is a one-sided conversation. "Don't worry. I'm still *only* yours." God, I want to see him. Fall into his arms until I feel better. But I can't. I'm too close now. "I love you."

I end the call and then move back to the bathroom to take a shower. I have to be to work by six. I have only nine hours to revamp my plan to get information. Getting him drunk and talking isn't working, but maybe the right combination of biker buddies and a whole hell of a lot of booze will do the trick. I'll try just about anything at this point because I'm ready get what I need and go back to Mason.

---

## MASON

The sun is almost down by the time I head out of the training center for home. I think Rex and I set a damn record for longest sparring session. Usually I don't train this hard on Saturday, but with Trix tied up and my brother and Jessica taking up most of my place, I need to be gone and keep myself busy.

I drove by Zeus's last night around seven and saw her car in the lot. It was near torture knowing that she was just inside, separated from me by a wall of brick and mortar while men, possibly even this Hatchet guy, were in there enjoying my woman's body. I could've put a hole through my damn dashboard, but, instead, drove up to our spot in the mountains and lay in the bed of my truck, thinking about her.

When it was quiet and I was left to nothing except my own thoughts and the infinite stars, I prayed. I've never been a religious guy, but Trix is rubbing off on me. Either that or I'm desperate with nowhere else to turn. Hell, I'd do anything if it keeps her safe. Including praying to a God I'm only now starting to believe in.

I pull out my phone to call Drake, but notice I have one new voicemail. How the fuck did I miss that?

I freeze in the parking lot, halfway to my car, when I hear her voice.

"He's back. Don't worry. I'm still only yours. I love you."

"Fuck!" I speed walk to my truck, throw my shit in the back, and peel out of the lot toward her house. Deep inside, I know I could be fucking up all her plans, but hearing those three words lights a fire in my chest. I need to touch her, to lay my hands on her, feel her warm skin and her beating heart behind her ribs to know she's okay.

It doesn't take long before I'm parked in her driveway next to a gray Smart car in the driveway. Not what I'd expect a guy named Hatchet to drive, so I jog to the door and pound hard.

The door swings open to reveal a smaller brunette. She's dressed in conservative pants and a professional-looking button-up collared shirt, untucked. "Can I help you?"

A man comes up behind her. He's average height, dressed similarly, with glasses and a frown. "Kim, you know this guy?" He glares at me.

"I'm looking for Trix. Is she here?"

Her eyes narrow. "And who're you?"

My chest warms at how protective Trix's roommate seems to be. "I'm her boyfriend." It's bold, but fuck it. It's the truth.

The brunette, Kim, shakes her head. "No, she's not. I'm pretty sure she's at work, but I don't know. We don't cross paths often."

Work. Of course. It's Saturday night. "Okay, right." I shake my head and step back. She's fine, at work. Safe. I force my pulse to slow. "Sorry to bother you."

"Wait." Kim holds up her hand and disappears back inside while her man watches me intently. When she comes back, she hands me a Zippo lighter with an eagle engraved on the side and a black Harley Davidson tee. "Are you looking for these?"

I flip the lighter over in my hand then shove both items back at her, fighting the urge to roar. "These aren't mine."

"Oh, oops." She flashes an embarrassed smile, hissing through her teeth. "I'm sorry. I thought . . . Never mind."

"No, thought what? What did you think?"

Her gaze darts to her boyfriend's and then back to mine. "Well, I mean you know Trix. She uh . . ." She chews on her lip.

"Guess you weren't here for the party last night?" Kim's boyfriend chimes in, a sympathetic smile plastered across his dorky face.

"No."

"I just assumed . . . wow." She rubs her forehead. "This is embarrassing."

"No, it's okay." It is so *not* fucking okay. "I knew she had a party."

I swallow hard and take another step back. Did he spend the night? Here. With her. I've never even spent the night here.

Without saying good-bye, I turn toward my truck, not moving nearly as quickly as I was when I got here.

Fine. He spent the night. But she said she's still mine, so no sex. Does that include her mouth on his—fuck, no. I can't go there. Not even in theory.

This is torture. Absolute fucking torture.

I growl and stifle the urge to put my fist through the window of my truck. How will we ever be able to survive this?

At this rate, we won't.

# THIRTY-ONE

## TRIX

Angel, Kayla and I pulled up to Caesars Palace with Santos in tow. Hatch was right. After a call to our boss and what I'm sure was a massive money exchange, we were cut from our shift early and picked up by a limo.

Memories from the last time I was here pierce me with regret, and I swallow the lump that forms in my throat. So much has changed since my first run-in with Mason. Walking through the giant doors into the casino, I'm not the same girl I was before he crashed into me.

Back then I was floating, unsure of what I wanted. And now, I'm dead set on my future. With this last obstacle keeping us apart, I plan on ending this as soon as possible and putting us both out of our misery.

"I can't believe how much this job is paying," Kayla whispers between Angel and me as we all follow Santos to whatever room we're supposed to report to.

Angel rocks into my hip with hers. "Two grand each, plus tips, and you're still thinking of quitting?"

She lifts an eyebrow, daring me to say yes. "We could walk in on a bunch of asshole pervs. Would the two grand still be worth it?"

"Fuck yeah, it would." Kayla giggles at her own enthusiasm. "I've never made this kind of money without having to suck dick."

Angel cackles and gets a glare from Santos that says *High-class, ladies. Let's try to act like it.*

She leans into my shoulder. "What's his problem," she whispers so he won't hear. "He's been funky all night."

"He just needs to get laid." Kayla rolls her eyes as if the solution to all men's problems is just that easy.

The girls quietly giggle the rest of the walk to the room, while I steel myself and muster up courage for the night. Hatch will expect me to drink heavily and pay a lot of attention to the men he's trying to impress, I'm sure. It'll be difficult to get more information out of him, but if there's one thing I've learned about these parties, they're great for eavesdropping.

When powerful men get together, they're all so busy trying to out peacock the other they don't even consider the dancer rubbing her tits in their faces is listening to every word they speak.

Diversion by sexual persuasion. PI work at its finest.

We make a turn and stop at a set of double doors. Santos checks the number to his phone then puts it away to knock.

"Holy shit!" Kayla whisper yells. "This is a villa." Her wide eyes study the door. "I've always wanted to see the inside of one of—"

The door swings open, and a guy around my age stares openly at the three of us without greeting, completely ignoring Santos. Dark brown eyes peer out beneath his overgrown hair and rake along our bodies from feet to tits.

I throw a hand on my cocked hip. "You gonna let us in, cowboy?"

His lips curl into a crooked grin. "Hatch!" He calls over his shoulder.

Hatch appears at the mouth of the marble foyer. He barely spares us a glance, and if I'm not mistaken, it looks like he avoided looking at me altogether. "Yep, let 'em in." He disappears deeper into the place or, rather, palace.

The ceilings are taller than I've ever seen in one of these suites, and everything is decorated with an old-world flare that screams rich and pretentious. We stick close to Santos as he follows the younger guy down a long hallway and into a room. There's a pool table and a bar, similar to the last place, but through the patio doors are a pool, spa, fire pit, and another bar that, even from this distance, I can see is fully stocked.

"Who the hell has this kind of money?" Angel whispers form behind me.

"No clue." But certainly not Hatch.

"They're in a meeting. Help yourself to the booze." The guy who answered the door doesn't look like anyone I'd ever seen hang around the MC guys. He's too clean. Too young.

Kayla busies herself behind the bar while I do a slow walk through the room. It's late, and yet we're the only ones here? I thought this was supposed to be a party. Unless there's a separate wing to this place where all the people are stashed . . . I wouldn't be surprised.

Kayla comes out, holding three drinks between her two hands. "Lemon drops!"

We all grab our shots, and with the lingering throb of a hangover, I choke it down.

"Let's play pool!" Angel says, and Santos starts to rack up the balls.

"I'll make more shots!" Kayla grabs my glass and heads back to the bar for round two, which, knowing her, will turn into three and four.

The guy who let us in moves back to a room at the far end of the villa, turns his back to the door, and stands like a guard.

Ah, so that's where all the people are. Who the hell is behind that door and what are they talking about that's so important it takes a guard to protect it?

Another drink is shoved into my hand, and I throw it back, this one easier than the first. "One more."

Kayla squeals and heads back to the bar while Angel takes her first shot at the pool table.

I don't know what's going on here tonight, but something tells me whatever it is could bring me closer to finding Lana's killer.

And back to Mason.

## MASON

"You sure you'll be okay?"

Jessica's plopped on my couch beneath a blanket with the remote in one hand and a saltine cracker she's been nibbling on in the other. "How long will you guys be gone?"

Fuck, not any longer than we have to be. "I'll get him home as soon as I can."

She blinks rapidly, as if she's fighting tears. "Do you think . . .?" She swallows hard. "Do you think he'll let him go?"

Drake's dad let him out of the family business? Funny, the asshole never acknowledged Drake as *being* family until the guy was old enough to do is his bidding. Prick.

I blow out a long breath and drop to the couch at her feet. "I have no idea. But I'm going to try my hardest to convince him to."

She studies the glowing screen of the TV. "The pregnancy changes everything."

"The *baby* changes everything, yes."

Her tired eyes meet mine and her bottom lip quivers.

"It's okay, Jess. You just worry about taking care of yourself. There's food in the fridge. Help yourself to whatever you want and try to get some sleep."

Drake's heavy footfalls sound as he barrels down the stairs, freshly showered. "Let's get this shit over with."

I nod to Jessica, and her gaze slides to my brother. "Be careful. Promise me you'll be careful, Dr—"

Her words are cut off as my brother presses a kiss to her lips, cupping her jaw with a tenderness I've never seen between them before. I push up and move to the kitchen to give them some privacy.

"I'm not giving up on us, Jess. Not you or our baby, understand?"

She mumbles something I can't hear.

"We'll get back as soon as we can." The sound of him kissing her mixes with the sound of her sniffing back tears.

I don't know what Drake's dad has planned for us tonight, but my guess is it'll be nothing more than a stern talking to about me staying out of Drake's life, keeping my mouth shut about what I've seen, and Drake trying to convince the man that his baby is worth him letting him go for.

I've always known D's dad had no soul. I only hope he's finally grown one. If not, Drake's fucked.

—

"This is it." Drake nods toward the huge doors to a fancy-assed suite of some kind.

Music filters through the doors, hard-hitting bass that would rattle the fuckers if they weren't made of solid wood.

He hits the glowing orange doorbell, opting out of a simple knock, knowing it won't be heard over the music. Voices call out, and soon the locks click and the door cracks open to reveal a guy who's vaguely familiar. One of Drake's crew.

"Jase, man. What's up?" Drake shakes hands with the guy, and they pull together for quick back-slapping hug.

"Drake, glad you could make it." Jase opens the door wider to let us in.

"Like I had a choice?" Drake laughs, but there's little humor in it. "This is my brother, Mason."

I nod to Jase, and he doesn't offer to shake my hand, which is good. I'm not sure who's an enemy and who's a friend yet, but if this guy is on Drake's dad's crew, he's an enemy.

"Nice to meet you. You guys got here just in time." Jase bounces his eyebrows, and I deduct a few years off my original age estimation.

Fuck, these guys are recruiting high school kids. Great.

"My dad around?" Drake asks while Jase leads us through what looks more like a mansion than a damn hotel room.

"He's here. Been meeting privately with some of the guys, but my guess is they should be finishing up." Jase continues to head toward the direction of the music. Male voices blend with the occasional girls, no different from a typical Vegas party.

We turn the corner into a large living space filled with partygoers. I scan the area, noting the distinct mix of people. Most of the guys look similar to Drake or me, dressed in some variation of the west-coast semi-casual attire of loose-fitting plaid and Dickies. But the rest are distinctly different. Denim, leather, and in desperate need of a razor, bikers are sprinkled throughout the room.

It's a damn sausage party in this place, although there are women, but they're heavily outnumbered. And most of them seem to be of the *working* variety. A few lean in to men and talk close, and there's another moving to the music and—holy fuck.

Strippers.

My eyes frantically bounce from a familiar redhead who's in nothing but her bra and underwear to a brunette who is topless and—dammit, it's Angel.

Hesitantly, I move deeper into the room to a back corner that's lined with couches and a small crowd of people. I hear my brother ask where I'm going but wave him off as my feet carry me forward.

The music throbs in my head, matching the pace of my pulse as I push through bodies. My steps falter, and I take in the view before me.

“No fucking way.” Drake’s voice mumbles at my shoulder, surprising me that he followed. “Is that . . .?”

Motherfucking shit.

“Trix.”

# THIRTY-TWO

## TRIX

Stupid fucking lemon drops. How many did I have? Five. No six? I retrace my steps and count in my mind while I rock my body against Hatch. He's basically ignoring me, talking to the guy next to him, but he keeps a firm grip on my hip to keep me from toppling over.

If only I could feel my legs, then maybe I'd be able to hold myself up from Hatch's lap rather than falling into it every time I try to dance. I didn't intend to drink so much, but the only way to tolerate what I have to do is to be inebriated. Not so much that I can't think, just enough to go numb.

I've been eavesdropping on every conversation I could get close enough to, and all I've learned is that this is some kind of celebratory party thrown by some bigwig dude who has his hands in more illegal shit than I could keep up with.

Apparently, his guys are going into business with Hatch's guys, and they've all gathered in Vegas to shake hands, toss out threats, and kiss each other's asses.

Nothing new. Total waste of my time. And damn, I'm so sick of being drunk.

As if on cue, my ankle twists, and I drop into Hatch's lap. A giggle bursts from my lips, and Hatch grabs my hair and pulls my face to his.

"If I didn't know better, I'd say you were looking for something." He flexes his hips, grinding his hard-on into my ass.

"No, Hatch." I pull my head for him to free my hair, and he does. "I'm not."

Whipping my hair around, I give him my back and sway my hips along with the music. If I weren't so drunk, I'd be asleep out of sheer boredom.

A firm grip pinches my thigh. "Ow!" I move to slap the hand away, but meet Hatch's glare that brooks no argument.

He pulls me to him, turns me around, and pulls me down to straddle his crotch. His hot breath pants in my ear. "You're pissin' me the fuck off." Strong fingers bite into my side.

I close my eyes, locking down my jaw to avoid whimpering. His hand tangles in my hair, burning my scalp. "You're . . . hurting me."

Where the hell did this come from?

He growls against my neck. "Lying little bitch." He emphasizes his words with a firm tug that wrenches my neck.

My heart races with panic.

"Get your fucking hands off her." The menacing voice stills my blood, and I shudder in Hatch's hold.

Anger melts from his expression and is replaced by something that almost looks like excitement. I follow the line of his gaze, and my heart slams so hard behind my ribs I fall back onto Hatch's chest.

Mason. And Drake? What . . .?

Oh my God, Mason. I scramble off Hatch's chest only to be slammed back down onto his lap, this time facing away from him. His arm comes around my waist, holding me to him. "If it ain't my two favorite brothers."

Mason doesn't take his eyes off me, pinning me with a glare that screams complete devastation.

Drake hooks Mason by the arm and tries to pull him away, but Mason shakes him off easily, stepping closer in the process. "I'm only gonna say it one more time. Let her go."

My spine goes straight, panic and fear making me want to run. I don't want Mason to see me like this, half naked and straddled over another man.

"Who the fuck invited you dipshits?" Hatch laughs then slides me off his lap to his side so that I'm pressed between him and the biker guy named Cage he was talking to.

How does Hatch know Mason? Why is he here?

Paralyzed with shock, my booze-fogged head tries to sort out what my eyes see, but I come up short, refusing to believe Mason would ever associate with guys like Hatch.

Drake moves forward, glaring. "Where's Elijah?"

"Lookin' for Daddy? How sweet." Hatch motions to the mysterious door at the opposite side of the room where people have been coming and going all night.

Mason shakes his head as if he has no idea he's acting out the one word his mind is probably screaming. A single tear builds and spills over my lower lid. Unable to hold his accusing glare for another second, I drop my head into my hands.

"Shit, you gonna toss?" Hatch's hand grips the back of my neck. "If so, get your ass to a bathroom."

I nod, feeling the acid from my stomach rush to my throat. He shoves me to standing and I take two quick steps, before my shoe snags on the carpet. I fall forward. My hands move to brace my fall, but two arms wrap around me, and I'm slammed into a wall of muscle.

The scent of fresh grass and honey surround me. "Mase—"

"Shh," he says into my hair while guiding me through a crowd.

"Stop, don't." I try to wiggle out of his hold, but his grip only tightens. "Let me go."

"Can't. Not until we talk." He guides me to a door and pushes me into a room, plunging me into darkness when the door closes.

I whirl around, searching for him, grateful when the light finally clicks on. I squint against brightness and turn to catch my reflection in the bathroom mirror. My top is made of fishnet, and my shorts cut up high on my ass, lacing up the back and leaving very little to the imagination. God, he must think the worst of me.

"What are you doing here?" I'd hoped the question would come out more accusatory than desperate. "Did you follow me?"

His jaw is clamped down in barely concealed rage. "That's your fucking source? That guy?" He practically spits the words through clenched teeth.

"Yes, but . . ." I blink up at him, thoughts whirling and trying to put the pieces together. "You know each other?"

He runs a hand through his shaggy hair, gripping it tight at his scalp. He's not denying it.

"Mason . . . how?"

He spears me with a glare that has me stumbling back into the wall. "This is over. Tonight."

"What? Why? You said—"

"That guy, your *boyfriend*—"

"He's not my boyfriend! You know why—"

"Almost killed my brother."

A gasp rushes from my lips. I press against my chest to push back the feeling that my heart is about to leap from my body. "How does Drake know Hatch? Wait, why are you guys even here?"

I shake my head as if somehow mixing up all the information will help it to finally align to make sense.

"It's over, Trix."

I jerk my eyes to his at the non-negotiable tone in his voice. "No, it's not."

He takes a step toward me, his icy-blue stare sending chills across my skin. "It is."

"How can you say that? He just came back."

He moves in more until the heat of his breath is on my lips. "It's over."

I grip his T-shirt, shoving him back and at the same time dragging him to me, needing my space as much as I need to crawl inside him. "It's not over yet. No!"

Lightning fast, he whirls me in front of him, pinning my hips to the counter top from behind me. He grips my chin, forcing my eyes to the mirror, and growls in my ear. "Look at yourself." His eyes are wild, glistening with rage, and his jaw throbs with tension.

Possessive, violent, and breathtaking.

He flexes his hips, pressing mine deeper into the granite vanity until the pinch of pain brings my eyes to the mirror.

My untamed hair is tossed around my shoulders, purple streaks like roadways across the net shirt that displays my naked breasts. I blink as my eyes travel lower. Mason's possessive hand is splayed across my bare stomach.

"Is this what you want, Trix?" He jerks my chin. "Look at yourself now. Is this what you want?"

I shiver in his hold, knowing the right answer is no, but holding onto the last thread of hope that I could help bring my family peace and Lana's killer to justice.

He tilts my face up, catching my eyes, and I fight the urge to recoil at the darkness I see in their depths. "I'm done with this. Not doing this anymore."

"What . . . why?"

His hand roams up, stopping at the tender underside of my breast. "Can only take so much. Thoughts of you with anyone else are fucking torture." He grazes my neck with his fingertips, brushing my hair back. "I know you're doing your best to respect what we have, but I don't give a fuck anymore. It's not enough." Hot, wet kisses paint my shoulder and neck until he nips at my ear. "You wanna know why this is over? Why I'm putting an end to this bullshit?" His breath beats heavy in my ear and he grips me hard. "Because you're mine." His declaration rumbles against my skin seconds before he turns me and drops to his knees.

My hands brace against the counter behind me as he throws one leg over his shoulder. Rough hands grip the thin material of my boy-shorts, pulling them aside.

"Mase . . ." My words dissolve on a moan as he buries his mouth between my legs.

He nips at me with his teeth, punishing me before slashing me with his tongue in a brutal and delicious assault. I lean back, leveraging as I dig my heel into his back, encouraging him to have his way. Opening myself to his fury. He growls against my over-sensitized flesh, whether in frustration or approval, I'm not sure. I'd take either.

He slides one big hand up the back of my shorts, grabbing my ass so hard it's sure to leave a mark. "It's over." His teeth graze, lips pull, and tongue lashes against me.

I roll my head on my shoulders, trying to stay upright and at the same time wanting to fall into the strength of his hands. *No, no, no . . . it's not over.* My voice can't find the words as his mouth has robbed me of breath.

So close, the sensations coil deep in my belly. I rock myself against him, joining in the rhythm as his hand at my ass guides me, rewarding me. Loving me even through his anger. Reminding me what I've given him and what he claimed. Proving that I'm his—that he owns not only my heart, but my body too.

I fist his hair, holding him exactly where I need him. My teeth sink into my bottom lip as my orgasm shreds through me, full-body and overpowering. My thighs quake, and a low whimper of ecstasy pours from my lips. Panting, I breathe through the aftershocks of my release. His tongue moves still, in lazy but purposeful stokes, coaxing me back to earth.

My heart beats to the chant of my soul: I'm his. I'm his. I'm his.

My ankle wobbles on my high heels, threatening to give out. He pulls back, hoisting me up to the countertop and settling between my legs. His arms wrap around me, and his lips kiss a pattern against my neck.

My eyes burn with tears. The combination of seeing him here, having a front row seat to his disappointment then his punishment, and having more questions than I have answers, only intensifies the pain.

A mournful cry falls from my lips as all the years of my searching seem to dissolve in this moment. I don't want to live with this hurt anymore. Don't want to push away my one chance at a happy life. Sick of selling my soul for hope that Lana's killer will be found, I'm tired of pushing Mason away.

"Beatriks, baby . . ." He smooths my hair off my face. "You gave yourself to me, and now it's my responsibility to keep you safe. Those guys, *Hatch*, they're dangerous, and I'll give you the choice, but if it's not the right one, I'll make it for you." He runs the pads of his thumbs along my jaw, his blue eyes piercing mine. "Walk away from this with me."

He's right. I've prolonged this long enough, and before, when my heart was empty and I had nothing else, it was easy to convince myself that this is what I needed to do. But my heart is full now and my search seems pointless.

I nod. "I want to. I really want to." I hold him close, burying my nose into his chest and breathing in his earthy sweet scent. "I love you, Mason."

"Love you too." He rubs soothing circles against my back. "Hate seeing you here; hate all this."

"Wait . . ." I pull back enough to see him, blinking through the fog of my tears. "How do you know Hatch?"

His eyes dart to the side of me, and I lean over to catch his gaze. "Tell me."

"Caught him and some of his guys fucking with Drake. Thought they'd kill 'em. Jumped in. They put Drake's debt on me."

"Drake's debt. What did he owe?"

"Drugs."

My eyes narrow as I put two and two together. "So . . . you had to give them drugs?"

"Basically, yeah."

A gasp slips from my lips before I can catch it. "You're a . . . drug dealer?"

"No, I delivered drugs to some assholes who tried to kill my brother so that they'd fucking leave him alone."

"And did they?"

He shrugs. "We're here, aren't we? No clue what Drake's dad has in store for him tonight—"

My eyes widen as realization of their earlier conversation finally dawns. "This guy, the one behind the door, is Drake's dad."

He nods. "Shit with this Hatch guy runs deeper than just an MC. He's in bed with Elijah, who is the worst combination of criminal: greedy, psychotic, and no fucking soul."

Nausea rolls through my stomach, and the lemon drops threaten a second appearance. I shiver in his arms. "Drake's in deep?"

"Trying to shovel his ass out, but yeah, he is."

I shake my head, worrying my bottom lip with my teeth.

"Whatever you need from this Hatch guy isn't worth you putting yourself in this kind of danger."

He's right. "You're—"

*Bam-bam-bam!* "Open up!"

My eyes pop wide, and my pulse pounds between my ears. "Oh shit. It's Hatch."

# THIRTY-THREE

## MASON

Son of a bitch.

What started off as being just plain shitty has turned into a clusterfuck of epic proportions.

The man, or men, who killed Lana are now tied somehow to Drake's dad? I help Trix from off the counter, make sure she's put back together, and at her nod, swing open the bathroom door.

"Fuck's going on here?" Hatch scowls between Trix and me.

I step in front of him. He's not a small guy, but I've got a good few inches on him if push came to shove. "Where's Drake?"

Hatch stares me down, and the heat of Trix's body warms my back. "He's with Elijah. They're asking for you."

I reach back and grab Trix's hand then move toward the door Hatch motioned to earlier.

"Where the fuck do you think you're going?"

I turn around to tell the guy to fuck himself.

"I'm going with him." There's a resolve in her voice that makes my chest swell with pride. She's not intimidated by this guy, which is insanely brave or naïve.

"The fuck you say?" He laughs, the sound like tumbling rocks. "You've been paid to work." His eyes narrow. "Do your fuckin' job."

She juts out her chin. "I quit."

In a move faster than I'd think possible for a man his size, he grabs her by the hair and pulls her from me. "You don't get to quit—"

I grip his throat, forcing him to release her so he can fight me off. He swings. Lands a solid punch to my jaw that I can't feel through my rage.

"You're a fuckin' dead man." I pull him by the throat into a flying knee that doubles him over. "Touch her again and—"

"Enough!" A booming voice radiates through the room.

I shove Hatch, sending him stumbling backwards, but he recovers with a glare that says *this isn't over*. I'm reluctant to take my eyes off Hatch. He could pull a knife or a gun, and the way Trix is clinging to my body puts her in just as much danger.

Hatch glares at Trix. "Understand now why you haven't been fuckin' me."

She curls deeper into my body and I tuck her in close.

"Hot, but . . ." J.P.'s voice is mocking. "Little trashy for your taste." He's close, too close to Trix. I bounce my gaze between him and the biker trash. "Mason, seems all you touch turns to whore."

"Fuck you." Hate this piece of shit. He was a cocksucker in high school, and he's a cocksucker now.

He grins, as if pissing me off is his greatest joy. "Nice to see you again too, asshole."

I contemplate beating the shit out of both J.P. and Hatch, but think better of it. Each man has a crew of guys around them demonstrating where their loyalties lie.

He jerks his head toward the office. "Come on. He's waiting for you."

I move to follow him, but his eyes cut to Trix. "Leave the girl."

"No."

His mouth forms a tight line. "I said, '*leave the girl*.'"

"And I said, '*no*.'"

He tilts his head, studying Trix as she clings to my arm.

"I got her, Mason." I turn to see Santos, who is flanked by Angel and the redhead. All of them look worried, although Santos doesn't seem nearly as threatening as I've seen him in the past. "I'll get her home."

She'll be safe with him. But not home.

I pull her to my front and wrap her in a hug, putting my lips to her ear. "My house. Go."

She stiffens. "No, I'm not leaving you."

A groan rumbles up from my throat. "Please, I can't do this if I'm worried about you. You need to go."

She swings her gaze to Santos and back to me, her chin high. "I'm not leaving. I'm going to wait for you."

I grab her upper arm and yank her. "With who? Hatch?"

She gasps.

"Go with Santos to my house. Don't fuck this up." God, why can't she just fucking listen?

"Mason, man, we don't have all night," J.P. says with a frustrated growl.

She scowls. "Why are you forcing me to leave?"

"Think you've proven you can't keep yourself safe." I nod to Santos and he moves in to take her.

"Come on, Trix." He hands her a tight dress, and she slips it over her head with a demeanor of pure hate radiating from her violet eyes.

Fine. Let her be pissed. As long as she's safe. We'll both live through this to fight about it later.

"Now, if we could get this fucking show on the road." J.P. sweeps his hand toward the open door of what I'm assuming must be an office or conference room.

I head back, but not before I make sure to see Santos and the girls leave the villa, the door closing behind them.

I follow J.P. into a room that has a long table surrounded by chairs. Elijah's sitting at one end, his eyes cast out the floor-to-ceiling window that overlooks the Vegas strip. I take a seat next to Drake, who's sitting with his head in his hands. Shit, this doesn't look good.

J.P. doesn't say a word and leaves the three of us, shutting the door behind him.

"Seems you two assholes are fuckin' things up for me." Eli's voice is stern and non-feeling. "Interfered in a little transaction we'd worked out between us and the Wild Outlaw MC."

So this is the shit Drake's dad is into. From surf gang to MC ties that walk way outside of the law. "If you're referring to me saving your son's ass and replacing the shit he owed, yeah, I guess I interfered." *You motherfucker.*

Eli spins in his chair, and I'm struck by how similar he and Drake look. Dark eyes and hair, athletic build, but whereas Drake's style reeks of California wannabe gangster, Elijah's is more mafia with a sprinkling of biker and a dash of serial killer. Even with their similarities, their body language couldn't be more different. My brother has never looked so beaten, and Eli's snarling. "Big shot superstar thinks he can talk shit to me?"

My muscles tense as the urge to wrap my hands around this guy's throat becomes overwhelming. "You called me here. Now tell me what the fuck you want."

He pulls a gun faster than I can track and points it at me. "Your slut mother never taught you boys any respect."

Adrenaline races through my veins, half anger, half nerves, but the anger wins. "You're wrong. She taught us to give respect to those who earn it."

My gaze darts to Drake, who still looks lost in his own head. I don't know what happened in here before I walked in, but whatever it was clearly wasn't in Drake's favor.

"You're not gonna let him go, are you?" I stare at Eli, refusing to break eye contact.

He seems to grasp hold of what little control he has left and holsters his weapon. "I have a proposition for you."

"I only came here to talk about you releasing my brother—"

He burst into an evil laugh that pricks against my skin.

"Mase." Drake's voice is beside me, but faint. "I already tried."

I glare between them. "What? Why not?"

"Because he took a vow when he joined me." Eli shrugs and stares at his son. "No getting out. He knew that from day one."

"What if he refuses?" No man can *make* another man do anything he doesn't want to.

He pushes up from his seat and moves around to drop his ass on the table next to Drake. "We terminate those who don't stay loyal."

My flesh crawls at the seriousness of his words. "You'd do that to your own kid?"

Eli tilts his head. "You sure you want the answer to that question?"

I throw an arm out, pointing to a downtrodden Drake. "He's your son. How could you expect this of him? You wanted nothing to do with him for most of his life. Now you're so devoted you can't let him go?" Even if it means so that he can raise his child? I avoid giving all that away. After all, knowledge gives them power.

"Mason, stop."

I turn my glare to my brother. "Stop? Stop what? Defending you? Fighting for you? Dragging your ass out of the bed you made for yourself? I can't do that. I'm your brother, your family—"

"You're not part of *this* family—"

"Fuck you, Elijah." I push up from my chair and grab my brother around the bicep. "We're done listening to whatever you have to say."

"Don't walk away from me, boy." Eli's voice shakes with rage. "No one walks away from me."

"Yeah? What're you gonna do? Shoot me in a hotel suite in the heart of Las Vegas?"

"There are worse things than getting killed." His words drip with threat.

"You leave my brother and me the fuck alone, and we'll keep what we know from the cops."

"Don't handle threats well." Elijah leans forward, his fists balled.

"Well then, this should be good practice." I drag my brother from the room, refusing to look back or at anyone until I'm out of the suite and into the elevator.

It's only then I slam my brother against the wall and get into his face. "What the fuck did you do, huh? What did you promise these guys that they're refusing to let you go?"

He shakes his head, studying the floor as if the tacky carpet will reveal the answer.

"I've always been there for you." I shove him and he doesn't resist. "You owe me something here. All I'm asking is how the hell you got in so deep."

The elevator doors ping and an older couple joins us. I move to the opposite wall and try like hell to calm my breathing. I don't know what happened in that room before I got there, but Drake didn't leave the same man.

Once in the casino, we head straight out to the valet and wait for him to bring up my truck. I dart my eyes to my brother, who's acting as if his skull has doubled in weight and keeps his chin down.

I pull out my phone and hit Trix's contact info. It rings until her voicemail picks up. Shit.

I hit "end" and type out a quick text.

**On my way. Stay put. We need to talk.**

The valet pulls up with our ride, and I toss him a few bucks and climb in, Drake doing the same while still playing mute.

It's a silent but tense ride home. I jog up the stairs from my garage, eager to get Trix in my arms. This shit isn't over with my brother, but at least I have my woman back.

The place is dark. Not at all what I expected. I check the couch then turn to head up to the loft when my phone rings.

I check the caller ID.

"Hey, Trix, where are you?"

"Hey, Mason . . . sorry, I didn't end up at your house."

"Yeah, I know. I'm here. Where are you? I'll come to you."

She clears her throat. "Oh, um . . . about that. I'm with Angel, and Santos agreed to stay with us."

"What? Trix, just let me come get you. We can—"

"No. Mason, look. I need some time, okay? A . . . a lot has happened, and you're making decisions for me. I just . . . I need time."

Is she out of her mind? "Decisions? When it comes to your safety, it's my job to make decisions."

"No, it's not. I uh, I need some time to think."

"Wait, hold on, is this about me refusing to allow you to continue with this suicide mission you're on? Or telling you to go with Santos?"

"Please, don't make this harder. Time is all I'm asking for."

"How much time?"

Silence stretches between us.

"Trix, I don't understand. I thought things were good. I thought . . ."

"I'm sorry." Her voice shakes with emotion. "I have to do this."

"Do this? Do what?"

"Maybe I'll see you around."

"See me around . . . Beatriks, stop."

"Good-bye, Mase."

"What?" My pulse pounds in my ears, sucking the breath from my lungs.

"You heard me. Good-bye."

"No—" *Good-bye?*

The line goes dead, and I stare at the phone in my hand, not seeing it.

She told me she'd never say good-bye. I'm sure her learning that I dealt drugs to that biker piece of shit of hers was a jagged pill to swallow, but Trix is strong. She of all people knows what it's like to be backed into a corner and forced to do things we're not proud of for our family.

No, fuck this. We said no good-byes.

I need to see her. My legs carry me three steps before I realize I have no idea where Angel lives or the slightest clue how to get in touch with Santos. That means I sit on my ass until the morning and start hitting up her house and Zeus's until I find her and force her to give me some answers.

"Why now?" Jessica's voice comes from the stairs that lead down from my bedroom. "It's the middle of the night."

"Business is taken care of, why not leave now?" Drake has her bag slung over his shoulder and his keys in hand. "You can sleep in the car, okay?"

I eye my brother. "You're leaving?"

He only nods.

"You don't have to leave now. Get some sleep and take off when you're rested, man."

"Can't sleep." He heads to the front door. "Driving will be good for me."

Still dressed in her pajamas, Jess turns toward me with a sleepy smile. "Thanks for letting us stay, Mase." She waves, and Drake opens the door for her then guides her out by the small of her back.

"Drake, you sure you're okay?"

For the first time tonight, he looks at me, but there's no emotion in his expression. "Did I ever tell you how I got this scar on my face?"

"Yeah, you got in a fight."

He shakes his head. “Not exactly. I was cut in. Cut in to Eli’s crew.”

I cringe, wondering how bad that must’ve been to leave that deep of a scar.

“These guys aren’t fuckin’ around, bro. Believe me.”

“I do, but I’m not going to let them take down my family. Not if there’s something I can do to protect it.”

His chin drops to his chest, and he mumbles something that sounds like “that’s what I did.” He turns his back on me, but freezes in the doorway. “Mason, just know that . . . I’m sorry.”

“Don’t be.” I squeeze his shoulder. “We’ll figure this out. You just focus on getting your girl and your baby home safe, yeah?”

He nods and slinks away, leaving me standing in my doorway, wondering what in the fuck my next move should be.

# THIRTY-FOUR

## MASON

The next morning I'm racing to the Youth Center. It didn't hit me until last night after staring at my ceiling fan for two hours that today is Sunday. I called Blake, whose turn it is to run the MMA class, and it didn't take much convincing to get him to give me his shift.

My tires squeal as I pull into a parking spot, scanning the lot for Trix's car. I don't see it, but maybe she parked out back. I jog to the door and Sylvia jumps when I rush in.

Her hand flies to her chest. "Take it easy on an old lady. You scared the heck outta me."

"Sorry. I'm sorry. I'm here from—"

"Yes, I remember. Mr. Mason, right?"

I nod and run a hand through my hair, anxious to get back into the gym and find Trix, put my hands and lips on her to know she's okay.

Sylvia pulls out her clipboard and slides on her glasses. "Hmm, okay, let's see here . . ."

I practice my deep breathing and wait until she gets her fucking shit together.

She peeks up at me from over her glasses. "You remember where to go, right?"

"Yes, I do." I point back down the hallway that leads to the gym, but my feet are already moving.

"Your nametag!" She waves, but I'm halfway there. "That boy's in a hurry."

She has no idea.

Once in the gym, my eyes search out the huddle of dancing girls for the flash of platinum and purple, but come up empty. Maybe she's not here yet? I walk around, scouring the place from the mats to the tops of the bleachers and everything in between.

Still nothing.

Last night was probably rough on her. Maybe she slept in? I head over to the kickboxing area and drop to the mats, keeping alert. I don't know how much time passes, but a small group of kids slowly makes its way over. I greet them without taking my eyes off the gym at large when there's a tug on my shirt.

I peer down and find Denny, whose mouth is turned into a frown. "Mr. Mason?"

I kneel to his eye level and hold out my fist for a bump. "Den, what's up?"

His dark brown eyes meet mine. "She's not coming."

My chest constricts. "Who?" I ask, although my gut tells me I already know.

"Miss Trixy." He sighs. "She's not coming."

My pulse hammers in my neck. "How do you know that, Den?"

He kicks at the mat then shrugs. "Because she always gets here early to bring me breakfast."

My heart pinches at the rejected sound in his voice. "Maybe she's sick?"

He shakes his head. "Nope. She's never sick. She shows up sick just to bring me breakfast."

The pain in my chest turns into the rapid throb of panic. "Huh, well, why don't you get your gloves on and start shadow boxing while I go talk to Miss Sylvia, okay?"

He nods and his eyes get watery before he dips his chin and heads to the gloves. "Den, buddy, I'll find out what's going on. I promise."

He doesn't respond, but straps on gloves that dwarf his tiny hands, and the same feeling of foreboding I had last night hits me again hard. With an urgency for answers on my heels, I jog to the front desk where Sylvia has her nose pressed to a computer screen. I knock on the counter to get her attention rather than scaring the shit out of her again, which I'm liable to do with the way I'm feeling.

"Sylvia, did Trix call in sick today?" My stomach flips over on itself as I wait for her answer.

Her eyes scrunch up along with her mouth. "Yeah, funny huh? As long as she's been here, she's never missed a day."

What the fuck? "Right. Did she say what was wrong?"

Her face turns sad. "Yeah, she had to go back home, something about having to take care of her sister."

I grip the counter, suddenly lightheaded. "Her sister?"

"As long as she's been volunteering here, I never even knew she had a sister."

I swallow and fight the urge to rub my temples. "She has a few. Did she happen to say which one?"

"No, she just said she needed time off and was looking forward to getting out of the city and into the Majestic Mountains."

"Where?"

She pushes up her glasses. "Where she's from. The Majestic Mountains? I've never heard of it, but it sounds lovely."

What the hell is she talking about?

"Great, okay." I pat the countertop. "Thanks."

She nods then goes back to her computer.

I return to the gym, but feel disconnected as my mind attempts to process.

Last night she needed some space. Today she's headed back to Los Gatos. Maybe one of her sisters is sick, and this is all part of the space she needs to figure things out. I pull my phone from my pocket and dial her again, the call going straight to voicemail.

Something isn't right. And I'm not giving up until I figure out what it is.

—

## Three days later...

This is bullshit.

All of it.

They say there's a thin line between love and hate, and I've been fucking living there for the last seventy-two hours.

I've practically worn holes in my damn phone from my repeated calls and text messages, none of them returned. I've driven by her house and burst in past her roommate only to find that she hasn't been there in days. Calls to Zeus's are pointless. For whatever reason, maybe company policy, they can't tell me shit.

Which is why I'm heading over there now to find Santos and torture the motherfucker until he tells me every single thing that happened the night he took her out of that villa.

It's not even seven p.m., and there's a line to get into the club. I push past to the front, and the bouncer holds his hands up. "Gotta stand in line with the rest of them."

"I need to talk to Santos."

"Don't give a fuck. Still need to wait in line." He nods to the back of the line, but fuck him. I've waited long enough.

I move from the front door and around the building to the back. From what I've noticed, Santos usually handles the girls' side of the club rather than the customer side. The back door is used for exit only and is locked from the inside. If I wait out back long enough, Santos's sure to pop his head out eventually.

The bass throbs, and I pace the length of brick wall, waiting. No matter how many times I check the parking lot for Trix's car, I find myself jerking to attention every time a new one pulls in or even fucking passes by. My arms tense and my legs burn with unspent energy. I'm antsy as hell and getting more impatient as every second passes.

The sun disappears and the air cools, letting me know I've been out here for a while, when suddenly the back door swings open. I rush over just as Santos' face appears and a group of men tumble out.

He catches sight of me, and I don't miss the slight reaction on the usually stone-faced bouncer.

"Santos, I need a minute." I rush up the steps and brace open the door.

"Workin', don't have a minute." He tries unsuccessfully to shut the door.

"What happened the night you took Trix from the villa? Ever since then, she won't talk to me. Guess she went home, but . . ." I blow out a long breath, suddenly feeling pathetic for being here. Guy's girlfriend dumps his ass, and he chases after every person she knows searching for answers. I rub the back of my neck. "I'm sorry, I know this sounds crazy, but I can't help but wonder if maybe she said something to you about being pissed at me? Something doesn't feel right."

He doesn't give anything away by his expression, but steps outside. I release the door, and he catches it before it slams shut, grunting as if holding the thing open is causing him pain. His eyes close and he clutches his ribs, breathing through his teeth.

I've been around injuries long enough to know exactly what that is. Broken ribs.

"Rough night?" I nod to his ribs, but he ignores me.

"Rough few days."

He steps under the light, and it's then I notice a fading black eye and a scab on his lip. "What the fuck happened to you?"

"Got messed up with the wrong people." He stares at me in a way that has me shifting on my feet. "You know what that's like?"

"I do."

He nods. "Yeah. You do. So does she."

I shake my head, feeling the weight of defeat crash over me. "So you're saying she thinks I'm the wrong people?" Fuck, I knew it. She thinks I'm a drug dealer and a participating member of B3. What she saw at the beach, knows about my ties to Elijah, and the way I man-handled her at that party, she has all the evidence against me.

He taps his temple, his eyes wide. "Think."

"I—"

"Think."

Think about what? "When you see her, will you please tell her to call me? It's cool if she's over us." It so fucking is not! "But I need to hear her say it."

His eyes dart to the lot behind me, his jaw hard. "Think harder."

"I know I fucked up."

Why the hell does he look so disappointed?

This was a mistake. I wave him off and move back down the steps. "Speaking in riddles, what the fuck?"

He mumbles something that I can't make out, but my guess is whatever it is will only make me angrier. I hop in my truck and head over to Rex's for poker night, feeling like I've lost the other half of my soul.

Now I get what Trix was talking about when she'd mention Lana's death. Losing someone you love is horrific. Knowing it happened is bad enough, but not knowing why is excruciating.

If she'd just let me explain, I could fix all this. Whatever she thinks of me is wrong and doesn't justify this kind of punishment.

Is this it? Did I lose her?

---

Rex reaches two hands into the middle of the table and rakes his winnings toward him. "You forget to take your meds today, Baywatch?"

"That's not funny." Gia, who took Talon's spot at the table tonight after the guy called to say he had last-minute pussy to slay, his words, not mine, slaps her man on the arm.

He cringes and stacks his chips in nice even towers. "Sorry, baby."

I swig off my beer while flipping a chip over my fingers.

"Mase, man, Rex's is right." Lane leans back in his chair, scowling. "Someone kill your kitten?"

How do I even answer that? No, fuckface, but my girl, the one you so proudly fucked, promised me she'd never say good-bye and fucking left my ass. Yes, I'm a pussy-ass bitch, but love'll do that to you.

"I'm good." I shrug and motion for Lane to deal the fucking cards already.

I feel the steely gray eyes of Gia as her glare bores into me. First thing I did when I got here was ask if she'd talked to Trix. She said she hadn't, but judging by the look of pity on her face, I'd say she knows things aren't good between us. Thankfully, Lane showed up before she was able to question me further, but I can see by the way she's studying me she's itching for more information.

A few more beers later, and we've managed to play poker without the subject of Trix and me coming up. I threw back more booze than I should've, and the game wasn't holding my attention, so I ended up losing all my money. I've never been readier to go home and pass out, hoping I wake up tomorrow with my girl in my arms surrounded by her clean floral scent with her blond and purple-streaked hair tossed across my chest as if this is all just some shitty dream.

"Think I'm getting a Harley," Lane says, pulling me from my thoughts.

"Sweet." Gia leans in. "What kind?"

"Fat Boy. Guy I know is sellin' one."

She moans. "Ohh, yeah. Fat Boys are sweet."

Lane nods. "You ever ridden one?"

Rex visibly tenses, but Gia's too wrapped up in the conversation to notice.

"No, but I've ridden on the back of one. Super smooth ride."

Rex clears his throat. "Oh yeah, how smooth?" He tugs on the barbell through his eyebrow so much so that I have to look away, afraid he's gonna rip the fucking thing from his skin.

Gia sits back, her face draining of what little color it has. "Rex—"

"Come on, Gia." He leans in toward her and something about the way he's doing it makes me want to jump in between them to protect her. "Why don't you tell us how fucking *smooth* that ride is, huh? We wanna know."

She shakes her head and drops her gaze. "I'm sorry. I—"

"Sorry what? That you brought this shit up *again*?"

Her chin jerks up to glare at Rex. "*Again*? You never let me talk about it. Ever! It's like you brought me home and just expect me to dive right into your life and leave everything that happened back in Denver!"

"Drop it." Aggression rolls off Rex in waves that make the hair on my arms stand on end.

She throws her hands in the air. "See! There you go again!"

"I'm not talkin' about this right now," Rex growls and flicks a rubber band at his wrist.

"Fuck you! I didn't do anything wrong, and you treat me like what happened back there is some dirty secret."

He fists two hands in his hair, and Lane takes this opportunity to excuse himself to the bathroom. I'd do the same, but feel the need to stay in case these two start really going at it.

"I don't want to talk about it."

She throws out an arm. "You never want to talk about it. Ever. But guess what? It happened." She presses her forefingers into her sternum. "We both fucked up, and it happened. I know you want to hate Hatch for what he did, but—"

I slam my beer bottle against the table, getting both sets of eyes. "What did you say?"

The tension in Gia's shoulders dissolves instantly and she blushes. "I'm sorry, Mason. You shouldn't have to listen—"

"How the fuck do you know Hatch?"

Rex's body instantly goes rigid. His fists ball up tight against the table.

Gia turns her body toward me. "Wait, how do *you* know Hatch?"

We all stare at each other for silent seconds, and the feeling that things just went from really fucking sucky to the worst shit ever hits in atomic levels.

"He came back for Trix—" Before the 'ix' leaves my lips, the table is gone, tossed by Rex across the kitchen to shatter against the concrete island. "Rex, man, talk to me." My voice is vibrating with rage, fear, fucking full-blown panic at the total loss of control I see in my friend's eyes.

"Where is he, Mase?" I hear the question, but I'm stuck staring at Rex whose eyes have gone vacant. "Mason!"

"How the fuck should I know?"

Rex pants like an overheated dog, his lips curling back over his teeth. "Call Trix right fucking now. Ask her where he is."

"I can't. She's not taking my calls. She's . . . I don't know, she's pissed at me and—"

Gia moves to stand in front of me, her hands on my shoulders, demanding my attention. "What do you mean she's not taking your calls? When did you see her last?"

I run a hand through my hair. "Almost a week. It's weird, everything seemed okay, but shit went down and now I don't know where she is."

"He came back for her, she's gone, and you don't know where the fuck she is?" Rex is practically vibrating.

"Mason . . ." Gia's bottom lip trembles. "Where could she be?"

"She went home. I think. I mean . . ." She said good-bye.

Said she'd never say good-bye, but . . .

She had to take care of her sister in the mountains.

Out of town.

The Majestic Mountains?

Santos took her home. Said he'd keep her safe.

Black eye, busted lip, broken ribs.

Like a blowtorch to my flesh my body heats and breaks out in a sweat.

"Oh shit, this whole time . . . she's been trying to tell me." I set eyes on Gia as I feel the blood drain completely from my head. "He took her."

# THIRTY-FIVE

## Four days earlier...

### TRIX

"What the hell was that all about?" Angel bounces alongside me as we make our way out of Caesars at a quick pace.

"I don't know." I'm only half lying. I do know that Drake is involved in some bad shit, and because Mason is always protecting his little brother, he's been dragged in by default. What I'm confused about is Hatch's aggression.

He's always been a take-no-bullshit guy, but I've never felt unsafe with him. He's never forced me to do anything against my will, and even after everything that happened between him and Gia, she made it clear he never took away her choices. But tonight was different, and for the first time, I felt genuine fear that he'd hurt me.

"Sucks we had to leave. I was having fun!" Kayla giggles, still drunk and completely oblivious.

Santos punches out a quick text, and by the time we exit the casino, our limo is waiting for us. We climb in, and even though I'm now safely inside the luxury car, I'm unable to take a full breath.

Mason's still up there, which means anything could be happening. Going by the expression on Drake's dad's face, I'd say things are going to get worse before they get better. Mason's not the type of guy who backs down when challenged. I just hope he doesn't do anything to wedge himself in deeper with these criminals.

It's a semi-quiet ride back to Zeus's, except for Kayla who sang along with the radio while dancing in her seat. Too drunk to drive, the other girls will get a ride home in the limo while Santos grabs my keys and ushers me to my car.

"Come on." He opens the passenger door and I slide in, grateful he's driving me to Mason's rather than dropping me at home.

He pulls out of the lot, and my mind tumbles over everything. I can't help but feel like this is my fault. If I'd just backed off, ignored Hatch when he came back to town, given up on my quest, then Mason and Hatch wouldn't be out to kill each other.

The Las Vegas lights streak by my window, and I close my eyes from the sensory overload. My head spins and my heart aches. I just want this all to be over.

Not sleeping, but somewhere in between, I register that we should've been to Mason's house by now. Wait, how does Santos even know where Mason lives? I blink open my eyes and dread falls heavy in my belly. We're headed out of Las Vegas.

Fuck! How did I not see this coming?

I swallow back the urge to scream and fear looking at the man next to me. The person who has been responsible for protecting all the girls at Zeus's. The man who has protected me, been my friend, for nearly four years.

There's no use in playing stupid. "How long have you been planning this?" The fearlessness in my voice shocks me.

He doesn't answer right away, so I turn to him then and fight the urge to burst into tears. His jaw ticks, and I swear if I didn't know better I'd think his eyes were glistening.

"How long?" My heart crushes, and the pain seeps into my limbs.

He clears his throat. "Not long."

I nod and return my gaze to the inky black night. "Hatch?" It doesn't make any sense. He knows where I live, slept in my house. If he ever wanted to kidnap me, he's had plenty of opportunities to do it before now.

"No." His hands tighten on the steering wheel.

No? I blink and rake through every possible explanation as to why I'd be an asset to anyone. But rather than come up with an answer, I only settle on one question.

I turn toward him again. "Why?"

His lips pull into a thin line. "They have Diane."

"What?" My questioning shriek fills the small car. "Who does? Where is she?"

He shakes his head. "Don't know."

"Santos—"

"I can't talk about this with you. Please, just . . ." He shakes his head. "I'm so fuckin' sorry, Trix." A single tear races down his cheek.

Shit, this is it. "It's okay. I understand." And I do. He's protecting someone he loves. I'd do the same thing. "I'm . . . I'm not mad at you. You did what you had to do." My last words are spoken on a whisper.

I need to call someone. 911. Without being too obvious, I walk my fingers toward my clutch that's between us on the center console. If I could just get to my phone, I might—

"They took your phone."

All the air rushes from my lungs. "Are they going to kill me?"

"They said no one would get hurt." There's doubt in his voice.

So that's it. I'm completely at the mercy of God knows who.

That leaves me with only one thing to do.

I close my eyes and dip my chin.

*Dear Father in heaven . . . help me.*

"Call him." Hatch tosses me my cell then pulls a chair up so close his knees touch the bed.

"Tell me where we are so he can pick me up, and I will." After a short drive out of town, Santos pulled over to blindfold and handcuff me. He apologized the entire time, and I was done not being mad at him.

Now I'm furious.

I would've told him as much, but after one last apology, he left me in the car alone until I was joined by someone else. The person didn't speak, but I could tell by the smell of his cologne it wasn't Santos. My first response was to be terrified. Santos would kidnap me to save his wife, but he'd never really hurt me. I believed that with every ounce of my being.

Now that he was gone, I was in trouble.

And as much as I should sob and beg, I can't. I'm way too angry for that.

I throw my phone on the scratchy polyester comforter. My shoulder aches from being handcuffed by one arm to the bed. Blackout curtains and only a single crappy lamp make it impossible to see anything that would identify where I am other than a shitty motel room.

Hatch growls and shoves my phone back into my hand. "Don't fuck with me, Trix. You're lucky you're still breathin'. Call him now. Break shit off with him. Tell him whatever he needs to hear to know you're safe but you're movin' on."

I lean toward him until the muscles in my locked-up arm pull tight. "Fuck you!"

He jumps from his seat and presses the barrel of his gun to my temple. "You know how easy it would be to end you right here? Wrap your dead body up in this piece of shit bedding? Cost us nothing more than the price of replacing a comforter."

I swallow back the urge to cry, refusing to give him the satisfaction. "Why are you doing this?" Human trafficking, prostitution, plain ole sick pleasure, all the reasons have filtered through my head, but none of them seem like Hatch.

How well do you really know him?

"Tell me why you're doing this to me."

"Pick up the fucking phone."

I turn my head so that the barrel is now pressing into my forehead. Eyes fixed to his, I press in, making the gun dig so deep it's bound to leave a bruise. "Why are you doing this, Hatch?"

An emotion flashes across his eyes, something akin to fear mixed with regret, but he pushes it back. He reaches into his back pocket, pulls something out, and drops it on my lap.

I blink down at the small piece of paper. A photograph with a watermark on the back. My pulse throbs in my throat. Is that . . .? I flip it over and slam my lips closed to avoid giving away a gasping response.

"You've been playin' me." Hatch punctuates his words with a shove of his gun.

"I don't know what you're talking ab—"

He grabs my chin and jerks my face to his. "Don't fucking lie to me. You think I'm stupid? Think I don't see the family resemblance. Shit, Trix."

I try to rip my head from his grip, but he won't let me, so I close my eyes.

"Lookin' for information, huh? Gotta say loved the fact that you did that using your mouth and your pussy. No man with a dick n' balls would pass up that kinda opportunity."

He goes on to say more, but his voice fades to static. He recognized Lana. I'd never opened up to him about my personal life, never shared Lana's story, so seeing her photo shouldn't have raised any suspicion, unless he knew her.

My breath catches in my throat. "You were there," I whisper.

I can't look at him, can't face the man who watched my sister get tortured to death and *did nothing* to save her.

"Didn't touch your sister."

Doesn't matter. Watching it makes him just as guilty.

"But you were there." Pain slices through my chest like phantom knives.

He doesn't answer. "You share your investigative work with your pretty boy?"

"Tell me who did it." The words come out of my mouth but sound nothing like me, more like a woman possessed. My veins pump with the urge to kill as the monster within rages for vindication. "Give me his name!" I lurch toward Hatch, but he steps back. Heat lances through my shoulder and arm as I tug at my restraints. My fingers itch to wrap around his throat and crush his larynx, to feel his life slip away from beneath my hands. A low grumble builds in my chest and escalates to a full-blown roar. "Fucking tell me—" My head jerks to the side, cheek inflamed by the powerful smack of his palm.

Without permission to do so, a single tear leaks from my eye and the fight seeps from my muscles.

"Now you know who you're dealing with." The weight of my phone presses into my hand. "Call him. Or you're both dead."

---

It's morning. But only just barely.

Light shines through the one corner of the window where the blackout curtains pulled loose from their binding. I roll to my other side, having to go back and forth all night to keep blood circulating through my arm.

After talking to Mason last night, I finally allowed myself to cry. Telling him the one thing I promised him I'd never say—using the word *good-bye*—was my only hope at alerting him that something's wrong. I hope to God he picked up on that.

I search the space of the small motel room and don't see Hatch. He came and went a few times last night, but only for minutes here and there. Motorcycle engines roared throughout the night, and it would seem some of the other rooms are occupied by members of his MC. I wonder if they know I'm here. Would they do anything to help me if they did?

I close my eyes and try to concentrate on the path we took out of town. If only I'd paid closer attention. It seemed we headed south, or southwest? Maybe thirty minutes. I growl in frustration.

Hatch was smart enough to get rid of all the logos or clues in the room that might give away our location. Even the telephone has been removed. Fuck!

The sound of a motorcycle engine rumbles and gets louder before it goes quiet. I roll to my side to face the door, nervous about who might walk in and praying it's Hatch rather than someone from his crew. As sick as it sounds, I'm safer with Hatch than anyone else. Lesser of two evils.

The door opens and I squint against the light. Hatch props open the door with his foot and kneels down to get something he'd placed on the ground. There's a tag hanging from the door handle. Do not disturb. A logo. I blink, trying to focus against the bright light.

Majestic Mountain Inn.

"Got breakfast." The door slams, and Hatch moves to the small table to drop a bag and two insulated to-go cups.

Majestic Mountain Inn. Majestic Mountain Inn. It said Majestic Mountain Inn.

He turns toward me, his eyes raking up my bare legs to my ass that's on display from beneath the skin-tight and too-short dress I've been in since last night. "You look fuckable all tied up like that."

If I had food in my stomach, I would've puked. Instead, I flip him off with my chained-up hand.

He chuckles and comes over to me, pulling a key from his pocket and holding it up for me to see. "You make one more call today, be a good girl, and I'll let you eat and take a shower. Deal?"

Phone call! I nod. "Yes."

He reaches behind one panel of his cut and pulls out my cell. "That place you work with the kids. Call—"

"How'd you know about that?" I never talked to him about my volunteer work, did I? It's the only part of my life that was really and truly me, something I kept to myself.

He runs a callused finger along my lower lip. "I know everything, Trix." His lips tighten and he drops his hand. "Call 'em. Tell 'em you're out of town or taking care of a sick relative. Don't give a fuck; just do it." He presses the phone into my palm and then sits at my hip, watching.

My muscles protest as I push up to lean against the headboard. Nerves tick beneath my skin, and I wish I could do this in privacy. After all, how much can I say with Hatch sitting six inches from my face? With a trembling finger, I dial the Youth Center.

"LV Youth, this is Sylvia."

I clear my throat. "Hey, Sylvia, it's Trix." I keep my eyes on Hatch.

"Trix, hi. What's going on?"

"Listen, um . . . I have to go out of town for a while, um . . . sick family member." I swallow. "My sister."

Hatch pins me with a glare, and his jaw works back and forth.

I shrug and mouth *I'm sorry, it just came out*. Which is total bullshit.

"Oh, no. Honey, I'm sorry. Is it serious?"

"Serious? Yeah, I'll probably be gone for a while, but I'll let you know."

"Okay, sure. Yes, family first. I'm sorry to hear that."

Hatch gets up and moves to the table to grab his coffee.

"It's alright. I'm kinda looking forward to going home." I fist my hand around the phone.

"Where's home again?"

I pinch my eyes closed and hold my breath. "Majestic Mountain."

I brace for Hatch's punishing slap.

"Where's that? I've never heard of it."

"Just outside of town—" My throat constricts with the power of Hatch's hand wrapped around my throat.

"Sounds lovely.

My mouth opens and closes, but I can't breathe enough to get a word out. I watch as Hatch tries to figure it out, his eyes darting around the room, searching for something he missed.

"I'll get you covered here. You let me know when . . ."

Her words dissolve as black invades my vision. My eyes roll, and the phone falls from my hand as I fight for consciousness. He shoves the phone to my ear and releases my throat enough to suck in a quick breath.

"Oh, honey, don't cry. Your sister'll be okay."

"Thank you."

He mouths *say good-bye*.

"Good-bye."

"Bye, Tri—"

He rips the phone from my ear. "Nice try."

This time I see his fist coming, but it's too late to brace.

I barely register the pain before everything goes black.

---

I wake up to a rumbling in my belly and a killer fucking headache. The room is dark, but that means nothing. It could be high noon and I'd have no idea. I roll to my back and groan as my head swims and my jaw aches. My arm is attacked by pinpricks as blood rushes to my numb fingers.

"Nice of you to wake up." Hatch, that motherfucker.

I ignore him until something he tosses at me lands on my belly. I look down and tears spring to my eyes.

My phone. Shattered into multiple pieces.

"You did it to yourself." He stands and moves to the bathroom.

Finally alone, I allow the tears to flow freely. I'm never going to see him again. After this, Hatch won't let me live. He knows I'll go to the cops, turn his ass in, and tell them everything I know.

My search for Lana's killer has become my death sentence. I'd laugh at the irony if it wasn't so fucking sad. This is going to destroy my family.

The sound of running water muffles my cry as the reality of my situation hits me square in the chest. I wonder if this was how Svetlana spent her last few days: crying, begging for mercy that never came. Hoping beyond hope that God would deliver her. Or maybe she was strong. She always was, and she had faith that even the worst situations could never shake. Did she look her killer in the eyes and grind her teeth against the pain? Challenge them with her determination to die without giving them the satisfaction of knowing they'd broken her.

Hatch grabs my arm and frees me from the bed. "Come on, sunshine. Let's get you cleaned up."

Part of my brain registers that this would be a good time to fight. Being free means I could claw at him, find his gun, and scream at the top of my lungs until he put a bullet in my head.

But I'm weak and tired. So fucking tired.

He carries me to the bathroom and sets me down. He lifts my dress over my head and pulls off my boy shorts before motioning to the steamy cascade. "Go on."

I half expect him to follow me in, rape me, at the very least demand something from me, but he doesn't. Instead, he drops the lid on the toilet seat, sits down, and lights a smoke.

My toes hit the warm tub, and the heat sucks away every last bit of my energy. I sink to the floor of the dingy motel tub, pulling my knees to my face and wrapping my arms around my shins.

*Dear Father in heaven, if this is it, if these are my last few days on this earth, please let them pass quickly. Have mercy on me in my death that it won't be painful or messy. Comfort my family. They'll need you now more than ever. And please, God, please . . . let Mason know that I love him, that he's the only man I've ever loved, and that, even in death, I've dedicated my heart to him wholly and completely. Svetlana, moya sestra, moye serdtse. I will see you soon. Amen.*

# THIRTY-SIX

## Present day . . .

### MASON

Could it be this easy? I stare at my phone and read the words again. Majestic Mountain Inn. Thirty-six miles outside of the city.

Unease stirs my gut, screaming that something ain't right. This has to be a set up, but even if it is, I'll walk right into a firing squad for the chance to get Trix back. I shove my phone into my pocket and watch as Rex spills a shoebox of ammo onto the table.

He tosses me a blade that I catch on the fly.

"We have to get the cops involved." Gia stands off to the side of Rex, his rage making it clear to keep a safe distance.

Lane, who interrupted Rex's full-fledged freak out, ended up being sent home with a sore jaw. Rex is radiating fury like I've never seen before only mirroring my own.

"No cops." He pops a clip in his Sig and shoves it behind his belt.

Agreed.

"Rex, don't risk—"

He slams his fist against the table, his glare aimed at her. "He hurt you. Who knows what the fuck he's doing to Trix. I owe that woman my life for finding me when you were gone. No way we're callin' the cops. Not until I rip that fucker apart and beat him with his bloody limbs."

The robotic tone to Rex's voice matches the same detachment I feel in my head. It's as if my body is protecting itself from total self-destruction, allowing it to stay separate from the whirling feelings that threaten to send me into chaos. No, this is a time for clear thinking.

Like the hours before a fight, calm, focused, a calculating predator with an appetite for annihilation.

The doorbell rings and Gia jumps.

"It's alright." He continues to fill his pockets with knives and ammo. "It's Wade."

"That's good." Her shoulders relax a little. "He's level-headed. He'll keep you from killing someone—"

"He's not coming with." Rex moves to the door while I continue to pace the kitchen, every second that passes another second we're not getting my girl. "He's staying with you."

"What?" Her eyes pop wide and the tension in her shoulders returns.

"Just a precaution." I try to speak as calmly as possible through the turbulence of fear and anger that coils in my gut. "This could be a set up to draw us out of town so he can get to you."

She stares between Rex and me, shaking her head. "He's not like that. He'd never hurt me."

"Don't you fucking defend him in my house!" Rex's roar practically shakes the walls.

Gia cringes before her shoulders sag. "*Your* house?"

He recoils and crosses to her in long strides. "I'll be back by morning." He moves to touch her, but she pulls from his hold. Reaching again, he loops her behind her neck and presses a hard kiss to her lips before releasing her. She turns and stalks to the bathroom, slamming the door behind her.

"Fuck." He takes a long, exhausted breath. "Let's get this over with."

It's about time. I move to the front door, tossing Wade a quick nod.

"Can't believe I'm gonna miss this shit." Wade shakes his head. "If you get a chance, grab a video."

"My hands'll be busy." Killing. Maiming. Choking the life out of whoever stands between Trix and me. I eye Rex, who's stuffing his pockets with weaponry. "Hate to rush this, but my woman's out there."

"Don't get yourselves killed," Wade mumbles to me as we pass.

Ha, if saving Trix means my death, it'll be worth it.

---

We pull into the mostly abandoned motel parking lot less than thirty minutes later. From the outside, I'd assume the place had gone out of business years ago with its weed-ridden, cracked sidewalks and Bates-esque broken neon sign.

The No-Vacancy sign hangs to one side, only three of the nine letters visible. I flick off my headlights and pull the truck into the surrounding wooded area, inching around the back to a spot where we can get a clear view of the strip of rundown motel room doors. Only two cars are parked in the front, a mid-range compact with Nevada license plates and a rusted-out Jeep. Sticking to edge of the lot and out of sight, I park, shrouded in a canopy of shadows created by overgrown trees.

Rex grabs for the door handle before the truck comes to a complete stop.

"Hold on."

He freezes and whips his head around, eyes wild like an animal who's been locked in a cage for a year too long. "No, let's go get this fucker."

"We have no idea what we're headed into here. Which door do we hit first? If they panic, they could throw her in a car and be gone in seconds. We gotta be smart about this. I won't risk losing her again."

He blinks, and the animalistic fog fades to logic. "You're right. Okay."

We sit back and watch the sleeping motel, checking windows for lights or curtain movement. Minutes pass and feel like hours. I know there's a good chance Trix is just behind one of those doors. But which one?

The place is smaller, roughly twenty-five rooms. More of them face the highway, but I can't imagine her being stashed over there where Hatch could be freely seen coming and going by people on the highway.

The clock ticks, and almost an hour passes before I catch movement to the far left of my vision. "Someone's there."

Rex follows my glare, and we watch a man emerge from a room on the far end. I squint, trying to make him out, but there are no lights in the lot or along the motel walls.

"He's headed to another room." Rex's gaze tracks him right along with mine.

The closer he gets, the more he starts to come into focus. He's wearing a baseball hat pulled down low, so I can't make out any features, but something about him is familiar. Maybe he was at the villa the night she was taken.

"Dammit." I squint when all but his legs are hidden from view beneath a fallen overhang. He stops at a door at the opposite end from where he came.

"I can't see shit." I keep my eyes on his feet, waiting to see who comes out of the room and where they're off to. I hold my breath, hoping like hell it's that motherfucker Hatchet so I can barge over there and beat the living piss out of him.

The door opens, and Rex and I lean in, but I can't see enough to make out anything other than him disappearing into the room.

Fuckin' hell . . . now what?

## TRIX

"Come on." Hatch's growl comes from the other side of the tiny two-person table. "Eat up." He presses a whiskey bottle to his lips, taking a few long pulls of amber liquid.

Even after days of his barking commands, my stomach still twists every time he snaps. These last few hours he's seemed tenser than usual, taking phone calls that require one word answers and end with a string of curses.

I'm cuffed by one arm to the leg of my chair while I pick at a cold cheeseburger with my free hand. "I'm not hungry."

My heart burns at the memory of the last cheeseburger I had with Mason, how life had seemed so complicated then. I was so stupid. I had everything I never even knew I wanted and turned my back on it all for *this*?

Being held captive has given me time to think, to face my own mortality, and to pray. I've gone through every emotion possible, wringing them all dry until I'm left with only one.

Remorse.

I wasted so much time. I could have been living but didn't, and Mason . . . God, I should've thrown myself at his feet when I had the chance. Now I don't know if I'll ever see him again.

"Eat!"

My eyes dart to Hatch's, and the telltale glaze of inebriation coats his glare.

I pop a cold fry into my mouth and chew it until it's liquid, my throat refusing to open and take food into my belly. I dip my chin, hiding my face behind my ratted hair, and try to hide my disgust.

"It's almost over." He tilts his head, watching me. "Soon, this'll all be over."

"I don't even know what this is, Hatch." I try to take a few sips of water, hoping it'll ease my queasy stomach. "You haven't told me anything other than you know who killed my sister but refuse to say."

My gut burns as anger ignites my blood.

He chuckles, but the sound clashes against the pain that twists his expression. "It'll all be over soon."

God, why does he keep saying that? And furthermore, what does that mean? I answer my own question and my stomach revolts. They're gonna kill me.

I pick away at my food in silence, and Hatch drinks while punching out the occasional text. Since when did he get so popular?

A knock on the door makes me jump, slamming my knee into the table.

I study Hatch, who doesn't seem surprised by the visitor. I haven't seen another person besides Hatch since he brought me here.

A sheen of sweat breaks across my skin, and I pull helplessly against my cuffed wrist. Equal parts panic and hope explode in my chest as Hatch cracks the door and speaks in a hushed voice.

I lean to try to peek around his massive back, but I'm at a weird angle and unable to see past him.

Seconds pass before he steps back and a man enters the room. I can't make him out at first, other than he's wearing a baseball hat and his lack of leather and denim tells me he's not a biker.

Once inside, the guy steps closer to me, and the dim lamp light reveals his face.

I choke on a gasp and cough through a sob.

"Drake? Oh God, Drake!" I pull hard with my arm, pushing my seat back and standing up to launch myself into his arms. "Get me out of here." I stand and move toward him, dragging the chair with me.

He peruses me with narrowed eyes, seeing me in nothing but an oversized T-shirt and hair that hasn't been brushed in days, but says nothing.

Dread trickles in, cooling the warmth I'd felt upon first seeing him. My head spins as I try to piece it all together, and when he sets his dark and frigid eyes on mine, it all clicks into place.

I drop back into my chair. "You did this?"

He closes the space between us, but sits at the foot of the bed, just outside arm's reach. Smart. I'd claw his fucking eyes out. "I did."

I swallow the lump forming in my throat. "But . . ." I shake my head, looking between Hatch and Drake. These men aren't strangers. Hatch was a friend and Drake is my boyfriend's brother. "Why?"

He takes off his hat and runs one palm over his cropped hair before popping it back on. "I needed out."

I swing my gaze to Hatch, who throws back more booze, ignoring me. "What does that have to do with me?"

"Blood for blood. A life for a life." He says it with zero feeling, as if he didn't just sign my death warrant.

"My life"—I take a few seconds to process—"for your life."

"Yes."

I should feel something, a wave of rage that crashes over me and takes away all thought and turns me into some kind of feral animal that will risk my very breath for the chance to escape. Instead, I'm strangely numb, as if the concept is too much for my heart to take. Too complex for my mind to assimilate.

"But . . . Mason."

Drake nods, as if he'd considered that too. "He'll get over you."

*That's it? He'll get over me?*

"No, he'll kill you," I spit between clenched teeth, the primal beast inside waking to the idea that by doing this, Drake will cause Mason pain.

He sighs and leans forward, his elbows on his knees. "He'll believe you left him. He's been through it before. He'll get through it again."

No, he won't. Maybe he has in the past, but what we have is different. What we have is forever.

The last band that tethered me to sanity snaps, and I cover my mouth, trying to force back the beginnings of crazed laughter.

His eyes narrow and he takes me in, cautious, as if at any moment I'll morph into a rabid beast. A giggle bursts from between my lips and quickly matures to full-blown laughter.

A chuckle grates from Hatch as I double over in my seat, letting the absurdity overtake me. Tears spring to my eyes as I suck air into my lungs. "He's so gonna kill you."

"Shut up!" Drake's jaw ticks.

I hold up my hand, silently asking him to give me a second, but the giggles continue to roll from my lips. "He's done . . . everything . . . for you." More laughter.

Anger twists his features, his scar turning light against his fury-flushed skin. "I said shut the fuck up!"

"If you kill me . . . he'll find out." I wipe back tears as a sob rolls into a hiccup while the chaos of emotions tumbles through me. "He'll never give up until you're dead."

As sick as it is, the laughter makes me feel better about dying. Maybe it's the stress release or the confirmation of what I knew to be a possibility, but either way, I know Mason will dedicate his life to finding out what happened and make the fucker pay.

I lean back and slide deep into my chair, my T-shirt riding up high on my bare thighs, and smile. "You don't deserve him."

Even beneath the bill of his hat, I can see the war that wages behind his eyes.

"He actually loves you." I tilt my head, stare, and glory in the way he squirms. "Probably the only person who really does."

Drake pushes to standing so quickly my heart jumps. "Don't have to listen to this shit." He pulls something out of his pocket and steps behind me. "Let's get this over with."

Cloth presses against my mouth. I force my lips closed against the intrusion. He wraps a hand around my neck, squeezing tight. "Open. Now."

"Fuck y—" Fabric presses between my teeth and pulls tight. I wince as Drake ties it around the back, ripping hairs from my head in the process.

Another strip of cloth grazes my forehead before the room is plunged into darkness.

"Pull the car around." He releases my cuffed arm and presses between my shoulder blades. "Get the fuck up."

I stand on wobbly legs as he pulls both hands behind my back. The click of the cuffs sends dread swirling in my belly.

Robbed of sight, speech, and mobility, I'm at the mercy of these psychos and marching to the beat of my death sentence.

## MASON

"Shit!" My legs throb with restrained energy. The urge to race out of here, kick that fucking door down, and rage has me jumping out of my skin. "Fuck this. I'm going."

Rex doesn't say a word, but climbs from the truck with me, and we move toward the door. Adrenaline races through my veins, and I have to fight to stay upright as the flow makes me unsteady.

I don't know what's going on behind that door, but I swear to God if they touched a hair on Trix's head I'll kill them with my bare hands and paint the walls in their blood.

My vision clouds, fading to tunnel vision with my focus on that door. I'm vaguely aware of Rex at my back, grateful that he's letting me take the lead on this. We close in when suddenly I'm grabbed from behind. Arms like pythons tighten around my body, and one big hand covers my mouth.

Oh, fuck no.

I leverage my weight, step to the side, ready to sweep the asshole's leg.

"Baywatch." Jonah's voice hisses in my ear. "Calm the fuck down. We're not the enemy."

He releases me, and I spin to see Blake releasing Rex from a similar hold. They motion to a nearby dumpster and we jog there, staying low to the ground.

"You dickheads almost got shot." Rex shoves Blake, who only grins.

"How'd you find us?"

Blake and Jonah share a look I can't read before Blake lifts an eyebrow. "Wild guess."

I run a hand through my hair. "Gia."

Rex groans. "Swear to Christ that woman is gonna be the death of me."

"Can't believe you dick-lickers were gonna keep us out of this." Blake bounces a scowl between us.

"Feels like déjà vu." Jonah's arms bulge against the black fabric of his long-sleeved shirt, like coiled snakes ready to destroy. His jaw clenches. "Gotta say I'm lookin' forward to finally putting this cocksucker down."

Blake, dressed similarly in all black, rolls his head around on his neck. "Fuckin' love beatin' up fat bikers, man. Like punching marshmallow."

"Don't want you guys getting involved in this." I prop my hands on my hips, needing to give them something to do because knowing my woman is possibly only yards away is making me fucking schizo. "You're married, got kids. Let us—"

Blake presses his finger to my mouth. "Shush, babycakes. Let the adults take this one."

I practically spit off his finger, and his cocky grin makes me want to throat punch him, but there are more deserving people just inside this motel.

"Right, so what are we about to face?" Jonah's expression takes on a feral glint. "Please tell me you guys have a better plan than just storming through the front—"

The creak of a rusty motel room door has us all ducking, moving like shadows in unison for a closer look.

"Well, if it isn't our old friend, that tubby fuck." Rex growls and I move, only to get hooked around the bicep and pulled back. "Where's he going?"

"Baywatch, don't be an idiot." The low timbre of Jonah's voice snaps me back.

Blake holds up a hand. "Let's wait. We don't have a visual yet."

I shake my head. "No, I can't wait." I point to the room Hatch just exited. "She could be in there with some fuckin' guy right now!" I stand to move forward, not caring if any of those assholes catch wind of me. If anything, the very idea of getting spotted sends a thrill through my muscles as they stretch and prepare for a fight.

The low rumble of a truck engine catches my attention, and I crouch instinctively. An older Jeep Wrangler, brown, lifted, with no top and huge KC lights comes from around the corner with Hatch behind the wheel.

"Shit, they're moving." Rex motions for us to head back to my truck.

"Wait, why not just take this asshole down here?"

"Patience, man. They have a gun on her, see us coming; we don't want to risk that." The anger in Jonah's voice is palpable.

"If she's even here." Blake doesn't take his eyes off the door as Hatch heads in to the motel room.

Come on, baby. Come on. Let me see you.

Seconds later he strolls out, his eyes scan the surrounding area, and then he motions for the man behind him to follow.

It's dark, and the man in the baseball hat emerges with a woman.

My heart throbs. Vision blurs. But nothing can mistake the platinum and purple streaks.

"Fuck!" They have her. As anger boils so does relief. She's alive.

T-shirt. Bare legs. A growl gurgles up from my chest. Guided by the other guy, she's blindfolded and gagged, but seems unharmed.

I fish my keys from my pocket. "Call the cops. Now."

"They're thirty minutes away."

I rip my gaze from Trix to set it on Blake. "Perfect. They'll get here in time to clean up the bodies."

# THIRTY-SEVEN

## TRIX

"Get down and stay down." Drake hooks my neck and pulls my head to his lap.

I resist, but he's stronger, and my cheek crashes against his thigh.

He chuckles. "Aww, come on. I know this position ain't new to you."

I try to grind my teeth but only meet the unforgiving fabric of my gag. The engine roars, and we reverse in a quick jerk. Drake's hold on my shoulder is the only thing keeping me from tumbling to the floorboard. I track our movements. Three left turns before we finally reach top speed.

The wind is warm, howling in my ears and whipping my hair around my face in stinging slaps. We're on the highway, and judging by the hoist I needed to get in the car, I'd say we're in some kind of all-terrain vehicle. My guess is we're headed further outside of town, and the sick roll of my stomach worries about being taken to a more secluded location.

The smell of Drake's cologne pollutes the fresh air, and I wish I could curl my arms around my stomach to keep myself covered and shielded from the wind. I flex my fists and focus on the burn of my handcuffs hoping to take my focus from the ache in my chest.

Mason's brother is behind my kidnapping. That two faced son-of-a-bitch! My fingers itch to wrap my hands around his bitch-ass throat, choking the life out of him before throwing him to the highway like roadkill.

Part of me almost feels sorry for him. After all, Mason's not stupid. However this ends, Mason will figure it out, and he will destroy his brother for it.

I don't know how much time has passed, but it feels like forever before we slow and turn right. The sound of tires crunching on bare dirt fires panic in my blood. We're not in the mountains. If anything, I sensed a descent. We must be in the desert.

I focus on my hearing, searching for some source of help, the sound of other cars, people, anything, but I'm met with silence. The only smell I can detect outside of Drake's cologne is dirt.

We slow and I'm tapped on the shoulder. "We're here." Drake helps to push me up and brushes against my knees as he climbs out in front of me. "Here." He grabs my biceps to lead me out.

My head swims. Lack of food and getting up too quickly throw me off balance. My bare foot catches. I tumble forward, the gag preventing me from calling out. My shoulder slams against something sharp. Pain splinters down my arm.

"Fuck." Drake scoops under my arms, twisting me at an odd angle to pull me free of the back seat. He mumbles a curse. "You're bleeding."

Panic taints his voice. Why? He kidnapped and took me to the middle of nowhere to be killed, and he's upset because I'm bleeding?

He leans me up against the vehicle, and he touches my bicep. "Shit." Turning me around, he releases my hands from the cuffs. "Don't do anything stupid."

My shoulders ache, but I move to inspect my wound. Still blindfolded, I run my fingers over the torn cotton shirt to the wet and ragged skin beneath. I wince and follow the trickle of blood that flows down to my wrist.

He fumbles with the tie at the back of my head. "Here, let me—

I slap his hand away, yelling get the fuck off me, but it's all gibberish from behind my gag.

A growled sound of frustration reaches my ears at the same time his hands go back to my head. "Trust me, okay?"

*Is he out of his fucking mind?*

The gag is pulled free. I work my jaw back and forth to squelch the ache then move to pull free my blindfold.

"No." His hands hold mine still. "Not yet."

My arm stings as he wraps what I assume to be the gag around my wounded arm.

"There. Come on." He grips my wrist and pulls me forward.

I take a few steps, cringing against the pain of jagged rocks beneath my feet. I stumble as something sharp pierces the ball of my foot. I hiss through my teeth and trip, but strong arms keep me from falling.

Another huff of frustration and I'm off the ground, pressed against a solid chest. The scent of leather and highway give Hatch away as he cradles me and moves with heavy steps. I try to reach down, to tuck the length of the T-shirt I'm wearing over my bare butt.

Hatch chuckles. "Don't bother. Too dark to see shit out here."

"Where are you taking me?" I don't expect an answer, but I have to ask. At the very least I need to keep them talking.

"You'll see soon enough." His voice is cold, harder than I'm used to hearing; although everything about Hatch has changed.

Low murmurs of male voices prick my ears and send my pulse skyrocketing. More of them. A lot more of them.

I wiggle, fighting for Hatch to release me. I don't care how much it hurts. I'll run. They might shoot me in the back, but I have a feeling a quick death would be better than what they have planned.

"Please, let me go. I won't tell anyone, I promise." I fight harder only to be locked down tightly to his chest.

"No way. I need this and"—he gets quiet, as if he's struggling with what he's about to say—"so do you."

My mouth hangs open, prepared to launch at him for saying I *need* to be murdered, but before I can get the first word out, my feet are dropped to the warm desert floor.

He swings me around so that my back is to him, his hands placed firmly on my shoulders. Then he's gone.

I sway, disoriented now that I don't have something grounding me. I reach for my blindfold, knowing that if someone is close enough they'll stop me, and if not, I'll run.

Slowly, I peel back the fabric, and when no one stops me, I push it up to my forehead. Fuzzy silhouettes come into focus, and my eyes grow wide as fear chills my blood.

All men.

Some I recognize as Hatch's crew, others I don't. They're all standing in a circle around me, each one with the stone-hard face of a killer. My pulse pounds in my neck, and my legs feel like they're filled with concrete.

The ring of bodies parts to let through a man I don't recognize. Overgrown dark brown hair with a hint of gray around his sideburns, he doesn't look all that threatening. His average height and slightly muscular build scream every day guy, but the aura of pure evil that reflects in his black glare tells me all I need to know.

This dude is dangerous.

"Job well done, son." His words are directed at Drake, who I've noticed isn't standing in the circle along with the others, but is a few feet behind my left shoulder.

Drake simply nods.

Son? Drake kidnapped me for his dad?

Memories of what Mason told me about Drake's dad filter through my mind: criminal, psychopath, soulless.

I blink, the confusion and utter ridiculousness of this making my head swim.

Drake's dad spins on his heel to address the group. "You've all pledged to join me, to make my friends your friends and my enemies your enemies." He prowls in slow circles around me like a predator stalking his prey. "Tonight we make a blood oath."

They all grunt their agreement.

"We shed blood to prove our loyalty and our commitment to the club and to each other. If one goes down, we all go down." His eyes pierce mine and a slow smile curves his lips. "This lovely sacrifice has been brought to us by my son." His gaze swings to Drake. "You've proven you're ready to move on, and after tonight, you have my blessing."

Drake winces as his dad grips his shoulder. "And if you tell anyone about what you know, I'll have you as an accomplice to murder." He smiles at his son as if he just wished him good luck on his SATs.

His attention shifts back to me, and I search for Hatch to plead that he save me, but his eyes are downcast in avoidance. I turn to Drake, whose expression is a blank wall. He nods, and when I turn around, his father is less than a foot from me.

I gasp and lean away from him.

He hooks the back of my neck and pulls me toward him until I can feel the heat of his breath on my face. His hand slides around to cup my jaw, and he runs the pad of his thumb along my cheek in tender swipes. "Incredible . . ." His eyes twinkle with wonder, and my insides meet his compliment with nausea. "You look just like her."

Everything stops. My breath. Blood. Heartbeat. All of it suspended for a moment in time, everything except his lips.

"Now you'll die like her."

—

## MASON

"Why the fuck are we just sitting here?" I whisper to the guys as we crouch low behind a gathering of large creosote bushes.

Blake and Jonah share a look, something they've been doing often, and it makes me want to knock their skulls together.

Jonah studies me, and I can't miss the flash of pity I see in his eyes. "We're outnumbered. There're at least twenty of them, and they're most likely armed."

"So what? We just sit here with our dicks in our hands and wait for the cops? Who knows what could happen to her before they get here?"

We'd followed the rusty Jeep, maintaining a good distance to keep from getting spotted, and once they turned down the secluded desert road we had to pull even further back. At one point, I thought we'd lost them, but thankfully the sandy dirt tracks were an excellent giveaway.

"Got a better idea?" Blake's eyes stay forward, his body tense.

I turn back and calculate how long it would take to grab my truck parked about a mile away behind a large boulder. They might have guns, but if I drive fast enough, I could burst through their little Kumbaya circle and grab Trix.

"Yeah, I do." I turn to head to my truck.

"Whoa, hold up." Rex snags my elbow, pulling me back to the bush. "Do you see that?"

We all lean in, squinting through the sparse leaves. The circle of men has split into a large U-shape, and in the middle is Trix. Her stark white T-shirt glows in a pool of inky black night. She's still, not being held in place by anyone or anything physical, but stuck nonetheless. Her body sways, but her feet stay planted.

"She drugged?" Jonah growls and the tension between around us escalates.

One guy steps forward, clearly visible now that the circle has opened up. He's talking, using his hands to motion between Trix and the men who stand around bouncing on their toes in anticipation.

"This is bad." I squint for a better look while the guy waves his arms around. "This is really ba—*what the fuck?*"

Elijah.

Fire ignites in my veins and pushes me to stand. The guys hiss at me to get down, but it's too late. Simple static fills my ears as I move forward. Hands grip my legs, my arms, but I shake them off as if they're nothing while my focus zeroes in on Elijah.

They must hear me coming as, all of a sudden, the eyes of the enemy swivel toward me. Trix stares blankly at nothing, not registering my approach. The weight of the knife in my pocket warms my thigh, but I don't reach for it. My fists ball, and I prepare to destroy the man who's been fucking with my brother since birth, the man who's tormented my mom, and now the man who's fucked with my woman.

"Mason?" My stride slows, and my stomach hollows out at the sound of Drake's voice. Him too?

He steps into my line of sight, standing as a barrier between Elijah and me, locking Trix behind him.

I blink and force my lips to move, processing his hat, his shirt, his . . . It was him at the motel. "*You*? You did this!" Adrenaline bursts like sweet nectar into my blood and feeds my anger. "My own fucking brother!"

I move to the echo of my roar as it acts like a war cry to my soul.

He puts his hands up, but it's too late. "No—"

My fist connects. The sickening crack sends him skidding across the dirt.

Chaos breaks out behind me, but I only have eyes for the man in front of me.

Elijah grins, daring me to move. I lunge. He moves and pulls Trix to his chest. "One more move and the girl dies."

I fix on her eyes, no longer vacant but now aware and filled with fear.

"Mason . . ." Her lips whisper and fade into a whimper.

Blood. All I see is blood. Her upper arm is wrapped and blood-soaked from an older wound. My stomach lurches. A slow stream leaks from where the tip of Elijah's knife is pointed at her neck.

"Back the fuck up or she's dead." He says it like a challenge more than a threat.

He *wants* to kill her.

"Don't hurt her." I step back, keeping my eyes on hers, and hoping like hell she can find strength in them. "Let her go."

"Fuck you." Spit shoots from his lips.

There's a scuffle from behind me, feet pounding the dirt and the sickening thud of fists and flesh. I say a quick prayer that my friends come out of this uninjured, but don't dare take my eyes off Elijah.

"Please." I hold up my hands as Trix trembles in his arms. "Walk away, Eli." My patience is tethered by a thread as he jerks her head back hard.

"Can't do that." I see a flash of panic in his eyes. "She knows too much."

I meet Trix's gaze, asking the silent question. They widen with primal ferocity. What's she saying?

"It was him." The confession darts from her lips with an undertone of absolute fact.

More blood pours from the tip of Eli's knife.

"Snitchin' whore." A sick smile curls his lips. "Just like her sister."

She cries out, and the sound slices through my chest.

I blink and shake my head, sure I misheard. "*What* did you say?"

Trix cries out. More blood. She claws at his arms, but he doesn't let up.

Dread and fear and anger mix in a volatile cocktail of hate.

"You fucking heard me, asshole." He rips Trix back farther, her bare feet skidding in the dirt as they search for purchase. His eyes are wild, like I've seen Drake's when he's high and paranoid. "She's a snitch."

I step forward, watching the blood drain from Trix's face. Her legs wobble and Eli hoists her up.

"You killed Lana." Uncertainty gives way to rage. "It was you—"

I'm grabbed from behind, the cool metal of a gun shoved into my temple. I struggle against it. A thick forearm wraps around my neck.

Two guys have me locked down. I don't allow my eyes to move from Trix's.

"End him. Now." Elijah says.

Trix lurches forward. "No—" Her voice cuts off with a vicious tug at her head. My heart pounds.

I struggle again, but I'm overpowered. I throw everything I have left into getting to her, but gain zero distance. Fuck, this is it.

"Kill him!" Elijah's eyes are bulging from his head; the knife he's holding to Trix shakes in his hand.

One of the men holding me back groans. "Fuck."

The gun cocks.

I struggle harder, hoping one of my guys gets to me before Trix has to see my brains blown out over the desert.

"Mason, no!" Trix flails in uncoordinated kicks until the neck of her shirt is soaked in her own blood.

The visual rockets through my veins.

Fury rolls, swelling. Svetlana died because of what she saw, now so will Trix. Just like her sister, she'll be cut and sliced.

It builds, raging in a violent crest. Ripped from everyone who loves her. Taken from me with one swipe of that blade across her neck.

Madness ramps as the weight crashes.

First Lana, now Trix.

Tortured.

Destroyed.

Lost forever.

I roar and rip from the hold. The flare of a shot fired doesn't slow me down. Elijah's eyes widen seconds before I hit. Trix's body falls limp to the ground as I tackle him. His knife jabs, but I feel nothing except for the passion that rages for justice. Every hit connects. The battle with flesh and bone mirror the battle within as I release years of anger on the man who's hurt those I love.

The heat of fresh blood coats my hands, and I can't stop. Voices call out, hands try to grab, but my obsession for revenge spurs me on. His arms drop limply, his head lolling with every punishing blow. But it's not enough.

Wind whips around my head, kicking up dust to coat my blood-soaked arms with grit. Registering on some level that he's out, I can't pull back my fury. Can't cage the beast that's out for revenge. For Trix and for Lana.

He deserves to die.

Lights shine brightly all around, but it's fogged, tempered by my mania.

My lips curl back over my teeth, and the metal tang of splattered blood feeds the fire. More, more, I'll never stop. I don't fatigue. Left-right-left-right, every punch energizes the next.

Can't . . . stop . . .

My muscles lock up. Fuck! Heat stuns me still. I'm knocked to the ground. My body flops without control. I struggle to get up, to finish what I started, but my muscles spasm and ignore my efforts. I try to look around, but even my eyes are doing their own thing.

Soft hands cradle my head. Trix's eyes fill my field of vision. Tears stream down her face. "Shh . . . it's okay."

No! I try to force the word, but nothing comes out. She must know as she cradles me closer, rocking. "It's okay. Everything's going to be okay now."

She's not safe. Not yet. Not until every motherfucker here is dead. I fight, push my body to react to my brain's commands, but get nothing.

"It's over . . . shh . . . stop fighting it." Her voice soothes as I come back into my body. "It's okay," she calls out to someone. "He's okay." The last word cracks with emotion.

Twitching, I force my muscles to respond. I reach up and wrap my hand around her neck, her blood tacky against my palm. I flex my fingers into her neck, trying to communicate. *I'm okay, but you're bleeding.*

She holds my grip to her wounded skin. "I'm good. I promise." She runs her fingers through my hair and keeps her eyes locked with mine. I'm unable to release her neck. Feeling her pulse flutter beneath my fingertips is the best fucking feeling, and I hold them there until our heartbeats align.

No one's coming after us. It's over.

This could've ended so differently. My stomach turns, and I slam my eyes closed to keep from puking like a little bitch. What the hell happened to me? My fingers flex again against Trix's neck. She's here. Alive. That's what matters.

My muscles calm and I move to sit up. Pain slices through my arm, but it dies quickly when I study my surroundings. "Holy shit!"

Helicopters and SWAT teams litter the once-dark desert floor. I scan the area, able to make out faces that are now illuminated as spotlights shine on every space.

Jonah helps a man to his feet, only to hand him over to be cuffed. Blake's arms are crossed over his chest while he's deep in conversation with a guy who looks completely out of place in a suit and tie. I search for Rex, but can't find him.

Fuck! My stomach lurches again and I push up further. "Come on. Where is he?"

Trix's grips my forearm. "Who?"

My eyes continue to survey. "Rex. I . . . if anything happened to him . . ." Dammit, he has to be okay.

"There!" She points over my shoulder to a cop leading Rex away in handcuffs.

I push to stand, but fire stabs through my arms and my side. I groan and drop back to my ass.

"Mase . . . you're hurt." Her hands move over me in tentative touches, but I can't take my eyes of Rex, who's being loaded into the back of a van.

"Sorry, man." A SWAT guy dressed in black tactical gear steps in front of me. "We had to tase you."

"Why is my friend being arrested?" I motion toward the van whose doors just slammed shut.

"Looks like you've got some injuries." The cop studies my arms and torso.

I tilt my chin and see multiple puncture wounds in my arm. Eli, that fucking asshole. "Why is Rex being arrested?"

The cop swings his gaze to the bloody heap of a man at my side then to another mound of blood and body across the way before turning back to me. "I'm afraid you and your friend have some explaining to do."

I didn't have to hear him say the words to know what we'd done.

Elijah and Hatch are dead.

# THIRTY-EIGHT

## TRIX

Everything is so fucked up.

While I'm sitting in a hospital waiting room, unable to see Mason, who's in a hospital exam room guarded by cops, Rex is at the police station. They've both been arrested for murder, but Mason's stab wounds had to be attended to before—I take a shaky breath—before they take him to jail.

I've answered all the questions and given them all the information I have, everything from the night Svetlana was murdered until now. They know the truth, and even though they see me suffering for answers, they've given me none.

The door to Mason's room opens, and Detective Hodgeson, the man who questioned me both at the scene and again here at the hospital, strolls out. His eyes latch on mine, and he waves off the cops who are with him. They nod and leave, and he heads over to take the seat next to mine.

I shift and wipe my palms on the fresh scrubs they gave me when I arrived. I was able to clean up a little in the bathroom, washing the blood and dirt from my arms and face, but the smell of death still lingers on my skin.

"Miss Langley." With his dark hair and kind eyes, he smiles at me so sweetly that I almost cry.

No, hold back. I have to be strong for Mason.

"Is he okay?" I fist my hands in my lap.

He nods. "He's fine. He'll be sore, and I'm pretty sure they lost count of how many stitches he got, but he'll be okay. Luckily, the knife missed all his vital organs."

I exhale and my shoulders droop. "Oh, thank God."

"You were very brave tonight." The edge of anger tinges his words. "Things could've gone differently if we'd had better intel." He shakes his head.

From what I understand, Jonah and Blake called the cops, and if they'd been even five minutes later . . . A shiver slithers up my spine. Detective Hodgeson's words finally sink into my sleep-deprived and traumatized brain. "Wait . . . intel? What do you mean?"

He tilts his head, studying me. "I think you need to talk to Mr. Mahoney."

I jerk my gaze from him to Mason's hospital room door. "What? Can I? I mean they said I couldn't."

He shrugs one shoulder. "I think it's okay. I'll need to talk to the DA, but something tells me charges won't be filed. Everything else you need to know you should probably hear from him."

Taking that as permission, I shoot to my feet and move toward the door. His chuckle makes me pause, and I realize I was rude not to thank him. "Thank you," I call over my shoulder then speed walk through the door that the guards had opened for me.

My heart pounds wildly as I step into the sterile room. My gaze goes to the bed, but it's empty and looks like it hasn't even been sat on. I move deeper into the room, but Mason's nowhere to be found. Moving back to the hallway, light from the cracked bathroom door catches my eye. My cheeks heat, and I contemplate waiting until he's finished, but the sound of his mumbled voice pulls me to peek inside.

I cover my mouth to keep from gasping aloud at the sight of Mason. His hands are flexed, fists braced on the sink, and his wide and powerful back ripples with tension. White gauze and tape litter his flawless skin in patches over his left bicep, forearm, and ribcage. My gaze slides down his muscular back to the swell of his backside, which peeks up from above the loose-hanging scrubs. I gawk shamelessly at him, this warrior.

*My* warrior.

"Trix, baby." His soft whisper brings my eyes up to find him staring at me through the reflection in the mirror.

Time ceases as our gazes fuse in an unrelenting hold.

He studies the gauze wrapped around my upper arm and then drops his gaze to my neck, which is wrapped in bandages, with a few stitches underneath.

To think he was stabbed, could've died there in the middle of the desert as I held him to me. I'd never have survived that. My hand goes to my throat, realizing how quickly both our lives could've been over. Tears prick my eyes, and I roll my lips between my teeth to keep them from quivering.

He turns and crosses to me in long strides. "No, baby, don't cry."

Pulled tight to his chest, I wrap my arms around his hips.

"Shh. Everything's okay." He rubs my back, pressing firmly to loosen the tense muscles. "My brave surfer girl."

The warmth of his bare skin on my cheek fills me with a sense of belonging. "I'm so sorry, Mason. This is all my fault. I should've walked away like you said. I should've—"

"No." He grips my chin and tilts my head back to meet his glacial eyes. "Don't say that. Don't ever fucking apologize for them, do you understand?"

My eyes dart to the side. "Prison, Mason. I know what the detective said, but what if you end up in prison because of me?"

His eyebrows drop low beneath the shag of his blond hair. "About that . . ." He shifts me, and with his hand splayed at my lower back, he leads me to the bed. "There's something you need to know."

Whatever calm I'd found dissolves, and my blood turns cold.

He crawls onto the bed, motioning for me to join him on his right side. I curl into him, and he wraps an arm around me, settling in deeper.

"What is it?"

He clears his throat. "We got played."

I jerk my head up and wince as pain slices through my neck. "What? By who?"

He presses my head back down to his chest, resting his big hand on my neck as if to soothe it. "Jessica's pregnant and—"

"Oh wow, really? That sucks." I shrug. "Spawn of the devil and all." I can't help but hate Drake after everything he put us through.

His thumb runs along the tender skin of my jaw in a way that feels like he's trying to placate me. "Drake wanted out of his obligation to Elijah, but they made some kind of blood oath, a life for a life."

He doesn't have to explain more. This is the part of the story I already know. "I was the life."

"Yes, and also a sacrifice that would bond an alliance he was forming with some new guys." His fingers flex against my neck. "But apparently everything that happened tonight was put into motion months ago."

Months?

"Your buddy Hatch was on the run in Mexico—"

"I know."

He makes a sound deep in his chest, half groan, half growl. "Right, but what you don't know is the cops found him."

I peek up at him. "Really."

"Mm-hm." He presses my cheek back to his chest. "Turns out Hatch confessed to his crimes, and in order to get a more lenient sentence, he agreed to lead the cops to someone they'd been after for a long time now."

"Elijah."

"Exactly. So when Hatch realized Drake was Eli's kid, he made sure to organize the drug deal that I stupidly interrupted."

"Okay, so Hatch was working for the cops, but why did they kidnap me?"

"Drake wanted out; Eli wouldn't let him go. After Drake found out Jess was pregnant, he went to the cops. He told them that he'd share all the information he had if they'd make sure to end Elijah and his crew and never tell them who'd outed their operation."

"Oh my God, so . . ."

"The cops agreed, let D in on the fact that Hatch was working with them, and together they figured out a way to get Elijah and the majority of his crew away from the city and together where they could be taken down."

"So they used me as bait."

"Once Hatch found that picture of Svetlana at your place"—the growl in his voice demonstrates that the very idea of Hatch being in my place still makes him furious—"he'd found his golden ticket." His thumb rubs my jaw again. "He knew all along Eli killed your sister, baby, and he knew once that piece of shit Eli knew you were snooping he'd never resist the urge to take you out too."

My breath catches in my throat, but Mason's warmth and soothing touch releases the tension. "Drake and Hatch were working for the cops, but that doesn't mean things couldn't have backfired."

"Right." His muscles tense. "I'll never forgive Drake for using your life in this sick fuckin' game."

Relief washes over me. "If not me, then who?"

"Excuse me?"

"I mean, if it wasn't me they took, it would've been some other girl." I shrug, suddenly more grateful than ever for the past few days of my captivity. "I'd never wish that kind of fear on any woman. Can't even imagine how scared

Lana must've been." Tears burn my eyes, but I push them back and hold Mason tighter.

"Amazing." The word drifts from his lips with an exhale. "I keep waiting for you to break down, for this all to be too much and for you to spiral, but you never do."

"Just because I don't wear the gloves doesn't mean I'm not a fighter like you."

A low chuckle rumbles in his chest, making me grin. "No, you're ten times the fighter I'll ever be, Beatriks." His lips press softly into my hair.

"Poor Gia." To consider what she must be going through makes my heart hurt. She always said Rex would kill Hatch if he ever found him. She'll never admit it, but as much as she hates what Hatch became, I know she feels some kind of friendship with him.

Just as I did.

"She'll be okay, Trix." Another kiss to my head. "And so will you."

His words remind me that this could be our last time together. He took human life with his bare hands and could be thrown in prison to pay for his sin.

"What's going to happen to you?" I whisper.

He sighs, long and heavy with meaning. "I don't know. I guess I'll get officially arrested, be taken to jail. Hodgeson says the DA won't prosecute and the cops are hoping all this shit is seen as justice served."

I wrap my arms tighter around him, and he grunts, but when I try to pull my arm away, he holds it to him. "I'm sure he's right." No way could I stand to lose Mason to jail time. If I could somehow physically fuse our bodies together, I would. "Hatch's involvement explains a lot."

"Yeah, Detective Hodgeson said he's requesting solitary—"

"Wait, what?" I plant my palm on Mason's chest and push up to sitting. "Hatch is alive?"

He rolls his eyes. "Unfortunately, yes. Rex knew what he was doing, thought a lifetime in prison would be a better punishment than death, not to mention the cops needed as much info as they could get out of him. Can't get shit from a dead man."

"But Eli . . .?" I'm afraid to ask, but want to make sure I didn't misunderstand.

"Elijah is dead." A shadow passes through his eyes followed by resolve. "I killed him, and I'd do it again if it meant saving you."

## MASON

Saying good-bye to the Las Vegas County Police Department less than twenty-four hours after being taken there was better than I expected. I don't know who pushed my case to the front of the line, but when I shove through the glass door and out into the desert sun, the grins on the faces of the three men waiting for me gives them away.

"Baywatch, welcome to the LVPD Ass Rape Club." Blake loops an arm around my neck and thumps my back. "Now you gotta learn our motto." He stands up tall, puffs out his chest, and cups his crotch. "You fuck with the law; they fuck right back. Protect your junk and your ass crack."

I scratch my head, my lips curling. "I'll pass on the membership, but if it's okay, I'd like to transfer it to my brother."

Blake laughs just as Rex approaches.

"Glad you're out, man." He shakes my hand but pulls me in for a quick hug.

"Hey, I have one question." I scowl between Blake and Jonah. "Was it just some crazy coincidence that Hodgeson and Blake have history and he's the one who orchestrated the whole takedown?"

I wait for them to fill in the blanks, to sate my curiosity.

They share another look and I shake my head. "See, that shit right there. What do you guys know that you're not telling me?"

Blake steps forward. "Gia called us right after you two took off. I called Dave and he told me what was going down."

Jonah shoves his hands into his pockets and shrugs. "Couldn't let you face that shit alone, brother. Hodgeson told us to hold back, let them do their job, said they had a shit ton of undercover men with Elijah and Hatch's crew."

No wonder that night didn't end up a bloodbath. We thought we were outnumbered. But some of them were cops. Makes sense because none of us should've walked away.

"I made it clear that wasn't an option." Blake shifts his gaze from me to Rex. "We have each other's backs. Always."

Fuck if all this shit doesn't make me want to cry like a pussy-ass baby. "So that's why you guys kept holding me back that night. You knew the cops had a plan and—"

"We didn't want you to fuck it up by getting killed." Jonah slaps me on the back of the head. "Looks like your official."

"Officially what?" I rub my injured arm as the wounds seem to flare with the reminder of that night.

He crosses his arms over his chest, looking lethal. "One of us."

I absorb the warm feeling of belonging that seeps into my veins. All I've ever wanted is to be an equal member of the UFL Team, but from day one, I felt like an outsider, like a pledge who had to prove himself to be accepted.

I mirror Jonah's stance. "So that's it? All I had to do is kill someone?"

The air wires with tension, as if what I said was inappropriate or disrespectful. I'll never regret what I did. Not a single day of my life will I feel bad for making it so

Trix, her family, Drake, Jessica, and my niece or nephew, can all breathe easy knowing that evil bastard has been wiped from the earth. And if I serve time for that, I'll gladly take it.

The guys are still quiet, all of them darting eyes between each other.

I shrug. "What? Too soon?"

With that they burst into laughter and lead the way toward the parking lot.

"Nice to see incarceration hasn't changed you, Baywatch." Rex slaps me on the back of the head as he passes.

"Ow, fuckface! How 'bout you let up on the stupid nicknames." I rub my head. "If I'm an equal, why the fuck do you piss-suckers keep smacking me?"

"We like your hair." Blake pulls open the back door of Jonah's truck, ushering me in. "Come on, Hasselhoff. Quit being a bitch."

I pass him and into the back seat when another stinging slap comes to the back of my head.

Fuckin' hell, even though I'm tempted to whirl around and sink my knuckles into Blake's chest, I don't. Because brotherhood is about having each other's backs, fighting for what's best, and making sure your brother knows it.

Way my head's burning, I don't think I could ever forget it.

---

After the guys dropped me off at home, I took a long hot shower. Standing in the tiled space, my eyes closed, I remember the night Trix showed up in tears. How I wish I could go back, tie her up, and never set her free until she agreed to leave all that shit with Hatch alone.

If only.

With strict instructions to keep my wounds as dry as possible, I reluctantly shut off the shower and grab a towel when my phone vibrates on the bathroom counter. I grab it and move to answer when the caller ID catches my eye.

"Fuck." I wrap my towel around my waist, hit "accept," and head into my bedroom. "Got nothing to say to you."

"You answered, so there's a start."

"I'm serious, Drake. I get that this was all planned and you needed an out, but next time, use *your* fucking woman as bait."

I'm met with silence and then throat clearing. "Fuck, brother—"

"Don't fucking call me that." I stare across the room with the memory of Drake dragging my woman, blindfolded, cuffed, and gagged, to the desert for what she thought would be a slow death. "You've lost the right to call me brother."

"We're family."

"Family isn't dictated by blood. It's determined by loyalty, and you proved you're a selfish prick."

He huffs out a breath. "Alright, I deserve that."

"Fuck yeah, you do." The memory of Trix, fear flashing in those violet eyes, her shirt soaked in blood, assaults me. Yeah, Drake deserves a lot worse.

"For what it's worth, I'm really sorry. If I thought there was a better way, I'd have done it. They were gunnin' for Trix anyway. I knew she'd be safe as long as Hatch and I were with her. Elijah would've sent one of his goons if I didn't volunteer. I'd never let anyone hurt her."

A feeling akin to regret rolls around in my gut, but I push it back, unable to fully accept his reasoning, even if on some level it does make sense.

I run a hand through my wet hair. "Need time."

"I get that."

Silence builds between us.

"Right well . . . Take care."

I hit "end" and drop back to the bed. Fuck. He's right. I know he is, but even with time, will I ever be able to forgive him?

# THIRTY-NINE

## TRIX

No matter how many times I stare at the boxes in front of me, I can't help but feel like I'm forgetting something. Amazing how the last four years of my life fit in a dozen boxes and a suitcase. I check each label, making sure the ones that need to go into storage are clearly marked and the ones that come with me are too.

My stomach tumbles with excitement.

After I left Mason in the hospital two days ago, he ordered me to pack my things saying, "I don't know what's going to happen, but I want you with me until it does."

It didn't take much reading between the lines to understand what he meant: he wants to be together until the day they lock him up.

The thought of saying no didn't even cross my mind. If this last week has taught me anything, it's that life is fragile. From here on out, I'll take advantage of every opportunity, and when it comes to Mason, there's no place else I'd rather be.

Turns out that my moving in with Mason isn't only a comfort for each other, but it's practical too, seeing as I'm jobless.

I quit Zeus's. I didn't give notice, or even have to show my face. One call to my boss and he let me go and even said he'd give me a glowing recommendation. It ended up being a lot easier than I thought, but something tells me Detective Hodgeson had something to do with that.

Hodgeson wasn't aware of Santos' involvement in my kidnapping. Although Drake and Hatch were working closely with the police, Santos wasn't and turned me over without the knowledge that I'd be safe.

That information stung like a bitch.

I still don't blame him for what he did. Hatch's guys did have Diane, and from what I hear, they beat Santos pretty bad after he turned me over to ensure he kept his silence, but betrayal is still betrayal.

I move through the house one more time, ready to leave my old life behind and start a new one. The memories of this house will stay like ghosts searching for peace while I move forward without a backward glance.

My phone chirps with a new text.

**Hope you're ready. Once I get you home, I'm never letting you go.**

I grin and bite my lip, amazed that I can feel the sincerity behind his words by simply reading them.

**Even if you let me go, I'd never leave. No good-byes, remember?**

I hit "send" and hope that bringing up the breakup call Hatch insisted I make doesn't hurt him—my phone chirps.

**Good-bye? What language is that? I'm afraid I don't know what you mean.**

I let my fingers fly over the keys in response.

**It doesn't concern us. What does concern us is that I'm anxious to see you after two days, and if you don't pick me up soon I might explode.**

His response is instantaneous.

**Well then get your sexy ass out here. I've been sitting in your driveway for five minutes.**

My heart leaps in my chest, and I race to the door, swing it open, and find Mason halfway up the walk. We both stop, staring with wild eyes and devouring each other before I move. He must see it coming because he braces seconds before I launch myself into his arms.

He grunts from what I assume to be his stab wounds, but he doesn't let me go. One hand cups my ass, and the other digs into my hair, pressing my face into his neck. "Fuck, baby, I missed you so much."

"Me too." I run my nose along his neck, drinking in his earthy sweet scent with the knowledge that I'll get to do it every day from now until . . . I shake off the heavy feeling that comes along with an uncertain future and just hold on tighter. "Am I hurting you?"

"Nothing hurts when I'm with you."

I smile against his corded neck. "I mean your arm. Does it hurt to hold me?"

"Answer's the same." His hand slips up my thigh and under my cutoff shorts to grip my bare bottom. He groans, and his fist in my hair tightens. "Your roommate home?"

I chuckle, and the sound rolls from my throat thick with lust. "No, but I don't want to stay here for another second." Leaning back, I fix my eyes on him. "The next time I'm naked with you I want it to be in our bed."

The fog of desire clears from his crystal-blue eyes for a second, and love like I've never seen shines from their aqua depths. Just like floating on that surfboard and staring out into the infinite sea, locked in Mason's eyes I've never felt more a part of something. More needed, complete.

And finally free to hold tight to my forever.

# FORTY

## TRIX

The next few weeks pass in a blur. Mason and I have nothing but time to settle in to our new lives together. Mason's back to training at the UFL; bypassing doctor's orders to take four weeks off, he took one.

I've started working part-time at the Youth Center until something full-time opens up. If there's one look that could rival Mason's when he came to rescue me in the desert, it would be the relief and joy on Denny's face when I showed up at the Youth Center. His bright eyes and larger-than-an-eight-year-old-face-can-handle smile only solidified my purpose in life: to love kids who don't get enough at home.

Other than the occasional nightmares and Mason disowning his brother, I'd say life is good. Great even. Better than I ever expected.

Turns out Detective Hodgeson was right. The DA didn't press charges for Elijah's death, and all the guys came out of that night as local heroes. We were able to put the night behind us and focus on moving forward.

But, there's just one last thing I have to do.

I check the clock on the bedside table, waiting for the last number to click over from nine to zero when the strong arm that's tossed over my body tightens around my chest. One big hand cups my breast, and I'm pulled back into the cradle of Mason's torso.

"How long you gonna stare at it?" His groggy voice at my ear sends waves of goose bumps across my skin.

I sigh. “I’m willing it to freeze.”

“How’s that working?”

“It’s not.”

His low chuckle makes me grin. “Shooting ice with your eyes, huh?” His lips brush the shell of my ear. “Been watchin’ too many Disney movies.”

I turn in his arms, and he loosens his hold to allow me room before tugging my body flush with his. He slides his massive thigh between mine, and our legs tangle beneath the sheets. My body warms, and I’m amazed at how even the softest, most innocent touches feel erotic.

He kisses my forehead. “Nervous about today?”

I sigh and nuzzle into his neck. “I don’t want to go.”

“Then don’t.” His tone is serious and laced with anger.

“I have to. You know I have to.”

He nods, but the way his muscles tense says it all. He doesn’t want me to go.

After Hatch was released from the hospital and put in prison, his lawyer said they’d grant my parents and me a private meeting. I immediately turned them down, not interested in hearing what he has to say or bringing up the past that would only upset my mom and dad. But my parents insisted on going. And I can’t let them go alone.

“It’s fucked up I can’t be there with you.”

I peer up into the most loving and loyal set of blue eyes that soothe my frazzled nerves. “His lawyer set the terms. Besides, it’s probably best to keep you two separated.”

“Psht. Guy deserves to get his ass—”

I press my lips to his and hold them there until his muscles unclench and he exhales. “Let’s not talk about him.” I check the clock over my shoulder then turn back to the handsome and nearly naked man in my arms. “I have twenty-five minutes before I have to be in the shower.” I slide my hand beneath the elastic of his boxers and tease him with my fingertips.

He groans.

"There has to be a better way to spend the next twenty-five minutes that doesn't involve talking about Hatch, right?" I bite my lip to keep from smiling as he flashes me a crooked grin.

He grinds the long and hard muscle of his thigh between my legs, his hands moving to my ass. "I can think of a few things." He falls to his back, pulling me with him so that I'm straddling his leg. "But it'll take a fuckuva lot longer than twenty-five minutes." He nips at my mouth, dragging my lower lip between his teeth.

"Okay, I won't wash my hair."

He runs his smooth lips down my jaw to my neck, sucking gently.

"Mmm . . . or wear makeup."

He smiles against my throat. "So how much time do we have now?"

"Almost an hour." I bite my lip as his mouth glides against my throat.

"Oh, I can do plenty in an hour."

"Give me all you've got. I'll need it to get through today." My hips roll on their own accord, seeking out friction.

"Mmm." He sucks at my lips. "I'll leave you aching, baby. Sore and needy." He lifts his thigh, his hands on my ass, rubbing me to him. "Only thing I want you feeling today is me."

---

"It's not too late to back out." I watch through my rearview mirror as my mom worries her hands in her lap, her gaze fixed on a lot of nothing outside the car window.

She must know I'm looking, because she simply shakes her head. Her hair is pulled back in a low, loose bun, and the circles under her eyes speak of lost sleep.

"Dad," I whisper. "Are you sure this is a good idea?"

He reaches over and pats my hand. "We already endured the worst of the pain when we lost Lana."

"I know, but"—my eyes dart from the long stretch of highway to my mom, who's still gazing out the window—"is rehashing all this good for you guys. I mean I don't know if mom can handle reliving it."

"We'll see." He turns his gaze out the window, and in minutes, the signs for the State Prison of Nevada come into view.

I pull into the lot, remembering to breathe, not looking forward to being reunited with Hatch, and wishing like hell Mason were here with me.

We walk silently through the lot, and I can't help but notice the lack of color. The buildings are all the exact same shade of beige as the earth that surrounds them. The pale brown gives it a non-threatening look; like the desert, it appears benign, abandoned of life, when it's anything but.

We move through the screening process, and once we're deemed safe, a guard leads us to an empty room. The floors are concrete, and nothing is inside but a metal table and chair bolted to the ground, surrounded by a few foldable ones.

"Have a seat." The guard is all business as he motions to the flimsy plastic chairs. "Prisoner will be in shortly."

The door shuts behind him, and I jump as the sound echoes through the room. My dad takes the middle seat, and my mom and I the ones on the outside. His jaw twitches beneath his beard, the only sign of nerves or anger I've seen on him. Minutes morph into an agonizing wait until finally the door opens. My mom sucks in an audible breath, and my dad grips my hand and pulls it to his thigh.

A slender guy wearing a tan suit and glasses, with dark hair that's thin on top, steps into the room first. "Mr. and Mrs. Langley." He nods to my parents and turns to me. "Miss Langley." Another nod. "I'm Charles Yarner, Mr. Dusinsky's lawyer."

Okay, so Hatch's last name is Dusinsky. Not the most threatening biker name, I have to admit.

Neither my parents nor I do more than give a quick acknowledgment.

Two guards move through the door followed by two others. The last two flank a shackled Hatch. His face is still riddled in fading yellow bruises from the beatdown Rex delivered, and it looks like his nose is at a different angle from what I remember. His bright orange suit makes his large frame less intimidating, and his shaved head and face make him almost unrecognizable.

Hatch keeps his eyes cast to the floor as they move him to the table and deposit him in the bolted-down seat. I hear a clicking sound as Hatch's hands are manipulated behind him and handcuffed to his chair. Once done, the guards back away, but take stations at the four corners of the tiny room.

"Mr. Dusinsky has agreed to—"

"Charlie, I got this." Hatch's growled command is followed by the lift of his chin as he finally manages to look me in the eye. Remorse is heavy in his expression and his eyes soften. "Hey, sunshine."

My dad clears his throat, and Hatch's lips twitch before turning toward my parents.

"Mr. and Mrs. Langley." He shifts in his seat as much as he can while being locked to it.

"Feel good?" The question flies from my lips before I think better of it.

Hatch's eyebrows drop low, questioning.

I shrug one shoulder. "Being handcuffed to a chair. How's it feel?"

He doesn't drop his gaze from mine. "Not good."

Good.

"Mr. Dusinksy, we don't want to draw this out any longer." My dad speaks with a firm voice that calls the attention of the room. "We're here because we're interested in everything you know about the night our daughter was murdered."

My mom's answering whimper causes my chest to seize.

Hatch makes an affirmative grunting noise and, sitting tall, addresses my dad. "Figured as much." He eyes the guards then starts in. "I was working my first job with Elijah. We'd met before. I saw he was a bad dude, considered his crew partnering with my MC."

He sits back, his eyes focusing just over our heads. "I was meeting with a new contact. Pulled my bike off the road and stashed it in the bushes at mile marker sixty-nine. It was private, dark, no witnesses, the way Elijah liked shit done.

"Doing a pickup with a dude who didn't know what the fuck he was doing. Left his bike right there on the side of the road. Tried to make the deal quick, but he put a gun to my head and tried to take the shit he owed me plus the money. I was halfway to killing the asshole when a woman walked up."

"Svetlana." I can see it now, bike on the side of the road. She probably heard the man's cries of pain.

"We were in a gorge. Didn't even hear her pull up or see headlights. She asked if we needed help. It was dark, but I saw the moment her eyes figured out what she was seein' wasn't fucking legit. She started to back away, and the fuckface I was beating begged her to get help. I couldn't let that happen."

My dad leans forward, his arms on the table, and Hatch's eyes dart to my father's tattoos. "Are you telling us she witnessed you murder a man?" My dad's voice cracks with the truth.

Hatch sets his cold blue eyes on him, and there's respect in them. "Yes, sir."

My head swims with the intensity of the terror she must've felt. "Then what?"

He shrugs, the casual body language contradicting the twist of shame I see in his face. "I had to take her. Planned on scaring the shit out of her enough to keep her from talking. Elijah had different plans. Thought he'd use her to seal our partnership."

I shift in my seat, antsy, angry, and horrified. "How does that work?" Elijah mentioned something similar the night he died.

"Do something horrific; anyone who bears witness is just as responsible. We had each other by the balls."

Silence sweeps through the room as we all work out the story on our own.

"Did she suffer?" My mom's timid voice breaks the thick air.

Hatch's eyes move between my parents and me, a silent question blaring as loud as if he yelled it. *Do you want me to lie?*

My chin bobs once, the tiny movement so minor it's only registered by Hatch. He turns to my mom. "No, ma'am. Not at all. She was gone before . . ."

Before the cutting started.

It's a lie.

But I appreciate it more than I can express.

"You partake in this?" My dad's voice is steel.

"No. I'm only responsible for getting her there, but after that, I didn't touch her."

"You stood by while one of my daughters was murdered, and you kidnapped my other daughter to deliver her to someone you knew was a murderer. Even with police protection, so much could've gone wrong. You almost took two daughters from me."

"No, sir, I never would've let them hurt Trix."

My dad scoffs. "I have a hard time believing that."

"Understand you would, but"—Hatch's eyes move to mine—"Trix was my friend."

"Then why did you turn me over to him? Why not let me in on the plan you had with the cops?"

"Cops gave me one chance, Trix. I couldn't risk fucking it up. I knew once I found the picture of your sister that you had an end game. Good one, too. Never knew until that day you weren't into me. No such thing as a coincidence. Knew you were searching for the man who killed your sister. Knew Eli was searching for a girl. More importantly, knew if we got you to the location, I'd die before I let someone hurt you."

"*You* hurt me." My jaw still aches when I think about the punishing blows delivered by his hand.

"It's all relative. Not gonna lie, I was pissed finding that photo. Realized our entire friendship was a lie. Don't like bein' used."

"Oh, well, I'd care about your hurt feelings, but I don't have a single fuck to give!"

My dad squeezes my hand. "That's enough. I think we got all we came for." He nods to the security guard over Hatch's shoulder. "Mr. Dusinsky, I want you to know that what you've done to my family has changed who we are. There isn't a day that goes by that we don't miss our daughter. We had dreams for her, dreams to see her fall in love, become a mother, find her way through life, and blossom. We wanted so much for her, and you brutally robbed her of that. Robbed us of the joy of watching it."

Hatch's eyes shine and he sniffs.

My dad leans forward, never taking his eyes off the biker across the table. "I want you to know that we will walk out of here and never again think of what you did to Lana. We won't dwell on it, and we won't allow it to poison our lives. We love our daughter, but she's gone, and nothing is going to change that."

"I understand."

"But before we leave, you should know it's not too late for you. I'm sure you can tell that my past isn't clean." Hatch's gaze darts to my dad's full-sleeved tattoos then back to his face, but he says nothing. "Don't let the sins of your past rob you of the opportunity to do something great."

The biker sits stunned in his seat, and I smile wide at my dad, who manages to soften even the hardest hearts.

My dad grins and stands, pulling my mother up and to his side. "Thank you for your time. And Mr. Dusinsky"—my dad waits until Hatch meets his eyes—"we forgive you."

Hatch's jaw falls loose on its hinges. He blinks slowly and shakes his head.

My dad guides my mom and I follow. We move around the table toward the door, and I don't give Hatch the satisfaction of seeing me look at him. He is dead to me, and while my father may have forgiven him, I never will.

"Son . . ." Hatch jerks as my dad lays a hand on his shoulder. "If it's okay, I'd like to send you something in the mail. Looks like you're gonna have a lot of free time in here. May as well make it useful."

"Thank you, sir."

Those are the last three words I ever heard from Hatch. My dad made good on his plan to send something to him in the mail.

For every year that Hatch was incarcerated, he received a brand new Bible.

# EPILOGUE

## Three years later . . .

### MASON

It's fucking cold. I knew it would be, but I didn't realize how damn freezing the temps would be.

Why my gorgeous girl agreed to make our move this time of year isn't a mystery. Hell, when we got all the paperwork completed, we were both jumping out of our damn skin to get it done.

And here we are, standing at the threshold of a game-changer. A life-changer.

I grip Trix's left hand and toy with the diamond on her ring finger. She turns toward me, those violet eyes glowing with excitement and a little fear. Her cheeks and nose are flushed pink from the chill, and she flashes me a smile that almost sends me to my knees. "I can't believe we're finally doing this."

I lean in, pressing my warm lips to her cold ones. "We've been dreaming of this day. Now let's make it happen."

The first year after we moved in together wasn't easy. Thankfully, with the help of good lawyers and all the information Samuel Dusinsky, aka Hatchet, supplied, anyone involved in Hatch's MC and Elijah's crew was tried and imprisoned. Everyone except my brother. The information he provided to law enforcement must've been good because all he got was home arrest along with a lifetime of community service and the threat of imprisonment if he even looked at the wrong side of the law. Birdman, Jayden, and Harrison refused to cooperate and each did a little time for drug dealing.

"Wait." Trix tugs on my hand. "What if . . . I mean . . . what if they—?"

I silence her with a kiss. My heart warms at the tenderness reflected in her eyes. I cup her face and tilt her chin. My thumb brushes along the scar that runs the length of her neck and she melts into my chest. "Baby, are you getting cold feet?"

A tiny grin ticks her lips. "I can't feel my feet."

I chuckle and kiss the tip of her nose. "Do you regret not having family here with us? I know your dad wanted to—"

"No. I want it to just be us. It's important to me."

"Okay, so what is it? I know I'm ready, we bought a house, you're working full-time at the Youth Center, my job at the UFL is secure . . . we're ready."

Her hair, now naturally blond and free of purple streaks, whips around her face with the arctic wind. She tugs down her beanie. "You're right. We're ready. Plus, if we don't do it soon, we'll turn into icicles."

Hand in hand we stomp up the snow-covered steps to a large door.

"Here we go." She squeezes my hand one more time before I pull it open and usher her inside.

We're greeted by an older lady, who rattles off something in Russian. I've been studying for the last year, but her words are too quick to keep up with.

"My *zdes' dlya nashikh detey*." Trix's words come out just as quickly, and luckily that's a phrase I'm familiar with.

A grin tugs at my lips, and my chest is engulfed with warmth. *We're here for our children.*

## TRIX

I can't breathe. Stepping through the doors of the orphanage where Svetlana and I were adopted from, I'm overwhelmed with so much love. I don't remember my time here, but my soul recognizes it instinctually.

After we show the woman up front our paperwork and identification, she motions for us to follow her.

My hand is gripped so tightly in Mason's I don't know who is holding harder. The Russian language filters through from different rooms, echoing on walls along with the giggles of children. Each time we pass one, my heart leaps in my chest, conflicted between the feelings of joy that we get to take ours home and the knowledge of those who're left behind.

Mason must feel my tension as his hand releases mine to curl over my shoulder and pull me to his side. His lips touch the shell of my ear. "Don't worry, baby. God has a plan for all of them. There's a family waiting somewhere."

I nod and hug him to me.

*"Zhdi zdes',"* the woman barks, and she leaves us in a room that looks like a classroom filled with small desks and books.

"She said wait here."

I grin up at him. "Your Russian is improving, Mr. Mahoney."

"I have a great teacher, Mrs. Mahoney." He flashes a big grin; all those white teeth and full lips have me practically swooning, even after two and a half years of marriage.

I pull off my beanie and shrug off my fur-lined coat, suddenly melting from the inside. Unable to sit still, I pace the small room.

"Bea, baby," He leans against a bookshelf looking like the picture of calm hot dude. "Breathe." He's always so relaxed, solid, and constant. He's my rock.

Footsteps sound from down the hallway, and Mason comes to my side, his hand around my waist.

The woman appears, and when she steps aside, a four-year-old boy peers up at us, his big brown eyes wide with fear. My heart lurches in my chest.

I step forward and drop to my knees. "*Ne boysya, Feliks.*" *Don't be afraid.* I press my hand to my heart. "*Ya Beatriks.*" I'm Beatriks.

He nods, understanding, but his hand grips something behind him.

I lean over to see the dark eyes of a two-year-old little girl wearing a tattered frilly pink dress. Tears well in my eyes.

"*Moya sestra, Tatyana.*" *My sister.* He presses his free hand to his chest. "*Moya sestra.*"

My breath leaves on a rush, and I almost tumble backwards except for the powerful arms that come behind me to hold me up. Tears stream down my face, the rightness and power of the moment nearly taking me off my feet.

"*My zdes', chtoby otvezti tebya domoy.*" The deep timbre of Mason's voice as the words fall from his lips send renewed strength. *We're here to take you home.*

Feliks' eyes widen, but this time not with fear, with excitement. "*My oba*?"

"Yes, both of you. *Vy oba.*"

Tatyana steps out from behind her big brother, her head a mess of dark curls and skin as pale as the snow. "Feliks?"

The boy, our son, doesn't take his eyes off Mason. "*Mama i papa*?"

"*Da.*" *Yes.* The one word shakes from Mason's lips.

Both children take a step forward, eyes asking the unspoken question. I open my arms, and they fall into them with a force that sends me back into Mason's chest. Tears drip from my eyes as I hold my son and daughter for the first time, knowing that everything in my life has led up to this moment. Led here by not only Svetlana's life, but by her death.

My husband's arms wrap around us protectively. Comforting and holding us together as we allow the first few threads of our family bond to weave together.

As if I could feel her joy from heaven, my heart swells, knowing that Lana is rejoicing in this. Her death was not in vain if it meant bringing us to this moment.

Thank you, *moya sestra*.

We sit like this for a long time, as little hands hold us tight as if they're afraid this is all a dream, like we might walk away and they'll be stuck without parents, without our love. So we wait, we hold our son and daughter while leaning on each other, and we do it until they feel safe. If it takes days, we'll do it until they know that they are ours. To love and protect.

Feliks is the first to peer up, his eyes going right to Mason's. *"Navsegda, papa?"*

A tear drips down Mason's cheek to disappear between his smiling lips. He cups his son's jaw and nods. "Yes, *syn.* Forever."

**The End**

# ACKNOWLEDGMENTS

First off, I want to thank God for allowing me the ability to tell stories, even though I'm sure he rolls his eyes at most of what I write.

Thank you to my husband who is and always will be the only hero in my life. It's your love that inspires me and your support that anchors me.

Thank you to my babies, who have made me feel like I'm the greatest novelist the world has ever seen, even though they have no idea what I write. I love their blind faith.

To my parents and my brother for being the best pimps and my number one fans, thank you. I'd never have the courage to do this if it weren't for you.

A huge thank you to Evelyn Johnson for always having my back and for allowing me to drag her all over the country for signings and events. Your friendship and loyalty are unparalleled.

Thank you to my partner in crime, Cristin Harber. Your friendship has meant the world to me over these last few years, and I look forward to many more.

Big ole high-five to my Critter Crew: Claudia Connor, Cristin Harber, Racquel Reck, and Sharon Kay. You girls know I'd never publish a book without having your eyes all over it. I appreciate you all more than words can adequately express.

To my friend Amanda Simpson at Pixel Mischief Design, thank you. It's your creativity that has molded the face of my brand. Your brilliance and skill are awe-inspiring, and I couldn't have hand picked a better or more talented person to work with.

Always a huge thank you to the talented Elizabeth Reyes. I'd never have had the *cajones* to write if it weren't for your encouragement and support. Thank you for your time and, more importantly, your friendship.

Thank you to Theresa Wegand for editing and proofreading all my books and for not firing me for forcing you deep into the Urban Dictionary. It's been such a joy to work with you, and I look forward to tackling many more books together.

None of this would be possible if it weren't for the readers who've given my books a chance. There are so many incredible authors out there, and I'm humbled and honored every time a reader picks one of my books. Thank you for taking a chance on me.

Last but not least and probably the most important, thank you to all the Fighting Girls who support me and the books with the kind of steadfast love only an FG is capable of. I'd be nowhcrc without you girls. You mcan thc world to mc.

# FIGHTING FOR FOREVER PLAYLIST

"Shadow of the Day" by Linkin Park
"Hit or Miss" by New Found Glory
"Hold My Hand" by New Found Glory
"Shameless" by All Time Low
"Dance Inside" by The All-American Rejects
"Drunk in Love" by Beyoncé
"Thunder" by Boys Like Girls
"You Had Me at Hello" by A Day to Remember
"Work" by Jimmy Eat World
"I'm Not Okay (I Promise)" by My Chemical Romance
"Waiting Game" by Yellowcard
"Shadows and Regrets" by Yellowcard
"Stickin In My Eye" by NOFX
"Wasting Time" by Blink 182
"Caress Me Down" by Sublime
"Same In the End" by Sublime
"With You Around" by Yellowcard
"Surfer Girl" by The Beach Boys
"I Wanna" by The All-American Rejects
"About a Girl" by The Academy Is . . .
"Situations" by New Found Glory
"What I've Done" by Linkin Park
"One Grain of Sand" by Ron Pope

# ABOUT THE AUTHOR

JB Salsbury, New York Times Best Selling author of the Fighting series, lives in Phoenix, Arizona, with her husband and two kids. She spends the majority of her day lost in a world of battling alphas, budding romance, and impossible obstacles as stories claw away at her subconscious, begging to be released to the page.

Her love of good storytelling led her to earn a degree in Media Communications. With her journalistic background, writing has always been at the forefront, and her love of romance prompted her to write her first novel.

Since 2013 she has published six bestselling novels in The Fighting Series and won a RONE Award.

For more information on the series or just to say hello, visit JB on her website, Facebook, or Goodreads page.

http://www.jbsalsbury.com/

https://www.facebook.com/JBSalsburybooks

http://www.goodreads.com/author/show/6888697.Jamie_Salsbury

CPSIA information can be obtained
at www.ICGtesting.com
Printed in the USA
BVHW04s0945130318
510452BV00019B/70/P

9 781512 099102